NO FORGETTING PROVIDENCE

OBSESSED INTENTIONS

BOOK TWO

LEE WIMMER

NO FORGETTING PROVIDENCE

First Edition

Author: Lee Wimmer

Title: Obsessed Intentions- No Forgetting Providence

Identifiers: ISBN 979-8-9883334-5-6 (ebook) September 2024

ISBN 979-8-9883334-6-3 (hardback) September 2024

ISBN 979-8-9883334-7-0 (paperback) January 2025

Hightower Publications

Battle Creek, Michigan

www.hightowerpublications.com

Cover and Interior Design by Emilie Haney, eahcreative.com

To those fighting on the front lines of child trafficking and working to keep our children safe, I salute you, and thank you for your tireless work. Without your efforts hundreds of thousands more children and women would be endangered. While there is so much work left to do, we all owe you our utmost respect and gratitude. May our prayers and support be unwavering in light of the growing complicity to further enslave the defenseless. God bless you all.

Ablast of smoke and a sharp squeal of the tires informed Dr. Steven Ray, DR to his friends, that the charter jet from Sri Lanka had touched down. Somehow, the plane still felt like it was in the air as it continued the sideways shake. With the concrete runway shooting by them, an easterly crosswind pushed the plane hard. Then, after a heart-wrenching deceleration, the plane reached the uncovered FBO gate, the private-jet terminal at Kalamazoo/Battle Creek International Airport.

Despite the snow flurries, a small crowd managed to gather by the FBO hidden in the back of the airport. Waiting to deplane, he watched his companion's expression as she swallowed hard.

"Hey, honey. It's going to be all right. It's just a few reporters." Placing his hand on her leg, forcing a half smile, he wondered—Was it? When he sighted his mom in the waiting crowd, he felt it also, and for good reason.

"It's not the reporters I'm worried about. What if your family doesn't like me?" Debbie Holmes leaned her head on his shoulder, and long locks of gold fell across her face. She picked at the seat back in front of her, appearing lost in thought, her gaze shifting from one point to another, never seeming to focus.

"Oh yeah. I totally get that." Laughing, he elbowed her to show his fun side, maybe even take away her tension. Then he pushed her hair back, admiring her. "Hey, they're going to love you."

As they got the all clear to deplane, the copilot positioned a wheelchair lift above the airstairs. "Dr. Ray, give me just a moment, and we'll have you on the ground. I'm waiting for our ground attendant to finish getting ready for you."

DR drew in a breath at his own tension. The butterflies in his stomach were as big as the ones he'd seen in his vision of the afterlife with Habiba. When he left here just three months ago, he didn't think he'd be coming back to Delton, at least not this soon, and certainly not to live. Was he making the right decision? Now his own eyes were searching.

No. Stop it. Everything was going to work out.

"What, what did you say?" He shifted in his seat to face the man.

"We're ready for you, Doctor." The smiling copilot pointed to the wheelchair.

"Sorry, I was in la-la land." DR leaned over and kissed Debbie's cheek. Still, she stared out the window. All color had drained from her face. He patted her arm. "Come on. Let's get off this plane."

"Is that her?" While she kept her voice even to hide any alarm, her face was a dead giveaway as she strained to pick someone out in the crowd.

He craned over her shoulder. Willie stood beside Mike, his brother. They were bundled up and sort of leaning against each other as Mike's wife, Alyssa, did the same on the other side. If Debbie was looking where DR was, then his secret wasn't a secret anymore. "Is that who?"

She sat up. "Oh... I'm sorry I was thinking about something else. I've been on this plane too long. Ready?" Her color returned. Now, she seemed to be a ball of energy. Like him, she must be ready to get this over with.

After they hit the ground, the waiting crowd waved. Mom was out front just like he expected, Dad, his brothers, and friends just a step behind. Reporters called out to him, holding microphones stretched as far as they could reach, wanting questions answered as camera flashes fired and TV cameras rolled and recorded every word, smile, and frown.

Mike stepped in front of them to shield Debbie and DR.

Mom bent to the wheelchair and wrapped him in a bear hug, her tears flowing before she took his face in both hands and kissed his cheeks. "My baby is home." She shifted to Debbie, still smiling, and reached for her. "And who is this lovely young lady?"

Barely able to hear her amidst the reporters twenty-some feet away still squawking their questions, he clasped Debbie's hand. "Mom, this is Debbie, my girlfriend. She's going to help me heal up."

Out of the corner of his eye, he caught Willie staring as he reached up for his dad's hug. The wheelchair made him feel quite disadvantaged, if not captive. After introductions, "glad you're homes," and well wishes, they headed inside to warm up and find their transportation to Wall Lake. Then he promised Mom and Dad he'd see them soon, and he motioned for Debbie to push him. Soon, she had him trundling along as fast as she dared to go.

Mike jogged along with them, still nudging the reporters' microphones and cameras to the side. "My brother will hold a presser once he has a chance to get his legs under him. You have your pictures and video. I'll let you all know when he's ready. Thanks for coming." Placing his hand on the wheelchair, he bent down to DR. "Wow, that was some welcome, huh?" Then he made eye contact with Debbie and introduced himself and Willie, who had now caught up, the rest of the Ray clan further back, ready to go home. "Would you like me to take over, Debbie?"

"No thanks. I got this." She beamed, fighting the wind as her hair whipped about her face.

"We're so glad you're safe—and back in Wall Lake," Willie gushed, then clamped her hands over her mouth. The stiff breeze blew her long curly black hair too, but her headband held most of it back so only strands caught on her mittens when she covered her mouth before she fought to tuck them away.

"Uh, yes." Mike shot her a hard woolly eye, and his stone-cold face flashed piercing eyes before unthawing again. Now glowing with his trademark smile, he gave DR a pause. "What Willie is saying is we have everything back in place, except your wall décor. We also picked up a few things to make it easier for you. If you need anything, let me or Willie know."

He patted DR's shoulder and shook Debbie's hand, then half hugged her. His eyes shot the piercing look again behind Debbie's back at Willie, and he half held out his arm as if he could distance Willie from them, communicating his obvious displeasure with her.

DR smiled. Just thirteen days earlier, Mike had told him about Willie's infatuation or crush or whatever it was on him, a secret he hadn't shared with Debbie and a secret Mike wasn't supposed to share with him. It seemed he was the only one who could keep a secret, and keep it, he would.

How one likes the weather, the pace of life, and the feel of Wall Lake, often depends on where one is from. Gail, DR's deceased wife, loved the pace, but not the weather. So now he wondered—How would Debbie like it? She was from Chicago, so the temperature should be fine, but the pace may be too slow for her. Certainly, the locals would forgive her as they did Gail.

Although mostly confined to bed his first week home, DR cheated from time to time, slipped into the wheelchair, or sat on the deck with Debbie counting the stars. She seemed to enjoy the lifestyle he relished, the same one he enjoyed with Gail, the one Debbie expressed hopes of one day sharing.

The medication he'd been prescribed often caused him to drift in and out of sleep, even in his wheelchair. But Debbie was always there to push him back inside and help him get to bed. She'd become his lifesaver, a fact he shared with anyone who came by to visit, and he quickly fell in love— no, *they* fell in love.

This evening's sky was full of stars, and their breath drifted away on the cool, crisp night air. Slapping against the boat lift below reminded him of their recent adventure and all the mystery of the Indian Ocean. Feeling the heat from the chiminea burning hot only feet away, he spread a light blanket over them. "It's a beautiful evening."

"I can see why you love it here. The view is amazing." Her brown eyes glistened, aglow with the same joy now warming his heart. She squeezed their entwined hands, her approving smile saying she felt the way he did.

A hot mug of coffee cradled in his grip, his arm leaning ever so lightly on Debbie, he shared his contentment. "With you here, it's just about perfect. I could do this forever."

He put down his mug, let go of her hand, and slid his arm around her shoulders. Their eyes met. Maybe, just maybe Miguel had it right, and there was a—no, no, no. DR mustn't let himself get swept up in their fantasies. This was great, but it was just his turn.

Telling himself that, he leaned in until their lips met.

"About perfect?" She mocked and drew back after a brief, but amazing kiss.

"It gets better every day. I can't wait until I lose this wheelchair. Then I'll show you another part of the world I love." His eyes glazed while strands of her hair blew in his face, though her Bears stocking cap restricted most of it.

"I saw how much you loved sitting on the deck of the *DI*. It was as if you didn't have a care in the world. I've always been a city dweller, so it's going to take some getting used to." Laughing, she whisked the strands away and tucked them under the cap, then pushed back a lock of his sandy hair, breathing the essence of him. "I loved those nights out there with you, blue moon or no blue moon. I wished I hadn't become so impulsive." She sat up, cocked her head. "Do you hear that? Someone's at the front door."

"I think you're right. Would you mind?" He picked his coffee up from the end table, flashing back to the time Gail selected the patio set.

"Yep, I got it." Debbie rose to leave, turning in time to notice his appreciative stare as she walked away. A pleased smile stretched out her lips, eyes flashing like brown sapphires.

She returned an innocent smile, head tilted, taking all of her in. Then he leaned back into the love seat sofa and relaxed into the cool canvas cushion. At first, all he could hear was muffled voices. As they came closer, their conversation became understandable.

"We're outside on the deck. Let me show you," Debbie said.

"How are you, guys? Is DR getting his rest? I know you must be a lifesaver." Willie's voice carried the enthusiasm of a kid on Christmas morning, and she must've raced ahead of Debbie because she reached the patio doors first. "I love his deck. Gail and I used to spend hours out there."

Was Willie always so bubbly, so high energy?

"We're fine, he's taking it one day at a time, but he'll get there." Debbie answered as they stepped out onto the deck. "DR, sweetheart, look who stopped by."

Huh. She not only sugarcoated her voice but also appeared to grit her teeth behind Willie's back. No, he must be seeing things.

"Willie, come, have a seat. The chiminea feels great this evening, and there's not a cloud in the sky." He pointed over the lake, then extended a hand to offer her a seat near them beside the fire. But she came right around and gave him a tight hug, her brown eyes aglow.

Wow, he wasn't expecting that. He jolted back ever so slightly. They were almost cheek to cheek, her eyes squinted, and her cheeks rose as a surprised smile rounded them before she let him go.

Then she hugged Debbie too, whose arms flew out wide as she sagged into the hug. She must've been as surprised as DR. "My, you're a hugger. How nice." Turning her face away from Willie, Debbie communicated her surprise to him by widening her eyes and raising a brow. She probably did grit her teeth.

I guess she's not feeling it. Unless Miguel said something to her about Willie's crush. No, surely Miguel had more tact. Still, DR would have to remember to ask him.

"Willie, thank you for helping Mike get the old place back together." He nodded toward the house. "If I didn't know better, I'd say I never packed it all away. You must have a photographic memory."

As the ladies took their places, an uneasiness seemed to settle over Debbie. Meanwhile, Willie retained her Christmas-morning wonderment.

"Oh, it was nothing. I was glad to help. It reminded me of my time here with Gail and how she loved this place. But anyway, I had a good time. You know how we girls are when it comes to decorating. I'm glad you're pleased." She circled her hand out above her head, showing it wasn't a big thing, then rubbed her hands in front of the chiminea. "How is the healing coming along?"

When that wasn't being asked, he'd know he was well. He squirmed in the chair. "I'm still sore, feeling a little raw in my abdomen, but I'm getting my strength back one day at a time. Hopefully, I'll get crutches soon as the wound in my thigh is healing faster than my abdomen."

A dour expression flashed across Debbie's face. Seemed she was fighting something. So he wasn't the only one Willie caught off guard.

"Debbie, how do you like his king-size bed? Isn't that nice? Those posts must weigh a hundred pounds apiece." Willie tilted her head, squinting her eyes, almost like a sister asking fifty questions after a date. "The mahogany is so pretty, and the mattress, wow, it's so relaxing."

"I love it, not that I've felt the mattress." Debbie's lips turned down at the corners, and the fire once roaring in her eyes now only seemed to flicker as if Willie had sucked the fun out of her evening. "I have my own room—just for now—so DR can get his rest." Sitting up straight, she perked up and shot him a toothy smile before shaking a finger at him. "Just for now."

It seemed like the ladies were sparing, each taking a turn, measuring their opponent. Time to change the subject. He flashed an exaggerated wink Debbie's way. "Overall, everything is great. I have so many caring, loving people stepping up to help me get better."

"How long before you get your crutches? And once you do, will you have to stay on them long?" Willie scooted sideways in her chair, leaning on its arm to get even closer, or so it appeared.

He tried not to shift back. "I should get them in a few days and hope I'll only need them for a week or so."

Debbie entwined her hand tighter with his. Willie's expression soured, and she even shut her eyes, exhaling deeply.

"By the way"—eager to distract the ladies, he drew out the words with the tone of a storyteller—"one of the passengers from my cruise is coming to stay with me. Actually, he's Gail's second cousin. Now there was a real shocker. He's coming over to work with Clyde on the artifacts until it's all wrapped up. Debbie's driving to Detroit to pick him up at the airport in the morning. I hate for her to drive so far alone, so I was wondering..." He smirked at Debbie. "Willie, would you mind going with her? It would give you two time to get to know one another." He suppressed a grin, guessing what Debbie was thinking by her sharp intake of breath and her glower piercing him for the blatant betrayal.

She twisted in her seat and let go of his hand. "No. I mean, it's not necessary. Why ruin her day too? Besides, you know how Ryan can be— he won't leave her alone." She elbowed DR softly so Willie couldn't see her, then leaned toward the other lady. "Willie, Ryan was always chasing after me on the cruise like some love-crazed Irishman. I don't want him to set his sights on you and ruin your life."

"What time do you leave?" Willie notched up her chin. "It might be nice, some girl-bonding time. I'm not worried about any man, and I can take care of myself." Her counterpunch sent a clear signal: she was in this until the end.

"Early." Debbie raised her golden brows.

"Great. Tomorrow is Mike's big interview with that best-selling author from Australia, so I have the day off. I was going to go in and listen in, but this should be more fun." Her eyes widened, and a telling smile beamed, her confidence unmistakable. "Just give me the time."

DR smiled. "Seven thirty. Right, sweetheart?"

"That's the plan." Debbie looked down at their hands again and squeezed tighter.

Willie rubbed her own hands on her thighs. "Seven thirty, it is. Do you want to meet at Marcie's Place? We can grab an éclair and some coffee. I'll treat."

"Sounds good." Debbie's fingernails clawed into his palm. Whatever she was fearing about tomorrow, she'd find out in the morning.

CHAPTER
TWO

Congress was experiencing chaos. Behind the scenes, the attacks, newspaper leaks, and bogus foreign complicity all being leveled against the POTUS were now having a horrible effect on the public opinion of the man and on his ability to lead. Senator Carl Brummengarten and Congressman Max Rice, both from Chicago, had their own fronts to attack him, but they failed in the biggest attempts yet.

Their hired terrorists bungled their attack on the American yacht, *Disillusioned Illusion,* in the Indian Ocean—all shown live on international television to deal a blow to the President's foreign policy. It was behind them now, but not in the eyes of their supporter, or rather controller, Mr. Jennings. He would stop at nothing to unseat the President, his former friend, even if it included killing other Americans, like the attack on the *DI.* "The man will undo all our gains. No way can he have another four years!" Jennings had been heard shouting.

Congressman Max Rice's entire political party had grown vicious, some even kicking administration officials out of restaurants and attacking colleagues with trumped-up accusations, and slander. One congresswoman told people to attack his supporters at grocery stores and gas stations, wherever they were seen.

"Mary, would you please get Mr. Jennings on the phone?" Max shifted in his chair, feeling the squeeze, and he didn't like it. Staring out his window over the road below, he shuddered. This wasn't a phone call he wanted to make, but everybody in DC had someone they had to answer to, didn't they?

"Kat is on line 1, sir. Can I get you anything?" Mary shut a drawer of her desk. One thing about her, she was efficient and dependable. Something special in DC.

"Thanks, Mary. I'm good." He jabbed the button for line 1. "Hi, Kat. How are things?" He reached into his bottom desk drawer and removed the half-empty vodka bottle and a glass, almost a necessity when calling Jennings.

"I'm sure I'm doing better than you, Congressman. He's pretty mad. He dropped a bundle on the live television coverage and now says your whole show made POTUS and his foreign policy look like a rock star. You know Senator Brummengarten passed the buck to you, right? Doesn't matter, though." She giggled, then cleared her throat. "So how do you think this is going to go?"

"That bad, huh?" He'd dreaded this call. Now, his intuition was being rewarded. Mr. Jennings always got his way, eventually. No matter who got hurt—even if it was an ex-wife or two.

"I've never seen him this mad. The last couple of weeks have been brutal, what with the impeachment and all. Well, here he is."

Max liked his mornings quiet. He liked to ease into his day. Not today. He poured the vodka to the top of the glass and gulped down a good glug.

"Max, how you been?" Jennings's voice sniveled through the speaker.

"Thank you, sir. I'm doing fine. How are you?" Max cringed, knowing better than to avoid the question. He took another gulp. Being a congressman was *not* what he thought it would be. He came in with high hopes, believing his party cared about their constituents, only to find out otherwise. Likely, his adversaries across the aisle in the House had owners too. Power brokers pushed them up their ladder, only to gain influence. He wanted no part of it, but he knew too much—now. He wouldn't be like his predecessor who accidentally drowned while out for an early morning March jog.

"Yes, I can imagine. What the—" The voice rose, then huffed. "Excuse me, Max." A coarse cough came through, then a loud, deep breath.

"Doctors tell me I need to control my anger, cut down on my love life, all the good things I like, and I still can't believe after all these years Kat doesn't like my language. What happened, Max?" A slam, like he'd struck his desk, sharing his anger, reverberated through the speaker.

Max cringed. Jennings was living on the edge. Often when Max met him, Jennings was with a different model type each time, usually a teenager, all while smoking cigars and drinking hard liquor. Hard to believe just years before he supported Max for his first run for office, he was Pentecostal, or so he confessed. But something snapped when Patsy died months after Max won his election. Not long afterward, Jennings was given a seat in Circle. Now he was a different person, with different goals.

"Funny thing about you politicians. Once you get to Washington, you think you're something special, forgetting who is *really* running the show, ofttimes trying to sidestep me. Well, how's the water in Lake Michigan this time of year, Max?"

Max could imagine the old man's smile, but he was joking, or so Max thought. Jennings wasn't who sent his predecessor to the dark abyss.

"Just joking, Max. But it does help keep you sleazeballs in line. But don't worry about it now. Your overseas friends deserved what they got. I'm sure you'll hear something as soon as the mourning is over." Another course laugh carried through the line.

"I don't follow, sir." Max set the empty vodka glass on his desk and turned to the window again. He rubbed his forehead to stop a headache. Life appeared so calm on the street. If only he could turn back time.

"Pick up the paper, man. It's front-page news." A cough resounded, then another coarse laugh. Then the phone went dead.

Max usually read his papers first, scanning the headlines. With this administration in the White House, things changed fast. But today, the call with Jennings was first on the list, and he'd wanted—*needed*—to get it over with. Now, he pushed the intercom on the phone. "Mary, are my newspapers still out there? Would you bring them in, please?" He reached toward the bottom drawer again, then stopped. Was he becoming a lush like so many of the others on Capitol Hill? All the parties and private meetings where alcohol flowed like water led many of his colleagues to the whiskey nose, at least that's what Mary called it. He jabbed the intercom again. "And maybe a cup of black coffee, please?"

Moments later, Mary strolled into his office, passed the coffee and newspapers to him, then slunk away like a beaten animal. She'd handed him four newspapers folded in the center.

Max set the coffee on his desk, closed his eyes, and whispered to himself. "Lord, don't let it be true." Eyes closed, he unfolded the first paper, opened one eye a bit, then the other wide. A shudder racked his body as he read the headline, then the second paper, the third, and the fourth. Every paper's headline blared a similar theme: US Assassinates Rogue General.

Max sat on the Armed Services Committee. They'd had no warning or briefing of the attack, usually customary. This administration had recently listed the general as a terrorist, a kingpin, a US enemy. That eliminated the need to give anyone a warning of the impending strike. The last administration and POTUS considered the general a friend, an ally who took care of their dirty work in the Middle East—secretly.

He put his head on the desk, mockingly banging it.

After the news had time to soak in, he pressed the intercom. "Mary, get me the White House, please." His trembling hand let the button go.

She knocked on his office door, then edged it open. "Sir, the White House isn't taking any calls from Armed Services Committee members. There's a presser scheduled for this afternoon."

He'd been studying the peaceful street, sipping his coffee. Now, he turned from his window to the only person in DC he hadn't caught in a lie. Just how did she keep her values?

"You know, Mary, ever since this foolish impeachment, things have gone crazy. If only they could've sunk that stupid boat." He turned back to the window. A busload of schoolchildren was unloading to tour the Capitol Building.

"What boat, sir?" In her reflection on the window, her eyes narrowed, and her brows cocked and rose as she smoothed out her blouse.

"Nothing. I was just thinking about something else. Thank you. That's all for now, but what time was the news conference?" He rubbed his forehead, now beaded with perspiration, the way he got when he was anxious. "And when you reach your desk, would you get Senator Carl on the phone for me?"

"Three p.m., sir." She stepped out quickly.

And he replayed the conversation with Jennings in his mind—"How's the water in Lake Michigan this time of year?" The snively tone rang fresh as if speaking now. He shifted, moving to stand behind a photograph of him swearing in. "Man, what was I thinking?"

He palmed his forehead again. "These people are brutal. Just because they gave me large donations, now they expect me to tow the party line, regardless of what I think. They only gave me money, a ground team, and connections. I did the rest. *I* had the ideas. 'How's the water?'" He ground his teeth and clenched his fists. "I have to get out, somehow, someway."

"Sir?" Mary's voice coming through the intercom snapped him back to reality. "Senator Carl is on line 1. Is there anything else you need?" Her typewriter whirred in the background as she waited.

"No. Thank you, Mary. That's all." He put his hands to his face in a praying fashion and inhaled several deep breaths before taking the call. With all the turmoil, would Mary see through it all and retire? Then he'd be in a pickle. She knew everything going on, at least here on the Hill.

"Carl." He spoke fast, too angry not to shout. "What's the meaning, telling Jennings I dropped the ball? The general was *your* friend—*your friend* screwed it all up, using that goofball, what's-his-name, Mekaastic. He wasn't a pirate, just a petty thief. How was he going to stop a heavily fortified yacht with sharpshooters on board? Losers, and you lied to Jennings. Do you know what he asked me this morning?" He stopped and jabbed the intercom button hard enough to bend his finger backward. "Mary, see if you could dig me up another cup of coffee. Thanks." He let go of the button just in time to hear the senator's reply.

"Whoa, and good morning to you." Carl laughed. Was he deliberately baiting Max? "I can guess. Besides, nobody knew the yacht was prepared for attacks. He must've had someone help him with the fortification."

A commotion rumbled on the other end of the line. Sounded like Carl was shredding some documents, an all-too-familiar sound. "Carl." Max gulped and dropped into his chair. "He asked me 'How's the water in Lake Michigan this time of year?' You know where he was going, don't you?"

Carl snorted. "You know the saying in DC, right? 'You can laugh or cry, but no one cares.'" Now Carl was the one laughing over the phone lines.

Max ground his teeth again. His fist slammed his desk's smooth walnut surface. "How can you laugh about this? I don't think he was kidding this time. These people are serious, for crying aloud. I should have stayed in the contracting business."

His door opened. Mary tiptoed across the room with his coffee.

"Thanks, Mary," he whispered.

"Don't worry," Carl soothed. "Above all, don't get your underwear in a wad. I've been in this business for thirty years, and I'm still kicking, aren't I? Besides, Jennings wasn't who did your predecessor in. That guy's dead—old age, I heard. He shouldn't have tried to leave Congress. He knew too much... just like us. Don't get all uptight. I couldn't take the heat for the Iranian thing. I've got something else coming down with the impeachment, something I'm sure he's not going to like."

"What's that?" Leaning back in his chair now, Max stared at the ceiling. This all seemed like a scene out of a crummy B movie, the late evening meetings spent holed up in the Capitol Building basement, trying to sink American boats for political points and lying about everything.

"Since you guys have sent us this thing, this piece of crap impeachment, I have to figure out how to go low and dirty up the POTUS, without making *us* look like buffoons again. I still can't believe you guys voted for this... this *thing*. There's nothing there. Nothing!"

The whirring noise from Carl's office had stopped. All became silent.

Max exhaled and ran his right hand through his hair. "Tell me about it. At least you weren't meeting at all hours of the night with those bozos, having it shoved down your throat or up your..." Max stopped. He didn't like the committee chairman, not even in Sunday-morning Mass.

The whirring had started again. The senator's tone returned to normal. "Anyway, Jennings is just going to have to get over it. There's nothing we can do. Oh, we'll put on a show, but at the end of the day, that's what it is, just a show. Did he mention the kids the people on the yacht rescued? The boat they were on was anchored during the attack, *my boat*. They were supposed to be here two weeks ago. So guess what? He's sending them to your club after they go back and grab them again—only this time, he's grabbing more. He's wanting to set a trap for the good doctor. For some reason, Jennings is blaming him for the whole fiasco. The old man might've lost it. I just hope when he does go looney I'm nowhere to be found. If he ever gets the lead position in Circle, we're in big trouble."

Max swished his coffee. Too bad, he couldn't shred this whole thing. "Why can't he just leave the guy alone? He's just a regular kind of a guy."

Then what the senator said registered in his mind.

"Wait? What? He's sending them to *my* club? Not again. This is getting harder and harder to explain to my wife." He and Leslie had already been at odds over his irregular activities when he was at home for a break.

"In his OCD, he wants to bring this guy down for ruining his big show. I've got to go. He'll let you know, probably before he grabs the kids. Talk to you later. Oh, don't tell him I said anything."

"Yeah... thanks for making my day." Max cringed, closed his eyes, and hung up the phone. "What have I gotten myself into? Jennings is coming unhinged. Now, I'm going to be in on murder too?" No doubt about it—a headache was coming on.

After Debbie left to meet Willie, DR tuned in to his brother's seven-a.m. radio show and his interview with the author, a first for DR who ran from anything Christian. But the man and his unique story intrigued him. Then his phone rang before the introduction, and he swiped to answer Miguel, his most trusted friend, who just happened to be the believer he most admired, a turnoff for DR usually. Somehow, maybe through charm, wisdom, shared love of sailing, or more likely a kindred spirit, DR has taken a liking to Miguel, also a passenger/crew member on the *Disillusioned Illusion*'s shakedown cruise.

"DR, feeling better?"

A child's voice chirped something in the background.

"Hi, my friend. I'm getting there. How about you? How's that arm?" DR sank back into his wheelchair, glad to hear from his friend and thankful Miguel's wound was only a grazing shot to his right arm. He pivoted his chair toward the sunlight shining through the patio doors, lighting the living room, making it seem much larger.

"It's nothing, just a scratch, but I'm milking it for all it's worth. You haven't run Debbie off yet, have you?" Corey, Miguel's seven-month-old grandson was crying now, hurt crying like he fell or something. "Corey, I told you not to climb up there. Hang on, DR. I need to get Kim to take him."

The phone went silent.

"Okay, I'm back." Miguel's quiet laugh rumbled through. "Corey's in the climbing stage and terrible at it."

"No, I haven't run off Debbie. She's still here—thankfully. I think this is going to work out. I was concerned when she got saved." DR let out a snicker. "But she's not playing the part, although I wish she would in some areas."

Miguel went silent. Right, he'd have other hopes for her.

"Anyway, DR, I'm glad you're healing well. There's another reason I'm calling. David and Lorenzo called me. Seems Luigi's brother is milking the *DI*'s repair like Luigi tried to stick it to you before. If I didn't know better, I'd say Raymond has been talking with and taking orders from Luigi. I wanted to give you a heads-up. Raymond has her out back in the boneyard. I'm going over there tomorrow to get this straightened out."

DR scrubbed a hand over his eyes. Luigi tried to take him for an extra hundred grand on the sale price. He'd have gotten it too if not for Miguel. Miguel had also told David, DR's first mate, and Lorenzo, DR's Mr. Everything, not to take the yacht back to Marsala, that Luigi wouldn't be anything but trouble. It appeared he was right, again.

"I was also wondering if you've gotten to see your uncle, setting things right for yourself?"

"I'll be going soon since I'm feeling a little better. Don't worry. It's at the top of my list."

A buck nosed around out in the distance. Then a doe sprinted along the lake's east shore, followed from afar by another buck.

"Remember, DR, that's more for you than for him. Call me to let me know how it goes."

Through pursed lips, he suppressed a smiled, thankful men like Miguel still exist, the kind of man he always strove to be, except for the religious part. "I don't know what I'd do without you. Thanks again, my good friend."

"No. Thank you. Thanks to you and our cruise, I have a broader life with high hopes of sailing around the world with you and the whole gang again. Well, I'm going to go find Kim and check on Corey. I will let you know about the repairs. Tell Debbie hello for all of us. God bless."

"Bye, Miguel." DR shivered as the phone went dead. God bless, indeed. *Where have You been, God? Why now? Why does everyone around me have to be religious? I feel like I'm fighting someone I can't see, the invisible man.*

CHAPTER
THREE

Following GPS directions, Debbie made light work of the drive to Marcie's Place to meet Willie. She'd taken the rental Mike arranged for DR, a four-wheel-drive Pathfinder. This time of year, the snow could pile up fast, so she'd rather be safe than sorry. Now she parallel parked outside the booming joint and reached over to open the passenger door as Willie, who'd been huddled under the awning, bustled over.

"Good morning." Willie slung her purse onto the floor mat and held up a take-out bag and a tray of coffees. "I hope you don't mind. They were so busy, so I went ahead and ordered my faves to save us time. My friend, Rachael, works here and expedited our order." In snug black ski bibs and coat, along with a white knit hat and top, Willie flashed her toothy smile, her breath appearing like the smoke from a fiery dragon.

"Thanks, yeah. We need to be on the road. I don't want to get Ryan's knickers all discombobulated. He's somewhat intense." As Willie maneuvered climbing into the vehicle with the goodies, Debbie reached out her hand to offer help, but Willie ignored it. "So what did you get us?"

"I love the chocolate iced éclairs—the long ones overstuffed with custard filling—and their pumpkin spice latte." She fit their beverages in the beverage holders, gingerly unpacked the éclairs, handed one to Debbie, then pushed back her long black curls, and unwrapped her prized possession. She bit into it before Debbie could get onto the road. "Mmm, it's so good. I hope you like it."

"I'm sure it will be fine, and I do like pumpkin spice." Remembering the latte she shared with DR in Marsala before the cruise, she unwrapped her éclair, took a bite, and wedged the vehicle into the traffic flow. "This is good." She stuck her tongue out to lick the chocolate off her lips while balancing her éclair on her leg, her left hand on the wheel.

"I'm glad you like it. So, DR said you lived in Chicago. Were you born and raised there?"

Okay, so this was an information-gathering operation for Willie. Well, Debbie could use it for the same. No one was coming between her and DR, so she'd gather more than she gave. "No. How about you? Always lived in Delton? And would you move away if another radio station wanted to hire you in a bigger market?" There, give a little, take a little more.

Willie's eyes widened and eyebrows rose. "Yes, born and raised, and I love it. So the offer would have to be substantially more than I make now." She faced out the window. "I hope we can become friends. I'd like to show you why I love Delton and why Gail loved it too."

As the two-and-a-half-hour drive progressed, Debbie sensed a strange bonding, neither wanting to trust the other or seemingly give up on their hopes. But Willie's comment on becoming friends had registered. Maybe the gal wasn't bad. Maybe.

As they discussed the cruise, Debbie described everything, eventually coming to the part where she was born again, "saved," after their experience in Saudi Arabia.

"You know DR doesn't want anything to do with religion, right?" Willie's tone became condescending as she folded her arms and puffed out her chest. "Even Gail didn't know how to tell him she'd become a believer. That's why I had to break the news to him." She opened the glove compartment and removed the manual, only to stuff it right back and close the compartment.

Was she going to play this Gail card forever? Enough already. "At the time, we weren't romantic. That happened afterward."

Willie fidgeted with just about everything. Now her pink manicured nails caressed the seam of her knit hat. Couldn't she sit still?

"You know you're unequally yoked, right?"

"What's that mean?" Sensing some sort of religious bomb, Debbie glanced sideways at Willie, not knowing if she was friend or foe. Was her comment about being friends just a distraction?

"Never mind. It's none of my business. I just hope you're able to win him over. That's the main thing. Gail told me he was the kindest, most softhearted person she'd ever known, that something big must've happened to turn him from God. Why else would he travel all the way to Spain for college, telling Gail he didn't want anything to do with religion or its do-gooders?"

Willie picked at the window button, accidentally starting it down. The sudden blast of cold air felt good, though, and broke the building tension.

"Who knows?" Willie sighed and powered the window back up. "Maybe he read Gail's journals and is ready to live for God now. I hoped and prayed for you all the whole time you were on your cruise. I know God answered some of my prayers. Well, at least the way I asked. As for the others, well, He answered them. I just haven't seen or heard the answers yet."

Debbie flexed her grip on the steering wheel, taking a sharp turn slow, taking the conversation slow as well. "I believe in God, but I still don't know what I'm supposed to do or believe Him for. My grandparents believed, or so they said. But they never shared any of it with me. When Joshua led me to Jesus, I didn't even know that was a requirement." She took a deep breath and pushed the rest out. "There seems to be so much to learn, and it'd be easy just to slide right back to where I came from. You know?" There, she'd let it all hang out. Now, she'd find out whether Willie was a friend or not.

"I helped Gail. I can help you too. Do you have a Bible?" Willie twisted to look into the back seat as if she expected one to be there. "Have you read any of it?"

Huh. That settled it. Maybe a friendship with Willie could be possible. For the rest of their drive, they discussed the cruise and how

Debbie had dreams along with DR that somehow connected them to saving the children, even giving them directions on fighting the terrorists.

"Wow." Willie let out a soft whistle. "That's sounds like a thriller. You ought to consider writing a book. It'd be bestseller material to the Christian world. I watched the loop where they were attacking the yacht. I gotta say the way you all stayed so calm, well, it had to be a God thing."

Willie's true admiration twisted things up inside Debbie. God had put her main competitor in her hands. Wasn't that the way? Was He testing her to find out if she was worthy of love?

They went on to talk about Ryan McNeilly and his antics while trying to win Debbie's affections. She warned Willie because soon the overly aggressive guy would be their passenger.

The deer gone, his phone call ended, DR relaxed back into his wheelchair, blindly watching a fire dance in the corner fireplace. Debbie was gracious enough to build it before she left, knowing how he loved sitting in front of it looking out the large glass windows onto the deck with the lake backdrop. He often got lost there, deep in thought, especially since Gail had passed. Today, he didn't. Instead, he resumed listening to his brother's radio broadcast.

"The pastor of Back to Christ Church, located just outside Sidney, Australia, is with us today. His best-selling book, *How God Brought Me Home Again*, has been at the top of the nonfiction category for twenty-four weeks. Please, join me in welcoming Reverend Taylor this morning."

Easily, DR could picture his brother taking a sip of coffee during the pause, waiting for the reverend to answer, and hoping this interview would put him at the top too.

"Thank you, Mike, for a glowing introduction and for having me this morning." The reverend's voice rang through clear and strong. "I'm happy to have this opportunity to share my story with your listeners."

Their line of communication was sharp, not dragging, so the satellite was working fine again. "Before we get into your story, what do you think is driving the phenomenal sales your book has achieved?"

"I give God the glory. Not only has He inspired me, giving me my life back, but also, if given a chance, I believe He'll do the same for those who read the book. It's a story of 'all things,' like from the Scripture."

A dog barked. A door closed.

"Sorry. My lab gets a little rambunctious when he hears other voices. I want to add that God also has provided me with the opportunity to do dozens and dozens of interviews, like this one. I believe those interviews are where God reaches those needing the book. After all, I've learned the lesson. Now, I just have to hang on tight to it."

DR shifted. That answer ought to get the audience engaged or not.

"In our telephone conversation three weeks ago," Mike broke in, "you told me you've had thousands of cards, calls, and even threats since the publication back in May. What drives the threats?" As a Christian DJ, Mike had confessed to DR that he'd faced haters, though not to the level the reverend had described.

"As you've seen in my story, it's all about control. Especially today, governments are enacting laws pushing agendas, and voters are allowing things unheard of a decade ago, not only in Australia and America but also all over the world. We're in an unprecedented time where all things are acceptable, to some. Those who like it that way, those pushing a godless agenda, are doing it so they can gain control of a clueless population. But I have news for the clueless—control is only an illusion. We can no more control our circumstances than we can control when we need to go to the bathroom or get randomly shot, especially in the larger cities."

DR sat up at that. Was it about control? Was that at the root of his problem? Maybe even what caused his problems? His dad tried to control the gossip, what others might think. That was it, wasn't it?

"Control, like slavery?" Mike asked.

"It depends on how you define slavery," Reverend Taylor responded. "If you include addiction, mind control, political unrest, and the lack of morals, then I say yes, slavery. Watch the protestors. Most don't have a clue what they're protesting. They're just mad. Without a moral compass —*God*—there is no right or wrong, so all things are on the table, permissible. Love becomes empty. People become narcissists."

DR's phone rang again. "Really?"

He swiped to answer his mom.

"DR, I just wanted to check in. It's been several days since I've heard from you."

Dad was saying something in the background.

"I'm fine, Mom." He pushed himself back in the wheelchair seat. "Sorry I haven't called, but hopefully, we can get together soon. Hey, I was listening to Mike's show this morning. Do you mind if I get off here and listen to the rest?" He could imagine her joy hearing that. She'd been on him about God for twenty-some years.

"Sure, I didn't mean to bother you." Her voice came across low, missing its original enthusiasm.

"You're not bothering me. It's just Mike's interviewing someone. I'll call you later. Thanks, Mom. I love you."

"You too, son."

Just why did he want to hear the interview? Had Miguel, the cruise, or the dreams and vision infected his thinking? Whatever it was, something was pushing him to listen to a little more... just a little more.

"My family always loved God," Reverend Taylor was saying, "at least until my dad became an alcoholic. Then he started using the Bible to beat us, literally at times. He physically dominated my mom and whipped us kids, telling us God gave him the authority to discipline his family. I didn't want anything to do with a god who allowed that. I tried so hard, as did Mom and my sister, to live a pleasing life. But every time I felt I was living right, Dad would go on a binge. So I revolted." The reverend's voice sounded choked. "As soon as I graduated, I left, no looking back. My only regret was leaving my mom and sister behind to bear all his wrath."

"What changed?" Mike asked.

"Dad died. For a year, I felt nothing. Isn't that sad? But he'd let the alcohol destroy him and our family. After Mom remarried a godly man, I began to hear a voice inside me. I started going into my backyard, looking up at the stars and wondering—Is there a God? After a while, I pulled out the Bible, the same one Dad had hit us with. At first, it was emotional, but something kept drawing me. Finally, I started praying and studying the Bible, trying to find some sort of control, faith, or something on which I could rely."

"Where did all that praying and studying get you?"

"After about four months, it appeared nowhere. But I started noticing that, every time I learned something new from the Bible, I felt more built-up inside, power if you will. But each time, I was knocked down again. It felt like I was on a Ferris wheel. Unable to resist, unable to understand why I was facing so much pressure, unable to keep my growth, I'd begun a fight for my sanity."

A train whistle blew far off in the background.

DR glanced at the clock. The show wrapped up in a few minutes. How much more could they get in?

"How did you overcome?"

"I heard a voice, not aloud, but deep from inside." From Reverend Taylor's tone, his emotions were taking over. "It was a gentle whisper. 'Let me help.' That was all. I was busy making brownies at the time, and I realized I was just like the batter. I know it sounds crazy, but that's how it all happened. Sometimes we forget He's the Potter, the Creator. We're the creation formed for His good pleasure, to be His companion. He makes the calls."

DR snorted. Making brownies, was he? What kind exactly?

As if imagining his listeners' thoughts, Mike asked, "Was something in those brownies? Sorry..." Mike coughed, obviously embarrassed. "I didn't mean it to sound like *that*."

"No. Don't be. I get it." The reverend snickered. "And, yes, there was something in it. I'd dropped a piece of eggshell in. That's when I realized I was just like the batter. I couldn't get the junk out of myself any more than the batter could reject the eggshell. I can't make myself better. It requires the Holy Spirit for me to grow, to know God, and to live an empowered life—I have to open the door for Him to come in."

DR laughed. Wow, what a waste of an hour. So the good reverend was the nuts for the brownie. He turned the radio off, took a pause, and glanced at the chest of drawers through the master bedroom door across from the living room. He'd stored Gail's journal there when they returned.

Was it God who'd made all the connections, led them to their success? Was it God who saved the *Disillusioned Illusion*, giving him the connections with the Riccis in Italy? Saving the sex-trafficked kids by luring them there to rescue them through their dreams? Was it God who sent the message about the terrorist attack on the Port of Jeddah, Saudi

Arabia? Was it a prophet of Jehovah, the man who'd told Itasham to share his dream of the attack, saving them all?

His mind spinning, he flopped his head backward. Thank goodness for the wheelchair.

Then he spoke aloud, emotionally drained. "Then why didn't You save me from Bill? Why didn't Dad protect me? Why did You take Gail so soon? Why, God? Why?" He was beginning to feel like a marked man, unraveling.

Must be the meds. This would stop.

When Interstate 94-E forked off to the right, they only had forty-eight miles left to go. The conversation had changed. Now, they were talking about the cruise and Ryan. Debbie forewarned Willie. Whether Willie would be her friend or not, Debbie knew how impossible he could be.

At the airport, she claimed a short-term parking spot so they could find him in the packed Detroit Airport luggage area where they hunkered down. After watching for ten minutes, they spotted Ryan, his bright-red hair a beacon in a sea of humanity coming down the escalator for their luggage.

He scoped Debbie out too, waved over his head, and after finding his bags, walked over—straight into her tight hug. "Hello, gorgeous. I've been looking forward to this ever since DR asked me to come help him out. How are you?" He held her at arm's length, bending back to take a good long look, then ogled Willie, seeming to notice straightaway she was without a band of betrothal.

"I'm good, yes. Everything is fine. Ryan, this is my new friend, Willie. She works with DR's brother." Now she'd watch him pursue her. If he took up his old antics like how he'd attempted to get the chaises close to Debbie by the pool on their cruise, this would be fun.

Willie's black ski bibs were snug but unrevealing. Still, his gaze appeared to bypass all restrictions as he sidestepped Debbie and scooped Willie into a hug. The poor girl's expression showed his boldness shocked her.

Debbie smirked. *Better get used to it, girl. This is just the beginning.*

Before they reached the car, Ryan's interrogation had begun. Debbie laughed to herself, feeling sorry for her new friend, just not *too* sorry. Maybe this could slow her pursuit of DR.

"Is Willie your real name, or are you, like most radio personalities, using an alias on air?" Ryan settled in the back of the Pathfinder, but he mustn't have buckled his seat belt, as he was as close to her as he could get without climbing over the front seat.

"Willie was a name I picked up when I started at the station. My name is Tonya... Tonya Gottey. You're the first person who's asked me that in years." Willie kept facing the front, probably not wanting to encourage his endless barrage.

"Ryan, really?" Debbie winked at her new friend. "Give the girl a break. There'll be plenty of time to get to know each other. How was your trip over?"

"Just trying to make conversation. That's all." He paused and turned his head toward the complex as they passed by the casino alongside the interstate. "Besides, I don't see a ring on her finger. For your information, Tonya is a lovely name. You should use it more." He rested into the back seat's cushions. "You aren't seeing anyone, are you?"

"Ryan, can we at least get out of the airport parking lot before you hit on her?" She shot him a woolly eye in the mirror. One thing you could say for the man—he was consistent.

Seemed Willie was warming up to his questions now, though. "No... it's okay, Debbie. Thank you, Ryan. It is a pretty name, but Willie was the name they hung on me at the station. Then I guess it was easier just to go with it in my personal life as well." She appeared confident, her brows rose, and an air of attentiveness came over her.

Debbie tsked, shaking her head. *Girl, I hope you know what you're doing. He's a real tiger.*

CHAPTER
FOUR

DR rested for an hour or so, then called his mom back, sorry he brushed off their call earlier. "Mom, it's me," he said once she'd answered. "I'm sorry I couldn't talk earlier. How are you and Dad?" The clock—a nice piece Gail picked up with an anchor for its hour hand—displayed eleven ten. Debbie should be back in an hour or so.

"Steven, I'm fine, just concerned about you." Mom talked slowly, as if picking and choosing her words. "And now your dad—it looks like his brother is getting ready to pass away, and he's taking it hard."

DR clenched his teeth. "I was wondering about that. Three weeks ago, Mike told me Uncle Bill wasn't doing good and Dad was looking worse because of it." He wanted to push it, but something inside him, maybe the Michigan Strong thing, kept him from pushing his mother, from upsetting her. He'd never let on he knew she knew about *the night*. He pulled at his hair, an old habit, one he'd set aside for seven years during his time with Gail. Now, it had returned. Every time he thought about *the night*, his nerves came alive. "Got to stop this," he whispered to himself.

"Stop what?"

She must've heard him. "Just talking to myself. Mom, I was thinking. Maybe Debbie and I could come over to see you guys soon? Staying cramped up here in this house is starting to make me edgy. Would that be okay?"

Great. He scowled at the mirror above the hall table. Now his hair was standing straight up from all his pulling. He fingered through it, straightening it.

Something clunked on her end. Had something fallen?

"Are you all right, Mom?"

"Yes... yes, I'm fine. Just dropped a book. Oh, son, I'd love for you two to come by." Her voice readily shared her joy. "I'll talk to your dad. Maybe we can have dinner or something for you. How's that sound?"

He swallowed hard, fighting the anxiety over his intentions. "Okay, Mom. That's just what we'll do. I'll get back to you on the day and time. Tell Dad I love him. Love you too, Mom."

"I love you, son."

After disconnecting, he paused. Time to set things right. Time to confront those who had hurt him when he was nine. First Bill and then Dad. This had gone on long enough. The secret had to be exposed, at least among all those involved with it.

Confronting them wouldn't be easy, but his conversation with Miguel showed him how important—how *freeing*—forgiveness could be, at least for him. Remembering all those lonely nights—scared, lonely nights— brought back fresh tears. Somehow, he had felt at times like he deserved it. More recently, he'd heard lots of victims felt that way at times, that it was their fault. But that was nonsense. No one deserved it. Kids shouldn't be messed with, and that was that. He would end this now, once and for all.

The girls arrived around an hour later with Ryan in tow. And just like on the cruise, he came in with arms wide open, heavily accented words well preceding his entry. Debbie and Willie followed right behind, Debbie jokingly cringing.

"Well, isn't this some place you got here, cousin? Living here, I'll bet you're happy as a Larry, for sure." Ryan grabbed DR for a hug, then let him go after he winced. "Sorry, I guess I'm overzealous, happy to be here.

Hope I didn't hurt you." He retreated to the porch, then rolled in two bags of luggage, and parked them by the door.

"I'm good, thank you. Just a little shock. That's all. How was your trip? Were the girls decent to you?" DR patted Ryan's back. "Come in. Let's have a beer to celebrate. That is what you do back home in Dublin, right?" He started rolling the wheels on the chair, but Ryan got hold of it and took off with him.

"We'll hire a car to take you to your room. I'm sure you're pretty tired by now." DR cut Debbie a glance, then caught a glimpse of Willie. "Debbie, were you going to take Willie to her car?" He motioned Ryan to wheel him to the refrigerator, then reached in, extracted a Stout for Ryan, and held up two more bottles. "I'm sorry. Would you ladies like a cold one?"

"Thank you, but I shouldn't." Shaking her head, Willie tossed her hair back. "Is Ryan staying in the hotel near the highway? If so, I can ride back with him to get my car. No need in Debbie having to go out in the cold again." She cut Debbie a smile.

"Sounds like a jolly good idea." Ryan took a drink from his beer, then nodded his agreement, his bright-red hair flopping onto his forehead. "I'd love your company too."

A car showed up shortly, and after a round of goodbyes, they were on their way.

DR placed his hand on Debbie's on the wheelchair handle as she began to push him into the living room. "Sweetheart, I need—no, want—to go by the hospital tomorrow to see my uncle. Would you like to ride with me? I've made arrangements for a transport to pick me up at ten a.m. We can grab lunch afterward if you like."

She stopped halfway. "Sure. Is he okay?"

"No. He's on borrowed time." He ducked his head, then glanced sideways to see her out of the corner of his eye. "I have to tell him something. I just hope he's still alive when we get there."

"Oh... That's sad." She took him the rest of the way, then helped him out of the wheelchair onto the large red chenille sofa and propped a few of the many colorful pillows around him.

He was getting stronger now, mostly able to do it by himself. Still, it was nice having her help. In a couple of days, he'd see if the doctor would let him use crutches to get around. It sure felt like it was time.

Later, when they retired to separate bedrooms, his call, he lay awake for hours, wondering, playing his time with Bill in his head—over and over again. He hadn't seen the man in at least—What? Fifteen years or so. How would he handle it? Would the emotions flood back in? Certainly, that's undeniable. Would he get mad? Would forgiveness ease his anger?

A star shot across the sky, outside his window. Was it a signal?

Maybe confronting those who hurt him also meant confronting himself. Was he ready? It had made him feel dirty, broken, used. Could he confront those feelings? If he was to get over the guilt, he'd have to face the demons tormenting him. He snorted. Some hero he was!

Sleep did come, but slowly.

When morning awakened him, he had a fight on his hands already. The fight to overcome his fear. It arrived this morning like a roaring lion, even though he'd figured everything out the night before. Now the gunshot wounds seemed to hurt much worse. Yes, it was his mind and his demons playing tricks on him. Still, it was there to overcome. After the breakfast Debbie prepared—coffee, toast, and fruit—they headed toward the hospital in the transport.

"Sweetheart, I hope you don't mind"—he rested a hand on her knee —"but I need to talk with my uncle alone. I need to work out something with him, in a little one-on-one time." As a half smile crossed his lips and his eyes squinted, he must've appeared nervous.

"Is everything all right?" Her hair hung in a ponytail under a white ball cap. Her eyes appeared to glisten with hope, her love shining through them. She patted his hand on her leg. "Sure, no problem. I can wait in the waiting room for you."

At the hospital, they headed to the fourth-floor ICU unit, and the nurse directed them to Bill but added, "I'm afraid he doesn't have long, so be quick. And please don't get him excited." Her downturned lips and eyes told him everything.

Debbie wheeled him to the door, opened it for him, then kissed his cheek. "I'll wait around the corner. Good luck with whatever you're doing."

She turned and left him to it.

With Bill asleep, DR lingered by the door. He took a deep breath, and his entire being screamed inside him. For twenty-three years, he'd lived with it. Now, he rolled into the room as quietly as he could. He maneuvered his wheelchair around to the side of the bed against the window. There, rays of sunlight slithered between the half-closed blinds to give a false impression of life, and the room filled with the sound of machines doing the living for Bill, a constant whirring.

He whispered his forgiveness speech again before realizing Bill's eyes were open, watching him, his face stone-cold expressionless.

"What do you want, boy?" he wheezed as best as his dying body could push out the words. A dry cough followed like a death rattle.

"I came to forgive you."

Bill was but a shadow of a man, his body a mere skeleton, not the strong man of the past. DR felt sorry for him, the fear left him, and now his upbringing, Michigan Strong, came into play. Compassion is stronger than anger, stronger than revenge. Forgiveness is a love that trumps all things—his grandfather had taught him that. Now he would find out.

"You forgive me?" Bill faked a shallow laugh. "Forgive me, boy? That was just payback for what your dad did to me, how he ruined my life. That's all... nothing else." Bill's breathing became more labored, his wheezing louder.

"I don't understand." Pressing back into his wheelchair, DR tugged at his hair, trying to understand. He fought to maneuver closer, but too many things were in the way. "What did Dad have to do with it?"

"Boy, I don't have enough time left to tell you the story. Ask your dad. I know one thing, though—your dad doesn't deserve a son like you." He seemed to disappear further into the bed, as if his body was giving up the ghost, it's strength, word by word.

"Still, Uncle Bill, I came to forgive you and to set myself free from this bondage I've been carrying around. So I forgive you." Tears streaked down DR's cheeks. Was this Michigan Strong? Was it okay to cry?

The man's eyes released their own tears.

Bill pushed the nurse's button on the remote in his hand. "Boy, if you're finished with your forgiveness, you'd better leave. I don't think this is going to be too pretty." Bill's eyes closed, and his ribs rose into the air as his struggle to cross what Mom called the Jordan began. A doctor and a nurse came running. DR wheeled himself out of the way and headed to the door. There, he whispered "I forgive you" one more time.

He sat in the hallway outside Bill's room, composing himself, getting ready to start a new chapter. Debbie awaited him, so he'd better get to her.

As DR introduced Clyde McMillen, his friend, employee, and fellow archaeologist, to her and Ryan that evening over cocktails at his house, Debbie played the perfect host. While she served the drinks, Clyde didn't attempt to hide his surprise. "I'm glad you're back and all, DR, but I had no idea you were adding someone." He accepted the glass she handed him, a low mutter coming from his throat, probably too low for anyone else to hear. "What's he thinking, introducing someone who has *no* experience in the field to the project?" Then he fell silent, maybe sulking. Yes, she'd say he looked nervous.

DR's mom then called. Bill had indeed passed on, and DR's father was torn up. The family, she said, would get together privately the next evening but wouldn't be holding a funeral or memorial.

DR agreed to go, then cut their little introductory party short, leaving it to the two men to figure it all out.

The next morning, they took a transport to the shop where Gail and he once processed the pieces of Indian artifacts together. There, Debbie stood to the side, witnessing him basking in a flood of happy memories, even though he'd previously said they worked hours on end. Obviously, it was their joy, their discovery. Now, it appeared the flow was much slower, but crates still trickled in—about two a week, DR said. There, they cataloged and restored the pieces before sending them on to the museum for payment, which was made to the village and DR. The museum took care of the rest for him. Debbie wandered while he, Ryan, and Clyde went over things from the night before. She paused by a stainless steel table and eyed the guys. Clyde's mannerisms again suggested he wasn't happy.

DR patted Ryan's shoulder. "Ryan, I don't want you to do anything but watch this week. There's a lot to learn, and Clyde is an excellent teacher. The main thing is we do it right, every time, following our process. Okay?"

"Got it." Ryan winked. "Do it right—every time. You can count on me, cousin."

Clyde scuffled a crate around, his actions a little much. "Well, I've got to get to it, Boss. Come on, Ryan."

When Clyde strolled further into the spotless workshop, Ryan shrugged and followed. So Debbie brought DR home to rest for his planned meeting with the family. "Probably a bunch of religious rigmarole," DR groused as she wheeled him to meet the transport that evening. "I don't need that, but I'll endure it."

"Good on you—you're a trooper." Smirking, she kissed the top of his head. At least, he hadn't insisted on her going with him. How could he? He obviously didn't want to go himself. She'd pour a glass of wine and relax with a copy of *Scientific American.*

"I hope I'm released to drive myself soon," he said once she'd tucked the wheelchair in the rear.

After he left, dusk settled in and deepened to nightfall. She stood by the window, sipping her wine as the sun hid itself under the horizon, Wall Lake shimmering as if a million diamonds danced on her waters. She hugged an arm around herself and let out a contented sigh.

DR was right. This place was spectacular.

Then the doorbell rang.

She glanced over her shoulder, scowling at the door. "That better not be Willie or Ryan. I can't deal with them right now." She crossed to the door and peered out the glass side pane.

Clyde? What on earth? She'd just met him the night before.

She pulled the door inward and pushed a smile into place. "Hi, Clyde. How can I help you? Would you like to come in?"

Did the guy *ever* look happy?

"Yeah... thanks. Is DR home?" He surveyed the room as he entered and stepped aside, waiting with her to close the door.

"No, but he should be back shortly. I'm having a glass of wine. Would you like one?" She probably shouldn't have offered. He smelled of alcohol already.

"Sure. That sounds good. Thank you."

His stare burned into her from the chenille sofa as she strolled to the kitchen for his wine. Breathing deeply, closing her eyes, she whispered a quick prayer, then returned with his glass. "How was it working with Ryan today? He's quite the interrogator."

He turned up his glass and drained it dry. "The guy is a nutjob—that's what he is. And that irritating accent. Why would DR hire the guy? The chief must've said something. I don't know, but I do know DR is the luckiest guy around."

His eyes scanned every inch of her, making her feel naked.

"He's had his breaks." She perched on the arm of the nearby love seat. "But from what I know of him, he's worked hard and gone through a lot of hardships too."

"Maybe." Clyde's attitude and purpose seemed to shift as he glared at her. Then his smirk said it all. "All I know is he married the sexiest redhead I've ever met, found buried Indian treasure with her, and became an internationally acclaimed archaeologist. Then she died, more millions in insurance, and he meets you. I'd say that's pretty lucky. Meanwhile, I'm working my butt off to make ends meet, and now I have to work with Ryan. Not a great outcome for me, you think."

He scowled at the bottom of the wine glass as if studying his options. "But maybe I can feel better about my circumstances...." He set the glass down and stood. His eyes seemed to have a weird fire about them as he leaned closer. "If I do you, maybe I'll feel better about all this."

"Clyde..." Her heart began to pound, adrenaline kicking in. "You need to calm down. DR will be here shortly. You don't want to make matters any worse."

"Oh, I don't think so. I'm going to see what we have here." He reached out to grab her shoulder, but she jerked away, scrambling to her feet. "So, I got a fighter on my hands. Well, I like a challenge." He stalked around the upholstered chair between them and shoved her against the wall beside the fireplace.

"I am warning you, Clyde. You're going to get it if you don't stop this." She'd been taught the best defense was an offense. She slid out from between his arms trapping her and ducked down to get away.

"Oh no, you don't. I'm getting what's due me." He dove to grab her, ripped her blouse, and tore her bra off one shoulder. "You're not getting away that easy."

"I'm warning you: take your hands off me—now!" She spun and slapped his hand from the other side of her blouse.

"Or what?" He wrestled with the blouse.

"Don't say I didn't warn you. Now you're going to get it." She whacked his hand away again.

"You're right. I am going to get it. You can count on that!" he jeered. His eyes glazed like an out-of-control madman, given over to his alcohol-induced intentions.

Marcie's Place was packed for a Monday night, their pumpkin spice latte very much in demand here at the beginning of the cold winter. The men driving DR's transport were anxious to get home, but they gladly stopped for the promise of a latte. The man on the passenger's side ran in to pick up DR's call-in order. Minutes later, he climbed back into the van and handed his partner a tall coffee and then DR a bag with two éclairs and a coffee tray with two tall cups of the pumpkin magic.

"Thanks, Jack. You guys are a lifesaver. Debbie will enjoy this." He looked out the window as the van pulled away and other customers scurried about with their own prized treats. While he sipped his coffee, a warm sensation came over him. With the whole thing about his uncle behind him, having said his piece, now he could focus on Mom and Dad.

Good thing he had the transport. He didn't want to wear Debbie out with errands and carting him around. Besides, she'd be glad she'd stayed behind tonight. His dad was a mess. Something just wasn't right. DR had to get to the bottom of it.

Wall Lake became a different place in the winter. For one thing, one could see the houses much easier without the leaves blocking the view. Now, he could see his home, a mere half mile away across the lake. As it came into view, flashing red lights lit up the area—two police cruisers, a medical rescue vehicle, and a fire truck—giving it an ominous look through the light fog shrouding the water in between them.

"Hurry. Something's going on at my house." Thoughts raced through his mind. "Please, hurry!"

CHAPTER
FIVE

efore a police officer could come out to stop him, DR was already on the ground in his wheelchair, the transport technician efficient in his job.

Now, the officer held his hand up in the universal stop signal. "Sir, I'm going to have to ask you to stay. This is official police business."

"This is my home. I live here." DR gripped the wheels, ready to roll around the officer if necessary. "What's going on?" He glanced from side to side to decipher what was happening. Clyde's car was next to their Pathfinder, and the sprawling lake house was lit up with lights on in almost every room. A dog barked its disapproval of the disturbance from around the lake's shore.

"I'm sorry, Mr. Ray. I didn't recognize you. There's been an assault. Come with me." The officer reached for the wheelchair handles to help him inside.

"Wait just one second. Here, Jack. This is for you both." DR handed him a fifty-dollar bill. "Okay, let's go, Officer."

While the officer wheeled him inside, DR's heart pounded much like it had during the attack on his *Disillusioned Illusion* just weeks earlier.

In the living room, Debbie sat on the sofa, talking to an officer. More importantly, she appeared unharmed, except for her top and somber expression. When she saw him, she got up and came over. Once in his arms, she wept.

DR stood, opening his arms. "What happened, sweetheart? Are you all right?"

Some of the furniture was still overturned as if a bar fight had taken place.

"Clyde... was drunk. He attacked me." A sob escaped her throat as she tried to straighten her blouse, still hanging down from the left side even though she'd pinned it up. "All I could think about was the terrorists attacking us." She squeezed him in her arms before taking his hand and helping him back into the chair.

Then she returned to the sofa. "He was mad, Officer. DR had brought someone else on board to help him, and for some reason or other, Clyde just went off. He kept saying how lucky DR was and maybe he should just see what DR had for himself here, meaning me." She squeezed DR's hand and shivered at her own words. "Clyde tried to rape me, honey."

How calm she stayed for someone who'd just been violently attacked! It was the same fearlessness she'd shown on the cruise. She glanced over her shoulder after hearing the other officer and medic talking while walking in with her attacker.

Clyde was led out, cuffed, and bandaged, his face showing he was the loser. His arm hung in a sling, and gauze bandaged his face below a swollen left eye. And the bloody shirt and swollen lip still testified of his suffering.

DR's rage rose. He pushed himself out of the chair to stand, then pointed at the door, his hand shaking. "You're fired. Get out of my house. I don't ever want to see you again."

Of course, the not-seeing part wasn't an option. Clyde still had access to the shop, and some pay was due him.

Debbie reached out to restrain him and return him to his wheelchair. Clyde just kept his head down and walked out to the police cruiser.

"It's okay. No need to get excited. He got his." She smirked, then winked. "I told him he was going to get it."

"Can you tell me where you both were standing when this all started?" The officer surveyed the fallen furniture Debbie had left upturned.

"He was sitting here, on the sofa, when I got him a glass of wine while he waited for DR. When I returned from the kitchen, I gave him his wine and sat there, on the love seat."

"Then what did he say or do?" The officer jotted it down in his report.

"After he guzzled the wine, he started to get angry, threatening me. Soon, his rage was out of control." She rubbed the red mark over her shoulder from the bra strap as she recounted what happened next.

A tremor went through her, and DR squeezed her hand to comfort her.

"Go on," the officer prompted.

"He said if he did me, maybe he wouldn't feel so slighted. I told him to stop or he was going to get it. He said, 'I'm going to get it all right.'" She stopped and composed herself. "Then he grabbed for me again, so I gave it to him. First, the lip. He licked it, and the taste of his blood seemed to drive him even harder. He grabbed me again. Then I threw him down, but he shot right back up. After a tussle and a few more facial punches, I snapped his arm. That did the trick. That's when I called you guys and DR, only my call to DR went straight to voicemail." Pursing her lips, she ducked her head, probably for his sake.

"Honey, I'm sorry." DR reached for the back of his head, but caught himself, stopping short. "I didn't check. This whole thing with Bill has thrown me out of sorts."

"Wait a second!" The officer quirked his lips, as he laid his pen down, extending his hand. "I recognize you, now. You two are from the yacht attacked on the Indian Ocean. I thought you looked familiar." He sprang to his feet and shook their hands. "I saw the whole thing on the news. That was some battle. Dr. Ray, the way you dove in front of those bullets—that was top shelf. I know it probably saved Ms. Holmes's life."

"Yes, that was us." DR cut her a look. "And we're still working it off, so to speak."

"I can't begin to tell you how proud we are to know a resident from here in Wall Lake was part of saving those kids. And you"—the officer nodded to Debbie—"how you stayed calm and took down those terrorists. Wow. We don't see that kind of action here, and I'm thankful. You're both heroes. Thank you for saving those kids. Kids shouldn't be used like that."

"It was all by accident, I assure you." DR shifted in his chair. "We still have no idea why anyone would want to attack us."

"More like a divine appointment." She smirked, tugging at his sleeve. "Remember, we had those prophetic dreams—they weren't by accident, I'm sure. And they helped draw me and you together too."

"Ms. Holmes, where did you learn to fight?" The officer studied her size and conditioning. "To beat up a man his size is quite an accomplishment for anyone, but especially for a lady of your stature."

"I lived in Japan until I was fourteen." She drew back and lowered her gaze, her words coming out rather quietly. "I studied under the leading ninjutsu master."

"How many years did you study ninjutsu?" Pen back in his hand, the officer continued his questioning.

"Eight years, plus I've had a few refresher courses in Chicago. Where I'm from, you never know when you'll need to defend yourself or from whom." She rubbed at her arms again. "It appears the same can be said for Wall Lake."

DR's brows rose, and his eyes widened. Once again, he reached to the back of his head. Still, he resisted the urge to tug his hair and exhaled instead.

"This isn't a usual thing here, ma'am. It's only the third attack this year, and that's still a rather high number for the Delton and Wall Lake area." The officer closed his notebook and patted it. "I think I have all I need right here. You'll be around if we need something else, won't you?"

"Yes, she'll be here." DR rose and put his arm around Debbie. "Thanks, Officer."

The officer let himself out as they watched him leave.

Then DR kissed her cheek. "You forever surprise me. Is there anything you can't do?"

Turning and facing him, she draped her arms around his neck. "You'll just have to wait and see."

In Albion, Tammy Rae Ray was at her wits' end. The years of heartache over her oldest son had built to its crescendo. She wanted DR, her Steven, to be part of their lives again, part of a family he deserted long ago. Mike Sr. was going to have to listen to her, and that was that. But she needed a plan, a good one.

When the screen door squeaked its announcement of his arrival home from work, she had about five seconds left. She'd pull out all the stops now. Tonight, she'd get her way. It had been over twenty years, and with Bill dead, her husband had no reason to continue the charade.

She rushed around the kitchen. The table was ready, as were the candles, steak, and dessert. Not to mention she'd dolled herself up. It all looked perfect, even if she had to say so herself.

"Honey, I'm home," Mike called out, coming down the hallway as if he didn't know she'd heard the squeaking door. He strode into the kitchen, then paused. His eyes widened at the wonderful setting she'd prepared—just for him.

"Welcome home. How was your day?" Trying to remain bold, she raised her chin and pushed her shoulders back.

"Steak on a weekday?" He looked from side to side, put his arms around her neck, and kissed her lips. "What's this all about Tammy Rae?"

"I wanted to please you."

"Tammy Rae..."

"We need to talk."

"We are talking. But we don't need steak to talk, do we? I feel like I'm being basted and wiped down for roasting. This must be something big." His right hand slid down to the small of her back. His left held her back so he could look into her eyes.

"It's about Bill... and Stevie. I need to know what happened and why you didn't stand up for Steven. I miss my son, Mike." A tear slid from her left eye. She brushed it away on her sleeve. She'd told herself to stay strong. Strike 1.

"Not again. How many times are you going there?"

"Bill's dead. What can it hurt to talk now? He won't get in trouble now, Mike. What happened? I want to know." She twisted loose from his grip, walked over to the kitchen sink, and gripped the countertop. Her back to her husband, she leaned over the sink and peered out the window. "I want to be a part of our firstborn's life again. I want *us* to be a part of it before we die." A gasp escaped her lips. Strike 2.

"Can we eat first? I'm hungry, and there's no use letting all this food get cold."

Good. He must've realized she had a point. She loosened her clenched grip on the tiled counter.

He walked over to snuggle against her back. "You wore my favorites too—dress, perfume, lipstick, stockings, the works. You look lovely, by the way. I must be nuts letting something from so long ago keep me from loving on you."

Heat burned behind her eyes, but she blinked back the unshed tears, spun around, and kissed him on the lips. Her eyes closed, and her heart beat wildly. "Let's eat."

This was far easier and nicer than she'd prepared herself for. She was ready to go to the mats. Now she'd get to the bottom of it. After dinner, she took his hand and guided him to the living room. The lines on his face showed his age due to the stress he must've been feeling.

"Relax, honey. It's just you and me. How bad can it be?" She kissed his cheek. "Maybe we can play tag later, and I might just let you catch me." She winked, eyes narrowing to show her playful side.

"I've always caught you."

"Did you ever think I wanted to be caught?" A giggle escaped her lips as she nudged her husband. "Now, tell me what happened so we can get it over with."

Mike let out a shuddering breath. "When I was ten, Bill was seventeen. He was touted as the best football player Michigan had produced in twenty years, a high school five-star recruit, the top of his class at his position of cornerback."

His shoulders sloped, and he ran a hand over his face. "He was my knight in shining armor. He always looked after me. I wish I wasn't so immature and selfish. There was a scouting camp I wanted to go to, but Dad wouldn't let me go by myself. So he made Bill go with me over his objections. I found out later there were rumors about the camp leaders. They... they supposedly abused some of the children and teens."

"What's this got to do with my son?" She wiggled on the sofa.

"Give me time to finish." He held up a hand. "I told you it's a long story. Anyway, the rumors ended up being right. That night, when everyone went to bed, they went into Bill's tent and molested him. I could hear Bill calling out, but no one went to help. Neither did I. I was scared. But the authorities did get involved, and the leader got a slap on the wrist. Meantime, it caused Bill to go off the deep end. He gave up everything and ran away to California. No one even saw him for five years. It destroyed him." Tears wet his collar, pent-up secrets and emotions let go of.

"I still don't know why you didn't punch him out, call the police, something. He stole Steven's life." She was crying too, remembering the horrible night.

"I did do something." He groaned and rubbed his right leg several times. "I went over to his shack on M-66 and beat him up. Still, I couldn't call the police. I felt responsible for ruining his life. And he just laughed at me afterward, saying 'a life for a life.'" He bent over, putting his head between his knees.

"But your little boy—look what all this did to him."

"I know!" Mike's whole body jerked. "Believe me, I know. I loved taking Steven fishing, watching the games at the Big House. But I couldn't get over ruining Bill's life just to go to a stupid camp. When he came back from California, he was a drunk, a shell of the person he was. I felt shame every time I saw him, especially as he was dying."

Tammy Rae could almost feel her husband's hurt. He was crying, and anyone who ever knew her man knew that was a no-no. So she let it go. Now was the time to make plans to reunite them. Reliving the past was over, and only the future lay ahead.

"Can we have them over, Debbie and Steven, Saturday, and get this worked out? I told him we'd have them over for dinner. He said he'd like that." Patting his leg, she raised him up to look him in the eye.

"What did you have in mind?" His face contorted, and the lines etched deeper.

"Just the four of us, we'll have fried chicken, Steven's favorite, and all the fixings. Even some of the raspberry cobbler you like. Then you and Steven can go outside and talk this thing out. I'll keep Debbie busy inside with girl talk and a photo album or two. It'll be fun. You'll see."

The next morning at DR's home, things were much calmer. He sat sharing breakfast with Debbie. The beautiful woman across from him looked the same, but apparently, he still didn't know quite a bit about her.

"Honey, I'm sorry I didn't see that coming." He shifted in his wheelchair, still angry. "Maybe bringing Ryan over wasn't the best first move. After all, he's inquisitive and sometimes downright pushy. Tie that together with his accent and slang, well, I can see how it could infuriate someone."

"It's not your fault. How could you have known Clyde was a ticking time bomb and I just happened to be convenient? A bad choice, but convenient." Her smile brightened, and she tilted her head. Then a giggle escaped her lips, and her brown eyes squinted and appeared to dance. "You know, Dr. Ray, being around you seems to be a dangerous proposition."

Rising out of his wheelchair, he embraced her. *God is good.* Whoa! Where did that come from? He must be losing it.

"So how old were you when the court took you away from your mom and dad?" It was time he learned everything about his beautiful girlfriend.

"I was six. Granddad accused my parents of being druggies, and the strict Japanese courts agreed with him. After that, I only saw my parents a couple of times a year. Granddad did everything he could to keep them away." She sighed. "Even now, I haven't seen them in over fourteen years. I would love to see them, to find out what happened."

Her faraway look told him to change the subject.

"Hey, we can talk about this later." He returned to his chair. "I'll bet Clyde was surprised. I'm thankful you know how to defend yourself."

"I'd say he was surprised, but he was right. He was going to get it, and when I busted his lip, it felt so good. I don't get many chances to use my training. He fought back, but after I broke his nose and arm, he was done." She shook as she laughed.

"I know I'll be watching my *P*s and *Q*s." He winked and pushed his hair back.

She bent down and kissed him. "All you have to worry about is loving me, Dr. Ray."

CHAPTER
SIX

At WREAL, Willie read the news from the night before off the state police press report. Then she let out a gasp. Could that account of a local arrest be right?

"Mike, you need to see this." She waved the report.

"What? I need to see what?" He shuffled through the day's emails and on-air notes. He hadn't even taken his coat and scarf off yet, and notes from Saturday's interview still littered his desk. Besides, he knew as well she did that nothing of much importance ever happened in Delton.

"Look." She rushed across the small office and thrust the report in front of his face. "This. It's about Debbie—Dr. Debbie Holmes. Your brother's girlfriend."

"Let me see that." He skimmed the page before settling on one arrest report. Then he dialed DR and shot Willie an I-don't-know woolly eye.

The phone rang three times before a female voice answered.

"Hi," Mike responded. "Is this Debbie?" He gestured to Willie and pointed to the receiver as if Willie hadn't heard.

She stifled a smirk. She did radio for a living, for crying out loud.

"Yes, this is she."

"It's Mike, DR's brother. Is everything all right over there? Willie and I just saw an arrest was made there last night. What happened?" He switched to speakerphone and squinted as he focused, obviously hoping everyone was okay.

"Yes, I'm fine. Which is more than I can say for Mr. McMillen."

"Mr. McMillen? As in DR's assistant, Clyde?" His jaw dropped, and he sat on the corner of his desk. "I saw DR's address and worried something happened between you two. Is he okay?"

Now Willie's smirk broke free. He was shooting the questions in rapid-fire like a seasoned reporter chasing down an interview.

"Your brother's fine. He must be up making his special coffee because I can smell coffee all the way across the house."

Debbie giggled, and it settled Willie, helping them relax.

"Oh... you better not drink that stuff, especially if he says it's his special sailors' blend."

Mike snorted. "I well remember my first—and *last*—cup of it. I'm so glad you're okay. What happened if you don't mind me asking?"

Willie, trying to draw information with him, rolled her wrist around and around like someone giving parking directions.

Muffled voices came through the phone. Then a sudden rush of air as Debbie exhaled. "Wow... how many coffee grounds did you put in this? I can already feel my heart racing." Her loud laugh followed.

"Did you just drink some of his coffee? I told you so." Mike grinned at Willie. "Our friend just had her first taste of DR's Sailor at Sea Coffee."

"Yep. I was warned." Debbie's merry voice rang out. "Now I know why he says it wakes you up. There will be no sleeping today. Anyway..." Her voice dipped. "Clyde got mad because DR hired his second cousin, Ryan, to help with the processing of the dig artifacts. Ryan can have that effect, plus Clyde may have been cheating on the processing of the pieces." She then recounted her night before hurrying on. "I'm all right, though. I'll tell you more when I see you, but I need to go before this coffee gives me a coronary. Bye, Mike."

"Okay, I'll talk to you soon." The phone went dead as soon as he replied. So he clattered it back to his desk, processing. He shook his head side to side. "To be so small... she sure is a tough one." But then they'd seen her steely resolve during the attack on their yacht. "She can't be, what, more than five one or two? I wonder how she stopped the guy. I guess we'll find out soon enough."

"She's my size almost. I'd say she's five two." Willie's lips slid down at the corners, her eyes still stretched wide.

Mike touched her hand, likely knowing she hadn't given up on her crush on his brother yet. "You need to let it go, Willie. It's not going to happen."

She turned, not ready for that discussion. "I'm over it," she said softly, ending the conversation.

At the marina in Marsala, Italy, Raymond Cancio approached Lorenzo Loretti, the first mate on *Disillusioned Illusion*. The owner, Dr. Steven Ray had the yacht towed there after a pirate attack. Just over two weeks ago, Raymond's brother, Luigi, had tried to bilk DR for an extra hundred grand on the vessel's sale price, but Miguel Ricci interfered. Now, it was time to correct that.

No longer playing it nice like at their first meeting, Raymond wiped the grease from his hands as he planted himself in front of the first mate. "The *DI* is over ten years old, so some of the parts aren't as readily available for her electronic and navigational systems. It would be faster to upgrade the missing elements. Yes, it will cost more, but insurance should pick up a big part of it."

He placed the greasy cloth on the workshop counter, then walked over to the bay where the *DI* was docked, half under cover and half exposed, due to her size. For all her damages, she was quite the beauty. "Tell me what to do, or I'll have to put her outside on mothballs. I can't leave a dock space taken up by a vessel not under repair."

"I don't know what to tell you." Lorenzo shuffled his feet, kicking at a loose washer on the decking. "I need to talk to DR first. Insurance will pick up a big chunk, but he's going to have to bear the rest."

"Don't take too long. I'm putting her out back tomorrow." Raymond rocked back on his heels, hands on his hips, his firm attitude nothing like the friendliness of the day they brought her in. "My bays are valuable. Fortunately, I'm not swamped right now, but tomorrow could be a different story."

After Lorenzo left, Luigi came out to the service area. "Well, what did he say?"

"He said he had to call Dr. Ray. He can't make that decision." Raymond eyed his brother, the marina's GM. Yep, deep down, Luigi wanted this revenge more than his own breath right now. His brother's sly grin confirmed Raymond's thoughts. The pair had run the marina together for decades and had blithely gotten their hooks full of dark-red bloodstains as they sucked their customers dry at every opportunity. And this was an opportunity too.

"Miguel cost me before, but not this time."

"Don't get too greedy," Raymond fired back. "You lost the sale on the yacht because of greed, and we *need* this money."

But his brother was an all-or-nothing kind of guy. He'd rather retire at Momma Leone's retirement home and miss out on a French Rivera retirement for revenge. Not Raymond, though. He didn't need a total gut job, just a good appendectomy.

DR held onto the door handle to steady himself as Debbie wheeled in and out of bumper-to-bumper traffic. The road to Chicago, I-94, offered a bumpy and congested interstate highway, paved part of the way with concrete. Now, the Pathfinder's tires thumped over the joints in a constant roar on their way to visit Debbie's store in the Windy City. They'd stay overnight in her home.

"Whoa." He groaned. "Were you an Indy driver in a past life?"

"Are you going to squeal about every little thing?" She applied her brake as another car with intentions to occupy their spot cut in front. When he pressed his feet hard on the floor as if he could slow them down, she patted his thigh. "Don't push a hole in the floorboard."

"I'm not used to being the passenger. I just hope to survive the journey." He tried to smile, still unable to take his focus off the traffic.

"You're forgetting I learned how to drive in Chicago. We all drive like this. It's called survival." She pushed the accelerator to the floor and guided the Pathfinder into the far-right lane, then whipped back into the center lane of the six-lane section. "You either go with the flow or get run over. It's hard to slow down after all these years of driving pedal to the metal. Besides, it's no fun driving Miss Daisy."

She bit her lower lip and flexed her grip on the steering wheel. "What happened the other day at the hospital? Did you get to visit with your uncle before all the commotion of the doctors and nurses running in?"

"Yes." He cleared his throat. He'd never told her what he was there for. Apparently, she'd become curious. "I'm glad we went when we did. I would've hated not getting something off my chest. I've only told Miguel about this, I didn't even tell Gail, but it seems she kept a secret from me too. Anyway, it's the reason I went to Spain—I had to get away from everything, especially my dad."

He rubbed the cotton material of his jeans down, gathering his thoughts. "When I was nine, my uncle molested me. I told my dad, but he wouldn't call the police because he didn't want people at church to think badly of us. I don't know what he did. But my uncle came by our house several times two years later." He closed his eyes. "The other day, I told my uncle I forgave him, and he laughed. He said it was payback to my dad. But he didn't have time to explain. That's when his time came to an end."

She gulped, and a shudder went through her. "You poor thing. I'm so sorry."

He raised a hand. "I heard a voice each time he came by the house. It told me where to hide my brothers. I don't know why it didn't tell me where to run too." Moisture sheened his vision as he looked straight ahead. "The voice in my dreams on the cruise was the same voice. I don't know whether I made it up or if it was a voice from somewhere else. So, I went to the hospital to forgive my uncle because Miguel helped me realize I needed it for myself, so I could go on."

She caught his gaze, their souls sharing the hard truth.

"That's the reason I've had problems with religion, relationships, and liking myself. There were times I felt guilty, dirty, like I deserved it somehow." He twisted straight ahead again. They were getting ready to leave the highway and enter the downtown area. "My mom's dad always taught us boys something he called 'Michigan Strong.' It's not religion. It's about respect, respecting others, and yourself. He said the morals we hold dear, such as 'Do unto others as you would have them do to you,' are the only steadying force in which we could ever believe."

"Is that why you don't want to make love yet?"

"Sweetheart, I've told you you've got that wrong." *Here we go again.* "I want you more than you will ever know. But you're worth the wait. That's just the way my mother raised me. I–I think you're amazing, one in a trillion, and I want to treat you that way. Mom taught us that if a girl—a lady, in your case—meant anything, you should treat her that way."

A car from the left cut them off, and he slammed his feet on the floor again.

She laughed.

"Besides, my mother-in-law's life was changed forever when she had a relationship with a boy—just one time. When she got pregnant, her dad made her leave their house because church people would talk. So she moved to Malaga before Gail was born. Gail never saw her grandparents or extended family. All because of one tryst." He bowed his head, soul bared.

"Whew." Debbie whooshed out a breath. "I'm sorry. How terrible. I've never met anyone like you, so committed to your beliefs, even when it costs you something."

There is a way that seems right, yet we don't do it. And a way that seems wrong, and we do it. Where did he remember that from? His thoughts shifted like grains of sand in a Saudi Arabian windstorm.

Ryan changed the locks, gathered Clyde's possessions, at DR's request, and placed them by the front entrance. Once again, Clyde had made a bad decision, like when he left DR and Gail after working with them for two years off the Indian Coast. DR said that, less than a year after he left them, they found the Indian burial site. Now after attacking Debbie, he'd be out of DR's good graces forever.

When someone knocked, Ryan answered the door to Clyde standing there with his passkey out. He must've tried and found it no longer worked. At DR's urging, Debbie didn't want to press charges, but the district attorney went ahead with the case.

After posting bail, Clyde went by the shop to get his things. "Let me in, Ryan." He gestured with his hands.

"Hold your horses." Ryan fumbled with the new security bolt at the top of the door.

Clyde forced his way in as the door swung open, then pivoted to eye the new security measures. "It didn't take you long to get me booted out. New locks too?"

When he pushed Ryan, Ryan held his ground. "Me get you booted out? Excuse me, but I didn't try to rape Debbie." He smirked at the sling and bandaged face. Kinda hard to believe sweet Debbie could inflict all that damage. "And from the looks of it, you didn't get too far there, either. DR has been kind to you, and this is how you repay his kindness?"

"It should've been me who made the disth–covery," Clyde slurred, the alcohol's side effects showing. "He just got lucky."

It'd probably be best to get him on his way before more trouble. Bowing up, Ryan shoved his red hair back to the side. "Okay. There's nothing else for you to see here. Time to go."

"Yeah, you're right. Nothing else to see here. Just give DR a message for me. Tell him he hasn't heard the last from me." Clyde stepped backward.

Ryan pulled the door open all the way and helped/pushed him out the door. If Clyde's arm wasn't broken, he probably wouldn't have left so easily. Ryan shut the door and leaned on it, almost giddy. He was *the* man now. He'd take the rest of the day off. The museum professor and curator who handled the purchase and distribution of the pieces they processed weren't expected for a day or so. Then he'd knuckle down and get to learning how to handle ancient relics from a grave.

He headed over to Marcie's Place. Once his eyes adjusted, he recognized a familiar face. Tonya was here with another man. Ryan crossed to her table with the purpose and determination of a suitor. "Can a sham have a seat?"

Not waiting for an answer, he plopped down beside her and patted her shoulder while his eyes took memory shots of her.

"Uh, sure. Why not?" the guy with her retorted, his dropped jaw and raised eyebrows sharing his surprise.

Tonya shook her luscious black hair back over her shoulder, out of the way. "Mike, this is Ryan McNeilly, DR's second cousin, by marriage. They discovered that on the cruise." She then identified Mike as DR's brother. "So I understand your first two days at work have been... interesting."

"Oh yeah!" Ryan snorted, then reached over the table to shake Mike's hand. "Clyde messed up big time. DR's been good to him, but somehow, he felt entitled. He came by today to get his things, and he'd been drinking again. I hope he doesn't do anything else stupid."

"Ryan, it's good to meet you." Mike sipped his latte. "DR must be glad you're here. Especially now. Where are you staying?"

"I'm staying in the shop for now. There's an efficiency there. They had it put in back when they first started receiving crates since they so often lost track of time." Ryan drummed his hands on the wooden table, enjoying the atmosphere, especially the big fireplace with the roaring fire livening him up. "So, Tonya, what's good here?"

"I love the éclairs. How did Clyde look this morning?" She fidgeted, pushing around her chocolate treat on its paper doily.

Ryan flattened his palms on the tabletop. "You should have seen him. That Debbie's a firecracker, tough as nails to be as small as she is. She sure messed him up."

A server came over to check on them, then gave Ryan a wave. "I'm Rachael." She laid several napkins down, catching his eye also. "Can I get you something?"

"I'll have what Tonya is having."

"Okay." She jotted it down. "One vanilla latte, hot, and a chocolate overstuffed éclair, right?"

He grinned, enjoying their interaction. "Sounds good, Rachael."

"Tonya?" Mike finally questioned, his lips pinched in a half smile, and the corner of his eyes rose.

"Yes. Isn't that a beautiful name for a beautiful lass?" Ryan nudged Tonya with his shoulder. "It's way better than Willie. She's far too pretty to be a Willie."

"Oh... yes. It is a beautiful name, but I haven't heard it in several years. What brought that up?"

Glancing her way, Ryan sensed Mike would prefer her to answer.

Soon, Rachael returned with Ryan's order, and Mike stood and took his leave. "Ryan, it's been nice meeting you. Take good care of my brother.

It's time for me to get home to my wife and kids. Willie, see you tomorrow."

And just like that, he was out the door, and Ryan was alone with Tonya.

"Ryan, I was thinking…" She fiddled with her sticky doily, then balled it up. "If you'd like, I can show you around a little. There's not a lot here in Delton, and in the wintertime, it can be boring. But maybe I could show you Grand Rapids or Kalamazoo. Would you like that?"

She gasped and clamped her lips together as if she wished she could take it back as soon as it came out.

"That would be sweet. When do you want to get together?" He let his eyes glide over her, taking more pleasure.

"Maybe Saturday?" Was that a blush? Was she liking his attention, somewhat?

"Saturday, it is."

CHAPTER
SEVEN

Debbie's store was located on a busy street. Now, traffic whizzed by faster than DR liked, but at least, her private parking space wasn't far from the store. She took his wheelchair out of the back and helped him into it.

He smacked the right handle. "I'll be glad when I can lose this contraption."

"It won't be long. How's your thigh doing today?" As she bent forward to peer from behind, her soft hair tickled his neck, her eyebrows shot up, and her smile widened.

The sun washed across her face. Wow. She sure was beautiful, angelic. Smart too. "I feel good. I'm ready to get out of this chair. I believe the doctor will think so too. My side still hurts, but I haven't done anything since the attack. I need exercise too." He placed his hand on hers. Kinda amazing how quickly he'd fallen in love with her. That's it, wasn't it? He was in love.

At the front door, clearance signs covered most of the glass. The store wasn't wide, but it ran deep. A handful of customers browsed the clearance bins, and a gentleman strolled up and hugged Debbie. The pair swayed in the hug.

Then the man looked at DR. "So this is the lucky beau." He reached out and shook DR's hand. "I can't tell you how many hearts you're breaking. She's a special woman."

"DR, this is Johnny, Johnny, DR. Johnny has been with me for seven years and is my very best friend." She flexed her jaw as if trying to suppress her emotions. Then tears began to flow.

"Are you all right, sweetheart?" DR clasped her hand, cupping it to his cheek.

"Johnny is buying me out. I'm letting the store go." She sighed, exhaling audibly. "He's so good with it, practically running it since Mark was killed. This was our dream, Mark and I, but now, I've got a new one." She reached inside a cabinet, snagged a tissue, and wiped her tears away.

When he opened his arms, she climbed into them. She pressed her head to his shoulder, and her slight body curved to his as emotions overcame her.

"What are you going to do?" But this wasn't the time or place for that discussion. Was it?

She didn't answer him but let the moment pass. Johnny's face lost all color, and his mouth gaped. He must be worried about what his friend would do now.

"Can I talk to Johnny for a moment?" Debbie slid off DR's lap and patted his chest. "You can have a look around if you want."

"Sure. I'll roll myself around." He headed straight to the Neanderthal section. Some pieces were replicas of things he'd seen when studying archaeology.

After about fifteen minutes, she joined him and rested a hand on his shoulder. "When Mark and I opened this store, over a decade ago, we mainly carried small pieces from independent digs, some were ours. But we knew a plethora of other paleontologists from different parts of the world and from the conventions we attended. Being an archaeologist, you know how it is. How it's important to be connected. So we bought a lot of their pieces, along with these manufactured replicas." With her free hand, she picked up a small three-horn replica, a triceratops, from a shelf, pressed her fingertip against the horns, then placed it back. "I don't care for the manufactured pieces, but they're necessary. They help get kids interested too."

"Are you okay?" He slid his hand up to cover hers where it still lay on his shoulder.

"Just apprehensive. That's all. It's hard to let go." Her eyes misted, but she drew her shoulders back. "What did you mean a moment ago? When you asked what am I going to do?"

"Nothing really. I know you're struggling to let go of the store. Besides us, what do you see yourself doing, I guess, is what I was wondering. But this isn't the time or place. Sometimes my brain won't think before my lips march on." He lowered his head, not wanting to add more stress to her situation. He'd been there.

"Come on. Let's get out of here." She rolled him to the front entrance where Johnny was building a display. "Johnny, you take care. You're going to have a wonderful success here." She released DR's chair to wrap her arms around her friend once again, eyes closed. Her whisper drifted DR's way. "Love you, Johnny."

Then she turned—like a page in a book—and wheeled DR outside, not looking back. By the time they reached the Pathfinder, she'd composed herself as if nothing had happened.

"Are you hungry? I could use something to eat." He twisted in his seat to face the back as she put the wheelchair in the vehicle.

"I can eat. I'll whip something up when we get to my house. There should be enough there to get by on." A strange smile curved her lips, as if she knew something he didn't. The twenty-five-minute drive to her home on Chicago's northern side, not far from Lake Michigan, was as much an adventure as coming into the city. Though it wasn't as secluded as DR's home, the manor-style house hid behind a black privacy fence and security gates.

She pulled into the driveway and fished out a remote to open the gates. As they swung open, she studied him. "Our home was Mark's prized treasure, while mine was the store."

The brick paving up to the house formed a herringbone pattern. A three-car garage was attached to a colonial with round pillars behind a manicured lawn with mulched trees and flower gardens. Beyond the garage, he could just make out a hothouse.

"Nice. This is some place you have here. Must be labor intensive to take care of, though." He and Gail chose their home because of the ease of care. Mow the grass and trim. Voilà. All the flowers were perennials and needed little care or were growing wild, and they kept the environment as close to the surrounding land as possible.

"Mark aspired to run for political office, so he did a lot of things to make a positive impression on the local power brokers. One of his friends, Congressman Max Rice, was a local contractor until about the time Mark was shot. He has a house around the corner. You might get to see him soon." The twinkle in her eye hinted she was up to something. Then she grabbed his wheelchair handles. "Come on. Let's go in."

So she'd lived a big life. While he shunned the limelight, her deceased husband must've been quite the opposite. "Do you like socializing with high-society people?"

"I was intimidated at first, but I soon learned they're no different, except their money allows them to do things most people can't, won't, or shouldn't. Kind of like Miguel. My best friends are very wealthy, but you would never know it, unless you were looking for something not to like about them." She buzzed the lock open with an electronic key, then pushed the massive oaken front door inward, and held her hand out as if to extend an invitation for him to enter.

He cocked his head to eye the chandelier hovering over the foyer. "Who cleans this place and takes care of your garden?" He let out a low whistle and twisted in the wheelchair to see her face. "This must've cost a fortune. Is it something you can give up?"

She sighed. "I think so. I love it—don't get me wrong. But it's over the top for just me. Plus, a house this size needs a family in it, not just a couple. Mark and I had planned to have a family, but..." She shrugged. No need to say more. Mark was dead. After shaking her hair back, she ran her hand over a wall table and raised it to look for dust. "Maggie, my cleaner, does an amazing job."

"I can tell."

The intercom buzzed. "Debbie, we're here. Are we early?"

She smiled. "It's Dale and Karen, my best friends who live next door. They wanted to see the man who stole my heart and made me want to leave the big life I've been living. A few others are coming over as well. Hope it's okay. Besides"—she winked—"they're bringing food." She bent over to get a kiss, and he happily complied.

Then Karen nudged the door open, Dale following. She rushed to Debbie, and they embraced before Dale got his own hug as Karen studied DR.

"I can see why you're ready to move on, girl. He's a looker. DR, I'm Karen, and this is my husband, Dale. Debbie has been a good friend for a long time. You must be something special for her to leave all this and her friends behind." She waved her hand, palm up, as if sharing the place, then reached toward him, and DR shook it, then Dale's.

Debbie hadn't mentioned any parties or get-togethers. But as much as the quick intros took DR aback, the food sounded good. He was starved, and surely, she was too.

She waltzed over to wheel him toward the kitchen. "Let's go see the kitchen."

Dale led the way, Karen only a step behind. Then Dale put his finger to his lips as he turned the corner. What was that about?

Debbie turned the corner, and a shout rang out. "Surprise! Welcome home, Debbie." Over twenty people staked out in the kitchen with an attached eat-in area, all shouting. "Welcome home, mighty heroes!"

Balloons bobbed around a banner. Someone had gone to great lengths to share their love for her.

Debbie introduced him to everyone, including Congressman Max Rice and her late husband's other influential friends and associates. Then she took leave of him while he and Max talked, visiting the others who had come to wish her well.

"DR"—the congressman reached for his hand—"Dale and Karen tell me Debbie got religion and is putting her property up for sale. That must have been some trip you two shared. We've tried over and over again to fix her up with some of the eligible bachelors at our church from around Chicago, and every time, she spurned them." His eyes didn't seem to focus, but rather, his gaze shifted around the room, almost like someone fishing or someone who didn't want to miss anything. "And how did you ever defeat those nasty terrorists I saw on the television clip?"

A deep breath filled DR's lungs. Still, his lungs remained constricted. The healing wound on his leg throbbed as the memory twinged through him. "It was quite the trip, not quite the one I had planned. It all changed right before the terrorist attack on Jeddah. Someone warned us, and we got out of there just in time. Nevertheless, we all became good friends." What was bothering Max? The guy squirmed as if *he* was feeling the memory twinges shooting up DR's leg from his wound. "We had a good plan and some luck. You never know on the Indian Ocean, especially with the Houthis, Hamas, and all the other Iranian thugs."

A woman strolled over and slid her arm around the congressman's waist. Slightly shaking her head back and forth, she took inventory of DR from head to toe before speaking. "I must say, Debbie always did have good taste. DR, I'm Leslie, Max's better half." She kissed her hubby's cheek, then offered her hand.

"Leslie, it's nice to meet you." He shook her hand, feeling something like a specimen under a microscope.

"The place isn't going to be the same without our girl." She dipped her chin, lowered her glasses, and peered over them. "You take good care of her."

"I will." Just what had Debbie told everyone? DR swallowed hard. He wasn't even aware of the steps she'd taken to pursue their relationship. But what he'd learned today bolstered him. Yep, the future was looking up, and she was committing to their relationship full tilt. He spotted her across the room. Their gazes met, and she winked.

Then Leslie patted his shoulder and made her way around the rest of the room like a politician's wife, leaving DR trapped in the wheelchair as Max started what seemed to be a survey about the cruise.

"Where in the world did you get guys who could shoot like that?" Red blotched the congressman's neck. "Hired men?"

"No—well, David is my second mate. But the other shooter, Tom, competes in international shooting competitions. So I asked him to bring along a few of his toys, just in case. Looks like it was a good thing I did." The urge to stand overwhelmed him, so DR took care and eased out of the chair. He stood beside the cherry kitchen island with its granite countertop and leaned on it.

"Does it still hurt when you stand?" Max eyed him too closely.

"Just a little, not so much my thigh, but my abdomen is still sore. I hope to lose this contraption though on Monday." DR stretched across the countertop and retrieved a cold Coke and chip bag. He held the chilled can up for the congressman. "Would you care for some?"

"Sure, why not?" His lips quirked as he reached for the soft drink. "This is probably the first one I've had in a month that didn't have alcohol in it. Just don't tell Leslie. She's a teetotaler." He popped the top and guzzled the fizz down. "You said someone warned you. How did that happen?"

"My professor was giving us a tour of Mecca, and someone claiming to be a prophet told him to warn us. I thought it was a hoax, but the professor convinced me. So we left straightaway." DR crunched on a chip, then lifted the bag to read the brand. "These are pretty good. I don't think they have these on Wall Lake, but I've got to try to get them."

"Where did you go after Jeddah?" Max munched one of the chips DR shared. "Mmm, they are good."

"Miguel, a good friend who helped me fortify the yacht, wanted to stop in Aden, Yemen. I wasn't too keen on it, not with all they've got going on there. But we had a day to spend, and Miguel's persuasive. We went into the city, only to find more heartache. Someone had broken into a children's home and took ten of them. It broke our hearts." He shifted, balancing on his good leg and getting tired of the story.

"Ten children? Wasn't it ten that you rescued?"

Why did this guy sound more like an integrator than a future friend? DR set the Coke down and wiped his mouth with a handkerchief.

"That's what they tell me. I was a little unconscious at the time." He sat back down into the wheelchair and gripped the wheels, ready to roll away.

"I enjoyed talking to you, DR." The congressman clamped a hand on DR's shoulder. "Why don't you and Debbie call me, and we'll get together at my club over by the lake. Dinner is fabulous, and we can take the *Lucky Lucie* out for a nighttime cruise."

There it was again—that under-the-microscope feeling. DR ground his teeth. Maybe the guy was just looking out for Debbie. "Sounds good, Congressman." He squelched his misgivings and reached to shake the man's hand. "I'll get with Debbie, and we'll get back to you."

"Please, if we're going to be friends, just call me Max."

The get-together lasted well into the evening before everyone had their fill of good food, wine, and conversation, Dale and Karen being the last to leave.

"DR, it was a pleasure meeting you." Karen clasped his hand in both of hers. "We look forward to seeing you both soon." She released him and tipped her head Debbie's way, a motherly gleam in her eyes as she accentuated the word *soon*.

After closing the door behind them, Debbie leaned on it and exhaled. Then she walked over, bent down, and kissed his cheek. "That was some party, don't you think?"

"More than I was ready for." His lips quirked and brows rose.

"Sorry. I wanted to surprise you."

"Mission accomplished. It was nice, though, and the food was great." He grabbed the wheels of his chair and rolled to the window on the left of the entrance door, watching Dale and Karen stroll home through the security gate. "You have a lot of good friends."

"Yes, I'm lucky. I noticed Max spent a lot of time with you. He's always been trying to get me to come out to a club of his, Lake Michigan Men's Club, for dinner. But it seems a little weird to me." She took the handles of the chair and pushed him toward the back of the house. "What did he say to you?"

"He invited us to come over together. What sort of club is it?" DR sank back in the seat, watching the rooms she passed by.

"They have nice dining. I know that. But I don't know whether it's a golf club or a sleazy place old men get together to watch girls. I never asked." She yawned. "Mark never went there."

"He seemed awfully interested in the attack on us. Even preoccupied." Her yawn must've influenced him. He yawned too. "I'm tired too."

"I hope you don't mind sharing the same bed. I don't want to sleep upstairs." She peered around the wheelchair, looking for agreement.

"We'll just put some pillows between us somewhat like in that 1934 movie, *It Happened One Night*, with Claudette Colbert and Clark Gable. They shared a bedroom, they weren't married, so they used a sheet hung between them." He arched a brow and craned around to see her over his shoulder, catching her disappointment.

"So we're still there?"

"Just joking. We don't need the pillows." Though he didn't know how much longer she'd wait, he was unable to give up his beliefs.

After he got himself in bed, he waited on her. He could see her in the master bath. Man, she looked ravishing, her blonde hair a crown of glory, indeed.

"Better stack a few more pillows." She sauntered into the bedroom, her white robe open, exposing her pink puppy-dog pajamas, the same ones she wore on the cruise. She waved at them. "I thought you'd prefer this to my teddy."

"No. It's just better—*for now.*"

CHAPTER
EIGHT

n Marsala, Miguel asked Lorenzo and David to meet him at the marina shop around four o'clock for a talk with Raymond, the shop manager.

"The *DI* will not be put out back in their boneyard or any other, and that's that," he insisted. He'd seen enough, and the Cancios had damaged the marina's reputation already. If need be, he'd take over their lease.

Before four o'clock rolled around, he arrived to get a good look at the situation. Raymond was working on a Jet Ski, wiping it down with a rag. When the shop's entrance monitor rang, he rose and cleaned his hands off with a cloth while he headed to meet Miguel.

Miguel finished his walk around the forty-meter *DI* before the monitor sounded again and Lo and David joined him along with Raymond at the bow.

"Now this is some get-together. To what do I owe this pleasure?" Raymond's left eye twitched.

"You know what the pleasure is." Miguel rocked back on his heels, ignoring the hand Raymond extended to him. "Why do you and your brother always do this? Isn't it enough that the marina sales have tanked—thanks to Luigi's rip-offs? Now you have to destroy the shop's reputation too?"

"What are you talking about?" Raymond's twitch became more pronounced. "I spoke with the boy about this earlier. He knows what's going on." His gaze shifted between Miguel and Lo as he leaned back against a tool stacker, slightly moving it. He straightened up.

"First off, there are no boys here. Lorenzo is the first mate of the yacht, and David is second mate for my friend Dr. Steven Ray. They are heroes, and I would remind you to treat them as such." Miguel cut the pair a nod and wink. "Second, the *DI* is not going out back in your boneyard. Vessels there become bones. Not going to happen, Raymond, not going to happen."

"Miguel..." The man huffed a sigh. As he glanced down the length of the vessel, he appeared to shrink. "I can't leave her parked in one of my bays, waiting for parts. It costs me money. She's ten years old, so her parts are harder to come by. But if we upgrade them, I can get right to it. Replacement parts will take a week or two, and I'll have to pull her outside."

"We'll see about that." Miguel shook his head side to side, thick salt-and-pepper hair blowing in the slight breeze. He shoved it back. "A friend's coming over with his tugboat. We'll haul her out of here. If you have anything on board, now would be the time to get it off."

As if cued by a stagehand, an air horn blast signaled his friend's arrival, and Raymond jolted, knocking back against the tool stacker.

"Wait." He held up his hands. "Don't do anything rash. We can work this out." His gaze darted between them, and beads of perspiration popped out on his forehead. "I want this job."

"Seems to me you've already said your piece. What do you gentlemen think?" Miguel crossed his arms and rubbed on his shoulders, assuming an alpha position.

Lo and David looked at each other. Then Lo tilted his head, and his brows rose. "Yes, I think he has."

David nodded his agreement.

"Look, it's all Luigi's fault. He wanted to gouge the man because he lost the commission on the sale in the first place." Raymond waved both hands, palms up in a half-surrender position. "I want this job. I've got some of the parts. Maybe all of them. I can have it ready in two, maybe three, days. What do you say?"

Fiero, Miguel's tugboat friend, juiced the engines, emitting a loud rumble.

Raymond winced and spun toward the tugboat. When he twisted back, all color had left his face. "Please?"

"Two days, Raymond." Miguel thrust two fingers in Raymond's face, then lowered them. "Why didn't you just do the work? All this drama wasn't necessary." He waved to Fiero.

The man waved back, blasted his air horn once more, and backed out.

"Thank you. Thank you." After shaking their hands, Raymond took a cloth from his back pocket and wiped the sweat from his brow.

Miguel, Lo, and David all said in unison, "Two days!"

At last, DR was able to lose the wheelchair! And just as importantly, he could drive an automobile again. His doctor asked him to use a walker as much as possible, but his alpha mentality and hardheadedness limited the use of such an aid. He preferred to tough it out, especially the following Saturday when they went to his parents' house for dinner.

The weeklong wait had stressed him, but now, he'd get to the bottom of his dad not calling the police on Uncle Bill. Why had Dad been more concerned about what people would say than his son's safety? Friday night, DR had a hard time sleeping, his uncle's comments about payback swirling around in his thoughts.

He slid behind the wheel for the hour-long drive along the interstate from Wall Lake to Albion. The ground was clear, no snow had fallen to speak of yet, so the drive would be pleasant. Debbie seemed at ease, maybe because she was fully vested now, having sold her shop, put her home up for sale soon, and committed to making their relationship permanent.

At where he grew up, he showed her the college and explained how the downtown area made its survival off the college. Then he took her by the local hot spot, one of the college hangouts, a pizza restaurant, before driving to his parents' home on the town's backside.

"Not quite Chicago." He cut her a half smile, winking. "Most of my schoolmates moved away like I did. There isn't much here other than factory work, and that's no fun. They run them three shifts, almost seven days a week. It doesn't leave much time for a life."

Debbie sat, taking it all in. Certainly wasn't much to be overexcited about.

"Are you okay?" He pushed playfully on her leg.

"I was thinking about my friends. They were so nice to come by and give us a party. I hope we can make a lot of friends on Wall Lake. Maybe we'll meet some friends at Willie's church." Then her face scrunched as if she realized the slip and wished she could squeeze the words back into her mouth.

"Church? I don't go to church." Suddenly lightheaded, he tightened his grip on the steering wheel as sirens sounded in his imagination. He slanted a terrified look her way. "Where did you come up with that idea?"

"Forget it. It's just something she mentioned. It's not a big deal."

The sightseeing tour over, he spent the rest of the journey in silence. He wouldn't join in a conversation that may include him going to church. Not. Going. To happen.

His dad was a stickler for upkeep, always saying it was far better to take good care of your things than to replace them as they wore out. The gray siding looked fresh, even though it had been on their house for fifteen years. The greatest improvement they had made was gravel in the driveway, and Dad was proud of that.

As they pulled into the driveway, Mom stood looking out the front window. Then she let the curtain fly back and came out of the house, followed a few steps back by Dad. She was beaming, but Dad appeared apprehensive.

"There's my boy. I've been looking forward to you both coming all week. I hope you're both hungry." She took him in her arms and squeezed him tight for the longest of moments. "You're not using your wheelchair, and you're driving too. That's great."

"Yes, I was able to get rid of the chair earlier this week. You remember Debbie, don't you?" He peeled himself out of her grip, just in time.

"Of course." She tore around the car, taking Debbie by surprise. "Debbie, welcome. I hope you're a big eater. I'm so excited to have you both here, but we don't want to stand out here all day. The food is ready." She clasped Debbie's hand and tugged her along.

"Hi, um, okay. It's nice to see you again too." Debbie's widened eyes and raised brows shared her shock as she lurched forward. "I can eat." Half stumbling, she stepped awkwardly as Mom tugged her arm.

Dad shook DR's hand, then half hugged him before he caught up with the ladies. "Honey, I know you're excited, but there's no need tearing Debbie's arm off." He reached out and hugged her before Mom dragged her the rest of the way inside. Then he fell back with DR again.

"Your mom has been busy all day, just cooking away. She has all your favorites. You know how she likes to put the dog on." He shook his head, the corners of his lips turned up, and his eyes appeared to glow. "You'd think the king and queen of Sheba were coming."

"Don't pay him no never mind." Mom smacked at the air with her free hand, waving him off.

"You have dogs?" Stepping inside, Debbie turned in a circle, moved to stand beside DR, and bent down as if looking for signs. "I used to have a Pomeranian, but that was years ago. Where do they stay?"

DR's eyes crinkled, and a smile widened on his lips. Then a roaring laugh escaped as he and his dad both shook their heads. "No, honey. They don't have dogs. That's just an expression. He means she's been working hard to put her best foot forward for you. Like the candles on the table."

Debbie stared up at the ceiling, probably feeling punked, but she was smiling. Then she punched him lightly in the arm. "Now I know where you get it from."

"I like to keep things light around here." Dad smirked. "Tammy Rae can get too serious at times. Would you two like something to drink? We have Coca-Cola, milk, and water. We don't keep alcohol in the house."

"I'd like a Coke, Dad." DR eyed Debbie for her reaction.

"I'll go with a Coke too, Mr. Ray."

"Honey, you call me Mr. Ray, and I look for my dad. Please call me Mike or"—Dad elbowed DR and winked at her—"or Dad."

"Hmm, I like Dad." She winked back, giggling. "You're a wisenheimer just like your son, I see."

"You know what they say. The apple doesn't roll too far from the tree, but I always add that some do get a worm or two." He shook from laughing, appearing to be enjoying their banter.

"Dad... Are you saying I have a worm in my apple?" Unable to hold a snicker, DR almost snorted.

"Nooo, son. Not at all. It's just an observation. Some apples do get worms, but not yours." Dad chortled again. "I better stop before I get him all riled up. Tammy Rae, would you like a Coke? You've been working hard."

"Yes, that would be nice."

DR shifted, enjoying Debbie's banter with his folks. So far so good, but he hadn't come here just for a fun night. What would this evening reveal?

Over in Delton, Willie went by DR's workshop to see Ryan, who appeared busy through the security window as he opened a crate from India. She eyed the worktable midroom before he caught her waving. Then he laid down two pry bars and half jogged to the door.

She held up two cups of pumpkin spice coffee and a bag with éclairs, practically currency in her world, and stood back for him to open the door.

"Tonya... Oh, I'm sorry." His Irish twang rang deeper this evening. "I got so busy I forgot you were going to show me around. Please forgive me."

"It's okay, not like it was a date or something. We can do it another time." She leveled out her shoulders, trying not to appear disappointed, then offered the latte. "I thought you might like something to drink and eat." She brandished the éclair bag too before setting it down. She turned in a circle to survey the shop and peered over the lid of her coffee cup while taking a sip. "This is nice. How do you like it here?"

"Hmm, I'll tell you what's nice. These treats. This is awful thoughtful of you." He unrolled the bag on the éclairs, eased one gooey treat free, and bit into it, a delighted groan escaping. Then he nodded. "Yes, it is nice. Different from working in a church office. But I'm thankful for the opportunity." He slid a chair over for her and grabbed some paper towels to use as a plate.

"Is the work hard?" She peeped into the crate he'd been opening when she knocked. It was still full of packing material.

"No. There's just a lot to learn. And I've fallen behind because I'm not always sure of what to do, so I have to either call DR or wait on the university professor." His eyes closed as he took another bite of the éclair. "Mmm... just what I needed. You're the best."

"I know, right? They're delicious—and habit-forming." A giggle escaped her lips. "So when do you want to go on the tour? I'm free most days after three p.m." She wiped the crumbs off her hands and disposed of the tissue inside the take-out bag.

Ryan's lips quirked, and his brows rose as he tilted his head. "Are you asking me out on a date? Because that's what it sounded like."

"No." She cringed, her shoulders inching up by her ears, her face heating. "I mean, well... I just wanted to be friendly. That's all. I want you to enjoy our town, no, no. Not a date." Great, she was practically stammering.

"I'm just kidding, Tonya. I didn't mean to get your knickers in an uproar. Of course, I'd love for you to show me around. I'll even get dinner." He patted her shoulder. "Besides, I would love a date with you. I just can't go tonight. Can I have a rain check?"

"Just let me know, and we'll do it." To change the subject, she pried away some packaging from the box. "Is it okay if I look?"

"Sure." He pulled some from the other side and exposed pieces like platters. They appeared to be hammered.

"Oh, how beautiful. Are they hard to preserve?" She curled her fingers inward to keep from picking them up. Yep, she knew better.

"It all depends on the material, what it's made of." His eyes appeared to be finding pleasure in what she was made of.

She shivered at his admiration, but the male attention was nice, even if he was a little aggressive and crass. "Okay, I can see you have a lot of work to do, so I'll get going. Here. That's my phone number." She started toward the door. "Let me know when you're free, and we'll go on that tour."

"I'll have to let you out. After what Clyde did, we've put new security in place." He slid around her to let her out, then saluted her with his latte. "See you soon."

After dinner, while DR and his dad headed outside, Debbie settled in with Tammy Rae to investigate the family picture albums. As they thumbed through the albums, Debbie tried not to squirm with Tammy Rae's gaze intent upon her.

"You look incredible in that outfit. No wonder Steven is falling in love with you." She reached over the album and hugged Debbie.

"Oh... That's so nice of you to say." Debbie eased free. "You're so sweet. I see where DR, Steven, gets it from now. I love him too." While she tilted her head in modesty, she was confident. She wore the outfit—designer jeans and a simple white button-up shirt—to be comfortable and understated. No use wearing something that screamed "look at me." They would look anyway.

She flipped through the pictures, occasionally peeping out a front window to get an idea of what was going on. Mike Sr. sat on the picnic table, his feet on the bench. DR stood nearby, the body language she already knew so well suggesting his anxiety as he paced in front of his dad. She wanted to go outside, but Tammy Rae, seeming to sense it, shook her head.

"They need to work something out. Let's look at another album." She patted Debbie's hand, then raised her brows. "Do you have any pictures of your cruise on your cellphone?"

Oh! That would be fun. "I do. Let's take a look." Debbie wriggled her phone from her back pocket, glancing out the window again. "I wonder what they are talking about. Do you know?"

"Yes, and if Steven wants, he can tell you later. Now how about those cruise pictures?" With the corners of her lips upturned and her eyes glistening, she appeared happy.

At ease, Debbie unlocked her phone and brought up the trove. The first cruise picture was the last one she'd taken, when they were being rescued by US Navy helicopters in the Indian Ocean. She let out a shuddering breath. "They'd just taken DR and Habiba up in baskets, both unconscious. Now, it was my turn. I was the last one on the boat."

She tipped the phone to her companion, revealing a picture of a compartment door that hid the kidnapped children in darkness for days.

A message was scratched on it in small scraggly handwriting as if one of the children had written it.

The harsh reality of their plight had yet to hit Debbie after the cruise. It all happened so fast. It hit now. She couldn't suppress the sob. Then the floodgate swung open, and she fell on Tammy Rae's shoulder. She stayed there for what seemed like an hour but probably wasn't even a minute.

"Honey, what's the matter? What is it?" Tammy Rae palmed strands of hair away from Debbie's face when she left their embrace.

"I'd forgotten the intensity of it all, the dreams, the attack, the fear of nearly losing DR, and the horror of finding the missing children. Then to top it all off..." This time, her sob was a happy outburst. Yes, God had guided them indeed! She'd forgotten *Providence*, the boat, but providence had indeed found them.

"What's that on that compartment door?" Tammy Rae leaned closer, eyes squinting, mouth open.

Debbie handed her the phone, not needing to see. It had etched itself into her memory. She put both her hands over her mouth, covering most of her face.

"Is it writing?" Tammy Rae squinted long and hard at the phone before touching the screen, enlarging the picture.

"Yes, it is."

"It says 'Stevie was here.' What does it mean?" She returned the phone, then pushed to her feet. "Let me get you some tissue, honey. I'll be right back."

Looking out the window, Debbie felt a sense of belonging she hadn't felt. On that fateful day, DR dove in front of her and took two bullets meant for her. This man, this hero, would do anything for the love of his life—and he'd proved it.

So what was he fighting out there now?

CHAPTER
NINE

DR had stopped the pacing. Now, he stood with his hands in his pockets, once again the schoolboy who suffered the attacks. His dad sat on the picnic table DR and his brothers had climbed over as kids. Good days sandwiched between days he'd never forget.

Dad kept his head down, scrutinizing his hands, the same hands that held DR, hugged him, and perhaps missed him? "Son, I'm so sorry for everything. I don't even know where to start." He lifted his head and propped up on his elbows. Then his gaze went off into the yonder, and a tear appeared to be trying to escape.

DR shifted his stance, protecting his wounds—the recent ones and the ones inflicted so long ago. "Dad, I only have three questions. First, why didn't you call the police? Yes, I heard you through your bedroom door telling Mom you didn't want people to talk. Next, what could they say that was worse than what Uncle Bill did to me?"

He ground his teeth to suppress his emotions, but they wouldn't be held down. His voice became edgier. "And most importantly, did you know he came back two other times two years later?"

DR turned his head. Eyes closed, he pressed a half-clenched fist to his lips to contain the ugly urge or spirit pushing him.

When Dad jolted, DR reopened his eyes. Dad now sat up ramrod straight, horror flaring the edges of his eyes and dropping his mouth open. Apparently, words wouldn't be formed.

"Yes, Dad." DR ground the words out. "Two more times. Each time, I had to hide my brothers—or so, a voice told me. When Bill left, he always laughed, saying, 'Don't tell your dad, or next time, it'll be your little brothers.'"

He almost resumed pacing, unable to stand still with the memories burning his blood. "He'd go out laughing about dreamwalkers and tongue talkers. Did you think I was damaged goods? Is that why you didn't want people talking?" No longer babying his wounds, he pressed his feet hard into the ground to regain control, focusing on the reason he was here. "But no matter. I'm not here for answers. I'm here to forgive, no matter what." There, he said it. Miguel was right. This was for him. Dad would have to find his own escape, forgiving himself.

Dad exhaled a shaky breath. "I feel so ashamed. I didn't know Bill came by. But all of it is my fault. He only did it to get back at me—at least, that's what he said." His eyes searched the sky as if looking for a note from God on what to say next. He then related what happened to his brother. "He didn't come back home to Albion until after you were born, about ten years or so. By then, he was an alcoholic and a bum, driving that old Chevy Caprice and living out by Route 66 in a shanty, doing odd jobs to eat and drink. You know the rest."

Staring at the ground, DR kicked at a root and scuffed over the loose gravel, another boyhood habit never broken. The silence was intense, his father apparently as humbled by their predicament as DR was.

"Dad, I saw Uncle Bill before he passed. I went to forgive him, and I did." DR explained what happened there and how he now understood what Bill meant. He dropped onto the tabletop beside his dad, put his arm around his shoulders, and felt the strength in him. Looking out into the field just as his dad did allowed his mind to focus. "It wasn't your fault. You couldn't know the future any more than I can. I just know it's time we put this in our past. There's a lot of living to be done, and I want to spend it with you, like we used to."

Dad bumped his shoulder against DR. "I would like that more than anything, son." His voice caught, and he took a deep breath before continuing. "I cherished our time together at the Big House. Remember how you used to try to howl like a wolverine?" He chuckled, beaming.

DR's stiff muscles loosened. He gave his dad's shoulders another squeeze, then released him. "Those were good times. We'll do it again, Dad. I promise." Then, his lips quirking to one side, he shook a finger at him. "I may not howl, though."

His phone rang, so he slid it out and checked the contact—Tom. "Are we good, Dad?"

"Better than ever." Dad looked to the sky, and DR imagined he was thanking God. "I'll see you inside." After a man hug, Dad left him to answer the call.

"Hello, Tom?" DR strolled toward the driveway, his soul at peace.

"How are we, Gimpy?" A guffaw came over the line. "You healed up yet, or are you still milking it for Debbie's sympathy?"

"Ha ha. Aren't you the funny one? Strange, I don't remember you being a comedian."

A woodchuck scurried into his hole, hearing him coming. DR mimed holding a rifle and shooting him like he did as a boy.

"And yes, I'm still milking it, wouldn't you? I'm getting better by the minute, though. I finally got rid of that wheelchair, so life is good. So... just catching up, or is this business?"

"Does there have to be a reason?"

"Go on. Ask him!" Laurie's voice called out in the background, egging him on.

"What's up? I hear Laurie?" DR put aside the imaginary rifle and whispered, "Next time, Mr. Woodchuck."

"Did you say 'Next time, Mr. Woodchuck'?"

"Sorry." DR guffawed. "Just my imagination. So what be your pleasure today, Tom? Before Laurie busts a vein."

"How is Debbie?"

A scuffle came over the phone.

"Hi, DR," Laurie said. She must've taken the phone away from Tom. "Glad to hear you're okay and Debbie's still taking care of you, but I don't think that was ever a concern anyway, the way she clung on to you on the cruise." Something squeaked like a chair sliding on the floor.

"Is everything all right?" His ears strained to discern the situation. "Sounds like you two are getting at it."

"We're fine. Well, I am. So... in two weeks, Tom's having this competition near you in Gary, Indiana. He wants to come visit you, and we're thinking maybe you and Debbie could support him?"

DR started back to the house, watching Debbie laugh beyond the window. "Sounds like fun. Are you coming too? We'd love to see you both."

"No. My mom's under the weather, and I don't want to leave while she's not feeling well. At her age, you just never know. Besides, I'm just recovering from all the excitement of the cruise, you know. The thing with the kids and all really got to me. Here's Tom. Love you, DR. Tell Debbie hi." Her voice dipped as she spoke to Tom in the background. "There. It's all set. Go have fun."

"Hey, DR. I'm back. Once Laurie gets something in her head—look out. I'm stoked to see you again. Maybe we can take a look around Chicago if time allows. You could show me the sights maybe?"

"That should be fun. I'll talk with Debbie and work out the details. Let me call you back in a day or two, all right?" DR stepped onto the first porch step, ready to get inside to see what kind of things they'd been filling Debbie with.

"I look forward to it. Bye, DR."

In the house, Debbie waved her cellphone. "Come here." She took his hand and scooted over to let him sit between her and his mom. "I've got something to show you. I forgot all about it."

"It's going to be a tight squeeze." He sat, making himself as small as possible.

"Look. Isn't that amazing?" She showed him the picture and pointed at the words—*Stevie was here.*

"What is that? It looks like the outer door of a cargo compartment." He slid the phone from her hand. Then his heartbeat kicked up. The handwriting looked familiar, just like his. He gulped, afraid of the answer now.

"I took this picture on the boat the kids were hidden on, the boat they anchored away from our fight, the boat from our dreams. Its name was *Providence.* How do you think your name got on there?" She pointed up, her eyes enlarged, brows raised, lips curled. "You don't think...? No, it could be, could it?"

~

The next morning at DR's home, DR and Debbie relaxed on opposite ends of the large red chenille sofa. The colorful pillows that once occupied the sofa now lay on the floor, offering splashes of reds, blues, and pastels. He browsed a yachting magazine as she played on her cellphone. Occasionally, when she became entranced in an article, he picked at her. He was bored. Winter tended to do that to him, while she seemed content just to be with him, though she'd made it clear she preferred to be in the bedroom.

He got up and walked to the windows overlooking the lake, the nearby fireplace burning low. He threw another log on the fire, then stoked it to accept the log. He felt stronger today, almost back to full strength. Just his inner core still needed more time to heal the muscle damage. Since Thanksgiving just passed the day before he arrived home, the gloomy gray skies were here to stay—with no sunsets over the lake—at least for four, maybe five months. When he moved here with Gail, they had plenty to do, staying busy documenting and preserving the pieces from India. They'd had fun on the slopes after he started snowboarding. Back then, he didn't mind the weather much.

Now, trying to heal, there was none of that, not even working in the shop. At least for the time being. Good thing Debbie didn't appear of the same mindset, *bored*. Now twenty-four hours could seem like forty-eight, even with her company.

"What do you prefer to do in the winter, sweetheart?" He gripped the back of an upholstered chair, leaning over it and facing her and the question he'd never even asked himself.

She paused her internet search, her eyes moving from side to side, lips pursed. "I never really had to think about it before. I used to work at the store. I guess I just threw myself into my work." She balanced the phone on the sofa arm, got up, and walked over to him. Then she threaded her arms around his shoulders and reached up for a kiss. "I don't know, though. What do you like to do?"

"It was the same for me, especially when Gail was alive. We'd work fifty hours or so a week. Then we'd go snowboarding and then to Marcie's Place for a hot drink. But soon the work on the artifacts will be finished, and even Ryan will have to find something else to do."

He let go of her embrace and returned to the fireplace to stoke the log again. "I want to do something that makes a difference in others' lives. Maybe something with children? But not all the time. I'd like to continue the cruises. That was fun. But I want—no, I *need*—my life to make a difference."

She moved to the window. "I guess there's no better time than the present to think about it, to figure out what you want to be after all this is over. Hmm, what we want to be."

Beyond the lake, the trees were barren, most of their leaves lying on the ground by the shore. They created a blurred line between land and water, unseen in the large lakes like Lake Michigan, but here without a massive tide to redistribute them, the matted leaves would lay until they soaked into the water's edge.

"We'll just have to think about it. Something will present itself—it usually does." His phone rang. He picked it up, but the word *scam* splashed across the screen. He pushed the hang-up button and sent the obnoxious call into oblivion. "That reminds me. Tom called yesterday. The excitement of your picture and making up with Dad made me forget."

"How are they?" She threaded her fingers through his and drew him back to the sofa. Along the way, she ran her hand over the leaves of a palm tree alongside the sofa, then sat cross-legged, pulling him to her right.

Who could help but admire her beauty? She looked so soft and inviting in those warm cotton unicorn PJs, the same ones from the cruise. "They're fine. He's coming over for a shooting competition in Gary. He wants to spend some time with us."

"Where is he staying? Does he want to stay with us? It would be a long drive from here, but I still have my house. We could all stay there." She placed her hand on his leg as if for persuasion. "It's only about a half hour to Gary."

"That might be nice. It would save a lot of driving since the competition is spread over two days."

"Then it's settled. Call Tom." Her face glowed, her smile widened, and her eyes glistened big. "Once we know his schedule, I'll plan to fix my two favorite fellas a special dinner."

"Okay. Let's see. It's ten thirty here, sooo... it is three thirty p.m. in London. Here goes." He brought up Tom's contact and grinned when Tom answered. "Tom, it's DR. Debbie suggested we all stay together at her house. She has a beautiful home thirty minutes or so away from Gary in Chicago. How does that sound?"

"Sounds great. But I'll need to leave early to get my practice in. Is that going to be a problem?"

"I don't think so." He winked at her. "Debbie said she'd make us a special Chicago-style dinner too."

"Wow, thanks. I can't wait. I'll call you once I get my tickets with all the flight details and such. Probably tomorrow. Oh... should I fly into O'Hare?"

"Sure, we can pick you up at the airport. I look forward to it, Tom." He nodded his head side to side like it was on a pendulum and pinched his lips pinched into a smile. "Talk to you soon."

"Bye."

He scooped up Debbie's hands, jiggling them.

"How did he like the idea?"

"He loved it, just saying he'd need to leave early both days to get his practice in. I told him that wasn't a problem."

"Sounds great. I'll be able to stay in my home one more time before selling the place, and my mister won't be bored." She poked at him, but her eyes reflected the sadness of letting her home go.

In London, after hanging up the phone, Tom let out a loud yahoo.

Hearing his shout, Laurie came running. "Are you all right? I about dropped my laptop when you screamed."

Being twice her size, he scooped her up and planted a kiss on her lips. "Thank you, honey. DR just called. They're putting me up at Debbie's. Isn't that great? Three days with two of our good friends in the Windy City and no hotel bills." He spun her around and around in the air, her feet sticking almost straight out. "Are you sure you don't want to come? You can take a break from writing. It's not going anywhere. DR said Debbie's going to make us a Chicago specialty for dinner one night."

Laughing, she kissed him and swatted at his shoulder. "Put me down before you make me dizzy."

"What do you think, honey? Care to change your mind?" He obeyed her and closed in on her, noses touching, eyes wide. "Well?"

"I would love to go, but the timing's just not good." She walked over to the distressed island in the middle of their French provincial kitchen and leaned against the antique top. "I can't leave Mom. Dad's not going to take good care of both of them, so they need me. Besides, it'll almost be Christmas. You know how Heathrow is around then. It's a madhouse. No, I can't take the chance of not being home for my folks at Christmas. You go, have fun. I'll be here rooting for you."

"Okay." He rubbed at his forehead, then winked at her. "But when I have all that fun without you, don't say I didn't ask."

Who knew what kind of adventure he would get into with DR? His grin widened. Just think of what their last one turned into.

CHAPTER
TEN

After two days, Miguel went back to the marina in Marsala. A cool breeze forced him to pull up his overcoat collar as he walked along the pier—directly into a light sprinkle. What an ominous feel that gave the day! Too bad, he had to deal with Raymond. He whispered, "Dear God, please let us find favor here today, and if that's not possible, give me strength."

He stepped through the marina shop door and approached the empty counter. "Raymond, are you here? Raymond?"

He must be out back, so Miguel went to go out the back shop door, only to be confronted by Luigi. The *DI* was no longer in the bay, so she must be out for a little shakedown cruise.

"Hi, Luigi. Where's Raymond? Out for a test?"

A crooked smile quirked Luigi's lips. So Miguel closed his eyes, remembering his prayer. Best thing he'd done all day.

"He's not here. I gave him some time off to go visit his boys." Luigi shifted his weight as he leaned on an old wooden workbench covered with tools, oilcans, and soiled cloths.

Heat surged through Miguel's veins. "What do you mean you gave him a few days off? He was supposed to have the *DI* finished today. Where is she?"

"Sorry, Miguel. Since Raymond handles all the mechanical repairs and crew, I had to shut down for several days. We had her towed to the manufacturer. They'll tow her back in a couple of weeks or so unless you want her back unrepaired. But they'll charge for the two-way tow." Luigi's thin lips appeared to suppress a laugh as he tipped his head to the left, covering a fake cough with his hands.

"You know you can't legally do that, don't you?" That heat now scorched every bit of Miguel, but somehow, he kept his voice even. "What is wrong with you? Why do you always do this sort of thing? How do you sleep at night?"

He resisted the urge to move closer, but the urge to fight was far stronger than he liked. Placing his hand on the same workbench, he slid a pair of pliers to the side and took slow breaths to calm himself.

Luigi fumbled with an eyebrow, his nervous side showing. "If you'd keep your nose out of where it doesn't belong, no one would ever know. Now, would they? But no, you have to come riding in to save the day. Well, you can't save this one." He snickered and sidled back a step. "It's all in the contract the boy signed. Cut and dry. They should have just upgraded."

Miguel breathed deeply, focusing on the scenery. "You were right in sending her to the manufacturer. Now, Lorenzo will deal with them. Consider yourself relieved of the responsibility."

"Wh–what do you mean?" Luigi stuttered, the smile no longer ornamenting his lips. "We're the client on file. She's our consign."

"You were, but consider your contract void, revoked. The insurance company will be dealing with the manufacturer. We're not going to okay your added fees. We didn't ask that *DI* be sent there, so we can reject the insurance adjuster's numbers. We both know the manufacturer won't lay a finger on her without their approval."

Luigi shuffled on his feet to the left and then back to the right, apparently unable to talk.

"This is what happens when you only think of yourself—you get sloppy. When Marco gets back in town, we'll be seeing you, Luigi. You and your brother have dragged the marina down for far too long." As Miguel turned to go back out, he noticed a revolver partly concealed on the worktable's second shelf.

Luigi mumbled under his breath. "Dr. Ray hasn't heard the last from me."

Miguel met Lorenzo in front of the marina as he was leaving.

"Where's she at, Miguel? I didn't see her out back." Lorenzo paused on his way in, but Miguel placed his hand on his shoulder and turned him around.

"Let's get out of here before the stench gets on us too." He checked over his shoulder for Luigi. Good, he wasn't there.

"Is she ready?" Lo followed him out onto the pier.

"No. They sent her to the manufacturer for repair." Grimacing, Miguel shook his head to settle himself.

"Can they do that?"

"I'm afraid so. You signed their contract. But we'll stop it... somehow."

Their time in Delton had passed quickly with DR and Debbie growing closer, falling in love, and giving his wounds time to heal. Now just some tenderness remained in his abdomen, and his doctor released him with instructions to continue to stay away from any heavy lifting or strenuous activities for the next weeks. "No carrying Christmas trees or ornaments," the doctor had joked.

It was hard to imagine over two months had passed since the attack on his yacht. But since then, he'd committed to a permanent relationship. With Christmas in two weeks and Tom coming the day after tomorrow, DR decided to take the plunge and make their engagement, if she'd have him, a special occasion.

"Did you say you were meeting Willie?" He called over his shoulder to her while straightening the quilt on his bed.

"We're meeting at Marcie's. She wants to find out more about Ryan. Seems she has a soft spot for him." Debbie patted the door trim and twisted to what must have been an invisible beat.

"Hope she knows what she's getting into." Hard not to remember the crush Willie had on him, according to his brother, Willie's best friend.

"That's why she wants to talk. Besides, it'll help us to get closer too. I'd like a little girl time while living in this small world of yours."

"Small world, heh?" He smoothed the wrinkles away, inspected his handiwork, then caught her admiring him. Man, he couldn't wait to marry this woman. How nice it would be to mess the covers up again… with her in his arms.

"What are you thinking, Dr. Ray? Maybe I'm thinking the same thing." She giggled and cast her glance at the bed, then back to him. The corners of her lips rose, and her head tilted toward the bed.

He walked over, hugged, and kissed her. "We better get out of here before I lose myself in you." Taking her hand, he tugged her toward the kitchen and their awaiting coffee.

"I've got to go meet Willie anyway, so no time right now." She reached for him, one more kiss. "Be careful driving to Kalamazoo."

"Tell Willie hi for me."

"I will." Out, she strolled, her black leather boots clopping on the sidewalk. She checked over her shoulder to see if he was watching, then slid into the vehicle.

He closed the door, continuing to watch her drive out of sight. Her spending time with Willie, was that good or bad? Willie was the one who'd led Gail to God. He still didn't know how he felt about that. On the one hand, he was glad since Gail had passed—after all, maybe her beliefs were, well, sort of an insurance policy. On the other, if she hadn't died, his life would've fallen apart one day. And he didn't know how he would have— could have—handled it.

God was his one concern with Debbie. Would it strain their relationship? No, he wasn't going there. And since she did, he required her to be there fully. No concessions, kind of like being Michigan Strong. You stand for your beliefs, whatever they may be, no compromise. Period. No matter the cost, he required that, and he'd heard God felt the same way.

After grabbing a to-go cup of his special blend, he headed out the door. Driving to Kalamazoo felt like getting a lifeline back. The injuries put so much of his life in a different perspective and gave him an appreciation for the things he'd once taken for granted.

Meanwhile, things he'd never expected had come to pass these last weeks. He'd forgiven his uncle and his dad. Now, he could forgive himself. For years, he'd tossed *the night* around in his thoughts. Voices inside sometimes cast him as the villain, not the victim. He'd often heard how many victims had the same problem, but now, he felt the world had lifted off his shoulders. Now, he had a clean slate.

Wheeling his Pathfinder into the jewelry store's parking lot, he claimed a space and sat, hands in his lap. If he were a praying man, he'd have prayed. Instead, he simply paused.

But it was time.

He unbuckled his seat belt and let it flick back as he cast aside all restraints.

Inside, a pretty young redhead, all smiles, teeth whiter than the faux snow at the base of their Christmas tree, approached. "Good morning and welcome!" she sang out in a voice as bright and cheery as the carols in the background. "My name is Sienna. May I be of assistance?"

Her hair, nearly the color of Gail's, gave him a start. Was that an omen? A red flag or something telling him to stop?

He didn't. He wanted to marry Debbie. The past was the past.

"Hi, Sienna, and yes, you can. I'm looking for an engagement ring."

"How wonderful. Congratulations." She sized him up, either for the finances or the man part. "I am so happy for you. They're right over here, if you will follow me, please. I think we have something your girlfriend will love."

He scanned the different cases along the way.

"Does she like yellow gold, titanium, or white gold jewelry?" She lifted a ledge that acted as both a doorway behind the cases and a security barrier. "We have a large selection of all three. Plus, if you need something a little different, we also do custom work."

What did she wear? That small toe ring and those bracelets... "She wears yellow gold, mostly." He bent over the case.

"Dr. Ray?" A male voice behind him startled DR as Sienna slid out several boards, one of yellow gold and one of titanium. "Dr. Steven Ray?"

"Yes, I am." DR reached to shake the hand the balding fiftyish man extended.

"How wonderful it is to meet you! I'm Julius, the manager here. I didn't expect to see a real-life hero today. We're all so proud that a neighbor from Delton saved those children. And to fight those nasty pirates and terrorists to the death. Wow... You can't make that up." He gripped DR's shoulders. "Sienna, this is Dr. Ray, you be sure to find him whatever he needs." Then he thanked him again and left as quickly as he'd come.

Sienna's mouth dropped. She must've seen the news too.

"Sienna, are you okay?" DR asked the seemingly starstruck girl.

"Yes. Sorry I didn't recognize you. Let's find you that special ring." She appeared to hold herself differently, probably thinking he was a hero. Even more enthusiastic now, she gushed about the rings. "Is this for the lady on the cruise that you saved? She's pretty. Oh!" She clamped a hand to her mouth, then lowered her head and tone. "Sorry. That's none of my business."

"No, you're fine, and yes, it is." Until her death, Gail wore the ring he'd bought her right out of college. After scraping together all he could, he could only afford a quarter-carat diamond, since they were starting out together with other archaeologists. But she didn't care. She never allowed him to upgrade it, saying, "True love knows no price."

"Dr. Ray, are you okay?" Sienna tilted herself to get a better look at him.

"I'm fine, just some memories." A tear pushed at its boundaries, wanting out. "Excuse me for a moment."

He headed to the men's room. Inside, he found some tissue, leaned against a sink, and eyed himself in the mirror before removing the traitors from his eyes. He didn't want to appear soft, but he hadn't confronted this memory. Tears aside, he took a deep breath and mumbled, "You've got this."

Then he strode back to Sienna. "Sorry, I didn't mean to rush off like that, but—"

"Oh, you're fine." She waved a hand, and her smile reassured him. "Take however much time you need. This is something you want to get right."

"I think this is the one." He chose a yellow gold ring with a carat and a half diamond stone, then held it when Sienna suggested he exam it close up.

"Do you know her ring size?" Sienna gritted her teeth behind a smile above hands that seemed to be praying.

"Actually, I do. She wears a wedding band on a chain, so I was able to get the size while she slept." He smirked. "Sneaky, aren't I?"

"Her"—Sienna blinked—"her wedding band?"

"Her husband is deceased, as is my former wife." And he was giving all this information, why? Maybe to convince himself?

"I didn't mean to pry. Okay, we'll get this written up, and I'll be right back." She ducked her head and hurried off to the manager's office.

Several minutes later, she returned. "Dr. Ray, Julius said we could have this ready for you in the morning. He's expediting it for you, and we'll deliver it to your address tomorrow." She handed over the billing statement for his acceptance. "Does that work for you?"

He raised a brow, surprised by the gracious discount applied to the final balance. "This is... great. And generous."

"Julius said it was the least we could do for a real-life hero." She stood on one foot, the other held behind her, bent at the knee, eyes glowing. Starstruck again, it appeared.

"Thank you, and please thank Julius. You just made a customer for life." He shook her hand and walked out. Looking back over his shoulder, he could see her standing in the door watching him still. He waved goodbye, then drove home.

In Marsala, Miguel's phone rang.

"Miguel, it's me." His distant cousin, Monsignor Ricci, sounded out of breath when Miguel answered.

"Alexander, it's good to hear from you." Miguel settled onto a sofa, preparing for a good conversation. "What's the occasion?"

"It's bad... really bad." The monsignor paused, breathing hard. "Terrorists attacked the children's home. They took them all this time, Miguel—all thirty children. But that's not all... They killed O'Reilly. Walters may not make it, either."

Miguel closed his eyes, letting out a loud breath, but otherwise quiet. Faces flashed in his mind. The children—Habiba, Derifa, and Amal and so many others. The dear priests who'd cared for the children's home—Father O'Reilly, dead? Father Walters, the perfect Saint Nicholas if only he had hair, fighting for his life? "Dear God. What else is going to happen to those kids?" He drew in another breath as if he could draw in strength to face this reality. "I'm sorry about your friends. How bad is Walters?"

"He was still in surgery the last time I checked, about half an hour ago. They shot him three times, point blank. Just like they did O'Reilly. These people are cold-blooded killers."

"I can't even imagine how the ten children who were taken the first time are dealing with this. Habiba nearly died last time. I hope she has her enzymes and inhalers." Miguel put his head down, supporting it with the hand free of the phone. "Why did God put animals like this on the earth? Do the authorities know which group did this?"

"Of course they do—they helped. But it's more than the corruption. Everyone's scared. The war here has been going on for years, and they have families to protect. Besides, the kids were probably sold before they took them. They just take them and transport them to the buyers. Easy money."

After a few minutes, Miguel promised to get in touch soon. Maybe now the monsignor would reconsider his past offer to bring him to Marsala where he could have his own church.

Sinking back into the sofa, eyes to the heavens, he whispered, "Dear Lord, please protect and deliver these children. Kids shouldn't be for sale."

CHAPTER
ELEVEN

DR had just returned home. Debbie was still out with Willie at Marcie's Place. He grabbed the milk to fix a bowl of cereal, then sat at the island before his phone rang.

Great, perfect timing. Why was it that just when you pour the milk the phone always rang? His first inclination was to squash the call, then call back later. But the contact displayed Miguel's name.

"Miguel, I hope this is good news."

"I'm afraid it's the worst sort of news. Are you sitting down?"

"I am. That bad?"

"Worse."

After Miguel explained, DR lowered his head and closed his eyes for the longest time, before groaning. "That makes me so mad! How can all these bad things keep happening to those precious kids?" He stood up slowly, blindly searching for a place to finish the conversation, not wanting it to be real. "Do they know who is behind it this time?"

He took his stand by the window overlooking the lake, trying to gain some balance in light of another tragedy. Ever since Gail's death, his life seemed like one big roller-coaster ride.

"It's heartbreaking. It seems crooked cops blocked the road so anyone wanting to help couldn't reach them in time. They had a box truck and hauled them off like cargo."

Heat raged through DR's body, and his fists tightened. "I'm so mad, but I don't even know who to be mad at. And Habiba? Somehow, I feel like she's supposed to be here with me. She even called me Daddy because of our—her—dream." He slapped the wall. "That takes some of the pleasure out of my news."

"There's more. Do you want to hear it before you give me your news?"

"Feliz Navidad" came over the phone line. The Riccis must be gearing up for Christmas.

"Sure, go ahead. It can't get much worse, can it?"

"Luigi sent the *DI* to the manufacturer."

DR fell silent before asking, "What does that mean?"

"I don't know, but we won't have to deal with the marina anymore. I wish Lo had listened to my advice and had her towed to another marina. Live and learn."

A door shut, and a baby's voice called out, "Pawpaw."

"So, Kim is back with Corey. What was your news before I get ambushed?"

"If there are no complications with the jeweler, I'm proposing to Debbie tomorrow evening. What do you think?" He pressed his nose to the glass pane, feeling the coolness.

"I think you are a smart man. She is a fine lady and very much in love with you. Congratulations! I'll pass on the news to Kim and Marco. Give Debbie my love. Sorry to be the bearer of bad news, and don't worry about the *DI*. I'll help your crew get it right. But here comes my little one, so I'd better go."

At Marcie's Place, Debbie, Willie, and Rachael, a young woman who grew up with Willie, were bonding over their life events. Debbie discovered a lot in common with Rachael, who'd lost her husband when he was killed serving the country. Her life since had been a financial struggle, the opposite of Debbie's, but they'd both felt a similar heartache.

Debbie described her store, then fidgeted with the napkin, shredding it. "We did well, lived the good life. Then, one day, while I was picking up a display some kids knocked down in back, a gunman came in, shot Mark, stole two hundred dollars, and ran out the door."

"Honey, it's okay." Willie patted her hand. "You didn't have to tell us. We understand."

"Thanks, but talking about it helps. Anyway, he died in my arms, and I couldn't do anything. When DR stepped in front of those bullets, I thought the same thing was happening all over again. I thank God he's alive." She nudged the pile of shredded napkin under the lip of her saucer that once held an éclair.

Rachael smiled and, seeming on instinct, gathered their dishes together as if forgetting this was her day off. "So how are things with you two? It doesn't take a rocket scientist to see how in love you are."

Willie smacked at her hand. "You're off. Stop that."

Laughing, Rachael shrugged. "I guess it's just habit."

Debbie's lips quirked. "He told me he loved me."

"He wouldn't have let you take care of him if he didn't. He's a straight shooter, and Gail said they didn't have any hanky-panky before their wedding night. He insisted." Willie's eyes seemed to be searching, looking, probing.

So Debbie shrugged. "Nothing's changed in that area either, no matter how hard I try. We've both been married, so we've opened the cookie jar so to speak—I don't see the big deal. After all, *I'm* the Christian, not him." Oops. She cringed. Too bad, she couldn't take it back.

Rachael didn't seem to pay any attention, but Willie looked like she'd just seen the curtain rise. Her jaw dropped, just for a moment, but nevertheless, it dropped.

Willie sat up taller and cleared her throat. "Folks around here, especially the old-timers, call his living 'Michigan Strong.' They say you ought to live the right way regardless of the costs—and not all of them are believers. They may just come from strong Christian families, like DR."

Her jaw muscles flexed as she twirled her fingers in her long black hair, and Debbie tried not to squirm while Willie appeared to size her up like a boa constrictor. Apparently, she hadn't given up on her fantasy—or had she?

"I don't know how much longer he intends to keep me waiting." Debbie huffed. "I guess we'll be getting married first. I hope it's not too long." She looked out the window. A woman roughly her age was playing with two small children. At thirty-three, she suddenly felt her clock ticking.

Then Rachael's little girl came skipping up. The chocolate smeared on her lips testified another éclair had met its match, and now strands of blonde hair caught in it. Rachael laughed, picked up a napkin, and wiped her face. "Well, ladies, this has been fun, but it's back to reality for me. I've got to get home and get my little darlings' supper on. Let's do this again soon."

"Sounds like a good plan." Willie pushed from her seat. "I'm off too. I'm supposed to talk to Ryan about going to Kalamazoo. Bye, Debbie. Tell DR hi." She wrapped her scarf around her neck and strode out the door.

Only Debbie remained. She closed her eyes, processing the last hours with her newfound friends. Well, one friend and one prospect. Was the crush Willie had on her man gone or just in hiding? Her cellphone rang, and caller ID identified the call from Japan. This was the third time that number had called her. The first two times she simply refused the call, but this time, curiosity won out.

"Hello." She waited for a response, but could only hear breathing, then a hushed tussle, then nothing. She pulled the phone away from her ear and eyed the home screen. "That's strange."

Congressman Max Rice picked up his overcoat and looked around his office, feeling like he was forgetting something. The intercom buzzed. Laying the overcoat on a chair close to the door, he hurried over to answer while still glancing around. Just what was he missing?

"Yes, Mary. What is it? I was just preparing to leave."

"Sir, Kat is on line 1. I'm sorry."

"Don't be ridiculous. It's not your fault. Have a good weekend."

"You too, sir."

Without pausing, he picked up the phone. "Kat, to what do I owe this honor?" He patted his pockets, still confused as to what he was missing.

"Max, Mr. Jennings would like to have a word with you. Can you hold while I connect you?"

"Sure, I'll wait." Ah, that was it. He needed to stop at the liquor store for a little pick-me-up for his flight home. He much preferred his brand over the airline's. Now, that settled, just what couldn't wait till Monday morning?

"How are you, Max? I've got some good news—finally."

"I'm, uh, good, sir. I was just getting ready to walk out the door for the evening. How can I help you?" A numbness came over him. He was tired of this endless pandering to Jennings.

"Kat said you were getting ready to leave for the day. I'm glad I caught you. This will only take a moment."

"It's not a problem." He dropped into his seat. "What can I do for you?"

"Remember how I told you there'd be some payback coming? Today was that day. I just got news the shipment for the club was picked up. It's being processed and transported as we speak. You'll be getting a message about the status first thing in the morning. And, Max, gets some rest. You sound stressed. This isn't rocket science, so don't overthink it. Did you invite your friend and the good doctor to the club for dinner?"

"Yes, but how did—"

"How did I know? Max, Max, you're forgetting whom you're talking with. Little happens in your world that I don't know. Anyway, I have a little surprise for them. Good night, Max. Sleep well." A course laugh, followed by a COPD cough, signaled the conversation was over.

Max hung up. Jennings once told him how amazed he was by the weak-minded congressmen in Washington, DC, giving up everything for power they could never attain for themselves. *They don't realize, Max, that power is an illusion... without money."* It seared itself into his memory because the angry old man was right. At least DC right.

The flight home to Chicago's O'Hare was bumpy, changing weather conditions making the plane work harder against the wind pushing out of the northwest. Several drops in altitude caused the passengers to hold tight and suspended the food service. Good thing the call reminded him to stop for the pick-me-uppers. They came in handy, not only for the suspenseful flight but also for news about the shipment to the club, his club, in name only.

The club that shredded his relationship with his wife. The club that stopped him from attending church with his family because he instead found himself putting out fires there. It being a men's club wasn't lost on Leslie, either. She didn't know what went on, besides what Max told her.

"Here's to us, Leslie." He toasted, the other passengers appearing frantic while he maintained his calm thanks to seven small bottles of ten-year-old scotch, five down, two to go. It wasn't just his time away from family that was the problem—it was how he acted in the time with them. Guilt gave him an attitude. Now it appeared child sex trafficking and murder would be added to his résumé. Not bad... for a congressman.

Sadly, Leslie didn't even know he was flying home tonight. He'd planned on surprising her, hoping to shore up their relationship before their son's birthday. Not going to happen. Now, he'd head straight to the club and sleep there. Things to do. The boss always wanted the new "performers" ready forty-eight hours ahead of time to ensure things ran smoothly.

They'd need to be scrubbed-up, painted-up, and polished-up. Probably a hairdo or two and new clothes. Not to mention Jennings was bringing in two more trailers. Wait! He jolted upright in his seat.

"Two more trailers?" He said it aloud, rousing the curiosity of the other first-class passengers. "Sorry."

The club on Lake Michigan's shore already had one trailer with accommodations for eleven "performers," cages four feet wide, eight feet deep, and seven feet tall. Gorilla transport cages, to be precise. At least, that's what the men working with them called them. The performers were only allowed out during the day. But adding two more trailers meant a total of thirty-three cages.

Max covered his face with his hands, probably appearing like he was praying. He wasn't. He was absorbing this new level of depravity. Depravity he was supposed to stand against, but he couldn't or wouldn't. Because this time of year, the water was cold—in Lake Michigan.

A deep breath. Another.

The complex of trailers behind a men's club must seem suspicious, especially from the air. Good thing, Jennings's "officials" in the city and state looked the other way at the club's unlawful activities. Many of those same high-up officials liked the "performers," often visiting the club and taking advantage of its amenities, including the club's yacht casino, the *Lucky Lucie*. The best and the youngest performers worked there.

The lights from the Windy City were coming closer. His end might be just as close if he didn't find a way out. But were his morals and integrity too far gone? Was it simply self-preservation? He no longer had compassion for the kids involved, so maybe the old man was right. Maybe he was just overthinking it like Carl had said.

The next morning when the jewelry store courier brought his ring, DR watched for the delivery van across the lake after receiving their driver's text. Then he rushed to the door, trying not to be suspicious, leaving Debbie on the deck, bundled in a long winter coat and Bears toboggan, sipping coffee in front of the chiminea. He opened the door and stepped out to meet the courier to conceal any conversation.

"Dr. Ray, Julius wanted me to get this to you first thing this morning." The courier offered a clipboard for his signature and a black square box.

DR opened the box, examined the ring, then signed the form. "Thank you. And please thank Julius and Sienna for expediting this." He handed the man a twenty. "Have a great day." Then he strode along the stone drive back to the house. Inside, he hid the ring in the coat closet before he returned to the deck.

"What do you say we celebrate tonight?" He stooped to kiss the top of her forehead where skin peeked out beyond her hat. "With Tom coming tomorrow evening, we won't have any time to ourselves, and steak and lobster with a good bottle of wine sounds good to me." He then leaned down further to steal a kiss. But no stealing was required.

She slid to her feet for a real kiss, then sighed out contentment. "Lobster and steak, I'd be nuts to say no. What's the occasion... no more crutches or wheelchairs? You know... It doesn't matter. We'll need to do a food run and go by the liquor store for a good wine." She bounced up and down on her toes, reached up, and stretched for another kiss.

"No. No need. I've already planned it. I just hoped you'd agree. I want to show you how thankful I am and maybe spoil you a little, if that's okay?" He took her in his arms, making sure she stayed kissed.

The day seemed to drag forever, but then the smell of steak grilling filled the house. DR dressed for the occasion and asked her to do the same. Then he put on some soft romantic music and set the table with crystal and candlelight. He even lit the deck lights for the whole lake to see.

"Mmm... honey, this steak is so tender. Where did you learn to cook like this?" Her eyes closed as she savored her bite. "You keep treating me like this, and I'll never leave." Caught up in the moment, she didn't realize she answered his forthcoming question.

After pouring her another glass of wine and one for himself, he knelt before her, hand extended with the black box open. "That was precisely what I was going for. I love you. Will you do me the honor of becoming my wife?"

"Oh!" she shrieked. "Yes, yes, yes... I will!" She shuddered as he took her hand and slid the ring on her finger. It was a perfect fit. She closed her eyes, reveling in the moment. Then he pressed his lips to hers. Yes, she would stay kissed.

The house seemed to glow as they enjoyed their evening together. Happiness had returned to the lake house—or had it?

The next morning, Miguel called Lorenzo. Three things on his mind couldn't wait. The desire to get on with life without these little inconveniences was strong. But his spirit reminded him the little inconveniences were God's way of using him. To that end, he could be thankful for his newfound friends too.

"Lo, do you have a few minutes? I've got several things to share?" He stepped into his study, facing the stately grandfather clock across the room, its rich dark wood blending well with the bookcases.

"Miguel, sì, yes. I have nothing but time. Sis is still asleep. She got home from work early or late this morning—however you look at working through midnight."

"Do you want the bad news first or the extra-bad news?" Miguel ran a hand over his hair. Lo hadn't visited the children's home in Aden, met O'Reilly or Walters, or seen any of the kids at the hospital. Maybe that would soften the blow.

"Just lay it on me. If it's about the *DI*, though, I can guess how that's going to go."

"Then I'll save that for last. Are you sitting down? If not, you might want to." Miguel sat himself. The leather chair cushioned him as he shared the news his distant cousin had given him.

"How horrible." Lo let out a low whistle. "Have you told DR? He'll be plumb tore up."

"He knows. Oh... I do have some good news. Let me pass that on before I say more." Then he rubbed his jaw. "You know, on the other hand, it's not mine to tell."

"Really?"

"Sorry. Also, the marina sent the *DI* to the manufacturer. I'll call them on Monday. Can you get in touch with the insurance company and tell them we want to okay all charges?" He tapped his jaw. Was there anything else on that front?

"Unbelievable. What is wrong with those guys? Don't they want the business? I know, we should have listened to your advice. Sorry, Miguel, and thanks for helping us get all this straightened out. Does DR know?"

"He does, and he's been in your shoes, so don't worry. Now for the good news. We are planning our annual Christmas celebration. I don't know if you've heard about it, but it's a big deal for us. And we would like you and David to attend. Bring Cillia too. David can bring his girlfriend." He rose to his feet and walked to the window, admiring the front lawn covered in Christmas decorations and a nativity set. "Who knows, Lo, maybe you'll meet someone at the party. You can let me know when you make up your mind. Kim has been working hard on this with the staff at the children's center in town."

"Heard about it. That's all people have talked about in town for a month. I'll let David know, but I believe you can count us in. And if you need any help, give me a shout. And thanks, Miguel. It means a lot."

"You are welcome. I look forward to sharing it with you. I have to go. Pass all the news on to David if you would. Be blessed, my good friend." Miguel set the phone down, satisfied. Yes, Lorenzo was a good friend, as were the others on the cruise.

What was it Penny had said? Good friends were "worth several crappy trips."

Indeed, they were.

CHAPTER
TWELVE

On the next-to-last Saturday morning in the peak Christmas shopping season, Marcie's Place was hopping. Many patrons grabbed their orders to go, shopping being the main activity for most, but not all.

Debbie seemed out of place—she felt out of place too. She didn't even grab a coffee before sitting down, preferring to save a table for herself and Willie. Rachael was there also, but she was working today. Already in a mad scramble to serve their dine-in guest, as well as back up the take-out workers, she was too busy to see Debbie's pain.

Willie rushed through the door, stopped, and warmed her hands over the fireplace before she waved at Debbie along the back wall's partly concealed booths. Then she headed over, looking for Rachael.

Her steps slowed, and Debbie sighed. Yeah, it wouldn't take much for Willie or anyone else to guess something was wrong. Debbie's mascara had begun to smudge, tears working their way out. She hid her face.

"Sorry I couldn't get here sooner. I had something to take care of." Willie forced a smile, but Debbie saw through it.

Debbie stood and grabbed her, surprising Willie whose arms flew wide before she gathered herself to hug her back. A sob slid from Debbie's throat. After a long moment, she let go and hid her face—again—as she sat down.

"What is going on? Are you all right? Is DR all right?" Willie pulled a handful of tissue from her purse and passed them over.

"No. I'm not okay." Debbie wiped her cheeks dry, then rummaged in her purse for a compact. "DR proposed last night." Another throaty sob escaped. She put her head on the table and bumped it several times.

Willie reached out to stop her. "Honey, don't give yourself a headache. It'll be all right."

"I already have a headache, and I don't think it will be all right. Not after this morning. I don't know what happened. All I know is we had a tiff, and here I am." Her eyes closed tight, her lips suppressing more sobs the best they could, she dropped the tissues and propped up on her elbows, hands hiding her eyes and face.

"DR's probably at home getting ready to call you and ask you to come home right now. I'm sure of it." Willie leaned her head slightly to make eye contact.

"It's not going to happen. I closed that door."

Willie stiffened as if to brace herself. "What did you do?"

"He said we could go to the justice of the peace today and get married, maybe have a big wedding later—just so we could be together. I asked him if he was always going to be this ridiculous. Couldn't he let it go just this once, I asked. He said no. That's why he left home at eighteen to get away from the do-gooders who preach to others about things they don't do themselves. And he wondered what had ever concealed his eyes to my wanting to do the same thing. Well, you can guess how that made me feel."

"What did you do?" Willie's eyes were wide open now, her jaw hanging.

"I grabbed my bag, stormed down the hallway. Then I slammed the ring and his house key on the hallway table. Not looking back, I slammed the door just as hard." She slid her hands from her face and stared into Willie's eyes. "Oh... why did I do that? Why couldn't I wait a few more hours?" She returned to bumping her head on the table. "We could've been married. Why am I so impulsive?"

Willie made shushing sounds to console her.

"He's right, you know," Debbie whispered and rubbed at her temples. "I may be born again, but I have so much to learn. I thought that would make it easier, but it's gotten harder. I still get the same urges, desires, *needs* as I had before, and I have a hard time resisting now, going off the deep end. How do you do it?" Debbie lifted a pleading gaze, then picked up the compact and tissues to fix her makeup.

"Honey, I lived the Christian life since I was old enough to know." Willie closed her eyes and took a deep breath. Then her dark ponytail bounced with her headshake. "I let my emotions get the best of me one day over ten years ago, and I'm still paying for it. You have to control your thoughts, not get carried away. Listen to godly advice from others who know you." She waved to Rachael.

"I'd forgotten all about eating." Debbie sat up straighter. "I'm starving."

"She'll be right here. Don't forget to pray, pray, pray. I've been struggling lately myself, but God will get you—and me—through our problems. Give DR time, and yourself too. Who knows what God has in mind for you both? Pray you can learn to control yourself better and that he'll be more understanding."

"I don't know. I was pretty hard on him."

"So what are you going to do now?"

"I'm going back to my home in Chicago. I thank God I don't have a contract on it." She sighed. "A friend from the cruise is coming over from London to meet us, but I guess he and DR'll have to hang out together. We were all going to stay at my house. I ordered a ton of food delivered. At least I won't go hungry."

But how had she let things come to this? Yesterday was so wonderful. Could they ever go back?

The house on Wall Lake was beautiful last night, aglow with lights, smells, and the excitement of love. It was equally unsatisfying this morning, a ring and key on the hallway table a reminder of what could've been. If not for different moral values.

Love had always been complicated for him. Was it his Michigan values, something he'd learned in church, from his mother maybe? Or was it all because of *the night?* "Why is this so hard for me? Does anyone else struggle with this? Should I give up what I believe to satisfy physical desires?" Sitting at the kitchen island, he could still see part of the lake below. There, a neighbor's dog treed a squirrel.

He smiled, admiring the dog's determination. Then the squirrel jumped from tree to tree. At first, the dog tried to follow, finally giving up as the squirrel jumped to a tree on the other side of a small inlet, escaping, like love had just escaped him.

With Debbie's home off the list of places he and Tom would be staying, DR checked for a hotel to book as close to Tom's match as possible. Skylight Hotel and Conference Center and an indoor shooting facility even shared the same parking lot. The hotel boasted preferential access to the club as well.

If it still had an opening, that ought to ease Tom's mind. But no, the hotel was booked solid. Still, DR put his name on the cancellation list, just in case. He'd wait a few hours to see. After he hung up with them, the phone rang.

"So, when is the big day?" Miguel's voice rang out, not bothering with the niceties of hello.

A moment of silence passed, DR thinking how to respond. "Hi, Miguel."

"She did say yes, didn't she?"

"Yes... she did. But that was last night, and today is a new day." He turned his focus to the lake. The same dog was sniffing the ground, looking from tree to tree, hoping the squirrel would return maybe? Feeling a bit like DR probably. "That's not a good subject right now."

"Oh no. She didn't do the same thing she did on the cruise, I hope. I mean I'm sorry."

"What do you mean? What did she do on the cruise?" He rose and strolled to the window. Was the dog going to give up? Should he give up?

"It's nothing, just my brain putting my big foot in my mouth. That's all."

"Well, tell your brain not to stop now. It might help our situation." A cup of coffee might take the gloom off. He headed to the kitchen to make a pot.

"I hear water running. Are you making coffee?" A laugh came over the phone.

"You know me—coffee cures whatever ails. So tell me what happened on the cruise? What did she do?" Who knew where this may be leading? But maybe it'd give him insight.

"Remember the night after the day trip to the animal refuge outside of Kerala? Debbie didn't come outside and sit with you because she was mad, disappointed you didn't go with her. Something made her think you were playing games with her. That's why she changed into a sexy outfit instead of wearing more modest clothing. Long story made short, she was going to give up on your relationship before it ever began. I talked her out of it."

"I still don't understand."

"She let her imagination and newfound religion run away with her. I told her it was because of her new faith and she had to fight the impulses that would come to test and tempt her. Seems she hasn't learned."

"That's what I don't get. I told her we could go to the magistrate today and get married secretly, but she stormed out before we could even discuss it. She went five years before we dated." He huffed. "But she couldn't wait six hours?"

Head shaking, he placed the glass pot under the filter basket. Soon, black fluid splashed on its bottom. "It seemed like she was trying to take away my convictions, like they didn't matter to her."

"I'll pray for you both. I'm sorry. So"—Miguel's voice perked up—"when does Tom get in?"

"I pick him up in Chicago this afternoon. I still have to hunt a hotel for us. Right now, I'm on a waiting list for one near the tournament, apparently a popular spot for shooters because of a nearby indoor gun range." He dropped two spoons of sugar and two ounces of milk into his cup, then hovered over the brewing potion.

"I'd say that is a hard ticket to punch. Few facilities can offer that sort of thing."

"Probably not." He poured his coffee, tested a sip, and released an ahh.

"I'll let you get to it. In the meantime, don't worry. If it's true love, it'll work out. Take care, DR, and I'll talk to you soon about the *DI*."

"Bye, Miguel." He walked to the hallway table, picked up the key, and placed it in the table. Then he scooped up the ring and tossed it into the air and caught it. "Easy come, easy go."

He took the ring into his bedroom to nestle it in its box. Along the way, he glimpsed the bedroom Debbie had stayed in. It was straightened and clean. Too bad she hadn't left a note, something he could hold either as a promise or as closure.

"What are you thinking, Debbie? We could've been together today." He sat on the edge of his bed, sipping his coffee. Tears seared the backs of his eyes. He set the coffee on a nightstand and stared blindly at the floor. "Why, God? Why me? Why can't I let myself go?"

The roller coaster that was his life had picked up speed again.

Then a loud rattle, then a ring drew his attention. His cellphone rang on the kitchen island. He couldn't make it before the call went to voicemail, but he could see the call was from the Skylight Hotel. Fumbling with the buttons, anxious to hear the message, he dialed the service.

"Dr. Ray, this is the Skylight Hotel and Conference Center calling. I'm happy to announce we have one king suite available for two guests. Please call to confirm your reservation."

He returned their call at once. Reservation made, now all he had to do was collect Tom at O'Hare and the day would have righted itself, somewhat.

Three and a half hours later, after maneuvering the Pathfinder through holiday traffic, DR reached O'Hare's short-term parking. Only a couple spaces remained at the furthest possible distance from the terminal where Tom was arriving, of course. DR set out at a brisk pace. But soon his inactivity after being wounded caught up with him, and his breath became labored. Reaching the baggage area, he claimed an empty seat to rest while waiting on his friend and their long walk back to the vehicle.

Soon, a smiling Tom came into sight, waving above his head to get DR's attention. He reached him, looked around, then hugged him. "Where's that beautiful helper of yours?"

"Something came up. She's not going to be able to host us. I made reservations at a hotel in Gary. I'm sorry. She was looking forward to seeing you." DR pointed to a familiar suitcase. "That's yours, right?"

"Sure is. Is everything all right?" Tom's stomach rumbled. "The airplane food wasn't all that today. Want to get a bite?"

"Let's get out of here first. We can get a snack to hold us at a store down the road until we check in at the hotel. Then we can get some real food. What do you say?" Having finished the subject, DR turned and started walking away after Tom grabbed his bags. DR talked over his shoulder. "How was the flight?"

Oh, Tom had two more large bags. DR stopped.

"Like I said the food wasn't all that, and neither was the flight. A lady had two toddlers and one or the other of them was crying most of the way. I didn't get much sleep." Tom put his carry-on bag down and inserted his credit card into a baggage-cart vending machine. "Let me get this. It will make the walk more pleasant."

"I'd help, but I'm not supposed to do any heavy lifting for a while." For which he was now strangely thankful. DR smirked.

"No problem. I'm used to being alone. At least this time I have good company. I just hate that Debbie's not going to be around." Tom loaded the last bag. The first two having his firearms and ammunition were tagged for customs inspection. "Hopefully customs aren't backed up."

After clearing the customs inspection, they made their way to the Pathfinder, Tom taking it all in, appearing especially interested in the missing friend's whereabouts.

"You know I never got the chance to talk much with Debbie on the cruise. We were all so busy doing our own thing, especially Laurie and me. She seemed like a feisty little thing."

"Oh, she can take care of herself. Don't you worry about that one. My helper on my Indian dig tried to rape her—that was a big mistake." A chuckle escaped DR's lips. "He probably won't try that on anyone again."

"What happened?" Tom wiped the sweat from his forehead, then laughed. "How far away did you park? I should have gotten a taxi back here."

"We here." DR pointed at the vehicle.

"Well, of course, we are. There aren't any more rows." Tom nodded over his shoulder back toward the airport, indicating how far they'd come. "It almost felt like we were walking to the hotel."

"It's Christmastime."

After stopping for a snack, they were off to Gary, Indiana, and the

Skylight Hotel, a fifty-minute drive, according to GPS, but with DR on a mission, the drive only took forty-five.

"According to the hotel's literature, it is one of only two hotels in the country that has on-premises access to an indoor shooting range. Will that help?"

"Are you kidding—heck, yes—if I can get on it. There's going to be over a hundred fifty shooters competing from all around the world. Just getting a room this close was a miracle." Tom happily nodded in between words, chewing on a mouthful of beef jerky, apparently his go-to.

"I don't know how I got the room. They said it was a last-minute cancellation."

Time passed as they bonded again, Tom appearing to be having a blast, and DR thankful for the distraction his friend provided.

In a packed parking lot, DR parked under the unloading awning, and they went in, baggage cart straining under its load, a wheel squeaking as it rolled. They soon found out how lucky he was to get the reservation, and why.

"I'm terribly sorry, sir, but the hotel has been overbooked. We've taken the liberty to book you in the Ferrybrook Inn." The well-composed young man grimaced while facing the man in line before DR. "If those accommodations aren't acceptable, we must apologize. We've made every attempt to find a similar room to that which you booked. Since this was our error, the hotel manager has taken care of the costs for you, Mr. Michaels."

"I booked those reservations four months ago. Why didn't you tell me sooner?" Michaels blasted, setting his suitcase down.

"We had a last-minute, uh, situation, sir. It shifted all our reservations. Again, I'm sorry. Would you like to speak to the manager?" The young clerk stood up tall. "I've said all I can."

"Yes, call the manager." Michaels slid to the side, watching DR and Tom enter. "Good luck. They gave my room away." He covered his forehead with his right hand, appearing to try to regain his composure, then looked right at Tom. "I know you, don't I?"

"Yes, Zane. I'm Tom Hughes, from London." Tom held out his hand to shake the other man's. "We've competed before. Well... you've competed. I've been there. Sorry to hear about your misfortune."

The manager came out and talked to Mr. Michaels, and after a few tense minutes, Michaels took his bag and Sam Blythe's card, leaving none too happy.

Sam saw DR and Tom as he was preparing to go into the back office. He stepped from behind the desk. "Steven Ray—excuse me, I hear it's Dr. Steven Ray now. How have you been, you old globe-trotter, you?" He grabbed his hand and wrapped an arm around him.

"Sam, Sam Blythe. I'm great. It's good to see you. You manage this hotel?"

"I sure do, and when I saw the wait-list, I knew there could only be one Steven Ray, the world conqueror and international cruise operator." He guided them to the counter. "I figured for an old classmate I could make a little magic and get you a room."

So that's why the room opened up. Maybe luck was changing again. "So how is Carla, and I heard you have three kids. Is that right?" Shaking his head, DR turned to Tom. "Sam here married the prettiest cheerleader in Albion, lucky guy. Sorry, where are my manners? Sam, this is my good friend Tom Hughes. He's competing in the tournament this week."

"We had three kids." Sam's smile fell short. "They're all gone, living with Carla."

"What do you mean 'had'? Is she all right?"

"I don't really know and halfway don't care. She left me eight years ago, met some suave guy from over in Fort Wayne." He clapped a hand on the front desk. "Next thing you know, she's strung out on meth and taking money out of my checking account to support them all."

"How about your kids? Do you see them?" Holding back his disappointment, DR let a frown convey his compassion.

"Somehow, the court gave her custody and half my paycheck. They said it was mental cruelty. I tell you what it was—my lawyer ended up being a bum. She didn't present any of the evidence I had to defend myself. She simply rolled over." Sam scrunched his nose and raised his right eyebrow, an old childhood habit. "But Carla got hers."

"What do you mean?" DR braced an elbow on the front desk beside them. "What happened?"

"I loved that woman more than a man has a right. I don't take any joy in what's happened to her, but one of my friends from church saw someone who looked like her, though he said it was hard to be positive because she was spent. He said she was standing on a street corner, if you know what I mean. I hope it's not her, but if it is, she brought it on."

"I hope not too. So you have a good room for us?" DR peered over the counter, trying to ground the situation and move on.

"I got a great suite for you, two bedrooms. How's that sound? And some practice rounds next door for your friend here. I've got work to do, so Ken will get you signed in. Let's do dinner or something one night. Call me." After shaking their hands, he disappeared into the back office.

"Dr. Ray, you're in 109—left down the hallway, third door on the right. You'll find all the information to reserve your times at the range, and if I might, I suggest you book those as soon as you get settled. Those slots will go fast. If you need anything, just dial ten on the in-room phone, and I'll pick it up here. Enjoy your stay." Ken handed DR two keys and a Wi-Fi passcode.

DR glanced out the window as Michaels drove away to find his hotel. Was this fate or an ill omen?

CHAPTER
THIRTEEN

DR put his bag on the bed and began unpacking while Tom went straight to the computer, heeding Ken's advice, looking right past the big-screen television and recliners. "I hate to say it," Tom spoke up. "But I'm glad we didn't stay at Debbie's. Your friend fixed me up, and every time slot is open. All this practice time will help me get dialed in here, knock off a little rust, and focus."

"That's good news. I'm happy for you." DR shuffled through the tournament information, schedules, coupons, and news, relaxing in one of the recliners. "Your shooters' packet has an invitation to the tournament awards ceremony. It appears they're holding it at the Lake Michigan Men's Club."

He stuffed the invitation and schedules back into the envelope, dropped it onto his lap, then kicked out his feet. "I recently met the manager, a congressman from Chicago. He's a friend of Debbie and her deceased husband. This might be fun." He locked his hands behind his head, rocked his feet side to side, and stifled a yawn. "What do you think?"

"Might be, but I'll doubt I'll be claiming any awards."

"This must be quite the tournament. Just look at all the opportunities in your package." He held up the large, clasped envelope. "You should check it out."

"These guys are all world-class." Tom looked up from the computer. "The guy you saw in the lobby today is Zane Michaels out of Australia. He's ranked third in the world."

"Like you said, maybe the practice range will knock the rust off and you could win this thing."

"Sounds good, but not probable unless I can raise my scores by ten percent." Finished plugging in the time slots he wanted, he rose, and his lips spread into a Kool-Aid smile. "Do you mind if I run over and check out the range before we go to dinner? Suddenly, I'm not as hungry. Maybe I'll just grab an apple. What do you think?"

"Go on." DR pushed himself back in the recliner. "I can see you're excited. I'll grab a nap or watch some television. I need the rest after those long airport walks."

Two hours later, the entrance door clattered open and closed.

DR, who dozed for an hour and a half, jumped up, then settled back into the chair. It was just Tom.

"Sorry. I didn't mean to startle you. The door has a powerful spring on it. Did you get some rest?"

"About ninety minutes. I'm hungry now, though. You ready to go?"

"Yep. I only had a Coke myself, so they better have plenty of food."

"I found a place that's supposed to have a good buffet, so you can eat all you want." That would likely take quite a bit too.

Soon, they'd found the place, and their server took their drink order and left. After Tom and DR loaded up their plates, they settled down to work on them, neither breaking to talk much. Michaels and a handful of other shooters were there also. It appeared he was still fuming about the hotel situation.

"Not only do I have a longer drive but I lost all my chances at using the range." A fellow shooter consoled him by patting his shoulder, but he was having none of that. "If I knew this was going to happen, I never would have entered."

Tom, overhearing the men's conversation, along with DR, gritted his teeth behind lips slanted and closed at one end.

"Not our fault. That's on Sam. And I'm thankful." DR shoveled in another forkful. "You've got to try this meatloaf."

The man who consoled Michaels asked, "Are you still going to the awards ceremony on Lake Michigan? It's supposed to be a real shindig this year."

"Of course. I've got to make something out of this trip. I'm not giving up, but practice is what sets you apart in these things. The inexperienced never get enough practice." Looking directly at Tom and DR, he waved.

They waved back. "I guess that settles it. We're going to the ceremony whether I win or not. Sound good?"

DR nodded his agreement. "Sounds like something we'd regret missing."

Debbie awoke to a ringing cellphone. Seeing the call was from Miguel, she cringed. His timing was always perfect, wasn't it? As soon as she messed up, he was there to pick up the pieces. But not this time.

"Miguel, how are you doing? Is that arm okay now?" She swung her legs over the edge of the bed. Whoa. Her head sure was pounding.

"I'm fine. It's you I'm worried about."

"You shouldn't worry about me. I'm a big girl." A big girl who wasn't ready for fifty questions.

"Sweetheart, I know you are. But I'm calling with an invitation. You see it's Christmastime, and we Riccis love to celebrate with our loved ones and friends. And you fall into both of those categories. We'd love for you to come over and spend a few days in our home. Kim could use the help, and it would get you away. What do you say?"

"I was just going to lay low, maybe spend some time with my next-door neighbors." She wiggled her feet into a pair of fuzzy slippers and shuffled toward the kitchen. "That all sounds like fun, but I'd be a spoilsport."

"The Debbie I know could never do that. Besides, Lo and David will be here, along with Cillia, Lo's sister. And Kim said she'd love to see you again. She enjoyed having dinner with you out on the point. Come on. It'll be fun."

She switched the cappuccino machine on, tilted her head back, then rolled it side to side, seeking relief from the tension in her neck. "Sounds wonderful. But I doubt I could find a flight now that would allow me to spend much time there."

She retrieved a cup from the cabinet. Maybe, at least, if she went, there wouldn't be a need to explain her breakup a hundred times to her friends and face all their sympathetic words of kindness, reliving it the whole Christmas season.

"Kim will book you a good flight. It'll be a time you won't forget. When can you leave?"

"Let me see. It takes seventeen to eighteen hours flying direct if you can get a seat. Today is Sunday, the seventeenth. If I leave Thursday, I can shop for gifts and deliver them to my friends before I leave." She glanced at her phone calendar, calculating the days while sipping the cappuccino. Then she pulled out a couple biscotti. "Wait. Make that the twentieth. Wednesday. Then I can spend more time with Kim. She's such a sweetheart, and I love talking with her."

"I heard something in the background. Are you drinking a cappuccino?"

"I am, the best ever, even if I must brag. The biscotti's not bad, either."

"I'm jealous." He chuckled. "So we're set then, Wednesday morning? I'll get Kim right on it, and she'll call you with the details. I'm looking forward to seeing you."

"Me too. Bye." Sitting at the kitchen island, she nursed her cappuccino. She'd go. She was always flexible and ready to enjoy herself. So why'd she have such a stiff backbone when it came to Dr. Steven Ray?

Tom had never shot better. He was relaxed, dialed in, and making the final cut to the three-man shoot-off after two grueling days of competition. At six foot five and two hundred and forty-five pounds, he was one of the larger men in the competition, but still agile. Holding his body still to make the shots for several days was the hardest part of the competition. The championship round on Tuesday consisted of silhouettes at 475 meters, clay pigeons at 50 meters, and behind-the-line events, squeezed around air pistols at 25 meters.

All three contestants excelled at the silhouettes with virtually identical scores. Air pistols were a toss-up too. But the clay pigeons cost Tom first place, the first-place shooter scoring one more kill. Third place missed two.

"I can't believe it. That's the best I've ever shot." Packing up his gear, he was given a score sheet to look over and approve. "DR, you must be my good luck charm. It was the practice range. All that shooting relaxed me, knocked the cobwebs from flying off me. I can't wait to tell Laurie. The eight grand will pay for my trip and then some."

"I'm impressed. That was some amazing shooting. Just like on the *DI*, you were unstoppable." DR cuffed his friend's shoulder. "I'm going outside to give Max Rice a call and let him know we're coming to the club for the trophy presentation. You take care of everything here, and I'll meet you at the car."

Outside, DR fished in his wallet for the congressman's number, finally finding his business card behind a credit card. "Hello, Congressman?"

"Yes, this is Max Rice. How can I help you?"

DR leaned against the Pathfinder, remembering Max's appearance. "This is Dr. Steven Ray, DR. I met you at Debbie's party."

"Oh yes. DR, how are you?"

"I'm good. I hope you are. I know you're busy, so I won't take up much of your time." He played with the side-view mirror. "I just wanted to let you know my friend placed second in a shooting contest and they're having the awards ceremony at your club tonight. We plan to be there. Are you in town?"

"I'm in town, but it's going to be a family night. I haven't been home as much as I'd like. I hate that I won't get to enjoy your friend's celebration with you, but I'll let the staff know. When you arrive, tell them you're my guests, and they'll make sure to attend to everything you need."

"Thanks. I'm sorry we'll miss you. Maybe next time, then." DR patted the top of the mirror and shifted to see if Tom was coming.

"Maybe next time. But I'm sure this is going to be a special celebration."

"Thanks, Congressman. Have a good one."

～

As soon as DR hung up, Max called Mr. Jennings. Maybe once this thing was done, everything else could get back to normal. Other than the fact that there were now three trailers and thirty-three cages. He just had to keep his eyes on the ball. That's all. Just like Senator Carl said, it wasn't rocket science.

Good. The phone was ringing. Kat answered but was a little short, maybe having a rough day. "Mr. Jennings will be with you in a moment." She put him on hold, not a normal practice.

"Well, hello, Max. What's the occasion for you to call me this late in the afternoon? Shouldn't you be out with your lovely wife and family?"

"Actually, sir, we're heading out to dinner in a little while." He lied. "But I have some great news. Dr. Steven Ray is going to be at the club this evening, with a friend, the one who was the sharpshooter on the cruise. Well, the guy placed second during the big shoot-off in Gary, Indiana. They're holding the awards ceremony at the club at seven o'clock." From his office, he could hear Leslie banging around in the kitchen. Hopefully, Jennings couldn't.

"Fantastic. Best news of the day. I'll get the detective and a few of his boys over there right away. They'll get the video ready to roll, and we'll get those party poopers. They're going to lose their hero status tonight. Ha ha. Thanks, Max. Finally, you're starting to earn your keep."

Max ground his teeth, holding the phone in his hand long after Jennings hung up. *"Earning my keep," he says? I'd be better off in Ray's place.*

The club on Lake Michigan gleamed like a frosted diamond. DR drove through the high entrance gate, passing the tall fence guarding the property. Beyond, the building offered a formal entrance, complete with columns, covered porte cochere, and attendants in red uniforms. Rather than brave the small wait for a valet as guests arrived for the dinner, DR pulled the Pathfinder to the parking lot. On the far side, the building wasn't nearly as fancy as its facade. Merely blocks covered in a stucco finish to brave the harsh Chicago winters.

As they walked the short distance to the club, DR rubbed his hands together against the cold. "We're supposed to inform the club when we arrive. They're going to give special attention to our needs." He shrugged. "Whatever that means."

They stepped into a nice interior, all tastefully dark beige with gold accents and chocolate-brown handmade pottery. Chandeliers hung in a pattern throughout the dining area. From the backside of the room was an extra-wide hallway where the servers delivered dinner to their guests and performers could assemble to stage. He hadn't expected such overt attention to detail, especially in the dining area, though it wasn't overly large, considering the building's size.

"Not bad for an awards ceremony. If the food is as good, we'll be all right." Tom turned in a circle, taking it all in. "I wonder what's for dinner?"

"The program said they were serving a few Chicago specialties, made right here in the club. They have Italian pastas, steaks, and a deep-dish pizza. But I'm sure, if we'd like, we could get something else." Names on the tables assigned each guest a specific seat. DR found theirs near the back hallway area.

"This is kind of strange." Tom frowned as he slid out the chair by his name. "You'd think, since I finished second, I would've been given some preferential seating."

"Maybe we'll get our food sooner, here." DR craned around to see if Michaels got the preferential treatment. As he guessed, he was sitting in the front middle. "It looks like they go by the world rankings for the seating arrangement, probably figured ahead of time who would win today. I guess they missed on this one." Snickering, he covered his mouth.

"You're probably right." Tom leaned back as one of the servers delivered their waters, asked what they wanted to drink, and left.

Dinner and the awards presentations went off without a flaw. The food was good, hot, and plentiful. The atmosphere was light, with lots of jokes, stories, and congratulations. DR relaxed, watching Tom enjoy it all.

But a few of the servers began to catch DR's eye. They all seemed to be sixteen or so. Several had bruises around their wrists or ankles. Going to the men's room, he met two girls coming down the hallway. One had a nasty bruise under her eye.

"Sweetheart, what happened to your eye?" With his left hand, he pointed the area out on his face.

"I was—"

Another girl put her hand to her mouth. "She ran into the bed last night in the dark." As she took the girl's hand and hurried away, her words drifted back. "Get a grip, Tina. You'll get us all in trouble. You don't want that, do you?"

They turned into the kitchen, Tina looking back at DR, appearing scared. Something wasn't right.

Leaving the men's room, he began to feel dizzy. Then everything went dark. When he came to, his hands and feet were bound to a chair or something, and he couldn't see. Someone must've slipped him something for some reason.

A cloth bag covered his head, and he was gagged. He tried to shake the bag loose, but it was tied below his chin. It only took a moment to realize he was no longer in the club, and he was cold, bone-chilled cold.

The floor and chair were swaying. Was he on a boat? But why?

Did Tom miss him, or did they take Tom too? He couldn't move against the constraints no matter how hard he tried. The chair was bolted to the floor, and the gag prevented him from calling out.

After about five minutes, the bag was taken off his head. A spotlight shone into his eyes, allowing him only to see the outline of his captors. But Tom was there too.

"Gentlemen, you're probably wondering what you've done to deserve this kind of treatment. I wish I could say you deserve it, but you don't. You had the misfortune of sailing into someone else's little political game, and now, you're going to pay for it. The attack on the Indian Ocean was by one of our POTUS's diehard enemies, staged to make the POTUS look bad. When you defeated those bozo terrorists, it made the boss comatose, so here we are. He wants payback." The speaker nodded to the two larger men flanking him.

The speaker's solemn voice brightened. "Please know I don't take any pleasure in this. On the other hand, the boys here can't wait. They love to see the struggle people make when their chair gets pushed overboard. It's going to take us a while to reach the spot for that, so you boys take this time to get your soul right with your Maker." Then he nodded toward the cabin. "We're going inside to stay warm."

This didn't appear to be the first time the yacht had been used for this type of activity. The deck was specially fitted to hold the chairs in place, and the three men seemed to have it down pat.

Unable to speak, DR and Tom looked at each other. Their eyes, wide and moist from the cold air, said it all. When the three men went inside, reality hit. It was twenty-eight degrees, and they didn't have jackets or coats. The cold began biting as the yacht steamed toward the middle of Lake Michigan. Where would their help come from now? No one even knew they were out here.

CHAPTER
FOURTEEN

The coastline grew fainter as the yacht engines ramped up.

At a soft noise, DR raised his head.

A little girl came out, and he jolted, recognizing her. She seemed to recognize him and Tom too. She ran over to DR, stopped, and took a long look, then blinked at Tom. She reached out and hugged DR before taking his gag out and holding a finger to her lips.

Shivering in her warm arms, he whispered, "Amal? It's Amal, right, honey? From the hospital?"

In Arabic, she whispered, "Don't speak. They'll hear us." She pressed her index finger to her lips again, then ran over to the corner where she'd hidden, and returned with a butcher knife. Their captor had used plastic strap cuffs to secure them. It only took her a moment to free them. Then she ducked down so as not to be seen and, using her hand, directed them to do the same. "Follow me."

"Where are your sisters?" DR asked.

"They're all in there." She pointed to the ship and guided them around the yacht's outer rail to the other side where they couldn't be easily seen or heard. "We can talk here."

Tom, who didn't know Arabic, held out his hands as if asking DR what was going on.

"Her sisters and maybe some other kids are inside. We can't challenge them now. We need to get warm."

A pistol lay on one of the tables beside a pack of cigarettes and a lighter. DR grabbed the handgun and tossed it to Tom.

"Amal," he resumed in Arabic, "we can't get your sisters right now. We have to go for help, somehow." He scoured the deck, not seeing anything helpful. "Have you seen the lifeboats?"

Now the yacht was a quarter mile out, the distance growing by the moment. Their lives depended on getting warm. Time was critical. She led them down to the next deck, staying in the shadows so they wouldn't be seen and pointing out the security cameras.

"How old did you say she was? She's a clever one." Tom watched Amal bravely lead them.

"I don't know, nine? She's been through so much. She's probably numb from it all." How could DR not admire the young girl from Yemen? The girl's sister had said he was supposed to be their dad. She heard it in the dream. He'd heard it too. Now, here she was.

Pulling down the lifeboat, DR whispered, "You get ready to jump, hold Amal, jump with her into the boat. I'll follow. We have to be fast, and you may have to fish me out of the lake." He then explained the same thing to Amal.

"Okay, but you come fast. You don't want to be in the water."

Off the backside, before they could be spotted, DR tossed the eight-person lifeboat into the water. At the same time, Tom took Amal and dove in, quickly followed by DR, who hit the water with his lower legs, but nonetheless made it in the boat, safely, holding onto the side.

With his lower legs wet, the cold was biting even worse. Time was running out on them.

They took the paddles and began paddling back to shore. Something strained in DR's abdomen, and he had to stop. So Tom paddled as hard as he could. Ten minutes later, they reached shore. Unable to go inside the LMMC, they climbed on board a boat that looked familiar to Tom and Amal.

"I know this boat!" Tom whisper-shouted. "It's *Providence*, the boat from the Indian Ocean where we found the kids." He then headed to the bridge, found the key in the ignition, and fired up the engines.

Amal knew the boat too. She'd been held there for two weeks in a secret storage area. Now she led DR to find something warm and retrieved the blankets from a couple of beds. She helped him get dried off and warmed up. Then she brought Tom a blanket as DR rested.

They sailed southward for about thirty minutes, to get away from the club and out of sight from the previous yacht—the *Lucky Lucie* as DR had seen her stern after they pulled away. Then Tom slowed *Providence* down to talk to DR, who was warming up.

"What was that all about?" Tom asked, wide-eyed.

DR, still shivering, felt much better. "He said it was related to the attack on us during our cruise. I don't know what to think—tied to the President was what he said, right?" Seeing Amal confused, he reached for her and hugged her thin frame.

Tom jerked a thumb toward her. "How'd she get here, anyway? And she said her sisters were inside the boat?" He closed his eyes and shook his head. "This is creepy."

"Whoever this is must've had them taken from Yemen. Maybe they're the ones who killed O'Reilly." DR sat on the bench seat alongside *Providence*'s helm. He bent over, trying to think, hands on the back of his head, tugging at his hair—the old habit wouldn't die. Amal sat beside him, all big-eyed, confused, and scared. "I can't believe the congressman I met at Debbie's had anything to do with this. But that's what it appears. How else would anyone know we were going to be there?"

"You mean you knew the guy? Whatever. We need to get to the hotel, warm up, maybe feed her, and call the police. This is way above our heads." Tom went back to the captain's seat and resumed their journey to Gary, Indiana, another thirty minutes from this point.

"The man said the staff would give us special attention. Guess his idea of special attention was a little different from ours." DR tried to explain their plan to Amal and how they were going to help her sisters.

As she sat at his side, a tear found its way down her cheek, then another.

"I feel for this child and the others. They've been through so much." He fought to hold back his own tears. "And it's not over yet."

～

Detective Shortman and the two men came outside when they reached the spot over half an hour after leaving their captives. Panicked, he kicked one of the chairs, shouting "Argh!" Somehow, someone had helped them escape. While searching the boat, one man called out, "Shortman, down here."

He and the other man joined him. A lifeboat was missing. Just great. Shortman closed his eyes and grunted. "Well, that's bad. The boss isn't going to like this." He hung his head. "I've got to go call him." Shaking his head, he returned to the main deck.

At nine o'clock, he didn't want to disturb Mr. Jennings. But he had to make the call, or he'd be going for a deep dive. The phone rang five times before a female voice answered, none too happy.

"What is it, Shortman?" Jennings demanded when he came on the line. "This better be important."

The woman giggled in the background.

"It's Dr. Ray, sir. He escaped—with his friend."

During a long pause, the woman stopped giggling, and a door slammed. "I guess not only the terrorists were incompetent. It would seem I'm surrounded by it. What the—What's wrong with you bozos? Can't you do anything right?"

"I'm sorry, Boss. I don't know how they got away. They were tied up tight."

"Don't worry. I knew something might go wrong. Tell Dingleman we're going to plan B. And as soon as he puts it in motion, have him check the cameras on the boat landing. I just heard the senator's boat is missing. And don't bother me no more tonight."

"Yes, sir." The phone went dead before Shortman could finish.

Arriving at the boat landing, Detective Shortman went straight to the club's office and found Dingleman, the club's assistant under Max Rice, watching a game show on television, flipping a pistol around his fingers over and over. He sat up, but seeing Shortman, Dingleman resumed his posture. "What's up? Everything taken care of?"

"No, they escaped." Shortman surveyed the office. The cleaners must've missed it. "Jennings said go to plan B."

"Is that right?" Dingleman's lips quirked, his eyes widening. He rasped a dark-skinned hand over his shaved head. "Are you sure? Did he say anything else?"

"Yeah. After you implement plan B, you're supposed to look at the camera video of the boat landing. He thinks that will show who took it."

"Okay..." Dingleman rolled his chair back from the desk. "Step outside the door for a moment. I need to get something." When Shortman was in the camera's view, Dingleman rose and fired a shot at Shortman's leg and three more shots that missed intentionally.

"What the hell are you doing?" Shortman grabbed his leg and rolled on the floor, cussing at first. "You *shot* me. Are you nuts? Argh!"

"Just doing what you told me, plan B." Going to the camera, Dingleman removed the thumb drive storing the surveillance video of the boat landing. He took it to the office and inserted it into the desktop computer.

"What are you doing? Aren't you going to call someone for me?"

"You're a big boy. Call it in as an officer down. We'll pin your shooting on the good doctor and his friend. CPD will eat them up for us. Mission accomplished."

When the trio reached the Skylight Hotel, DR planned to call the police first thing. But Tom turned on the television. A bulletin was posted on two fugitives shooting an officer in the line of duty. DR's and Tom's pictures flashed along with a mention of possible child trafficking. Images showed Detective Shortman—the lead man on their attempted murder—being wheeled on a stretcher to an awaiting ambulance at the LMMC. The words *subjects are armed and dangerous, notify police immediately, do not confront* scrolled across the screen.

"DR, you might want to take a look at this." Tom thudded down on the sofa, jaw sagging and eyes wide.

Already gawking at the screen, DR swallowed hard. He may be unskilled at thinking like a criminal, but even he knew they had to get out of the hotel—fast. It would only be minutes before the authorities kicked in their door—and found them with Amal. "Someone's gone to great lengths to set us up. Grab your stuff, Tom."

Holding Amal's hand with one hand, his luggage with the other, DR headed out the back hallway to his Pathfinder, Tom in hot pursuit with his luggage and gun cases. A car came racing toward them dangerously fast, then slammed on its brakes just in time. The hotel manager, Sam, rolled down the window.

"Get in, now. Cops are out front looking for you." He checked the rearview mirror, the bright lights of the police vehicles lighting up the night.

"Pop your trunk!" Tom called out, then loaded up the trunk with his and DR's luggage before hopping in the back.

Sam drove away out the back to hit the interstate ramp. After they were a safe distance down the highway, he chuffed in a deep breath as if finally remembering to breathe.

DR followed suit.

"What have you guys done? Did you really shoot a cop?" Sam twisted in his seat, keeping an eye on the mirror at all times. "CPD is going to gun you down—no questions asked. Is this the one they say you are trafficking?" He nodded to Amal.

"Sam, we didn't do anything. This is an attempt by the same people who attacked us on the cruise, according to the cop who was shot by someone. We escaped. Now, they want CPD to do what they haven't been able to do yet." DR craned to peer out the back window. Good. No one was following them.

Hands behind his head, he fought the urge to tug at his hair, then shared what they knew so far.

Sam whistled. "That's some story."

"That's not the half of it."

"Where are you taking us?" Tom interrupted, the miles whittling away as they headed east on Interstate 94.

"I own a small cabin in Paw Paw. We can crash there for the night until you decide your next step." Again, Sam eyed Amal. "How does she fit into all this?"

"That's what I was getting at." Closing his eyes, DR gathered his thoughts. "She is one of the kids we rescued on the Indian Ocean. Her sisters are still on the *Lucky Lucie*."

"*Lucky Lucie*?" Sam's eyebrows rose.

"The club's gambling yacht. It appears they use it for child sex trafficking too." DR explained about the most recent kidnapping. "I think they're all at the club."

"Who shot the detective? You guys didn't, did you?"

"No, Amal here saved us." To paint the complete picture for his friend, DR explained their escape.

"You can't make this stuff up—believe me, I try," Tom said. "My wife and I have written a few thrillers, but I never thought I'd be on *America's Most Wanted*."

Sam had a funny expression on his face, his lips squeezed tight as he breathed in deeply, his gaze rotating between mirrors. He must be questioning his involvement.

"Why did you come for us?" DR asked.

"I don't know. I just had an unction you needed help, and now it would appear I may be on the *AMW* too." Sam chuckled and flexed his grip on the wheel. "Tom, you're right. You can't make this stuff up. And every police force in the country is going to be looking for you—me too, now."

"What's your place in Paw Paw like?" Tom twisted in the front passenger seat to face DR in the back with Amal.

"It's just a one-room cabin with a bathroom, indoor plumbing, heat, and electricity. I have five bunks in it for hunting and fishing. Very basic, but it does have a refrigerator. So I'll stop and pick up a few things to eat before we head up the hill." He reached for his wallet and thumbed through, finding only twenty-two dollars. Then he pulled out his credit card and waved it in the air. "Emergency-use only."

"Wait. You can't use a credit card. They'll be looking for you too. By now, they've pulled the hotel's video. Tom, how much cash do you have?" DR rummaged in his own pocket and found several hundred dollars, but they'd have to stretch it.

Tom had quite a lot more since he was traveling. "I have five hundred and eleven dollars."

"Good. Give Sam a hundred dollars to get supplies. How much gas do you have, Sam?" DR craned to see the gauge, but the steering wheel blocked his view.

"I filled her up this morning, so we're good. I'm not going to get a lot, maybe some microwaveable food, water, and snacks." Sam raised his gaze to the rearview mirror. "How's that sound?"

"Perfect, but maybe get Amal a lollipop. I think she'd like that." In Arabic, DR asked what flavor she liked. "Make it a cherry lollipop."

DR shifted in his seat. Why were they being played? Was this to be his portion in providence?

CHAPTER
FIFTEEN

Jennings was at home in California, trying to stay focused on his female guest when Dingleman returned his call. "I've got some bad news, Dingleman." Jennings left the room and walked to the kitchen across the way. "I talked to Max a few minutes ago after he heard about Shortman. Max may be a loose cannon, a loose end." He placed a hand on the granite countertop, maintaining his view of the girl in the next room.

"So what would you like from me, sir?"

"Just keep an eye on him. These congressmen are a soft bunch. If he gets spooked, we may have to take him fishing, if you know what I mean." He laughed. Max just may have had a reason not to like his joke about the lake's water temperature after all.

"Not a problem, sir. I'm ready for the promotion anyway."

"That's what I like about you, Dingleman, always looking at the upside. Maybe you should be the next congressman from Chicago. How does that sound?" No, if Max went down, Jennings would need a new crew.

"I like it. I like it a lot. Don't worry about Max. If he acts scared, I'll let you know."

"You do that, Congressman." Hanging up, Jennings laughed even louder. No way would he ever make Dingleman Congress material. But it kept him in line and his hopes up. Ha ha. "Silly boy."

It didn't take long to see how basic Sam's hunting shack was. But he had a police scanner to track winter storms when hunting. One didn't want to get caught unaware of a snowstorm coming, especially since most seemed to start at night. The road up to the shack would be impassable when a hard storm hit. Tonight, the scanner fulfilled its original intent, following police channels.

Though the place had indoor plumbing, the commode and shower were in open view. Only a curtain hanging from a frame concealed them. The small refrigerator was full of old sandwiches and such. Tom went to throw them out the back, but Sam stopped him.

"You don't want to do that. This place is crawling with bears this time of year, bulking up before hibernation. Put food out there, and we won't get a wink of sleep." He pulled Tom back into the cabin. "Here, put them in this bag, tie it up, then bag it again. That should take care of any smell tonight."

Amal peered at the food on the table. "I'm hungry. Can we eat something?" she asked DR, her eyes pleading.

He tucked strands of her hair back from her face. "Sure, honey. What would you like?"

Sam spread the goodies on the butcher-block countertop for her to choose from. While she took an egg salad sandwich and unwrapped it, Sam handed her a water to wash it down. "We had better all eat something and get some sleep. We can make our plans in the morning."

"Sounds good to me." DR stifled a yawn. "This has been a long day. Sorry, Tom, that your day was ruined. You shot well this week. I'm proud of you." Taking a bite out of his sandwich, he saluted Tom with his water bottle.

"I wonder, though. Would we be in this mess if I hadn't competed? Where would they have gotten back at us otherwise?"

"I don't know, but here we are. Let's just take it one day at a time." DR swept the hair out of Amal's face again. When she looked up appreciatively, he could feel himself warming up to the nine-year-old. Somehow, they just had that effect.

Sam seemed to understand a bond was growing too. "Where is Amal from, and what happened to her parents?"

"The priests said she and her sisters were from Yemen. Maybe Aden. Her parents were killed by the Houthis or some other terror group." DR let his eyelids slide practically closed, either because of the sadness or because he was just plumb worn out. Whatever it was, he had no energy to analyze it.

The police scanner came to life when Sam started searching channels, finding one channel carrying the communications between the CPD and the FBI. What sounded like Detective Shortman on one end began to check off the facts and sent subordinates looking for connections and resources of the trio now wanted by the police and national law enforcement agencies, including the ATF, since Tom carried professional sniper weapons into the country.

"Skychief 1 to Mobile Intel. Come in, Mobile Intel."

"Mobile Intel. Go ahead, Skychief."

"Mobile Intel, has the property report on one Sam Blythe come back yet? And, if so, can you send a digital copy to my phone?"

"Skychief, I'm working on it. Some of his records weren't fully digitized, inheritances and such. It may be in the morning before I can get all that. I'll send you a copy as soon as I can. Mobile Intel, out."

The channel went quiet.

"We'd better get that sleep. Sounds like company's coming soon." DR surveyed the cabin, then nodded at the blankets and quilts. He took Amal's hand after she'd finished eating and led her to a bunk beside the wall, not far from the heat. Spreading the covers, he tucked her in, kissed her forehead, and whispered a good night in her language.

The three men all followed suit, climbing under some covers on their own bunks.

"You know"—Sam spoke out in the darkness—"growing up watching all those cop shows, I always wondered what it would be like to be a fugitive. It's kind of exciting and scary at the same time. I just hope the good guys really do win. We are the good guys, right?"

"Of course, we are. Get some sleep."

DR rolled over on his side, eyes wide open. This wasn't just some bad-luck scenario. The man who ordered the kids' kidnapping and the terror attacks on them was psycho. He wanted payback from his victim. How stupid was that—or sick?

How far would this man go?

No matter what, DR had to get Amal away, at least saving her. Then, maybe, they'd see about the others.

While the authorities had a difficult time finding Sam Blythe's other residential holdings, DR's was much easier to gather. Through motor vehicle records, they pinpointed his residence on Wall Lake, also arriving not long afterward at his workshop in between Delton. FBI, ATF, Illinois State Police, Michigan State Police, and Delton personnel surrounded each location, only to find them empty. They searched every drawer and closet in both locations, to find just one note about Tom arriving from London at Chicago O'Hare for the competition, nothing new.

The trail had grown cold. Meanwhile, Jennings leaned on every law enforcement official in his camp. He called the governors of both states, sharing the video of Shortman being shot, applying political pressure to bring the men down, dead. Only the suspects weren't in the clip—the camera angle just showed the victim. After he saw the club's video of the men taking *Providence* with a small girl in tow, he wanted his performer back. He didn't share *that* video with authorities. But he'd send all the other performers to his club in downtown Chicago for safekeeping.

Michigan State Police followed up at DR's parents' home and his brothers' homes, though they didn't manage to scare Tammy Rae and Mike Sr. into believing their son may have done something bad.

After midnight DR smelled the old food—the sandwiches left in the cabin a month or so ago. Although Sam said it would draw bears, it had to be better than dying from asphyxiation. He rolled out of bed and threw the rank bag outdoors, then climbed back into bed.

Around three thirty a.m., three bears—a sow and two eleven-month-old cubs—began tearing the bag open and leaning on and hitting the back door, waking everyone inside.

"I'm sorry, everyone." DR held up both hands. "I didn't listen. I put the bag of old food outside." He reached for Amal, patted her hand to quell her fear, and told her what was happening.

Sam switched the lights on. "Won't be any sleeping now. They'll be here for hours." He walked to the front cabin windows. "No bears here. Wait... Oh no. We've got to go—and fast. Get dressed, everybody. The cops are down in the hollow coming this way. We've got about three minutes to scram." He raced to put on his jacket and grab their food.

"Good thing you put that food outside. The bears knew." Tom jammed on his shoes, then helped DR hurry Amal too.

"I've got an idea, Sam. Let's buy ourselves some time. You all go get in the car, and I'll let the bears in the back door. The cops might think it's us and take more time getting inside to check." DR peered out the window. "Hurry. They're not too far down there. Better not turn the car headlights on."

After the others ran to the car, trying not to draw the bears' attention, DR opened the back door and threw some food on the floor just inside. When the bears started his way, he switched the lights out before heading out the front. A glance over his shoulder showed all three bears had made their way inside, working on the food he threw down. He ran to the back door and shut it, locking the bears inside, and then sprinted to the car.

"Go, Sam, go." He slid into the back seat. "Get us out of here."

"I hope they don't mess with my pickup truck. I just got it back from the shop. I only use it for hauling my kills, but I don't want to have my trunk impounded." Sam pulled out calmly at first to keep down any dust for the police to spot. Headlights off, he had to go slow, straining to see on the road going up the mountain. Below, the police lights almost reached the cabin now. Then Sam hooked the car around a sharp corner and headed down an incline toward a creek. The fence gate was closed, but he kept going.

"It's old man Simmons's property. He doesn't live here, just has some cows down in a meadow. Sometimes, he'll hunt here, but not this time of year." Sam angled the car, apparently to hit both parts of the gate at an equal spot, not to damage his car too much.

DR cringed. "Sam, I'm sorry about all of this. I'll pay you back for everything when this is over." Then a loud noise erupted, and he twisted backward. "Stop a moment."

Sam obeyed.

"Sounds like gunfire—lots of gunfire." The bears weren't going to make it, but better the critters than DR and his companions. He suppressed a shudder and took Amal's hand to comfort her, catching Tom's eye, where he was sitting in the front passenger seat. The cops didn't even bother to ID what was in the shack before shooting it up. A nod acknowledged Tom was thinking the same thing.

The car split the gates open and drove on, and the road took another hard downward turn. Then a creek came into sight. After their dry fall, the water level was below average, about a foot high, but Sam still navigated it carefully. The property owner had placed hollow-core cinder blocks turned sideways to cross the creek over. However, several had slipped out of place, probably washed-out.

Sam squinted and stopped the car. "I've got to take this careful, or we might get stuck in that hole between the blocks."

"Hang on a minute. Let me see if I can move them back." Tom jumped out. A shot fired now and again as he walked over the blocks to the hole to maneuver the blocks. Then, unable to budge the washed-out ones, he climbed back into the car, rubbing his hands together to get them dry and warm. "No use. The mud's got them lodged in the creek bank."

"Well, it's our only way out." Sam exhaled, swiping his hand down from his forehead over his face. "By now, the cops know we were there earlier since we left behind fresh food. Ohh... my cabin's going to be a mess. They slaughtered the bears right where they stood. Didn't they?"

Tom gave a grim nod.

"Okay, guys." Sam flexed his grip on the wheel. "I'm going to point the car and give it gas. We'll just have to pray we get across."

"Go for it." DR grabbed the handle above the door to steady himself and pointed out the handle above Amal's side for her to hold on also.

The car lurched forward. Trying to keep the car from spinning its tires, Sam held the wheel so tight his knuckles turned white. DR gritted his teeth. Then the car reached the hole. The passenger-side front tire dropped into the gap with a sickening crunching before it popped back out. Then the rear tire hit the same hole, repeating the process. Only there wasn't a noise like the first time. Instead, a loud scraping followed, and the car shook as something dragged across the edge of the two blocks on either side. After they reached the road, Sam stopped the car.

DR got out too. The car tilted precariously toward the passenger-side front tire.

Sam shone a flashlight on the front tire. The cinder block had ripped a sidewall. Now, the tire was seeping air.

"We better go as far as we can. We should make the road a half mile away. Then we can put the spare on." Sam slapped the hood, then walked back to get in.

DR climbed in and sniffed. "We have a bigger problem than the tire. It smells like the scrape was the gas tank."

The morning air held a certain chill as Debbie struck out to the airport, practically mirroring the dread in her heart. At least it wasn't foggy. She had enough of that in her head for everyone. Somehow, in her soul, she felt something wasn't right, almost like the feeling of leaving a kettle of water boiling and going away or leaving keys in your car ignition in a parking lot. With her spirit out of sorts, she couldn't put her finger on the *why*. Was it loneliness, wanting closure, or just plain out of hope for the future? It seemed like... like how she'd felt after her husband was shot.

Debbie had walked the floor the night before her flight, trying to work out in her mind what to say when she did talk to DR. She didn't want to give up on their love. She'd made a mistake, and it wouldn't happen again.

Each time she tried to call him last night, though, the phone rang and went straight to voicemail. "Is he screening my calls? Why doesn't he pick up?" she asked herself aloud, then huffed. "Well, two can play at this game."

She yanked her luggage along, second-guessing, judging him again. She slammed the luggage in the back. She only wanted to be with him, no one else. What was wrong with that?

This morning, she didn't bother to call again. She'd left him four messages last night and wanted to take the last two back. Loading her silver BMW, she swore she'd put this behind her and headed to the airport at five a.m. It would be a long trip. Now she wanted—needed—to get this off her mind, to stop overthinking everything. After all, that's why she was going to Marsala, right?

CHAPTER
SIXTEEN

Mom had called Mike and his brothers after the police left. Now, Wednesday morning, he explained it to Willie. Having prayed with his family the night before, he prayed with her now. "Lord, we don't know what circumstances surround my brother, DR, but You do. We ask You to keep him and his friends from harm. Guide them to do what is right and good in Your sight, Lord. Willie and I come in agreement and ask You to do whatever You deem necessary to vindicate them all. We know DR to be a man of good character, dependable, and strong. We ask You to help him remain so, Lord, and give him—and his friends—wisdom, strength, and the tenacity to accomplish what You have set before them. And we ask You to give their families peace, knowing this is in Your hands. In Jesus's name, we come, amen."

He hugged Willie. Then they both sat on the edge of his desk, pondering the thing they prayed for. Just how would God work all this out? "All right. Well, we better get back to work." He hopped off his desk and slapped his hands together. "We have a show to plan."

"Yep." She wiped a tear away and placed her hands alongside her mouth as she set out to go to her desk outside.

"Willie, wait." He gripped her arm. He held her steady, intent on her every move. "You don't still have a crush on my brother, do you?"

"Don't be silly." She slid her arm free and kept walking, ducking her face out of his view.

"Just checking. That's all. But if you do, you need to come to grips with it. He's got a girlfriend, remember?"

"Not anymore." She turned to go out the door. Then, her left hand on the doorframe, she raised her chin and shook her black hair away from curtaining her face. "She left him on Saturday." She continued out, moving faster, probably realizing he was coming after her now.

"Where did you hear that?" He sped down the hallway and followed her into her office, standing just inside.

"She told me."

"What? What happened? Did she say?" Mike's heart raced. Was this all tied together? Did he do something stupid? Debbie was a keeper.

"It was his morals, something she called stupid, his Michigan Strong morals. At least that's what she called them. Have you ever heard of them?" She blinked up at him. Was that hope in her brown eyes?

"Oh, I heard about them from Mom. Her dad had them, but he died while I was still young. DR used to spend weeks with him in the summertime. Mom said it nearly killed him when Granddad died." Mike tilted his head. Just where did Willie fit into all this? "Are you seeing that Irish guy, Ryan?"

"We've had coffee, and I showed him around. Why?" She slumped into her fancy office chair, complete with leather upholstery, and leaned back, appearing to await his answer.

"Just wondering. Keep praying." He headed back to his office. *What have you gotten yourself into Steven Ray?*

DR held tight as Sam fought to control the car and rammed through the barbed wire fence surrounding the pasture between them and the road. He had to keep the speed up as the front passenger tire began to go flat. At the pasture's other edge, he ran through the fence again. Upon hitting pavement, the front tire squealed.

No sooner had they gotten on the road than Tom pointed to a

helicopter through the trees. Sam clicked their headlights off, and DR held his breath. It would be over if they were spotted.

"There!" Tom shouted. "Pull under there. Maybe they haven't seen us yet."

Sam aimed toward the roadside table just down the road covered by a tree canopy. He leaned forward to look straight up in the air through the windshield.

The helicopter kept going.

"Wow. That was close." DR rolled down the side window, listening for the helicopter. Yes! The sound was growing fainter as it crossed the same mountain they'd just crossed.

Sam slumped back into his seat, turned the engine off, and closed his eyes. His shoulders shook as he took several deep breaths. "Let's get the tire swapped out."

"I've got it." Tom opened his door. "Pop the trunk."

Taking Amal's small hand and one of the blankets they'd grabbed in the rush from the cabin, DR led her to the picnic table. "Come on, sweetheart. Let's me and you get out so Tom can change the tire." They sat on the bench, a portion of a folded blanket under them, and he tucked the rest around her.

While Tom wrested the new tire into place, several bolts proving difficult, Sam came over and stood in front of DR. "Maybe it was good we had the flat. We might have been seen if we were further along." He scanned DR's and Amal's faces.

"Maybe." Not wanting to complicate this with faith, DR shrugged. "We need a plan, and I might have one. It's risky, but doable." He tilted his head at Amal, so Sam could see, thankful she couldn't understand English.

"What are you thinking?"

"First off, you have to decide how far you're in. This could get nasty." DR forced a smile. "You're not too deep. They may not shoot you—at least, I don't think they would."

"It's funny, but when this started, I didn't even think." Sam gripped his hips and rocked his neck side to side, lips pursed. "I just reacted to a friend in trouble. Now, I'm thinking, and I'm going to see this through. Risk or no risk."

DR reached up for a high five. Their hands met, and a commitment to each other formed. Tom, having finished replacing the tire, walked over, wiped his hands with a cloth, and high-fived Sam too. They were in agreement—they'd see this through, together.

DR patted Amal's shoulder. "If we're going to be treated as criminals, we'd better start thinking like them, the smart ones. We need to get rid of your car, Sam. Authorities will spot us in the daylight."

"This may sound crazy, but there's a school bus terminal a couple of miles up the road. School's out for Christmas." Sam rubbed the back of his neck. "Want to grab one of those?"

"School bus?" Tom asked.

"That would be different." DR arched a brow. Was he really about to agree to this? "They'd never think to look for us in one of them, especially if no one is supposed to drive the bus today, and it isn't reported stolen. Let's do it."

Tom covered his mouth, seeming to contemplate the matter. "Are you sure? Those things don't exactly blend. If they see us, we'll be sitting ducks."

"Wank, wank. Then ducks, we'll be." DR laughed.

They all laughed, a hollow laugh.

Twelve hours had passed since Detective Shortman called in the officer-down report and requested help. Now Jennings was mad, and of course, Max Rice was getting the brunt of it. If only he could just hang up, walk away. Instead, he squirmed, his heartbeat ratcheting up.

"Tell me something, Max. Is everybody over there incompetent? How can three bumbling, stumbling idiots escape the FBI, ATF, and just about every law enforcement agency in the area this long?"

Something shattered on Jennings's end. Glass breaking, maybe?

"I don't know, sir." Max cringed. "Luck?"

"It's incompetence, Max—you hear me? In–com–pee–tence. But don't worry. I've hired some boys who know how to get it done."

"Sir?" Max stiffened.

"I'm bringing in friends to take care of our rat problem. You and

Dingleman stay focused on the club. Take care of the girls and find out which one went missing. If things get too dicey, we may have to give them all a vacation, understand?"

Whoa. Wait a minute. Max jerked upright, slamming his knee against the underside of his desk. "One of the girls is missing?"

"Where have you been? Haven't you seen the news? We played it so it would appear Dr. Ray and his friends abducted her from somewhere. But I want her back—no loose ends. You understand?"

Max reached for a tall glass, his family still asleep. He hesitated, then put it back. "I understand."

"And, Max, when my friends arrive, stay out of their way. They tend to get impatient, if you know what I mean."

"Will do." Gladly. This ship was already going down, and Max didn't want to be on it. After all, it was cold this time of year in Lake Michigan.

He shivered.

The phone went dead. He strolled outside. It was cold, but he barely felt it.

DR saluted Tom as Sam pulled over by the school bus terminal and dropped Tom off with plans for him to pick them up down the road a ways, leaving Sam's car on the roadside. As the car drove away, Tom slipped through the open gate, staying low. DR craned his neck for a last glimpse. Someone's car was there. They appeared to be pumping fuel into the buses on the backside of the building. Tom would find a bus out of sight with a decent fuel level.

Soon, Sam parked. Only minutes passed before Tom pulled alongside them, DR hustling Amal onto the bus. Then Tom drove off after Sam retrieved Tom's weapons and their luggage from the trunk. "That was easy. The keys were right on the engine cover, and the fuel tank's full. Where to now?"

DR exhaled. "We need to let things cool down and get her to safety. I'm thinking a safe house."

Amal appeared calm, at least on the outside. Good thing she hadn't asked about her sisters. He wouldn't know what to tell her.

Sam sat sideways on a bench. "Where are you going to find one of those?"

"How about Greg and Penny's place?" DR shrugged. "It's a ways down there, but it should be safe. Besides, there isn't anyone here I'd put in harm's way—and I doubt it would be jeopardizing Greg and Penny. Hopefully, they will agree."

Tom scrunched his forehead. "Sounds good. We can get a good night's rest once we get there too. Maybe things'll cool down."

"Who are they?" Sam yawned. "Where do they live?"

"They're friends from our cruise, and they live in Birmingham. Birmingham, Alabama."

"That's a long way to go. Especially in a school bus."

"We'll have to get another car eventually. This bus will stick out in the south." DR's eyes felt beady. Tired, he rubbed at them. They all appeared tired, probably more from the strain and frustration, than the lack of rest.

"Great." Tom sucked in a deep breath. "Folks will ask me how I celebrated my shooting performance, and I'll say I stole a bus and a car... all while avoiding police to keep from getting shot." His voice became edgy, his face blotching red.

"Okay, guys." DR signaled with his hands to calm things down. "We're all frustrated, but we need to relax. Let's not get Amal upset too. We'll work this out one step at a time. First off, Tom, head toward Colombus, Ohio, take Interstate 94 east toward Marshall, then exit onto Interstate 69 south."

"How far is that?" Tom glanced over his shoulder.

"It's about forty-five minutes, depending on traffic." Sam stood and crossed to sit in the front seat on the passenger side.

It was only ten to six. Sunrise was still over two hours away. They'd be out of Michigan before daylight. DR settled Amal into her own seat, her blanket around her again. Then he leaned back against the bus's sidewall and napped as well. Tom and Sam talked, their voices a low rumble as they got to know one another while they streaked away from law enforcement, passing scores of police vehicles on the way.

~

The firm of Smithers, Manning, and Jones, headquarters located in San Juan, was the best of the best, an ex-patriot Special Forces unit. Often members of Circle, the elite establishment's public relations arm, used their services for their covert needs. Jennings made the call, and the firm moved fast to remedy the situation.

"Let's go. We need to be on the ground and in pursuit within eight hours. Time is money on this job. The old man is coming unglued." Smithers grabbed a duffel bag packed for quick deployment, slung it over his shoulder, and picked up their communication gear packed in a backpack, double-timed it toward the jet, and hollered again, "Let's go, gentleman."

"Where's our contact's information? I've already sent the coordinates to our air transport." Jones, rolling a stack of firearms and munitions in hard cases, hustled only a step behind.

"Here." Smithers stopped, set down his backpack, and handed him an iPad from the top of his pack. "It's recorded on here. The news accounts are there too. Our target—three white males transporting a nine-year-old. Gentlemen, we do not harm the girl. Understood?"

The four-man team, including O'Connor, an electronic surveillance specialist who only joined the firm six months earlier, boarded the jet headed toward the US mainland. O'Connor input the fugitives' last known locations and imported their pictures, descriptions, credit cards, cellphone numbers, and known relatives from the APB and the official online databases of the FBI, IRS, and other federal government sources. Soon, he'd created a profile of each target. "We've got their info. We'll have their location when they slip up or as soon as a surveillance camera captures their faces."

O'Connor read the three men's bios, then groaned. "Why do we always hunt the good guys? It would be fun if we could hunt terrorists like those we fought in the Middle East."

"Don't get caught up in the minutiae," Smithers scolded. "We are the good guys."

～

Ryan McNeilly unlocked the door to allow Willie into DR's shop, shaking his head. "What has my cousin gotten himself into now?" He shut the door behind her, hugged her, then pointed out how law enforcement opened crates, sifted through paperwork, and made a general mess of the shop seeking information on DR.

"We don't know what this is about." Willie handed him a picture from the AP wire photograph covering the story. "They showed up at his parents' home last night, claiming he'd shot a Chicago PD detective. There's a manhunt for him and two other men."

"Oh... I know the other man." Ryan's eyes widened. "That's Tom, from the cruise. He's a professional marksman. If he'd shot at someone, he wouldn't just hit their leg unless it was on purpose." He dropped the picture onto a stainless steel counter. "By the way, you look lovely today, Tonya."

"Thanks." She pulled up a chair. "You know he broke up with Debbie?"

"No. When did that happen?" He hopped up on a workbench, scooting a clipboard over to make room.

"Three days ago. DR proposed the night before. The next morning, she said she got mad and stormed out." Willie cocked her head. Did Ryan still have feelings toward Debbie? She bit her bottom lip, still not sure how she felt about DR. Or Ryan.

"She got mad he proposed?"

"No, about something after the proposal." She shifted in her seat. *That* was not a discussion she wanted with the hot-blooded Irishman.

"That crazy kid. She's so out there at times, but she's a sweetheart." Sitting on the table over her, he leaned in, his eyes searching her. "I think her husband's killing still affects the way she responds to tough situations."

Instinctively, Willie covered up, then relaxed. How would she ever get a man if she was always on the defensive? "I can't say I blame her. Holding your spouse in your arms and watching them bleed out? That would mess with me too."

"Changing the subject to happy." He drummed his hands on his thighs, maybe leading up to something. "Would you like to get some dinner sometime? I could use a little company. Delton's not exactly a hotbed of activity."

"What do you have in mind?"

"Nothing fancy." He released his eyes to roam her again. "Do you like hot wings?" His right eyebrow rose as he tilted his head to the left.

"I used to love them, but I haven't had them for a while. Where do you want to get them?" The last time she'd had wings was with Ashton, her high school boyfriend.

"Remember the side of Kalamazoo you took me to? There's a really good wing place there, and if you can eat a large order, they'll give you a piece of pie free. I had them last Friday, got the pie too." He grinned, probably proud of his accomplishment. "We can go tomorrow night if you want?"

"Sounds like fun, but don't expect me to eat a large order." She leaned back in her chair and patted her stomach. "I don't want to put it all right here."

"So it's a date?"

"Uh... Sure, it's a date." She stood, ready to go, then closed her eyes, already questioning herself.

"If you hear anything about DR, give me a call." Ryan followed her to the door and reached for another hug.

The hug felt good. The feeling of being in a man's arms, holding a man, pushed her own needs—her own desires to have a man—to the forefront. Outside, she exhaled. She didn't know how she felt about Ryan. She'd never dated outside of her faith before, and he was far outside of her faith. *It's just wings—that's all.* "Just wings."

CHAPTER
SEVENTEEN

When Max reached the LMMC, he headed straight to Dingleman's office. The call from Jennings had him on edge, that and the thirty-two "performers" now in cages in the trailers on the property's backside. And the fact Jennings expected them ready to take to his club in Chicago or else unsettled him. Dr. Ray being on the loose brought its own headaches, but was Max ready for murder?

"Dingleman, what is going on? Has everyone gone crazy?" Max placed his hands on his desk and leaned over it, close to where Dingleman was polishing his pistol, eyeing him.

"If you want out, Jennings will just add you to the list. Right now, I don't think anyone is safe. Do you want out?" Dingleman buffed the pistol's finger groves, then twitched it as if to point at Max. "He's going to expunge my record and said, if you wanted out, that was okay. I could be the next congressman from Chicago. Congressman Dingleman." He raised an eyebrow and opened the same eye wide. "Has a nice ring to it, don't you think, Max? Ha ha."

Max gasped. "Did he tell you to off me?"

Dingleman laid the firearm down. "No... don't be silly. Me and you have too much work to do. With the new girls and all, we'll be busier than a one-legged man in a butt-kicking contest. He told me to shoot your wife." He picked up the gun and spun it on his finger. "Now you know I like Leslie, but if I don't do what he tells me, I'll be the one on the list."

Silence.

"So what's it going to be? You in or out?"

"I'm in. I'm in." Max leaned on the desk—now for support, not some attempt to intimidate his "underling." "Would you really shoot my wife?"

"Nothing personal." Dingleman shrugged. "I like Leslie. But if it's her or me—well, you know how that's going to turn out. And it won't be my first rodeo, either."

Max understood. Like it or not, they were in this thing together. Jennings had lost it. Having nothing but hate for his old friend and confidant, the POTUS, he'd do whatever was necessary to get him out of office. It made Max cringe. Jennings was part of Circle now, and there'd be no end to how low he'd go to stay there. These weren't just hard times. They were different times, and Max knew it.

The school bus took a hard right turn, and the back right wheels jumped a curb and squealed, waking DR. He shifted. He'd slept for almost two hours. Amal leaned against him, her left arm lying on his legs. She must have moved to his seat after he'd fallen asleep. She looked so peaceful, so beautiful as she slept, and a feeling of love rushed over him, one he'd never felt before. He'd wondered if he'd ever get to become a father.

They were in Indiana on Interstate 69 now, heading south near Angola. But the bus took the sharp right to leave the interstate, veering onto the last exit before going under the merging Interstate 90 overpass ahead, where the roadblock was.

"Sorry, guys. Sorry about the jolt, but I had to do it. Look there." Sam, who must have taken the wheel at some point, nodded toward the horizon and what appeared to be a roadblock about three-quarters of a mile in front of them. Good thing, it wasn't yet daylight, and the flashing police vehicles' lights strobed the air. But as they exited, further study showed it was an accident between a semitruck entering the highway and a potato-chip truck, Sam's paranoia getting the best of him. "Sorry, my bad."

Amal awoke, stretching, then wrapped her small arms around DR. She blinked up at him, so vulnerable, so full of love.

He almost melted. "Did you sleep good, sweetheart?"

She shook her head, smiled, then hung her head. She must be thinking about her sisters.

He ruffled her hair. "We're going back for them as soon as we get you somewhere safe. Okay?"

She closed her eyes and rested her head on his arm.

Tom came back to their seat, sat in the aisle across from them, and nodded to the girl. "No better feeling in the world, I imagine." He splayed a hand on the seat beside himself, rubbing the leatherlike material. "Sam and I discussed ditching the bus, maybe getting a car or something. What do you think?"

"Probably would be a good idea. Besides, we could use a bathroom break soon, maybe pick up some food." He nudged Amal's arm and spoke in Arabic, asking if she was hungry and needed to go.

"I was thinking," DR said after the girl nodded. "We could head to an Amtrak station. There's supposed to be several near here. I'm thinking we could scope it out. Why don't you tell Sam so he can think it over."

Tom moved back to the front seat. The two men discussed their options. Then Tom returned. "He said that sounded great. He's going to stop in a few miles. The bus is getting low on fuel, so we can get some food and use the bathroom there." He gripped the seat with his right hand while leaning over to admire Amal and her bravery. "That sound okay?"

Moments later, after Sam pulled into the diesel island at the Angola convenience market, Tom, DR, and Amal headed inside while Sam pumped just enough fuel to get them to their destination, then moved the bus away from the pumps. When they came out with their food and Sam's, he ran in to pay for the fuel and take a bathroom stop.

Along the way to the Amtrak station, the number of police vehicles began to increase, especially the ones going the other way up the highway, many with their lights flashing. At the authorities' extra attention, DR left Amal with her gyro and chips and went up front.

"Sam, how did you pay for the diesel?" DR eyed him in the large mirror on the shade flap.

"I used my credit card. I didn't want to spend all our cash." Sam met DR's eye in the mirror. "Why?"

Another Ohio State Police car went screaming in the opposite direction.

DR covered his mouth and closed his eyes, exhaling loudly. "That explains all those police cars streaming by."

"Sam..." Tom kept his voice low. "Didn't you remember? We told you they're tracking your credit cards too. That doesn't give us much time. We better lose this bus—and fast. How far to Amtrak?"

"Not far. What time is it?"

"It's almost eight. The sun's coming up." Tom slid out his cellphone. "How can we check for the train schedule?"

"Whatever you do, don't use that." DR snagged the phone away from his friend. "Or any credit cards. Look, guys, we don't have any experience at this, so we'll have to try to remember things from the police detective shows. We can't use phones or credit cards. Nothing that uses electronic communications to verify. Cash only, or we'll have to steal it."

Tom nodded.

"Steal it?" Sam's eyes grew large, his voice sharp. "Aren't we already in enough hot water?"

Seriously? DR ground his teeth. "Would you rather be dead?"

The Amtrak station came into sight, all quaint and cozy—small, but comfortable looking on the outside. DR and the others got off while Sam ditched the bus about a ten minute walk away so authorities wouldn't suspect anything right away. Then he made his way to join the others in the terminal.

DR stepped outside to meet him. "The train will be here soon. It's running early so we'll have to wait about fifteen minutes or so before it leaves. Here's your ticket. They took most of our cash, but we'll be good."

Sam tucked the ticket into his chest pocket and traded it for half a Snickers bar. "Sounds good."

Three of them sat at the back of the train station, against the back wall, while waiting to depart the station. DR and Amal sat on one side of the aisle and Tom on the other. Meanwhile, Sam explored, turning his head to look at the road constantly as he examined the memorabilia-covered walls. There weren't any vending machines or anything of that nature, just the basics. And there wasn't a television, so their pictures weren't being flashed at them—or rather, at the one agent working the counter. No one else came in this early, and the agent seemed more interested in his cellphone than his passengers.

Right on cue, the nearly empty train pulled in. The heavy holiday traffic wouldn't begin for a couple of days. They boarded the train and waited.

"I feel trapped." Sam squirmed, a state trooper's car flying by the station.

"Hang in there." DR hunched his shoulders. Hard not to feel responsible, even though he wasn't to blame. "Just a few more minutes, and we'll be on our way."

"These tickets say Charlotte, North Carolina." Sam fumbled with his ticket, jittering a leg in his aisle seat on the left side, by the window facing the road. "I thought we were getting off in Huntington?"

"Tom and I figured it might help keep the authorities off our track long enough for us to get our car and leave town. Maybe buy us an hour or two." DR smiled at Amal, then told her what they were talking about.

She smiled.

"Doesn't it feel wonderful, having a beautiful child love and rely on you?" Tom squeezed his lips in a tight frown.

"What's the matter?"

"Just thinking about my wife. Can't wait to get home."

The five-car train crept forward. No one else boarded, and the four of them stayed away from the few other passengers to keep from being identified.

"And we will get home."

~

Max called Senator Carl, who was just getting ready to leave DC for the holidays. He didn't plan to tell him much, just feel him out, find out what he thought. Now Max pulled his car to the side of the road to talk. "Carl, thank God, you haven't left yet. Listen, there's big trouble brewing here in Chicago. Have you heard?"

"What's going on? I thought you were enjoying time with the family. Isn't tomorrow Danny's birthday?"

"Yes, he turns thirteen. And if I'm lucky, I might get to see it." *Ah, didn't mean to say that.*

"What do you mean? Are you all right?"

"No. There's big trouble. We had it set up to get rid of that bozo from the cruise, but something went wrong." Through the rearview mirror, Max watched an elderly man as he updated Carl.

"Ha ha. I'll bet Jennings lost it."

"Oh yeah." He'd lost it all right. "That's not the half of it. He told Dingleman to off me if I wanted out. Can you believe that?" His nerves on edge, he toggled the up-and-down knobs on the door locks. "Now his goon squad is hot on their tails."

"Sounds like you should get lost for a while. Let the old man cool down until after the good doc and his friends are taken care of."

"It's my family." Max palmed his face. "I'm worried about my family. Dingleman was going to shoot Leslie if I wanted out."

"Better move them too. I've said too much. Got to go."

The phone went dead. The old man behind the car was gone too.

Smithers and company planned on flying into Chicago since Paw Paw wasn't far by helicopter, but after getting a patch into FBI communications, they changed their plans and arrived in Fort Wayne, Indiana, around two thirty p.m.

"Here's the way this is going to go down. Jones, you and O'Connor head to the LMMC in Chicago. Get the film and electronic surveillance data from Dingleman. Oh, and the boss doesn't want any loose ends. Find out where that congressman is." Smithers glanced from man to man. "Any questions?"

"We're good." Jones balled his fist around a duffel bag strap handle and stretched his shoulders. "Where do we rendezvous?"

"If things go according to plan, we rendezvous back here tomorrow early in the evening. These targets shouldn't put up much resistance."

The company split up then. Manning and O'Connor boarded a rented helicopter headed north to Chicago, and Smithers and Jones in another copter charted course to Angola, Indiana.

Jones, who logged over two thousand flight hours before leaving the service, landed the bird at the convenience store in Angola. The parking lot was empty, most of the commuters having already vacated. The police had finished their interrogation and quit the scene.

Smithers and Jones entered the store, dressed in civvies, fully packing. Smithers went to the counter while Jones checked the rest of the store. While Jones found one male employee stocking the shelves, Smithers flashed his identification too fast for the clerk to see what he'd shown.

"I'm Detective Smithers and my associate is Detective Jones. We're here to follow up on what our associates found earlier. Do you have a moment?" Smithers made eye contact with Jones who now had the other employee at gunpoint.

"Uh, sure. We already showed them the tape. Would you—"

Smithers snapped his gun toward the clerk's face. "I'd like to see it. Lock the front door." He stepped aside to allow the frightened clerk to pass him, gun held to his head.

The clerk led Smithers to the back, then slowed when he saw his friend, also at gunpoint, coming toward them. "It's back here. Look—we don't want any troub–ble. T–take whatever you need."

"Thank you. We are." Jones pushed his pistol against the second clerk's head.

Smithers pulled up the surveillance feed and took snapshots with his cellphone of four suspects on the school bus. One was the missing child from the LMMC. "Looks like we've got some runners here."

He waited, watching the direction the school bus left the parking lot so they could track them.

After tying up the loose ends, leaving no witnesses, they flew south to catch up with the bus. Monitoring the FBI patch and flying over the road south to the Amtrak station around one p.m., they were closing in.

"Ha ha." Jones laughed. "Not going to take long now. What an easy payday."

"Don't count your money during the show," Smithers warned.

The train was only a few minutes outside of Huntington now. DR had awakened and was talking to Amal. The other two men slept.

Thankful he could speak Arabic, he listened to her story.

"Mom and Dad were killed when I was three. The Iranians came into our country and made everything bad. The priest said our country was safer when the Americans came into port, but that was before my parents were killed in a street war."

"I'm sorry." He leaned down to make eye contact. "But we're going to get you to safety now. I promise. And don't you worry. Then we'll go back for your sisters, somehow."

But, how?

"I don't want to go back to Yemen. They blew up our home and shot both of the priests." Amal peered at him with big puppy eyes, pleading. "Besides, Habiba said you are going to be our dad. God told her so."

How was he to answer the girl otherwise? "Well, I'm sure whatever God told her He has a way to make it happen." Wanting the conversation to end, he kissed the top of her forehead, then closed his eyes, more torn than ever before.

Sam stirred across the aisle by the window. "I'm starving. How about you guys?"

Tom yawned and stretched, apparently awakened by Sam.

"I could eat." DR stifled his own yawn. "I'm sure Amal here could too. What about you, Tom? Are you hungry?"

Tom rubbed at his eyes, then rolled his neck side to side, probably trying to work out the kinks or shake off his sleepiness. "I can eat."

Cute little houses passed by beyond the train windows. DR stretched out his legs in front of him. "Whatever we do, we need to get out of the terminal as fast as we can and avoid the cameras if possible. Amal and I will go straight to the taxi stand and secure a car. You two go retrieve the luggage and meet us there. How does that sound?"

"Like a plan." Tom high-fived DR.

After the train stopped, the four of them tried to blend in with the other eleven disembarking passengers. There wasn't a police presence at the station, so per their plan, they met up at the taxi stand. DR inquired about area restaurants while the other two went to get the luggage. Now, the car pulled away, going to a local restaurant the driver recommended. A place beside a Ford dealership and a small strip mall. By three thirty, they finished lunch with what was left of their cash, deciding to visit the strip mall.

Finally understanding what a good criminal or rogue agent must learn, they checked out the parking lot for vehicles. With no promising options, they agreed to *borrow* a vehicle from the dealership. Burning as much of the daylight as possible, they went back to the restaurant to get out of the cold as they waited until dark, ordering coffee and sodas.

Around six o'clock, what appeared to be the last person leaving the dealership turned out the showroom lights, drove out of the parking lot, and put up a chain. Tom and Sam crossed over to the dealership and crawled over a low fence on the lot's backside, but they weren't alone. A cleaning crew detailing vehicles remained, leaving keys in several cars as they cleaned the other vehicles.

From his vantage point, DR watched Tom nod to a white Explorer. "Good thinking," DR whispered. The four-wheel drive would help if they ran into snow going through the mountains, and apparently, the cleaners hadn't taken the key yet. When the coast was clear, they drove the white SUV out. At the restaurant, Sam flashed the headlights, signaling for DR and Amal.

They'd seen a similar vehicle at the strip mall, a Chevy Traverse, and it was still there. After switching the Explorer's dealer plates for the Traverse's, they headed south toward Birmingham, Alabama. The large Explorer had a third-row seat, ideal for Amal to lie down and sleep or look out both sides of the vehicle. Tom sat up front as DR drove, and Sam claimed the second row by himself.

While everyone else slept, DR enjoyed the drive through the West Virginia mountains, having never been to West Virginia or any of the states south of Ohio or Indiana. Funny, but he had better knowledge of Spain than the country where he was a citizen. He enjoyed the rugged mountainside and the snow-covered peaks, though he wasn't crazy about the hairpin turns. Icicles the size of boulders coated the rocks as water trickled down the mountain, reminded him of his childhood growing up and those times Dad had taken him to the ice festival in Munising, Michigan. There, they climbed on ice, learned the craft, and had a full day of father-son fun.

Snow now fell harder, slowing their trip south, but at least they were away from the surveillance cameras.

As the miles melted away, DR relaxed, and his adrenaline dropped back to the normal range. They could do this. Surely, no one was on their trail now.

CHAPTER
EIGHTEEN

ndiana authorities found the school bus parked a half mile from the Amtrak station. Putting one and one together, the FBI on the scene checked the video from the station's surveillance cameras and discovered their fugitives had boarded the train with tickets to Charlotte, North Carolina.

Once the information was shared via radio to other units, Smithers and Jones began making their way to Charlotte. Hearing the same feed, O'Connor checked the train schedule. The train made a stop in Huntington first. He called Smithers.

"You don't think they'd have gotten off there, do you?" Jones asked.

O'Connor pulled up the cameras there while Smithers asked, "What time does it say the train left Huntington?"

"Three thirty." O'Conner huffed. "If they got off there, you'll never find them. They'll have a three-hour head start. I'll keep looking for camera feeds and let you know if I find anything."

"Doesn't matter. We need to check it out." Hanging up, Smithers cracked his neck and breathed in deeply. "See? I told you not to count your money too soon."

They flew into a light snow, and it became heavier as they went further south.

Jones craned over the controls, their surroundings buried deeper under the snow. "If this snow gets any heavier, we'll be spending the night in Huntington anyway."

～

Driving home, Max replayed the conversations with Dingleman and Senator Carl over and over in his head a thousand times. How it felt when Dingleman placed his hand on the pistol elevated things to a new level. Now he had to end this. He had to talk to Leslie, tell her the truth, before someone got hurt or worse—dead.

Why couldn't the terrorists just have sunk that stupid yacht? No one would've known he was involved, or... What was he thinking? They didn't deserve to die, and the kids—What would've happened to them? And now *he* was the one supposed to traffic them?

No, not going to happen! He slammed his palm against the steering wheel. *I'll go to the authorities first chance—yes, the first chance.*

He drove into his driveway and frowned. Leslie's SUV was parked outside of the garage. She never parked outside because they accessed their kitchen through the garage.

A chill took hold of him. Was he too late?

"Leslie... Leslie, where are you?" he shouted, running in the front door, then to the kitchen.

His legs wobbled when he found her and their children baking brownies and cakes. Right. Tomorrow was their son's thirteenth birthday, so they were putting all the goodies and presents in the garage for the celebration, due to a snow forecast. And he'd forgotten.

"What's got you in such an uproar?" She paused from icing a cupcake, a smidgen on her chin.

He walked over on noodle legs, took his right index finger, and wiped the icing off. As he held it to her lips, he savored her giggle. He then bent and slid an arm around her waist, admiring their children. "Looks like someone's having fun."

"Dad, wait until you see the basketball brownie Mom made. It's so cool." Hands on the countertop, Daniel jumped up and down. "*And* she put my jersey number on it."

"Stop that, Danny. You'll cause the cake to fall."

"Sorry. Mom." Twisting, he calmed a bit.

"I can't wait to see it. Hi, Dawn. How's my sweetheart?" Max went around the counter and hugged his son and daughter. Then he kissed them both on their cheeks. "Kids, I'm going to borrow your mother for a while. Can you handle everything here?"

"Dad!" Danny squealed.

"Too old for Dad's kisses? It's not going to kill you. Besides, no one knows but us." Max reached for Leslie's hand and guided her to their bedroom for privacy.

As he shut the door, he knew this was making her apprehensive. Things had been difficult between them lately, to say the least. "Honey, I don't know how to say this, so I'm just going to say it. I need you to wait until it's all out before you get upset. Okay?"

"Well, let's have it. When are you leaving for Washington, and are you going to miss Danny's birthday—again?"

"I wish it were so simple." With a heavy exhale, he lowered his voice, wishing it all away. "No, I'll be right here with the three of you. This is worse."

After he told her everything, she slapped his face.

"That's fair." He rubbed his cheek.

They sat in silence.

Then she put her arm around him. "Go to the authorities. Tell them all you just told me."

Hunched over, he hung his head. "It may be too late. I heard Dingleman talking to someone on the phone after our conversation, updating them. Jennings has called in one of his squads."

Leslie's mouth dropped open. "One of his squads? What do we do?"

"You and the kids need to go to that little Irish town we visited ten years ago when Dawn was a baby." He forced a tight-lipped smile. "That was a lot of fun, and it'll keep you three out of harm's way while I work this out."

"But they'll kill you." She straightened up and held her shoulders back. "No, we're not leaving you."

"Look..." He gripped her shoulders, shifting her to face him. "We don't have time to argue. You need to leave tonight. While I pull some strings and make the arrangements, you pack. I'll fly back to DC and turn state's evidence. They'll give me protection, and you'll be safely away." He released her, putting his hands over his mouth, his eyes looking but not seeing.

"No." She drew his hands down. "I'm not leaving you. We'll go somewhere and hide from them, just until this squad gives up and goes home. Then you can go to DC and do what you have to do."

He deflated. How wonderful that sounded! "But where? Where can we go that they won't find us?"

"I've been wanting to go back to the cabin where we spent our honeymoon." She gave him a come-hither look. "Remember how much fun that was?"

"How could I forget? I'm pretty sure we got Danny that week." He allowed himself to enjoy the brief thoughts from their honeymoon. Then he shook his head, his whole body shaking, really. "But, honey, that was in the summer. It'll be cold there this time of the year. Wisconsin is tough in the winter even in a house, but in a cabin? I don't know."

"Remember the pond?" She bumped against him. "It'll be frozen, and we can build a bonfire and ice-skate. It'll be fun, and we'll be off the grid. You can spend some quality time with Danny. He's not going to be around much longer for you to bond with. Maybe you could show him some of the coming-of-age things your dad taught you, passing them down another generation, like setting bear traps and things."

He exhaled, low and deep, fully emptying his lungs, even if he couldn't fully empty his fears. "Okay. But we have to leave first thing in the morning, at first daylight. You and the kids can start packing while I go get some cash." He kissed her lips lightly, then squeezed her, and pressed his cheek to hers. "I'll be right back and help load the SUV."

"Let's go tell the kids."

Would it be enough? Or was he putting his family in danger?

Driving from Huntington should've only taken seven and a half hours, but the snow added another hour and a half to their time reaching Athens, Alabama. By two a.m., DR was tired. Everyone had slept except him, and now he needed a break. He veered into a rest area in Athens to switch out with Sam, then get some sleep.

Their white SUV was the only vehicle on the parking lot's car side, far too conspicuous. Road-salt grime now coated the once snow-covered vehicle, making it hard to identify. Amal and Tom went into the rest center first. Trying not to make a big splash on the surveillance cameras, Sam and DR would follow once they got back.

DR shut his eyes for what seemed like just a moment.

But now, Sam was pushing on his shoulder. "Better wake up. We've got company."

Flashing red lights burned his sleep-filled eyes. A police cruiser had stopped behind them, blocking them in. They waited as the officer appeared to be typing something on his car's laptop before he came to DR's door and tapped on the window.

DR rolled the window down. "Yes, Officer, is everything all right?"

The officer peered into the vehicle, probably taking note of its passengers and only seeing Sam in the back. "I know you must be tired, but Alabama doesn't allow passenger vehicles to stay here overnight. An exit down the road a half mile has several inexpensive hotels."

"Thanks, Officer. We're not parking. Just going in to use the bathroom. We'll be on our way shortly."

Apparently in a rush, the officer tapped the top of the car. "Great. Welcome to Alabama. I hope you enjoy your stay, Mr. Thornton, and have a merry Christmas." He hurried back to his cruiser, climbed in, and headed back to the interstate.

DR and Sam both leaned back into their seats, relieved, as Tom and Amal climbed in moments later, after staying out of sight. "What did he say?"

"Welcome to Alabama, Mr. Thornton." DR chuckled. "I'm glad Mr. T didn't have any tickets."

Sam smiled at Amal, maybe thinking of his kids. "God must've been looking over us."

"Yeah. Well, I don't know about that, but I've got to go now." DR climbed out, shaking his head.

Yeah, God helped. Where was He when those guys were going to drown them?

DR glimpsed Amal through the window. If she hadn't been there, they'd be dead.

~

Dingleman liked the feeling of power, and he liked what Jennings had told him earlier. Maybe he would have his record expunged. He liked the sound of Congressman Dingleman, it had a nice ring to it. *Sorry, Max, but I've got to do for me and mine.*

Twirling the pistol on his finger, he tapped out a contact. "Mr. Manning? Hi, Dingleman here. Just wanted to find out your plans so I can make time to meet with you."

"You must be a psychic. We'll be there shortly. On our way right now. Can you get everything set up for us? Fire up the *Lucky Lucie* too. The old man gave us something to get rid of."

Guess I won't have to take care of Max after all. Dingleman snickered. "Consider it done. See you soon."

Following Jennings's other orders, he helped the men deliver the "performers" to Jennings's downtown Chicago club. An hour later, he returned to find the helicopter sitting near the club entrance.

"Manning, O'Connor, I'm back," he called out, entering, seeing Max's office light on.

"We're in Max's office. We're ready to take care of Jennings's little problem as soon as we get the video off the server. Don't want any loose ends."

"So"—Dingleman braced a shoulder against the doorjamb as they downloaded all the video, then deleted the computer files—"where did you guys get your training? Were you Special Forces or something?"

"Yeah, something like that." O'Connor scowled. "Mostly in hell, Afghanistan, Syria, and Iraq."

Loose ends. How funny. Dingleman liked that. *No, Max won't be a loose end, and soon, I'll be the congressman from Chicago.* "Sounds great. Let's get going."

The two men came out, shook his hand, and bagged the prized video thumb drives. "We'll grab those on the way out. Come on, Dingleman.

The *Lucky Lucie* should be ready by now. We know you won't want to miss this."

All smiles, Dingleman trotted after them to the landing. Then his steps slowed. Max wasn't in the chair. Before he could say anything, everything went black.

When he woke, his head throbbed. "Hey! What's going on here? What happened? Did you *hit* me?"

He reached to feel the sore place, but—oh no! *He* was *in* the chair, strapped in.

Manning stuck a cloth in Dingleman's mouth. "You didn't really think the boss was going to help you be a congressman, did you? Oh... that's too funny." Manning and his companion laughed. "No wonder the old man was laughing when he said 'Congressman Dingleman, not going to happen.' Instead, he purchased you a diving engagement."

Dingleman fought while his captors were on the bridge staying warm, but strapped down, it was no use. After twenty minutes, they came out. They must've reached the spot where Jennings wanted him released.

"I don't get my kicks this way." Manning shrugged. "But O' Connor loves to watch people's eyes. Sorry, Dingleman. Nothing personal." He unlatched the chair.

"Look at him." The other man laughed. "I think his eyes are going to explode."

"You're sick. Come on and hurry up, will you? It's late. Let's get him overboard and get a room for the night. We can find the congressman tomorrow."

As the chair fell toward the water and sank below the surface, Dingleman struggled until the deep overcame him.

Max and his family left just after first light. He clenched the steering wheel in a death grip. Were they already the target of Jennings's squad, even though Max hadn't tipped his hand? A cold front coming down from the arctic had moved into Wisconsin, heavy snow was forecast for later, and they were headed for Eagle River, a six-hour trip north from Chicago.

In his haste, he'd forgotten to turn off their cellphones. Now, Danny's phone was buzzing, someone texting him. "We've got to turn our cellphones off. We can be tracked by the towers that are pinged."

"Really, Dad. No cellphones? What will we do?" Dawn stared out the SUV window, propped up on her hands.

Leslie waved her left hand in the air. "Honey, it's just Danny's friends wishing him a happy birthday. Where's the harm in that?"

"Sorry, but we can't take a chance. Turn them off. There's no use going away if we leave a trail."

Snow became heavier as they neared the town. Now, it was one o'clock. Already, they'd been on the road seven hours for the six-hour trip. Max stopped at the grocery store to pick up more supplies. But he decided against purchasing licenses for Danny and himself to hunt and trap because the forms were submitted electronically at the store through the Wisconsin Go Wild program. He couldn't leave the electronic footprint.

With the roads almost impassable, he nearly slid into a ditch several times on the way out. His muscles tense, he parked by the cabin, three miles from the town. The place was just as it had been during their honeymoon. Off the grid, it offered no electricity or gas. The owners had upgraded with several solar panels, but in the winter, they'd be worthless, the sun most times hidden by a thick cloud cover.

Max and Leslie had shared the great outdoors with their kids, often going camping for vacation. But they had never extreme camped, no cellphones or electricity. Inside, he opened the cabin curtains to get light into it, found some wood the previous tenant left, and built a fire in the oversized fireplace, the cabin's best feature.

He pushed to his feet and dusted his hands off. "There. It'll be warm before we know it."

The added light revealed how barren it was. Guess that wasn't much of a focus those years earlier. "Come on, Danny." He slapped his hands together. "I need your help getting the cargo topper down from the SUV before the snow makes in impossible."

After half an hour, the vehicle was unpacked, Max's rifles and traps set in one corner, Danny's birthday gifts in another. They set about getting the birthday celebration going.

"Tomorrow, we'll go out and set some traps and maybe bag us a buck. It'll be fun. Go ahead, Danny, open your presents."

Further south, someone else opened a present, electronic facial recognition was made of Max while he was stuck near an accident scene. Television cameras reporting on an accident outside Eagle River inadvertently caught a glimpse of him as he slowly passed by. O'Connor was able to glean their location off the internet through the state's transportation reports.

Heavy snowfall was blanketing the Midwest and southeastern portions of the country, slowing getaways, and holiday travel. It also impeded Smithers and company, forcing them to ground their choppers overnight.

"I just got word from Jennings. You're right. That is our little runaway bunny in Eagle River, Wisconsin." Smithers watched the images of other holiday travelers on a laptop as he spoke with Manning. "Soon as the snow lightens up, you and O'Connor take care of things up there. We're still trying to locate our bunnies. Hopefully, we'll find something in the morning."

"Why couldn't this have been Florida?" O'Connor pined. "This cold is for the birds."

"Yeah, penguins." Manning snickered.

"We'll be back in sunny San Juan before you know it—with a big Christmas present," Smithers retorted. "Both of you stay focused."

"I hope so. I thought we'd be home by now. Not going to miss Christmas." O'Connor called out after hearing their conversation over the speakerphone.

"You find our bunnies, and we'll get home."

Gambling had been Ryan's escape since he was a teen, though he'd never been good at it. But surely, his luck had changed when he found his cousin and had been invited to work for him. Of course, no one knew Ryan had a gambling problem, except those he was running from and the priests at the Catholic church he was administrator for—all of nine months and two hundred and thirty thousand euros later.

"Mr. McNeilly, I'm sorry about your bad luck, but that's about to change." Simon Crouch, the casino manager, extended a manila envelope. "I've been authorized to offer you an increase in your credit line, a twenty-five percent increase. How does that sound?"

"Sounds good. I believe you're right. My luck's beginning to change already." Taking the envelope, Ryan withdrew the agreement. "Can I borrow your pen?" He placed the agreement on a table, signed it, and slid the top copy into his pocket. "Thank you, Simon."

As Simon walked away, Ryan smiled, then headed straight to his favorite game to win back the other twenty-five grand. "With this five grand, I'm back in business." He placed several chips on the red number. "Then Tonya and I can have a good time in Kalamazoo," he whispered as the wheel turned and the ball dropped into the black number's slot. His shoulders slumped, but he stiffened them. "Maybe the next turn."

CHAPTER
NINETEEN

DR and friends reached Penny and Greg's home three hours before daylight. Hunkering down outside of the security gate protecting the Nichols's property, they slept in their *borrowed* Explorer. Around eight a.m., Tom rang the bell.

"Who's there?" an unfamiliar voice called out.

"Tom Hughes. I'm a friend from the cruise." He looked back at the vehicle, holding his right arm in the air.

"One moment, sir. Let me inform the master there's a guest at the gate."

Tom waited.

"Tom?" Greg's familiar voice came over the intercom. "Tom, what on green earth are you doing here? This place was crawling with FBI looking for you all yesterday."

"Let us in, and we'll tell you."

"Hurry up. Come in." The gates swung open, and they drove to the front door.

Greg, in his PJs and slippers, stepped out and motioned for them to hurry inside. They obliged.

The men embraced, all except Sam. "Greg, this is Sam Blythe." DR patted Sam's arm. "He's an old high school friend. Now a coconspirator, I'm afraid."

"Good to meet you." Greg shook Sam's hand, then arched a brow at the frightened, but curious Amal now clinging to DR's leg. "We heard there was some trouble, something about you shooting a detective. What's that all about?"

DR guided Amal from behind his leg. "Remember this little one? Her name is Amal. She was one of the kidnapped kids we rescued." DR hurried to explain what happened at the children's home, finishing with: "They took all the kids."

"No." Penny screamed, coming out of hiding. "Not again." She rushed to Amal, partly scaring her, then took the girl into her arms, and held her tight as if protecting her.

Greg placed a hand on Penny's shoulder.

"I'm afraid so. The other girls were on the casino yacht where Amal saved our lives." DR caught Tom's eye, who nodded in agreement. "If she hadn't been there, Tom and I would be dead."

"Let's go into the kitchen and get some coffee. I'd just put it on when you buzzed." Greg offered his hand to Penny, who released her grip from Amal seemingly reluctantly.

"How did all this happen?" She instead placed her hand on DR's back to guide him toward the kitchen. There, she took the coffee from Greg and passed it to Sam. "Where's Debbie? Isn't she with you?"

"The guy who attacked us in the Indian Ocean is behind it all, the kidnapping, the attack, the frame-up—all of it." DR nudged the sugar and milk to Sam. "The guy owns a club, the Lake Michigan Men's Club, and uses trafficked kids to appease their guests. He attacked us to make the President's foreign policy look bad."

Penny's jaw dropped. "What kind of evil is that?"

"I don't know. But we have to get back to Chicago before they do something with the other twenty-nine kids. We came here hoping you could hide Amal and maybe help us with some money." He sipped his coffee as Amal pushed tighter to his side. "She says Abba told her sister I'm supposed to be their daddy. It's the least I can do."

"Where is Debbie?" Penny asked again.

"She's in Italy with Miguel for Christmas."

"Come on, DR." Greg slapped his hands together. "Let's take the car and put it in the barn. The FBI has been snooping around since yesterday."

"Probably a good idea."

"I'll get breakfast on the table in a half an hour." Penny clasped Amal's hand and nudged her toward the kitchen table.

DR slugged back his coffee.

"We'll help Penny," Tom volunteered. "Go on. Get out of here."

As Tom waved him off, DR followed Greg outside.

"Give me the keys. I'll drive." Greg stopped on the porch and waved upward. "We had a drone fly over several times yesterday. I didn't know what they were looking for then, but I do now." After catching the keys, he climbed in.

"I still can't believe all this is happening." DR tugged at the back of his head, pulling on his hair, not fighting it. "I can't figure out why someone would go to such lengths to kill me and Tom."

"Sounds like an obsession if you ask me. Especially grabbing the kids again, but isn't that what the priest said? Something like the wolf always returns to the henhouse if he isn't stopped?" Greg clicked his remote to the front gate. "Sounds like you're going to have to stop the wolf."

After work, Willie and Mike went to Marcie's Place for a late afternoon latte. Christmas now just four days away, they wanted to discuss their plans for the rest of the week. Marcie added a new decoration to celebrate the season each day. Now the small bistro was sparkling, sharing the message for the season—A Savior is Born.

"Any word on DR from Ryan?" Mike asked Willie, then raising his hand, beckoned Rachael over.

She acknowledged him and finished serving her other customer.

"He hasn't heard from him since Monday," Willie answered. "But not hearing anything might be good news. I've been praying for them. I don't believe DR shot a detective."

"I'm sure he didn't, but something's terribly wrong. Let me know if Ryan hears anything, okay?"

"You know I will." Willie shifted as Rachael made her way over. "Hey, girl."

"Hi, Willie, Mike. Did you have a good time with Ryan in Kalamazoo?" Her right brow rose, her head tilted inquisitively.

Willie scowled at Mike as if he'd asked the question, but he settled back into the seat with a yawn—feigned or real? Whatever it was, it was catching. One opened her mouth wide before she responded. "It was nice. I have a hard time figuring him out. It's like there's an invisible wall. Something keeps us from—What do you call it? Clicking?" She covered another yawn and waved at Rachael. "What do you think of him? You've talked to him a lot, right?"

"He's moody." Her eyes went beady, and she smirked. "Not my cup of latte."

"Could just be the Irish in him." Mike drummed the table. "Besides, he doesn't know many people here, and he's doing a new job. Not quite like working in a church with your friends. Give the guy a break." Then he nodded toward Rachael's notepad. "Can I get a large black coffee and a custard donut, no chocolate topping."

"Sure. How about you, Willie?"

"A large chocolate mocha with whipped cream and chocolate drizzle, but no éclair today." She patted her stomach. "I've been eating too many."

Mike chuckled. "I don't think you have to worry too much."

As Rachael walked away, Willie braced an elbow on the table and plunked her chin in her hand. "He *is* moody. Sometimes, it seems like he's afraid of being himself. When we went to Kalamazoo, I almost sensed he didn't want to be seen with me. And he asked me to go. Doesn't make sense."

"You can't expect him to be like your other boyfriends." Mike leaned back and locked his hands behind his head. "He's from Ireland, and that's a whole other world."

"Other boyfriends?" She sat up straight again, and heat surged through her. "You make it sound like I've dated a lot. I've had one steady boyfriend. The rest were one-time dates. I'm *not* a social butterfly like some other girls in town."

He smirked. "Harsh, throwing your whole gender under the bus."

"I didn't mean it like that—at least, I don't think I did." Her lips turned down as the self-righteous fire in her heart dimmed.

Rachael came back with their order. "Here you are. Enjoy, even though there's no éclair." She winked at Willie. "I'll catch up with you later."

After she left, Mike picked up his donut and held it before his nose, breathing in deep. "Man, that smells good." He bit into it and talked around the mouthful. "I'm glad you two have become friends. That's got to make life more bearable when you come in here."

"She's sweet, not at all like I made her to be in my mind." The mocha blurred before Willie, just frothy beckonings of clouds in the whipped cream and drizzle. "I wish I could've been her friend in high school. She's a good mom too."

"It's a shame, but since you know, it's not too late."

"I learned a valuable lesson, thanks to you and your big mouth ratting me out." Giggling, she pushed on his left arm laying on the table.

The jostling smeared a sugary glazed streak across his chin. "Big mouth?" He wiped his jaw, then chuckled himself. "I didn't mean to rat you out. I was only trying to help."

"Well, I don't know. You guys in Delton like to gossip." She snickered. "But I won't make the mistake of making up my mind on people without knowing them or what the facts are again. So I won't condemn you for gossiping, *and* I'm not going to make up my mind about Ryan just yet, either. I'll give him a chance."

Of course, it might not be so easy. All her life, she judged others based on what she thought was the truth, and all along, she'd been wrong. It wasn't her place to make anybody anything now, but still... she did.

Greg opened the pasture gate beside an old gravel back road, then pulled the car into the barn before going back to chain the gate. The house was a good quarter of a mile away, but in plain sight. Beginning their walk, carrying their luggage and guns up to the house, DR stopped and turned around in a circle.

"This is going to sound crazy, but I feel like I've been here before." A butterfly landed on a wildflower, not a normal sight in December, even for Alabama. "It reminds me of the dream I had after I went unconscious on our cruise. Do you ever remember your dreams? I can't get it off my mind."

"This is a special place. My granny grew up here. She always used to talk about the angels who looked over her here, how blessed we were." Greg shook his head. "She would come down here and spin around and around, face to the heavens. When I was young, she told me more than once I'd see the glory of the Lord here. Folks in town thought she was nuts, especially when she talked gibberish. She called it tongues, God's language."

"I don't know about all that. My folks are the same way, but this feels safe, like home." Dragging his hand through the tall wildflowers that should be dead by now, he remembered the Revivalist talking about tongue talkers.

"You're welcome to stay here as long as you like."

Inside the house, Penny delivered on her promise of a hot breakfast. "Come on, boys. Better eat before it gets cold. And no one likes cold grits."

Amal, Sam, and Tom were already gathered and waiting.

"Penny this all looks great, you shouldn't have, but I'm happy you did." *So glad we came here, so glad.* "I've never had grits before." Pulling up to the table, DR waited on the others to dig in first, taking it all in.

"Well, you'll have to try them. Boys, you better eat up. I don't want all this food going to waste."

Breakfast turned into a blur of smiling faces, clinking silverware, and happy voices. When everyone finished, barely a crumb remained.

"Penny, those grits were fabulous. I've got to learn how to make them." DR set his spoon down, having scrapped up the last morsels.

Johnson helped clean up as the men went into the study and worked to figure things out.

DR stared out a window. "We can't go to the authorities," he said, "not until we have proof we didn't shoot anybody. But we have to find Amal's sisters and the other kids first. This Jennings fellow will kill them if he thinks we're close."

He walked over to the fireplace with an ornate white mantel loaded with family pictures. "Those children deserve a chance like everyone else." He picked up a picture of Greg with his boys in the swimming pool, Kool-Aid smiles on their faces. All kids deserved to smile like these boys.

"You know what that means." Greg crossed the room and gripped DR's shoulder. "You'll be driving right back into the lion's den. Are you sure that's what you want to do?"

"Are you crazy?" Shaking his head, Sam appeared to be forgetting earlier he had wanted an *S* on his chest. Now, it seemed he simply wanted to slip back into his life. "They'll kill us. You heard how they shot up my cabin."

"We can't run all our lives." Tom sipped from his coffee, watching Greg's horses through a window. "We have to end it one way or another. Hopefully alive. Life used to be so simple. Then I met Dr. Steven Ray. What is it about you?"

"Just lucky, I guess." A Sunday school lesson taunted him. Something like "Your problems can become the solution for others—when you trust in God." Now, why did he think about that? What brought that up?

"So"—Greg slapped his hands together—"what's the plan?"

DR pushed away from the mantel. "Sam, Tom, if you guys don't want to go back, I understand. But I have to." He held up a hand to halt any comments. "I don't want to, but if not us—well, me—who then?"

"I'm in. You can count on me." Tom clattered his coffee onto a side table, then widened his stance. "How about it, Sam? Want to be our getaway driver again?"

Sam, seated on the sofa, propped his elbows on his knees, clutched his head, and rocked it side to side for a long moment. "Why not? My kids are already gone. I've got nothing to lose now—but my life."

"Okay, that settles it." DR nodded. "Let's get our plan together. Greg, we need you to help get us a car, a cellphone, some cash, and a few pistols. We have to hit this devil right where he lives. We're going to grab the girls."

Five minutes passed in planning. "It's settled. Greg and Penny will watch over Amal while we retrieve the children and end this." Tom picked up his coffee mug and grimaced at what must be the cold dregs. "I'd like to use the cellphone to call Laurie. She's gotta be worried stiff, especially if it's been on the news." He gestured the mug toward the window where sunlight splashed off the in-ground pool. "I'll bet that's relaxing."

"When you come back, we'll have a big party in the spring. Then you can tell me. We'll barbecue some ribs, grill steaks, and lobster. Do it up big, 'Bama style."

❧

After breakfast, while the men went into Greg's study to plan, Penny took Amal upstairs, let her shower, and found her some clean clothes. "You don't mind boys' clothes, do you?"

Since Amal didn't have any idea what she was saying, it was a little awkward. Then Penny grabbed her cellphone and clicked the app she'd downloaded for their cruise to translate Arabic.

Amal's eyes grew wide when Penny tried to speak her language. She leaned over the phone, read the words on the screen, then started giggling. They now could communicate and get to know each other. The back of Penny's eyes burned as the little girl reached for her.

Penny spoke into her phone. "Don't you worry, little one. We're going to take good care of you."

Moments after she finished, the phone repeated the message back, in Arabic, and Amal clapped, leaning over the words now written in Arabic on the phone screen. She probably wanted to speak into the phone, but she appeared to be at a loss for words. Instead, she buried her head on Penny's shoulder.

At the child's love, the motherly part of Penny's soul began to stir. She missed this. No wonder God gave grandchildren, to stir our love and nurture our kindness toward the world. "Thank You, Jesus," she whispered.

Surely, He would help them look after this precious child and save her sisters, wouldn't He?

Penny came down the stairs excited, smiling, and Amal quickly followed, tiny feet pounding the carpet. She looked fresh and relaxed after a bath and her new outfit.

"I know how to talk with her now." Penny waved her cellphone cheerily. "I had an app on my phone I downloaded for our cruise to translate Arabic and a couple of other languages. It works like a charm.

176

You should have seen her light up when she heard me speaking her language." She slid her arm around Amal's shoulders.

Greg winked at DR. "It seems like your plan is already coming together."

Penny packed food and snacks for their trip, and after explaining everything to a now-crying Amal, who didn't want her daddy to leave, they went on their way.

Just after noon at the rental car agency, Greg came out holding a set of keys, then twirled them in the air. "Be careful with this baby. The guy said she's his prized possession." When he hit the unlock button, a set of headlights flashed, and a shrill beep introduced the vehicle.

"A red Dodge Charger with black racing stripes?" Tom walked over to it and kicked one of the tires. "This is going to stick out like a sore thumb."

Greg held his arms apart, hands up. "They were out of their basic stock, something about folks driving north for Christmas—no, I'm not making it up." A snort escaped.

"Yeah, but it's sure going to be fun to drive." Running his hand over the hood, Sam, their car aficionado, swooned.

Yep, Sam loved the old fast cars back in the day. DR shifted his feet. "Didn't they have something else? Maybe something that would do better in snow?"

"Don't worry about the snow. I got it. We grew up driving fast cars in the snow, remember?"

"Yes, and I remember you sliding into a ditch." DR opened the car door, admiring the leather interior.

"Isn't she sweet? Ohh, I can't wait to drive it." Sam ducked down and looked at DR through the car from the other side, beaming.

Well, that settled it, then. Their reluctant getaway driver was happy. *Good work, Greg.* DR walked over to Greg and gave him a man hug. "I guess we'd better load it up."

The others pitched in, and soon, they were on their way. If only they could know what awaited them in Michigan and Chicago.

～

After several hours, the cellphone was charged. Tom caught it when DR tossed it over. "Thanks. I can't wait to hear Laurie's voice." The phone rang twice before someone picked up. "Laurie, honey." He waited for an answer. Instead, it sounded like the phone had fallen. "Laurie?"

"I'm here. I'm here. Where have you been? I've called your phone a hundred times. Why didn't you call me last night?"

"It's a long story. Suffice it to say I've been living out one of our novels. Remember the little girl on the boat who was unconscious? Well, her little sister, Amal, saved my life—our lives. Someone is trying to kill DR and me."

"Wait—What? *Why?*"

"It's the same person who tried to sink us on the cruise. Walters said if the fox isn't caught, he'd return to the chicken coop. Well, he did. And he killed O'Reilly, injured Walters, and took all the children."

Greg watched the interstate signs passed by as Laurie gasped. "Why would anyone do that?"

So Tom hurried to explain what they were planning. "Honey, if I go, I'm not going to be home for Christmas, but if I don't go, only God knows what will happen to those kids." He fidgeted with the seat's back. "I know it's a lot to ask, but I want your blessing."

Silence.

"Are you still there?" He hunched his shoulders as Sam caught his eye in the rearview mirror.

"I'm here. I–I wasn't expecting this. My parents will be over. They're going to wonder where you are."

"Tell them I'm researching our next joint novel. How's that sound?"

"Okay, but it better have a happy ending. I can't stand bad endings." It sounded like she blew her nose.

"It will. I promise. I miss you, but I'm glad you didn't come now and get yourself smack in the middle of this too." He searched the bag of snacks for something.

"How are DR and Debbie? Any news on their engagement yet?"

"I don't have time to go into it now, but I'll try to call you tomorrow. I love you."

"Love you too, bye."

He tapped DR's shoulder with the phone and passed it to him to make his calls. "I know it's only been two days. But somehow it feels like forever."

"This baby is fine. Driving her is almost worth it all." Sam pushed the gas pedal a little harder, and a throaty roar followed. "See how sweet that is?"

"Well, don't go getting a sweet tooth. We can't afford any speeding tickets." DR chuckled, and Tom joined in.

But it wasn't funny. Something as little as a speeding ticket could cost them their lives. Then what would Laurie do? And what would happen to those kids?

CHAPTER
TWENTY

Jennings's friend inside the FBI also kept tracking Max Rice, using the interstate surveillance cameras the state of Wisconsin had placed for traffic flare-ups due to bad weather, as O'Connor now followed. Jennings sent word to Smithers, who passed it on to Manning and O'Connor, even though they had a patch through to the friend also. So either Max was in Eagle River for Christmas, or he was running. To Jennings, it didn't matter at this point.

Upon returning the *Lucky Lucie* to the LMMC, another loose end tied off, the team of two cleaned up their fingerprints, took the thumb drive, and boarded their Sikorsky S-76 helicopter. Forgetting they'd cleansed the video feeds *before* tying off the loose end. Now the exterior dock camera light glowed red, showing the camera's video was streaming back to the computer storage file once again.

They refueled for the two-hour flight to Eagle River. "Snows falling pretty hard. Looks like the flight's going to take a little longer. We'll have to refuel in Rhinelander before we come back." O'Connor, setting their course, began looking for accommodations for the night. "GPS puts it twenty-three miles from Eagle River."

"I'd hoped we could get this done today." Manning rubbed his hands together. "But the snow is just going to be too much. I'm glad they had these birds for rent. At least, this one can take it."

At four thirty-five p.m., they began their trek to Eagle River. O'Connor called Smithers along the way. "We're going to have to spend the night in Eagle River. Snow is falling about an inch an hour." He craned toward the side window, watching their clearance as Manning piloted the helicopter safely from the fueling station.

"Roger that. We're in West Virginia. Our little bunnies have disappeared too—for now. We're spending the night here—need to find a slipup somewhere. Otherwise, this is going to run us into Christmas. Over."

Manning was shaking his head.

"Roger that. Over and out." O'Conner disconnected and huffed. "Well, doesn't that just take the joy out of a manhunt?"

At four o'clock Thursday afternoon, the red Charger was still performing flawlessly. DR crossed his arms over his chest, Sam appearing to love every minute of it. Already, they'd been on the road for over four hours, but they had a long way to go, still over four hundred miles.

"So..." DR turned in the front passenger seat to face Tom in the back. "Since Amal is at Penny's, we can take turns sleeping on the back seat. That'll help us break up the driving. We have about ten hours to go. Add in a few stops, and we should reach Delton by two or three a.m."

Tom stretched his shoulders. "Where are we going to stay until we know what we're going to do?"

"Well," Sam broke in, "we certainly can't go to our homes or my hotel."

DR was silent. Lips pursed, he closed his eyes. "I can only think of one place, and I don't want to go there. But they'll be watching our families."

"Where, then?" Sam twisted his grip on the steering wheel, taking a sharp curve with a smooth whir of the wheels. "We can't go to a hotel, not anywhere near Delton or Chicago anyway."

"The woman my brother works with might let us stay with her for a few hours or so." Good thing, they were on better terms. Willie had even become one of Debbie's friends, or so it seemed. Maybe she still had that crush. At this point, he wasn't sure whether to be happy or sad if she was over it.

"So how long do we need to stay there?" Tom perched closer to the gap between the front seats.

"Let's wait until around four o'clock tomorrow before we head out. Then it'll be dark when we get to the men's club." Sam changed lanes to pass a slower vehicle and chuckled. "Good thing this car has a cruise control. Otherwise, I'd have a hard time holding my speed down."

DR held up the cellphone. It would be ten o'clock in Marsala. "Going to make my calls. Hopefully, this all goes well." From his wallet, he pulled out a phone number scrawled on paper.

"Hello?"

"Miguel, is that you?" DR's pulse sped up.

"Hi, DR. Are you all right? Debbie has been trying to call you for two days. She thinks you're screening her calls."

"No—I mean I'm all right, but I'm not screening her calls. Tom and I are in some trouble. Listen, Miguel, those children?" DR took a deep breath, then pushed the horror out. "They're here, somewhere—all of them."

"Whew." Miguel let out a low whistle after DR had fully explained. "This sounds like one of Tom and Laurie's books."

"I wish it were, but it's not a fairy tale. That much I'll tell you." DR paused to catch his breath. "We're hiding from every law enforcement agency there is, and we have to find the children before Jennings, the bad guy, takes them for a midnight swim in the lake just to get rid of them."

"DR, Debbie is here. She's going to celebrate Christmas with us. She's worried stiff about you and what happened. Can I share this with her?"

"I don't see why not. It's like Tom told Laurie—he'd wanted her to visit us too, but she stayed home because of her folks and Christmas coming. Anyway, if Debbie had been here with me, she would've been in the middle of this." He waited, knowing Miguel would give God praise for sparing the girls.

"Sounds like God was looking over them and you too. What are the odds of Amal being there if He wasn't? But Debbie's terribly upset with herself. She said you two would be married by now if she hadn't blown a gasket. After all this, I think she was supposed to blow that gasket. Maybe she had a little help from above. Don't you think?"

DR rubbed at the quickening pulse in his temples. "I don't know, Miguel. My life just seems to have these high mountains and deep valleys. I love the mountains, but to be honest, I've had about all the valleys I can stand." He moved his hand to cover his eyes, then exhaled, and lowered it to his lap. "Is she there? Can I talk to her?"

"She went out with Kim. They're putting the finishing touches on our annual Ricci Christmas Gala on Saturday evening. Lo, Cillia, and David are coming too. It's a shame you won't be here. I'll tell them what's going on, and we will all pray for you."

"Any word about the *DI*?"

"Not since I talked to you last. It shouldn't be long."

"Okay, I better get off here. Never know what they can track. Give Debbie and everyone my love. Tell her I don't have my cellphone. The FBI and Illinois State Police are tracking it anyway. I'll try to call tomorrow."

"Godspeed, my friend."

The phone went dead.

Was it God, or was it coincidence that spared the girls? He couldn't decide, but somehow the script had to be already written. Was it destiny? Or Providence?

All day, the Rice family celebrated Danny's birthday. He opened presents, ate cake, and drank pop. They played games and spent time enjoying the togetherness. The kids occasionally seemed bored, unable to use their cellphones, even if they could. They were off the grid, so no reception until they went into Eagle River, three miles away.

Now at five p.m., the snow was over a foot and a half deep and showing no signs of letting up. Earlier, Max took Danny out and taught him how to set traps for large game. In Eagle River, that included bear, cougar, deer, and elk, among others. They shot rifles, using targets. Danny had never shot or hunted with his dad, who was always too busy as the boy matured.

"Wasn't it fun teaching Danny how to hunt and trap?" Leslie wrapped her arms around Max, giving him a light kiss.

"I wouldn't call it hunting. The snow is piling up—makes it hard to do too much. But it was nice spending time with him." He couldn't bring his eyes to connect with hers.

"What's wrong?"

"This just feels wrong. I feel trapped." He pulled away from her. "We should've gone overseas or something. Out here, there's no running away."

"Honey, no one knows we're here. They'll never find us." She pushed back against him, trying to comfort her man.

"You don't know these people. They reached halfway around the world to kill the people on that yacht, using people like me. They have connections everywhere—I'm talking law enforcement and politicians."

"We'll be okay. You'll see. Then, when things calm down, you'll go back to Washington and bring these jerks to justice."

He cupped his hands on each side of her face. "I hope you're right. I truly do. I just can't see it right now." He thought for a moment. "He's part of Circle, and there's nothing they won't do to control things. *Nothing*."

"What is Circle?" Her eyes moist, her mouth turned at the corners.

"They're people. Powerful people. I've only met one of them. But I know who they are and what they can do. That doctor didn't shoot Detective Shortman. They did it to get the police to hunt him down and kill him. Something they've tried to do twice and failed. But they won't stop. Eventually, someone's going to kill him." He hung his head. After all, he'd been in on the last attempt, even wishing they'd sunk his yacht. "And I'm no better than they are. I used them to get to Congress, and now it's payback time."

In Marsala, Friday morning, Debbie had breakfast with Miguel and his family out on their glassed-in patio, the sun just starting to rise over the ocean, the coast some two hundred meters away.

"This is so beautiful. It reminds me of the restaurant we all dined at before the cruise." She leaned back as a server poured her a glass of fresh orange juice.

"I love the ocean. My family has always loved the ocean. And before long, this little one"—Marco patted Corey's arm where the tyke sat in the high chair beside him—"will be out on a sailboat, learning to love the ocean, just like his ancestors before him." Marco then took Kim's hand and squeezed, all while beaming at his dad, proud to be a Ricci.

Miguel stretched out his legs, crossing his feet at the ankles. "So, Debbie, you came in after I retired last night. I wanted to talk to you about DR. He called, and he's okay." When Debbie opened her mouth, he held his hands up. "But they're in a lot of trouble—trouble he's trying to work out with Tom." As he explained, he kept an upbeat tone, saying horrific things with a smile while poking at Corey, probably keeping his tone cheery so he didn't upset the baby.

But such tactics couldn't help her. Debbie shivered and lowered her head. "I should have been there. Maybe I could've helped."

"I don't think so." He leaned toward the table, closing the distance to her. "I think it was providence for you and Laurie. If you'd been there, you may all very well be dead now."

"How can blowing up and storming out be providence?" The day had lost its glow from earlier. She scowled down into her breakfast, her appetite also gone.

"DR, he's a strong man with good values." Marco took a deep breath. "From what I've seen, he'll do right by those kids—again. And one day, you two will be together. I feel it in my bones."

She was thankful, but right now, it all seemed like hyperbole.

"I've got to learn to control these flight-or-fight urges. I don't know why, but when it happens, everything speeds up. It's like someone or something won't let me be."

Miguel laced his hands across his stomach. "Honey, that's just the enemy. The more you resist, the sooner he'll leave you alone."

She shivered, whispering. "It's hard to fight something you can't see—or yourself."

Now what would happen to them? DR had only just recovered from his last wound. Would he even make it through this? And what about those children *Providence* put in their path?

~

While Tom drove the last shift to Willie's house using GPS, DR drifted in and out of sleep. It was an easy drive with the roads clear. It snowed in Delton. But only a few inches, so nothing to slow their progress. Considering the storm in the south and the storm coming out of Canada, they'd spent very little time in the snow. The Charger performed flawlessly, although it did go through the gas. Along the way, each of them had time to rest. Now at three a.m. Friday morning, they waited again until Willie got ready for work.

Shaking off a stiff neck, DR peered out the back window. Willie's lit-up Christmas decorations made him smile. He swiped his hand across his face to wake himself. It was six thirty now, and lights were on in what must be her bathroom and bedroom. "I'm going to go knock. Wish me luck."

Sam, just waking himself, mumbled, "Good luck."

"Yeah, good luck," Tom said.

Willie lived alone, so she'd probably be apprehensive to open her door this early in the morning. Still, DR rang the doorbell and waited. Someone scuffled around, but the door didn't open. So he rang the bell again. Finally, he sighted her through a small window in the door.

The door slowly opened. She stuck her head out and craned around, whispering. "You?" She grabbed him by the shirt and half pulled him into her cottage. "What are you doing here at this hour? Are you trying to get me shot?"

"I'm sorry, Willie." He scrunched through the barely open door. "But we didn't have anywhere else to go. Why are you whispering?" To defuse the situation, he nodded to her small Christmas tree in her living area. "Nice tree."

"Thanks, and yeah, no reason to whisper. Who is we?" Her surprised look refused to leave. Maybe she was covering for her lack of makeup.

"That would be Tom and Sam. My accomplices, or should I say my fellow framees? Anyhow, the other two men who are going to help me clear my name and save some children." He jerked a thumb back toward the car. "Do you mind if they come in? Then I'll explain everything?"

"I have to go to work soon. I don't know what good that would do right now." She walked to the window and cupped a hand by her face to see past the glare on the glass into the dark morning.

"Look, we won't be any trouble—you can go to work." He widened his stance and crossed his arms. "We just need a place to hang out until this afternoon, and we'll leave everything alone."

"All right." She waved toward the car. "Go get them. I'll put on some more coffee and freshen up."

DR stepped out and waved for Tom and Sam to come inside.

Ten minutes later, she emerged from the bedroom, looking much better, the shocked expression having been scrubbed from her face too. "The cops and FBI have been all over Delton—your shop, Wall Lake, and your folks' house. This is probably the only place they haven't been. They said you shot a detective in Chicago and kidnapped a nine-year-old girl. Of course, none of us believed them. You didn't, did you?"

"Of course not. We're being framed." DR squinted his eyes and pursed his lips, sharing his annoyance.

She held out a coffeepot. "Would you like some coffee?"

"Where's my manners?" DR strode into the kitchen area to claim a cup. "Willie, these are my friends, Tom and Sam. Tom, here, was on the cruise and also on the yacht in Lake Michigan when someone named Jennings tried to kill me again. Sam, well, he's my friend from high school, and he made the mistake of saving our lives. Now they're trying to get him too." He took a cup and allowed her to pour his coffee.

"Willie," Tom spoke first, "it's good to meet you. Thanks for letting us stay here."

Sam nodded his agreement.

"Wait—I didn't say you could stay." Coffee splashed the linoleum as her hand jerked. "I have to go to work soon."

"Willie." DR snagged the coffeepot before she could scald herself. He placed it on the stove. Then he gripped her arm. "This is important. Lives hang in the balance, ours and the children's. Please, if you don't want us staying here by ourselves, can you call my brother and get him to cover for you?" Taking a napkin, he wiped up the spilled coffee from the floor. "Just don't say anything to him about this. Secrets tend to get loose when he hears of them. Maybe take a vacation day if you don't want us here alone. We just want to stay until this afternoon. We'll tell you everything. Our plans to save the children, everything." His eyes narrowed as he tilted his head, doing his best pleading impression.

"What children are you talking about?"

"It's a long story, one I'll tell you once you decide to let us stay or not. But it's too long to tell for no reason."

"You do like kids, don't you?" Tom leaned his tall frame to the side and lowered his head, searching her eyes.

"Of course, yes, I like kids."

Silence.

"Okay...I'll call Mike." Dialing her cellphone, she mumbled to herself, "I must be dreaming. DR, here in my house. Be careful what you pray for."

"What's that?" DR heard her mumble.

"Nothing, I didn't mean nothing." Red blotched her neck. She did mean it.

DR listened as she talked with Mike. "Mike, I need to take the day off? It's important. Can you cover for me?"

She tapped her foot nervously listening to her coanchor.

"I know, and I'm sorry. I'll make it up to you, but it's too much to go into now. I'll tell you later. Sorry didn't mean to cut you off. Are we good?"

She held the phone tight to her ear, all the time shaking her head.

"Thanks, Mike. I'll talk to you soon." She hung up. "I must be nuts. But he's going to cover for me. By the way, you owe me big time."

"I know. I promise, and when you see those kids, you'll be so glad you helped." He turned to Sam and Tom. "Isn't that right guys?"

"Absolutely," Tom said.

Sam, playing with a Christmas ornament, tucked it back onto the tree. "It will be the greatest reward you can imagine."

"Well, you can start rewarding me by explaining everything." She poured herself a cup of coffee and offered them another pour as well, then settled back in an easy chair near the Christmas tree.

DR, Sam, and Tom sat on a sofa across from her, a coffee table with her family Bible and coasters between them. "Okay, here goes."

By the time DR finished, Willie's jaw hung open, and her gaze skidded from man to man for confirmation.

"Yep, that's about the crux of it." Sam nodded at DR's story.

"Those poor children." She opened a coffee-table drawer, took out a box of tissues, and carefully wiped her eyes so as not to smear her freshly applied makeup. "Who could be so heartless?"

"You would be surprised," Tom responded. "It appears congressmen, Hollywood, and media moguls."

"And this all started as election interference?" Faking a laugh, she laid the tissue down.

"Well, that's what the detective told us right before he planned to kill us." Tom sipped his coffee. "But he wasn't planning on our escaping. And we know most of their plot now."

"So..." DR sank back in his seat, crossing one leg over the other as if he could stay if he just made himself look settled in. "We need to stay here until around three or four this afternoon. Then we'll head over to Chicago and be out of your hair and eternally grateful."

"Okay." She sprang to her feet and spread out her hands. "Well, I'm hungry. Would you like some breakfast? I have Eggos and bacon. Living alone, I don't keep a lot of food here."

Sounded fabulous. They all agreed.

But DR's stomach tightened. Would this be their last meal? And while they waited, were those kids being fed?

CHAPTER
TWENTY-ONE

Danny and Max went to check on their traps after breakfast. The snow, now around a foot and a half deep, added to the test, but it also helped them see if any animals were in the area. They only saw a few cat prints.

Max shared with Danny how his dad taught him to identify paw prints, explaining how he knew they were a cougar's, even though they're almost extinct in the area. While they were checking the traps furthest away, not having any luck, a helicopter circled above them. The passenger took a shot at them. Max returned fire and grabbed Danny, and they ran as the helicopter descended to land.

"Run, Danny. There! Hide under that pine." Max hustled Danny to the side furthest away from their attackers. "We can't hide our prints, but we can make them circle the tree before they see where we went under its canopy." Now Max had to rely on the things his father and grandfather had taught him as a boy.

"Look, see that ridge?" He pointed to where they'd just come from. "They'll be coming from there, if they don't split up first. We don't want to shoot at them too far away. It'll be hard to hit them good. So we wait until they get near this tree. Then we'll be able to pick them off far easier." He took Danny's rifle and checked the chamber.

"Dad?" Danny's eyes were wide open, and his jaw dropped over what Max said. "Are we really going to shoot them?"

"It's us or them, son. These are the people your mom and I were talking about. They're hired killers. They won't think twice about shooting us." Max handed the rifle back to his son. Poor Danny must be petrified. Max's own heart pounded in his chest like it was about to explode.

Someone screamed, shouting profanity.

"Sounds like someone found one of our larger traps. Good thing, we didn't finish checking them all." He tried to smile, but Danny could probably hear his heart pounding. Er, maybe not. Danny wouldn't be able to hear over his own. "One down. I only saw two in the helicopter, so there's only one to go."

"Won't he be able to get out of the trap?" Danny blew on his shaky hands, then put his gloves back on.

"Maybe. Depends if that was the one on the side of the hill. If it was, he'd have fallen down the incline. Then the chain would've just about snapped his ankle." Max closed his eyes, shook his head, and whispered a prayer.

They hid under the tree for what seemed like an eternity but couldn't have been more than ten minutes.

A twig broke. Then everything went black.

Danny tried not to scream out or move. Maybe the shooter didn't see him. He followed the shot angle up into a tree where a man in camouflage prowled. Danny took aim, balanced the stock in a steady grip, and squeezed the trigger. The shot rang out. Then nothing, not a sound, but the shooter was gone.

Danny sat still for a few minutes, then jolted. His dad was bleeding and needed attention, fast. He rolled out from under the tree, still able to hear the first man in the trap screaming for help occasionally.

He reached the tall tree where the shooter had climbed up and found him lying awkwardly on his head. His neck appeared to be broken.

Danny turned his head for a moment. When he looked back, he saw the man's left eye was missing. A gaping hole in his skull and a puddle of blood confirmed Danny's shot had hit its mark. He vomited. He'd never killed an animal, much less a person.

He ran back to the tree where his dad lay and struggled to pull his much larger form out from under its canopy. He had to get him the quarter mile or so to the cabin, and it would probably take every ounce of energy in him. The other man better have fallen like Dad described so he wouldn't have to fight another shooter. After a minute or so of him pulling, tugging, and dragging his dad in any way he could, a woman screamed. Then three shots were fired just as he was coming within earshot of the cabin. It had to be his mom or sister. He began to call out as he came closer. The snow had started falling harder again, making it difficult to see, the quietness so loud he struggled with it.

Then he gasped. That was his mom lying on the ground! Cold fear gripped him. No! Mom couldn't be shot too. He edged closer, calling out. His legs wobbled when she pushed off the ground.

After shaking the snow off herself, she started coming his way. She screamed when she saw Dad.

"Quick. Let's get him inside." She took an arm and lifted it around her shoulders.

Watching, he did the same. Then he saw what the three shots were for. An adult cougar must've tried to attack his mom, but before it could get to her, she'd shot it twice, missing the one time from the looks of the cat's wounds.

"Mom, what happened? Why were you outside?" His chest swelled. She'd sure shot well, but how had she ended up on the ground?

"I heard shots fired after that helicopter flew over. I worried something was wrong." She grunted, struggling to get Dad over the cabin threshold. "Looks like I was right. Where's the man who landed the helicopter?"

Dawn, seeing their dad being brought in, let out a sob. With one hand clamped over her mouth and tears following the curve of her cheeks, she dropped to her knees, taking it in.

"I don't know where he is. We heard a scream, and Dad said the man must've stepped into our bear trap. That was before Dad was shot." Shot! His dad was *shot*! A shaking started in Danny's limbs now that he'd gotten him home. "His bleeding is slowing now. Can we put a covering over it?"

"Yes, go take the covers off the bed pillows and bring them here. That'll help. It's going to be okay. We'll take him into town—to the hospital." Mom moved to the doorway and peered at the driveway. Narrow and winding, it was at least a quarter of a mile long, now covered with almost two feet of snow. "Let's lay him on the floor for now. We'll warm the SUV first. Dawn, honey, he's going to be all right. We all are. Can you help Danny wrap a blanket around him?" She took the pillowcase and wrapped his neck up, putting the pillow under his head.

"Can we make it down the drive?" Danny laid Dad's arm on the cabin floor, then rose to look for the keys.

Mom's voice followed him, squeaking and haltering, but brave. "We have to. I'll take it extra slow."

But would it be enough? And would Dad make it if they could get him to the hospital? And who had been shooting at them? Why?

DR watched Willie's attitude change during the six hours they'd stayed, especially after hearing the entire story. She appeared to have more admiration for the men, seeing a side often not exposed in the world, real men doing what's right for others. DR's chest swelled to have such companions.

Getting into the Charger, Sam and Tom laughed while waving goodbye to Willie. Then Sam snorted, poking DR's shoulder. "Looks like somebody has a crush on our friend."

DR started the engine and waved goodbye to Willie outside the window over the car's top as he pulled away. "Come on. She was just being nice, friendly." He checked her out in the rearview mirror. *She did seem to pay more attention to me. Ah... she just knows me better.*

"Come on, DR. Where's your eyes, your brain? That woman is smitten with you." Tom raised his left brow and tilted his head, leading DR. "Why fight it? Debbie left you, right?"

"Look, guys." DR flexed his grip on the Charger's leather steering wheel. "Debbie may have left, but as far as I'm concerned, nothing has changed. It's still up to her. I can't just change the way I feel because of one argument. So just forget about this Willie thing." No, he hadn't changed his mind, his love for Debbie. Maybe Miguel was right. That was just God's way of getting her to safety. But then again, Willie...

"How long before we reach the club?" Tom broke through DR's thoughts.

"It takes almost three hours." Sam stretched out on the back seat. "I sure wished Willie liked me like that. That's all I know."

"It's your cologne." Tom made an exaggerated sniffing motion, then winked at DR.

"Cologne?" DR flexed his biceps. "And I thought it was my manliness. What's so special about my cologne?"

"Yeah, what's so special about his cologne?"

"Just kidding." Tom sniggered. "You really don't know why she didn't give you a second look?"

"No, what am I doing wrong? I could use a pointer or two."

"Stop stripping every woman you meet with your eyes. Most of them don't like that. Don't you know that?" Tom laughed. "Didn't you see how she covered herself up? She felt naked in your eyes."

"Really?"

"Yeah, really."

As DR merged onto Interstate 94 West, the conversation went silent. He began trying to remember the layout of the LMMC and the parking lot where they'd seen the three trailers. The girls better be there. Then they could figure out a way to get them to safety. But with only three days till Christmas, he had to stop thinking about the plan and pay more attention to the bustling traffic.

"I've never liked this drive into Chicago." Sam jittered, playing drums on the back seat. "It's always such a hassle getting through the toll gate and then fighting your way to the right exit."

"Reminds me of London sort of, except there you have to watch out for the double-deckers."

"Sam, I'm glad you're in a good mood, but could you please stop drumming on the seat? I'm getting a headache." DR looked at Tom. "You mean the buses, right?"

"Yep, they'll run you over almost. Nothing puts them behind

schedule, but I'm sure it's a stressful job, being responsible for all those passengers."

After driving two hours, DR took the exit ramp for North Chicago, watching for merging traffic, thankful for the Charger's extra power. "We need to stop for gas before we go to the club. You guys want to grab some snacks?"

"Do you think that's wise? Maybe Sam should pump the gas and grab a few things." Tom shifted in his seat, obviously not wanting to be identified or seen by a policeman. "After all, Sam isn't as well publicized since he isn't accused of shooting Shortman."

"That's probably a good idea. Sam?"

"Why not? Ol' eagle eyes here doesn't miss a trick. Pop the tank."

After a night in Huntington, West Virginia, Smithers and Jones spent most of Friday morning searching the camera links O'Connor had sent the night before. Not finding anything, they'd come to a dead end. They could only hope the fugitives slipped up, using a cellphone, credit card, or something. After refueling their helicopter, Smithers tried to reach the other team in Wisconsin, to no avail.

Smithers banged on the chopper's door, his muscles tensing up. "I don't know if the storm in Wisconsin has taken down a couple of cell towers or what, but I can't connect with our boys. Since the snow's stopped here, let's head back to Chicago. Something will pop up. We can go over to the doctor's girlfriend's house, maybe get information there."

"Okay." Jones took a minute or so typing coordinates into the bird. "I plotted O'Hare into our heading. It's about two hours."

Jones lifted off, veering north. "See if you can get Manning now."

Smithers worked with the radio and then his cellphone. "Nothing."

"Ohh… I hope they haven't gone and got themselves dead."

"I'm sure they're fine, but if you want, why don't we go to the club first?" Smithers jammed his cellphone in a leg pocket on his cargo pants and snapped it closed.

"I didn't figure it would take long to get our marks." Jones steered the helicopter clear of air traffic around the airport. "I guessed wrong on this one. They must be watching too many *MI-5* television shows. Soon, everybody will know how to hide and fight back. I like them too, especially the ones with Tom Cruise. I like the stunts." He craned to watch the ground below. "Maybe we should've waited to take down the club's assistant. He was pretty helpful."

"We have the patch he gave us, so no, I don't think that would have affected anything. Just our little bunnies are the slippery sort." Smithers slapped his companion's knee as he searched the internet for clues. "Buck up, man. Nothing we haven't overcome in the past."

"Right. We'll find them." Jones nodded, not taking his focus from the changing landscape. "We always get our man. That's why we're the best."

That they were. Smithers smirked. Nothing had ever stopped them before. Nothing would stop them this time, either.

Leslie inched the SUV down the drive as carefully as possible, her hands trembling on the steering wheel. She'd made it halfway down, right where the driveway curved sharply. Then a deer jumped out in front of them, and she instinctively slammed on her brakes before she could stop it, causing her to push the car's rear wheels off the roadside. Now, as she fought to right the vehicle, she gave it too much gas. The tires lost traction and slid deeper into the ditch, and the vehicle came to a screeching halt.

"That stupid deer." She banged her head on the steering wheel. Max had slipped in the seat, and his leg was lying more on the floor than the seat. "Danny, can you put your dad's leg back on the seat? I've got to figure this out."

Danny climbed out of the rear driver's side while she thought, carefully going around the vehicle. Snow in the ditch wedged under the pearl-colored Escalade's body, a good two-foot-plus deep, and now a strong westerly wind was blowing in a cold front. The temperature, eight degrees, was starting to drop as evening neared. It was now four p.m.

"Mom, how much fuel do we have?"

She checked the gauge. She hadn't given the fuel much thought. After all, they were only three miles from town, but now that they were stuck, it became important. "A little under a quarter of a tank. Why?"

"We're not going to be able to get out of the ditch. And it's a long way back to the cabin, plus Dad needs to get to the hospital, fast." Danny scuffled around the SUV, then poked his head in the door, rubbing his gloves together. "Mom, I'm going to have to walk to town."

Dawn began to cry.

Leslie placed her hand on her daughter's shoulder. "Honey, don't cry. We're all going to be fine." Then she pressed cold fingers to her own throbbing temples. Eight degrees and night was falling. Not to mention the chance of cougars. She suppressed a shudder, then spoke to Danny standing outside, by the driver's window. "That's around three miles, in this weather? That's a long way."

"We don't have any other choice. Dad will die if I don't." He wiped his nose on his glove, now beginning to drain due to the cold. "Plus, the car's going to run out of gas, and no one comes down this road much in the wintertime. I saw a house about halfway when we drove out here yesterday. Maybe someone will be home. I've got to try."

The kid was right. Only a day older than thirteen, and her boy had grown up so much. She clenched her teeth. "Okay, if you're sure. Take a blanket out of the back and wrap it around you for more insulation and be careful." She leaned out the open window, hugged her son, and kissed his cheek. "We'll pray for you and Dad."

He opened the back, took a brown blanket, and bundled it around his head, neck, and body. Then he shuffled down the driveway, trudging through a foot of snow or more at times.

"I love you, Danny," she called out.

Beside her, Dawn swiped at her own tears. "Mom, are we going to die?"

"No, and don't you even think that way. We're going to be fine. Your brother is such a strong young man. He'll make it to help. You just wait and see." Closing her eyes, Leslie exhaled. Everything had happened so fast. She'd only had time to react, but now it hit her. She began to shake. Trembling, she took Dawn in her arms, and they both cried. Then Leslie righted herself, released Dawn, and sat back in the heated leather driver's seat. Just how long would the fuel last as the vehicle idled?

"Do you remember when we went to your grandmother's church, back when your dad was a housebuilder?"

"Yes." Dawn sniffled, her eyes still aglow with extra moisture. "I liked that church. Why did we change?"

"I like it too. But your dad wanted to change to Senator Carl Brummengarten's church so he could make better connections for Congress. Well, before we came here, your dad and I had a long talk. He's not going to seek reelection. He's going to return to private business." She ruffled Dawn's silky hair, admiring her beauty.

"That would be great!" Dawn gave a fist pump. It looked like hope had returned, and the girl was all smiles. "So we can go back to church with Grandma? I used to love going to the restaurant afterward with her. She has a beautiful singing voice."

"Honey, do you remember the prayer we used to pray in church?"

"There were lots of them. Which one are you talking about?"

Leslie took Dawn's soft hand. "The one that goes 'The Lord is my shepherd; I shall not want.'"

"I think so."

"Let's pray it."

"Okay." Dawn squeezed her hand.

Just minutes after their prayer and checking on Max they fell asleep.

CHAPTER
TWENTY-TWO

DR pulled alongside the LMCC's main gate, careful not to draw any attention to the already noticeable vehicle.

Sam went to the gate to open it, then motioned to an older keypad to the electric gate and sprinted back. "Guys, this is an electronic gate. What do we do?"

"Are the buttons worn? Can you tell how many of the numbers they use?" Tom fished for the cellphone.

"Yeah, four are really worn, but what good will that do?"

"Good thinking, Tom." DR turned the car's engine off. "We can try to figure the combination somehow, but how?"

Tom checked up and down the road, then refocused on the cellphone. "I'm going to do a search for popular number combinations. It'll give us a place to start. What are the numbers?"

"Um, 0852, but the one is worn some too," Sam called back in his quiet voice.

Tom asked Google for the most popular four-number combinations. After a moment, the answer returned. "Try 1234, Sam."

"Not it."

"How about 1111?"

"Nope."

"Maybe 5555?"

"I thought the numbers were 0852." DR craned over his friend's shoulder to see the screen. "Are there any popular combinations on there for those numbers?"

"Okay, try 2580. They should be in a straight line down the keypad."

The keypad flashed three times and clicked.

"We have a winner." Sam jogged back to the car as the gate swung open, then shut back after DR drove inside.

"Thank God for Goggle," Tom said.

They hurried over to check out the three trailers first, hoping against hope they were wrong about the trailers' purpose. The first trailer was unlocked.

Sam turned in a circle, making sure they weren't set up, before entering. "Someone is either trusting or thinking they didn't need to lock up since the front gate was locked."

"It's creepy. That's for sure." DR cupped his hands by his eyes to shield them from a glare, but the windows were covered. "Something's not right. What do you think, Tom?"

"I don't know. It feels like we're in a B movie or something. The guy trying to kill us owns this?" Inside, he swung a cage door closed, counting them. "There are eleven cages in here. Oh man. This is sickening. They're treating these children like animals."

DR stood just inside the door, grinding his teeth to get control of his thoughts. There was one bathroom in the trailer. Each cage had a chamber pot, small dresser, and a few of the children's personal items.

"It looks like someone was in a hurry to get out of here." Tom pointed to an overturned water bucket.

"Let's go next door." Sam went back outside, looking out over beautiful Lake Michigan. "How can such beauty be beside such an ugly...?" He slammed a fist against his thigh. "This makes me so mad!"

Next door was more of the same, further fueling their anger. Except Tom saw something. He strode over to the back-corner cage, the furthest from the door, leaned down, and picked up a girl's yellow pullover tee shirt. A puff-print puppy pranced on the front, and a similar kitten played with print yarn on the back. "This belongs to the little girl who was unconscious, the one who said God told her you would be their new daddy. What was her name?"

DR lowered his head, whispering, "Habiba."

"What?"

"Her name is Habiba." He walked outside.

The third trailer was a little nicer. The cages offered more comforts. It was obviously where the more *cooperative* children lived.

"I've seen enough." Tom kicked a can outside, rattling up a storm. "And some authorities know about this? That's one big cover-up. I don't know what we've gotten ourselves into."

"We didn't get ourselves into anything. They started it. We finish it—and set the children free in the process." The back of DR's eyes burned. "Let's check out the clubhouse."

They quietly walked three hundred yards or so to the LMCC front entrance, turning, and searching the area all around before trying the door. Just like the three trailers, it swung open. They slipped inside, as stealthily as possible and closed the door behind them. It was dark, so the place must be vacant. Counting on that, DR switched the lights on.

"With Christmas just three days away, you'd think this weekend would be huge for this type of club." The room was set up with the tables in diagonal rows, tablecloths alternating between red and green. Miniature Christmas trees decorated every other table, blooming Christmas cactuses on the rest. DR walked past several tables. "Those weren't on the tables Tuesday night. Someone is preparing for this weekend."

"All we need now is some spooky music," Tom said.

"No, I don't need that. I'm already spooked." DR pushed a chair under a table.

"OCD?" Tom snorted out his amusement.

"Probably." DR's lips squeezed tight, forcing a tense smile. "Let's check out the offices."

After a few minutes inside the two managers' offices, they went down the back hallway. Other than the telltale signs someone was working on the computers, everything appeared normal, no signs of struggle, violence, or anything.

In the kitchen, a half-eaten candy bar lay on a stainless countertop beside a Coke, but all else was clean and in order. Nothing unusual. Tom rubbed a finger over the Sub Zero refrigerators. "It's so clean you'd think someone just straightened out the entire clubhouse."

Sam jerked a thumb toward the lake. "Let's check out the yacht."

"The *Lucky Lucie*? Well, she was lucky for us, maybe not anyone else." Tom pointed at the video camera mounted on a column, its red light glowing. "Looks like the video is on. We better check it when we go back inside."

After boarding the yacht, which was swaying in the chop of the not-yet-frozen Lake Michigan, they tiptoed to the bridge. Other than a book of matches and the usual paperwork, nothing appeared disorderly. DR picked up the odd matches. The cover displayed the flag of the city of San Juan. It was from a club on Coronado Beach. He held them up. "Now, this is where we should be right now."

"Where is it?" Tom played with the yacht's wheel.

"A bar on Coronado Beach, San Juan. Maybe when all this is over, we can sail the *DI* there and visit for a week or so. What do you guys think?"

"Why wait?" Sam snorted. "I'm ready now."

DR pocketed the matches. "Let's check out the cabins. They've taken the children somewhere."

For the next twenty minutes, they searched the fifteen evenly-sized cabins. Each offered a full-size bed and small appointments, including a bedside night table. Digging through each cabin, they found massage oils, towels, personal items, and ashtrays with books of matches. The matchbook covers promoted a downtown Chicago nightclub. DR grabbed a couple books of the matches, tucked them in his pocket with the pack from the helm, and headed to the captain's chambers, just off the casino. They offered extra luxury, and the casino itself boasted a special money cage and lift system for security.

"Nothing here." Tom closed a cabin door. "Come on. Let's see if the video camera shows anything."

"I feel sleazy after being in those cabins." Sam shivered, noticeably shaking himself. "I hope there weren't any evil spirits hanging around."

"Evil spirits?" DR shook his head. "Really, Sam?"

"Yeah. Don't you remember what the preacher always said? He said each area around the world had evil spirits in them, trying to steal souls. I can't remember it all, but he used Scripture." Sam looked at DR, then let it rest.

Tom pivoted and walked backward a step or two, taking in the conversation. "Sounds kind of like your dream, doesn't it?"

"I'm trying to forget those."

"Maybe you should try to remember. Miguel said they may have saved our lives." Tom turned around and held the door open for them.

"Forget the evil spirits." DR gave him a woolly eye. "Let's find that video feed." Shaking his head, he wasn't going there.

Since Sam worked in hospitality, he was more familiar with the club's software than DR and Tom were. He took about ten minutes of fiddling to find the video, using a backdoor through the hospitality application to access the computer's video files.

"Look, that's the guy who was here the night of the banquet. Remember, he came over and introduced himself. What was his name?" Tom braced both hands on the desk, leaning over the computer screen. "Can you turn up the volume?"

"I don't know... Wait. Here it is." Sam clicked the mouse.

The video showed two white men following one Black man. After boarding the boat, they cracked him over the head with a large chrome flashlight. Then they strapped the unconscious man to a chair, gagging him.

"See, Sam." Tom slapped the desk. "That's where they had us, except they used drugs on us and bagged our heads at first."

The video rolled. "No wonder the old man was laughing when he said 'Congressman Dingleman, not going to happen.' Instead, he purchased you a diving engagement." Chuckling, they went to the helm and were soon taking the *Lucky Lucie* out on the lake.

Sam fast-forwarded the video to the *Lucky Lucie*'s return, slowing as she was docked. Only the two white men returned.

"Looks like Congressman Dingleman didn't make the return trip." Tom closed his eyes.

Walking by the camera, one of the assassins said, "One loose end down, one to go. Let's get to Eagle River and find the congressman. I want to get home early for Christmas."

"Is there a time stamp on the video?" DR leaned over.

"Yes, Thursday, the twenty-first, four thirty p.m., yesterday." Sam shut the computer off. "What do you think is going to happen in Eagle River?"

"Sounds like a loose end's going to be taken care of." Tom scraped a hand over his now-stubbled jaw. "I've got to remember all this. It would work great in a novel."

"Yeah, probably a bestseller. People like sick." DR sat in Dingleman's chair, propped his elbow on the desk, and covered his mouth with his hand. "We need to go to Eagle River. Max might be our only hope now."

"Are you nuts? You saw that. Those guys killed that man, and you want to follow *them*?" Sam paced to the door and back.

"DR's right," Tom seconded. "We have to go."

"Correction"—Sam groaned—"you're both nuts."

Danny had barely gone an hour, but he was cold. The wind blowing in his face made seeing and walking harder and harder. He had to push through the deep snow on the road, too, since only one vehicle had traveled the road that day. Staying in the vehicle's tracks helped, but the wind was blowing snow into the tracks.

To occupy himself, he played their gun battle over and over in his head, shivering at the memory of the man's blood spattered all over the snow where he'd fallen. Thinking about his dad energized him. And all those times Dad had been away while in Congress might be over now. He'd get his dad back. *If* he could get Dad help today.

He talked to himself while battling the wind and cold. What was it his grandfather told him about a king in the Bible? Granddad said the king encouraged himself in the Lord. Granddad was a good teacher and friend.

God, if You can hear me, please help us—help me get through.

As the road turned a curve, he neared the halfway point, but the house there appeared empty. He walked, shivering and afraid, through two-foot-deep snow. Had God heard his cry?

The house was locked and dark inside. He banged on the door again and again.

No help came. He sat on the porch behind a wooden column to

escape the wind. He almost fell asleep from sheer exhaustion. Only his hunger saved him.

He struggled to his feet, gathering his strength, and nudged his sleeve up far enough to see his watch. He'd been going for two hours. "Oh, Dad, please be okay."

He stepped off the porch and into the bitter wind, pushing on, not knowing how things were back at the car.

He groaned, his breath hovering in cold puffs as he talked. "Becoming of age and a man was not part of what the trip was supposed to be about." Now, it was about saving Dad. Leaving their warm home now seemed like the wrong thing to do. "After all," he muttered, "the bad guys still found Dad. But saving Dad and making this walk will make me a man."

DR shifted his cramped legs. Tom had taken the last shift driving to reach Eagle River. It was almost nine p.m., and they'd been on the road for six hours. Tired and hungry, they pulled into a convenience store and stopped by the gas pumps.

"You two go in, stretch your legs. I'll pump the gas, then park the car." DR opened the fuel cap, watching the road for police traffic. Thankfully, the weather kept folks home. After filling the tank, he parked the car by the front doors, then went inside, finding Sam and Tom over by a roaring fireplace.

"This is a nice place." Sam took off his coat. "They have hot food by order, so we ordered you a double bacon cheeseburger and fries. Is that all right?"

"Sure, we need to take a break." DR rubbed his hands together to get some warmth back into them. "Did you ask about hotels?"

Tom spread his hands over the fire. "There's one a half a mile down the road."

"Order number 21," a teenage girl called out from the restaurant counter.

Sam checked his number slip, then gestured with it to the empty place. He chuckled. "Guess that's us."

They took the table closest to the fireplace and divvied up the food.

"Five double burgers?" One of DR's eyes almost closed, and the other eyebrow rose as he shook his head. "Are we feeding an army?"

"I'm a growing boy. What can I say?" Tom grabbed two of the burgers and a large fry.

"You keep eating that much, and you will grow." Sam slathered mayonnaise on his burger, laughing while making fun of Tom.

They spent the next minutes talking less and eating more. Then a teenage boy struggled to push the convenience store door open. The clerk ran to the door after seeing the boy nearly frozen.

DR shifted for a better view. Then, upon also seeing the boy, he ran to the door to help.

"Hurry up. Get in here." The clerk beckoned, helping to support the boy.

DR reached the boy and took over for the young female clerk. "Here, I've got him. Come on, son. Let's get you by the fire."

"My dad... my dad." The boy passed out. DR carried him to the fireplace, the boy's feet dragging on the ground.

Twenty minutes later, the boy woke and thrashed around upon finding himself lying beside the fire, his coat and hat removed. "My dad! He needs help."

"Okay, stay calm." DR held up a hand. "We're going to help your dad. An ambulance is on the way. Can you tell me what happened?"

The boy's eyes found their food.

DR smiled, took the boy up by lifting him under his arms, and helped him to a chair. "Are you hungry?"

"Starving."

DR snagged Tom's third burger and unwrapped it, telling Tom to order himself another one, then slid half of his fries to the boy. "Sam, grab him a milk."

The boy chomped into a bite, then chewed, and swallowed. "He's been shot." He snagged the milk carton and pried it open. "Some men in a helicopter"—he hungrily chewed while talking—"hunted us down."

Sam rocked back on his chair legs. "Looks like he hasn't eaten for days."

"What's your name, son?" Tom asked around a mouthful of his other burger.

"It's Danny, sir. Danny Rice."

"Danny Rice." DR jolted upright. "As in, your dad is Congressman Rice?"

"Yes, sir." Danny glugged down half the milk, then wiped his mouth with the back of his hand. "My dad's in trouble, and these men came to kill him. We shot one of the men, but not before he shot Dad in the shoulder and neck area. The second one must've stepped in one of our bear traps. We heard screams but never saw the man." He stuffed fries in his mouth.

"How is your dad?" Holding his breath, DR almost wished he could pray Max was still alive. They needed him.

"He's lost a lot of blood. I don't know now."

DR pulled his coat on. "After you've had enough to eat, can you show us where he is? We'll go get him. It could be a while before the ambulance gets here."

"We can go now. Can I wrap this up for my mom and sister? They haven't had anything for a while, either."

"Sure, we'll take it all." Nodding to the others to help wrap it up, Tom abandoned his burger and thrust his arms into his coat.

"Miss, can you tell the police and rescue squad that we went for his family? Tell them to wait here for us."

"Mister, we're not going to make it in that car." Danny pointed at the Charger. The kid's face was getting its color back. "The road is covered, and only one vehicle has gone in or out all day."

"Sir, you can use my dad's Tahoe," the clerk behind the counted offered. "He's got chains and blocks in the back."

"Are you sure? It sure would help."

A red Tahoe waited in the corner covered with snow.

"What do you think, guys?" DR zipped up his coat. "There might not be no escape."

"We have to try. If something happens, we're in big trouble."

Sam nodded in agreement with Tom.

"Got the keys?" DR held out his hand.

The clerk rummaged through her bag, dug all the way to the bottom, and brought out a keychain with a large fish. "Be careful. The roads are bad."

"Thank you." He searched for her name tag. "Uh, Cindy. We'll be right back."

Danny hugged the girl. "Thank you, Cindy. You're saving my dad's life."

DR swallowed hard. He could only hope the kid was right and the congressman wasn't already dead.

Arriving in Chicago, Smithers and Jones went into the LMMC, and prowled the place for clues, then accessed the video. Their gazes met. Their mark had been *here* earlier also. Then they found the footage of Dingleman going fishing. Still unable to get their other team on the phone or radio, Smithers frowned. "All the action must be going down in Eagle River. Let's go."

He followed Jones out to the helicopter.

"Will you find us a hotel room and make reservations for us?" Jones fired up the helicopter. "It'll be late when we get there and too dark to see anything. Maybe check and see if Manning or O'Connor have reservations too."

Smithers shot him a look but started doing what Jones had asked. After all, Jones was right and couldn't fly the helicopter and make their reservations.

"We'll get into town around ten o'clock if this wind doesn't slow us down too much."

After making the reservations, Smithers pulled out his 9mm and started checking it, then pointed at objects on the ground, pretending to pull the trigger. The corners of his lips curled up, and his eyes squinted. "Bang, you're dead." Three of his favorite words.

CHAPTER
TWENTY-THREE

The Tahoe revved up on the first try. It looked worse for wear, but its bones were good and strong, and the motor sounded solid. DR took the wheel in his hands and closed his eyes before realizing Sam and Tom were watching. He quickly opened them.

"I said a prayer too." Sam rubbed his hands together as if trying to encourage himself.

"I wasn't praying," DR grunted. "I was merely getting my mind straight. You guys ready?"

Opening his eyes, Danny smiled. "Yes, sir. I'm ready now."

The blowing snow had filled in the tire marks from earlier. The Tahoe slipped and spun its way through the deep snow, but kept going, the strong tailwind helping. The three miles seemed like thirty, DR grinding his teeth and hoping against all odds they would make it.

"Mom slid into the ditch because a deer ran out in front of our SUV, and she hit the brakes to miss it." Danny leaned forward and nodded to a house as they passed. "I sought help there earlier. Huh, still no sign of anyone there."

"How much further?" DR switched the wipers on to knock off the blowing snow.

"We're over halfway. The turnoff will be on your left. It's not too far past the curve up there." Danny pointed with his left hand.

After reaching the turn, DR began down the narrow drive. He let out a deep breath when he parked by the pearl SUV. Snow had drifted against the vehicle, making it hard to spot at first. Tom and Sam retrieved chains and a snow shovel from the back. Then they made their way to the SUV, several steps behind Danny and DR. DR stole the shovel from Sam and started removing snow from around the driver's side, then gave the shovel back to Sam.

The Escalade was still idling. It hadn't run out of fuel. Danny knocked on the window, then pulled on the driver's side door, creaking it open.

"Mom... Mom, I'm back. I brought help."

"Oh, thank You, God." The tight lines went slack across her face. "Danny, I was so worried about you. Are you okay?"

"I'm fine. How's Dad?"

"He's hanging in there. We cleaned him up some, and the bleeding has stopped. The hit appears to be more on his shoulder than his neck, but he also has a nasty bump on the back of his head. We need to get him to the hospital fast. He lost a lot of blood." She wiped at the tears on her cheeks. "Who are the men you brought?"

Danny introduced them, adding, "They were at the convenience store. Oh, and here's some food they gave me. I brought it for you and Dawn." He handed her the bag of burgers and fries.

"Ma'am"—DR braced his hands on the roof above her seat, leaning in—"to keep the heat in, you might want to close your door while we get ready to pull you out of the ditch." He pushed the snow off her door's window. "Set your heat so it will defrost the windshield and heat SUV."

Tom hooked the chain to the Tahoe chassis and waited for Sam to clean under the Escalade so he could find the tow hooks and secure the chain underneath it too. Just moments later, he slid underneath the bumper and found them. Then Sam worked to remove snow from under the back of the vehicle.

Ten minutes later, they had the Escalade on the main road. Danny's mom gripped the steering wheel tight while listening to DR.

"We called the ambulance. They should be at the store by now. If they're not, you keep going to the hospital. There are signs to guide you there once you pass the store. Be careful. The road is dangerous."

"Thank you so much. I don't know how we can ever repay you." She nodded to the dash. "I'm low on fuel. I'll have to stop."

"Okay, we'll see you at the store."

Watching the Escalade make its way down the snow-covered road, DR mumbled, "Can it really be this simple?"

Mike and Willie worked on their lattes at Marcie's Place, while waiting on their food. His wife had taken their kids for some last-minute Christmas shopping, freeing him up to spend time with his cohost. Rachael brought their order to the table just as his cellphone rang.

"Sorry, I need to take this. It's my mom." He turned partially to his left to be respectful. Then, lowering his voice, he comforted his mom with news Willie had given him about DR, not giving any specifics in case the authorities visited them again. After several minutes, he finished his call.

"Mom and Dad are worried sick. They've been praying almost nonstop since this whole thing started." He surveyed the scenery, though he couldn't make himself see anything.

"I can imagine. I've been worried too." Her left brow rose. "Has your brother always been a protector?"

"What do you mean?"

"It's not something everyone will do, run into danger to free someone else. I saw it in his eyes—those kids mean everything to him." Her jaw flexed as if she was fighting back tears.

"He always looked over me and my brothers, if that's what you mean." Mike bit into his sandwich, chewed heartily, then paused. "I don't remember much before I was six. By that time, he'd changed." He resumed chewing, still talking. "I don't know why, but it must've been traumatic. Mom always talks about how he loved to go with Dad fishing and to football games in Ann Harbor. Don't forget DR's five years older than me. That had all stopped by the time I can remember. They seemed to have some sort of a rift, still do."

"Is that why he doesn't believe?" She propped up on her elbows.

"I don't know. Like I said, I was little. But Mom always said her daddy said DR had something called Michigan Strong." He squirted ketchup on his fries.

"Michigan Strong?"

"That's what Granddad called doing the right thing regardless of what it cost." Mike fully focused on the food on his plate.

Willie reached over and stole a fry. "I can see that. Those kids needed someone to stand up for them, and I believe, with God's help, he and his friends will save them."

"I just hope he doesn't go and get himself killed in the process. It would kill Mom." Mike slapped at her hand when she absently reached for another. "*What* are you doing getting into my plate? Aren't you going to eat *your* fries?"

"No... no, you can have them. I put too much salt on mine." She pushed her plate toward him. Uh-oh. The glazed dreamy look was back in her eyes. Having his brother around must've stirred her feelings for him again.

Approaching the convenience store, DR saw flashing lights a half mile away. "Gentleman, looks like we're going to need a little magic." Should he keep going or stop too? Not that he had any choice since they had to change vehicles.

"Cross your fingers." Tom edged forward in the back seat and let out a low whistle. "Two state trooper cars came with the lifesaving crew."

All were parked and waiting.

"They probably won't give us a thought." Sam held up two sets of crossed fingers. "A wounded congressman is pretty far away from that."

Leslie pulled the Escalade beside the rescue vehicle and got out, motioning to the rescuers that he was in the back. Two EMTs rushed over, and one carried a lightweight gurney.

"He was shot between his left shoulder and neck. Hurry. It's been over five hours." She stepped out of their way. "I think he hit the back of his head against a tree when he was shot. There's a large knot there."

"Ma'am, we'll get your report of what happened after we get to the hospital. Who are those men over there?" A state trooper waved toward them, and DR, heading inside, averted his gaze. But the lights on the red Charger blinked, signaling it had been started.

"They saved us. We got stuck, and they pulled us out onto the road." Her reflection shone on the convenience store window in front of DR while she rose up on her toes to see what the EMTs were doing inside the SUV.

"He's stabilized," one EMT called out loudly enough for DR to catch as he lingered, holding the store door open for one last moment. "But he's going to need a lot of blood. That's probably why he's still unconscious. Follow us to the hospital." One of the rescuers then lifted him out of the SUV to carry him to the ambulance.

Soon the rescue vehicle and one state troopers drove away, Leslie driving behind them. The other state trooper headed inside the store.

As DR returned the key, Cindy wiped a tear away, apparently the urgency of the congressman's needs tugged on her heartstrings. DR strode off, leaving her to put her key away. "Can I help you, Officer?" she asked.

He tipped his hat, being proper. "Yes, ma'am. Was that your vehicle they used to help the congressman?"

"Yes, sir. No way would their car have made it up that road." She pointed to the road they traveled.

"You did a good thing. Your folks will be proud of you."

"All I did was what anyone with a heart would do." She squeezed her lips tight, rocked by emotion again. "They're the heroes. They even gave up their dinner for that family."

"Nevertheless, thank you." He then walked over to DR and his friends.

Here we go. DR stiffened.

The officer tipped his hat. "Gentleman, thank you for helping the congressman and his family. I'll need to get your statement if I may."

DR tugged at his hair. "Would you mind if we did that at the hospital? We told Danny we'd come by before we leave town."

The trooper glanced out the window as if taking in the Charger's lights. "Sure, I need to go there myself. You can follow me, but give me a minute to radio into the station."

"Yes, sir. Just pull out whenever you're ready." DR nodded to Tom and Sam to leave.

Stopping at the counter, DR thanked Cindy again. "If he makes it, he owes his life to you."

She smiled, shaking her head. A tear fought its way onto her cheek.

"You take care of yourself, Cindy." Tom patted the countertop on the way out. Sam too.

Mr. Jennings hadn't meant for the takedown of an old friend to cost so much or his plot to bring attention to Circle. But the agents he employed only managed to make the POTUS look more like the right choice, even to those who hated the man. The hapless terrorists had made the President's foreign policy look brilliant, and now—well, Jennings was down a congressman, Dingleman was dead, and his best detective was out of commission with a gunshot wound to his leg. Meanwhile, the targets—a doctor, an author, and a hotel manager—were still on the loose.

Time to end this. He called Smithers.

Not waiting to exchange greetings, he spoke first. "Didn't I tell you to keep this clean, no loose ends? Bodies are popping up everywhere. Do you think they'll just sweep it under the rug?"

"Do you want this done or not?" Smithers's calm was almost irritating. "Half of your problem is gone, almost. We'll find the doctor. He's just getting lucky—wait a second. Something's coming over the radio."

Jennings waited, but his pulse beat like a time bomb.

"Good news. We just found out where the congressman is. He's in the hospital in Eagle River, Wisconsin. Our other team is there. They must've gotten to him. We'll join them in the morning and get that taken care of. Then all four of us will find the good doc."

"You better get to it. If he turns state's evidence, we'll all have a price to pay." Jennings disconnected, then called the Club Gauntlet in Chicago. He'd gone to a great deal of time and trouble bringing the kids from Aden to Chicago, using a lot of favors, and he wasn't just washing his hands of them. Not yet.

"Let me speak to Carrie." No hello, no niceties. He pulled the end ball of a Newton's cradle balance balls set on his desk, a five-ball metal pendulum of perpetual motion on a brass base. He let the ball swing free. All the energy released continued to transfer to the other balls. Just like how his hatred for a former friend caused him to lose control. But now that his plans had gone forward, *he* was the one paying the price, not the POTUS.

"This is Carrie. Who's calling?"

"Carrie, this is Jennings. I want my *performers* taken back to the LMMC. I'm sending Carl over to get them ready for New Year's. Have Toney and the boys use the yellow bus to take them all back at once."

"Yes, sir. That is good news. It's kind of crowded here."

"Thank you, Carrie. Sorry for your inconvenience. Tell the other girls I've added something to their pay."

He hung up. "Where are you, Dr. Ray?"

The steel balls continued to bounce.

He propped his elbows on the desk and supported himself, watching. Then, with his hands covering his mouth, he exhaled loudly. "And what are you up to?"

The Eagle Rock hospital gave the congressman a transfusion and IVs right away as he'd lost over 35 percent of his blood. Doctors reinforced the idea he lost consciousness after hitting his head on the tree where he was shot. He regained consciousness less than an hour after arriving. Now, four hours later, the emergency room doctor deemed him alert, ready to talk after having to fight for their lives.

"Honey, I'm sorry for what I've done." Max swiped a hand at his leg. "I'm ready to set the record straight before someone else gets killed."

Leslie, holding his hand, raised it and kissed it. "We're going to be okay —you'll see. After your term expires, we'll go back to being the family we once were. Dawn is so excited. I told her we'd go back to our church, no more politics."

He shook himself, trying to shake the fuzziness from his head. "How did I get here?"

"That's a long story. I'll tell you later, but three men here saved us all. They're outside." She nodded to the door. "One of them is named DR. The names of the other two slip my mind. It's been kind of a hectic getting you here and all."

Propped up in bed, he closed his eyes, not saying anything for a time.

"Are you okay?" She put her hand on his forehead to check his temperature. "Is everything all right?"

"Just thinking." He took hold of her hand. "How ironic is that? The man Jennings is trying to kill saved me from Jennings. He's the man I told you about. The one they framed for shooting Shortman." He sighed, closing his eyes.

"That's why they acted strange around the troopers." She squeezed his hand. "They were afraid of being identified. You've got to set things right for them—tonight. Before they get hurt or, worse, actually have to shoot someone." She straightened up, sucking in a breath of air for her own courage.

Around three a.m., a team of FBI agents came on the scene. Along with a Wisconsin state trooper, they took the congressman's statement and ordered tighter security for his room. Then one of the agents and the trooper went to the waiting room. Another headed outside to make a phone call while his partner delivered the good news.

DR waited with Sam and Tom in the hospital's small art deco waiting room. Its bold blues and deep reds blasted color from the seating as well as the art. Live palms and scheffleras cozied up the corners to create a cheery and comfortable ambiance. DR now stood before one of the photographs, and the perfectly balanced symmetry grounded him as Tom and Sam sat on the red upholstered armchairs.

"I'm sorry to keep you gentlemen waiting." The senior FBI agent spoke as he entered the room. "After talking with the congressman, I hope you accept my apology on behalf of the US government for the ordeal you have endured." Agent Collins reached to shake each man's hand. "All federal and state APBs are hereby suspended following the congressman's sworn statement."

"Yes, yes!" Sam cheered, balled his hand, and pumped his fist in the air. DR and Tom cheered as well.

Collins clasped his own hands together in agreement. "In the morning, we'll square this with CPD. Congressman Rice dispelled all the charges against the three of you, including child trafficking. Unfortunately, due to the hour, there won't be a notification or retraction in tomorrow's newspaper. However, all warrants and searches are called off, and you're free to go."

DR tossed a magazine from the rack on the wall and smacked at the air just minutes after the agents left. "Just like that—we're free to go? After everything we've been through—after we're nearly *killed*. 'Oh... it's just been a mistake.'" He sneered, and his sarcasm, even though Sam and Tom were elated when they first heard the news, soon seemed to become theirs too.

"I can't stand someone doing things and thinking a simple I'm sorry fixes it." Tom kicked the trash can.

"It feels good to be cleared, free, but I get it." Sam put his hands behind his head, stretching. "What about Jennings, the kids?"

"Nothing has changed. Jennings is still trying to kill us, and don't think he's not going to want you dead too, Sam." DR locked eyes with Tom. "He's the one we have to stop, or at least hurt, somehow. And we have to get the children."

Tom nodded. "No doubt about it—he's not going to stop, not unless we stop him. We can't go to the police because we don't know who's dirty and who isn't." He walked to the room's entrance to inspect the hallway. "After I call Laurie to tell her the good news, I can sleep here or in the car—your choice."

"I've slept in a car this week more than I want to for the rest of my life." Sam crossed to a stretch of three armless chairs fastened together and tested the depth of one. "Let's stay here and grab some breakfast in a few hours before we head out." He took his coat off to use it as a pillow.

DR picked the magazine up, crinkling the front cover. Then, while Tom found a place to sleep, DR claimed his own. "Guys, we know it's him or us, but I don't know where to start next. Do you?"

CHAPTER
TWENTY-FOUR

A black Ford Suburban pulled into the gate area of Greg and Penny's estate in Birmingham at eight o'clock Saturday morning. Greg barely glanced at the camera image on his phone as a man pushed the call button for the gate to be opened.

"May I help you?" his butler answered.

"FBI Agents Larson and Riddlehour. We'd like to ask Mr. and Mrs. Nichols a few questions."

"I'm sorry they're out. Can I take a message?" Johnson responded as Greg had earlier instructed.

"Do you know when they'll be returning?"

"I would suspect late this evening, but I can't say for certain." Johnson leaned against the nearby doorway, his gaze fixed on Amal as she played Greg's Xbox, still learning the controller while Greg used Penny's app to tell Amal what to do.

"Tell them Agents Larson and Riddlehour urgently need to talk to them. We'll come by later."

Johnson stepped away from the intercom, frowning at Greg. "What shall I do when they return, sir?"

"Nothing. I've already told the FBI everything I knew at the time. No need to update them, is there?" Greg took the controller from Amal and chuckled. "I finally found someone I can beat. She's not going anywhere."

"Very good."

"Who's not going anywhere?" Penny swished into the room, grabbed her phone from Greg, and looked up a phrase.

"Two FBI agents were at the gate. Johnson sent them away. We told them everything we knew already—at least before all this happened. Anyhow, how could they track them here?" Greg closed his eyes and shook his head. His man in the game died, and he slapped his knee. "No fair. I was distracted!"

"Are you going to lose... to a nine-year-old who's never played before?" Jabbing at Greg's arm, Penny snickered. Then she pulled Amal to her and rocked her back and forth, the one thing Amal easily seemed to know, affection—love. "And don't be a sore loser. You should be used to it by now."

"I haven't lost yet." His lips protruded, pouting. Sad-eyed, he handed Amal the controller and sat dejected, fake pouting.

Penny laughed while trying to say the phrase on her phone. "Would you like to go to the store and buy some new clothes and shoes?"

"Naeam." Amal's eyes lit up. "Naeam."

Penny pressed the button on her phone as Amal spoke. "She said yes. We'll go get her some things for Christmas this afternoon, after lunch." Leaning over, she kissed Amal's forehead, nodding to Amal, clearly loving having the little one in their house.

"Of course she wants to go shopping. She's a girl, isn't she?" Greg waved at the cute child, giving Penny a know-all glance. "Don't get too used to this, Penn. She'll be leaving soon, and I don't want you moping around for days."

Penny stuck her bottom lip out, making her eyes look big and mopey.

"And we're still not getting a puppy."

The sun shining through a window must've awoken Tom because he was now shaking DR's shoulder. "Wake up, DR, Sam. It's going on eight o'clock. We need to head out." Stretching, he moaned. "Aw, would've been better if we'd slept in the car. Maybe I wouldn't have another stiff neck."

"Hindsight is always twenty-twenty, but I agree. I feel like I slept on a rock." Sam patted the chair he was in, letting out a weak chuckle. "It is a rock."

"No use complaining now. I'm going to wash my face." DR pushed off the chairs and pulled at the hair on the back of his head. "I'm starved. Anyone else hungry?"

They must've been, because when he started down the hallway, the others followed.

"So what's the plan for today? Drive back to your place?" Sam picked up his pace to keep from falling too far behind his friends.

"Food. That's the plan." Tom patted his stomach. "I can't think before I eat."

"One thing at a time. We'll eat, then hit the road back to Wall Lake. How's that sound?" DR followed the signs to the cafeteria, then stopped, almost falling back.

"Like a really long drive." Sam, not paying attention, nearly knocked him down. "What's wrong?"

All DR could do was point. Blood splatters covered the wall behind the concession checkout. Trays were scattered across the floor where two kitchen workers lay. He bent over, closing his eyes.

Tom pulled the alarm, then went to check on the men, DR and Sam followed.

"Check for their pulse," Tom instructed, his first aid triage skills coming to play. "Be careful—don't disturb anything."

DR and Tom both checked a victim's pulse by their carotid artery. Sam went back into the kitchen, then came back outside. Closing his eyes, he shook his head. "There's a woman back here too."

Security ran in, saw the carnage, and called for medical backup before reaching DR, who shook his head, signifying they were dead.

"Guys, we're going to ask you to step outside," a security officer ordered.

Nodding, stunned, they gladly left.

They answered questions later. Then the security guard escorted them to the exit, but on the way, a report came over his radio. The sentry at the heliport on the roof had also been shot dead. The guard locked the exit after they went out.

Confused, DR pulled at his hair. Just what was the killers' goal? He could think of no clear leads. "Jennings?"

"I don't know." Sam frowned. "What did they gain? Nothing is missing. The congressman is safe and has guards by his door. Why the kitchen?"

"Let's leave that to the professionals. Besides, if this is Jennings, we better get out of here. I'm driving." DR climbed in the Charger, taking the keys from Sam.

"I'm still hungry. Stop by the C-Store on the way? Maybe their breakfast is just as good as their burgers." The corners of Tom's mouth turned as if he tried to fight a gnawing emptiness in his stomach.

"I'm on it." DR pulled the car to the left side of the store so they could leave easily when the time came, he didn't like to back out.

When they sprinted into the store, they were in luck—no one was ordering and all the customers either had ordered or were eating. After taking their order, the server asked. "Is this for here or to go?"

"For here?" Tom arched a brow at DR.

"Sam, I think we better get this man fed." DR clamped a hand on Tom's shoulder and jostled him. DR glanced at the field beside the convenience store through a window, seeing a large civilian helicopter on the other side of the lot. A man was tinkering with its engine. "That's not something you see every day. On second thought, we'll take this to go." He rose up over the counter to get the young lady's attention. "Ma'am, can you make that to go?"

"What's up with that? I'm starved." Tom snagged a handful of napkins and several forks and knives. "Do you know how hard it'll be to eat sausage, gravy, and biscuits riding in a car? We don't have these in London, so I'd like to enjoy them."

DR shook his head, moving to the window. "Think about it. The radio said a heliport employee was killed too. What do you think the odds are there would be another helicopter in Eagle River the same time as that one?" He pointed at the bird less than a hundred and fifty yards away. "Maybe they found another way to kill Max."

"No." Sam stiffened. "You think they poisoned him?"

"I don't know. But we're not sticking around to find out." DR grabbed their food from the counter and slapped a tip down. "Thanks. Come on, guys."

They strolled back to their car, trying not to draw attention. "Look, that guy is pointing at us." Tom slid into the back seat. "I'll sit back here. It'll be easier for me to eat."

"Yep, I'm on it." DR fired up the engine. Good thing they'd filled the tank when arriving in town the night before. In the rearview mirror, DR saw the two men rushing to complete whatever they were doing. He left the parking lot fast, not waiting to see if they were pointing at them or something else.

～

Leslie watched Max finish a hearty breakfast, and the way he especially enjoyed the small bowl of oatmeal with powdered sugar and peaches warmed her.

"You liked that oatmeal, did you? Maybe I'll have to get the recipe from the chef." She breathed deeply, closing her eyes, then shivered, thankful for their deliverance from the clutches of evil. "I'm glad you told the FBI everything. I feel like a burden has been torn away."

"There's still a lot to tell. I just told them enough, so they'd take down the APBs on DR and his friends. When I go back to Congress and this comes out, there's going to be a price to pay, for me, men like Jennings, and Senator Carl." He yawned. "Don't get too comfortable. Those people have seven ways from Sunday of reaching you anywhere."

"Sleepy?"

"You know how I get after a meal if I don't get going." He stretched. "This must've taken more out of me than I knew. I'm going to take a nap. I love you, honey. We'll make our plans later."

She leaned over the bed and kissed him. "I love you too. Get some rest." She walked to the chair by the window and sat where the sun shone through the partially closed blinds. Picking up the book she'd packed for their trip, she began reading the inspirational, but soon, she was asleep too.

When she woke an hour and a half later, Max's heart monitor's rhythm had slowed. Then an alarm sounded after his heartbeat fell under fifty-five beats per minute. A nurse entered the room and shut the alarm off before taking his pulse manually to ensure it wasn't a monitor failure. Once she finished, she called a code blue. His pulse was now less than fifty beats.

"His pulse is dropping. We're going to take care of this. He's going to be all right."

Leslie slumped against the corner to get out of the way. The team checked his oxygen and throat clearance and then placed twelve leads from the mobile echocardiogram to his body. His heart rate dipped below thirty beats per minute. Checking electrical activity, the test took too long. Then they injected epinephrine, but Max still flatlined. After another frantic ten minutes, which included defibrillation, the team gave up.

The lead doctor hung his head, breathed deeply, and signaled for his team to wrap it up. The team packed their equipment and whispered their condolences before leaving Max's side.

Leslie slid down the wall and hit the floor hard. It wasn't supposed to happen this way. Her whole body shook as she cried out bitterly, "Where were You, God? Why Max? Why?"

The red Charger raced toward Chicago down Route 45 south. Ten miles later, the helicopter came into DR's rearview mirror, rising over a hill. So they, too, were being hunted. "Guys? Looks like we've got some company. Tom, better get our guns out of the trunk."

"Where?" Tom twisted toward the back window and frowned at the helicopter. "Right. I'm on it." He finished his last bite and shoved the trash out of his way. Then he folded down the other side of the back seat to gain access to the trunk.

The helicopter passed them by and flew out of sight over a hill. Still, Tom handed Sam and DR their 9mms, took a rifle out for himself, and attached a scope.

DR was driving around sixty miles an hour when he topped the hill. The sun in his eyes, he lowered his visor. Ah, there it was—the helicopter hovering sideways, waiting for them. He slammed the gas pedal a split second before the helicopter passenger fired his shot. The assassin's first shot almost skimmed DR, hitting the head cushion right beside him.

Tom, seeing the bullet also hit the back seat, shuddered. He squirmed in the seat to look out the rear window. "I thought the APBs were dropped."

"These aren't cops." DR gritted his teeth. "They're Jennings's hired thugs again. They probably took Max out." He maneuvered through the light early morning traffic. Good thing this wasn't a weekday with commuter traffic.

Sam readied his pistol and took the safety off after checking his ammo. "Reminds me how we used to shoot cans in high school."

"I hope we shoot better today." DR craned around to find the bird. Up ahead was another sweeping curve. He tried to continue his acceleration through the end of the curve, coming out of it where the helicopter hovered, waiting for them.

The shooter mustn't have been ready for their speed around the corner. He fired four shots, but they all missed their targets, one striking the hood, one the top, and two the back window.

After the glass spiderwebbed, Tom used his rifle stock to pound out the window. The glass fell into the seat before he got a shot off himself, to no avail, but he continued to fire as the helicopter whirred in pursuit. Tom let off ten rounds at the bird and struck the windshield with eight shots, shattering it.

Meanwhile, DR was traveling too fast to make the next curve. The Charger sailed into the air toward the northbound lanes and landed hard in front of oncoming traffic.

Sam grabbed the handle above the passenger door, his gun falling on the floor. He scrambled for it as DR navigated against the oncoming traffic. A crossover lay a hundred and some yards ahead. DR positioned the Charger over the centerline and floored it, sideswiping several vehicles along the way. The other vehicles banged against the guardrails to avoid them.

Tom swept the broken glass off his seat and searched the sky for the bird. "Where did they go, DR?"

DR craned for a glimpse. Nothing.

Then a van tagged them on the passenger's side as DR steered across the crossover and back onto southbound lanes. He checked between mirrors and the windshield, making his calculations. "I don't know, but we've got to shoot them. They're not going to give up."

They approached a tunnel. Would the helicopter be waiting at the other end?

The windshield imploded as eight shots struck it, pieces breaking loose, one sticking in Smithers's thigh. He screamed and pushed hard back into his seat. Several of the shots hit vital components, one struck the engine's fire extinguishers, and another hit the chopper's ECLs, reducing fuel flow to the engines. Then an animated warning began: "Warning hydraulic failure, warning hydraulic failure."

Jones switched off the warning system.

"Get on them!" Smithers shouted. "We didn't come this far to stop now." He ground his teeth against the pain and slammed a fist against his unhurt thigh. Seriously, what was with a target that didn't quit?

"I can't control it. We have to put down."

Jones was right. Even Smithers could feel the wind from the rotors and the changing flight speed. But when Jones began searching out a place to land, Smithers pointed his gun at his companion and gripped the controls with his other hand. "I said get them. I'm not going to tell you again."

"You're going to get us killed. Let's go home. We can come back later." Jones shifted, but after a glance at Smithers's face, the guy must've realized better than to push it. Jones turned the bird, and they located the target.

"There they are. Get on them."

"I've got a bad feeling about this."

Ignoring him, Smithers fired ten rounds at the red Charger. The driver tried weaving, speeding up—everything. Still, several of Smithers's shots hit important targets, including a rear tire that began deflating. Another hit the gas tank, and fuel leaked on the highway.

The car hit the guardrail. Now only going thirty miles per hour, they were a sitting duck.

"Yes...yes!" Smithers gave a fist pump. "Don't stop now, Jones. We've got them right where we want them."

CHAPTER
TWENTY-FIVE

The helicopter passed over them again while positioning for the kill shots, flying out of sight for a moment. DR slammed the brakes and pulled over to the roadside. "Get your gun and get out!" He rammed open his door, his gun in hand. "They're positioning themselves for a better shot. Follow me."

Tom and Sam, unsure what he was up to, followed anyway, running as fast as they could after him across the road.

"Get behind here before they come back." DR dove behind a concrete retaining wall just in time to avoid being seen.

Without the spiderwebbed glass between them and the helicopter, he could see their assassins' determined faces. The shooter couldn't find his targets. The sun shining in his eyes as they came over the hilltop and the cold air also hindered him. "Fire away, guys. Let's take this bird down."

DR, Sam, and Tom began firing, sending twenty-seven rounds their way. Several struck the pilot's face and neck. The helicopter dipped forward as he fell on the controls, and DR's the last image of the passenger was one of unbelief and fear.

The chopper's rotor blades struck the ground, causing it to spin. Twisting metal and glass flew while it flipped out of control, right on top of the Charger as a log truck, loaded down and probably headed for a paper mill, exited the tunnel thirty yards away. Having nowhere to go, it slammed into the chopper.

The explosion scattered logs high into the sky, covering a hundred yards or more, nearly taking out DR, Sam, and Tom behind the paltry barrier. The logs blocked both the southbound and northbound lanes.

The gas on the road ignited and lit up the Charger's gas tank before a ball of fire threw the sporty car some twenty feet into the air. The helicopter wrapped around the front of the truck, which pushed it another forty yards down the road, and the chopper began to melt from the explosion's heat as the truck's front end rose in the air.

"We better get out of here." Tom stood, holding his rifle tight. "The law will be here soon, and we don't need that."

"That was one fine ride." Watching the car burn to oblivion, Sam nearly tripped.

"Let's go." DR started off. "We'll borrow a car further down past the first crossover."

Hawk-eyed drivers now sat stuck in traffic. Avoiding them, DR climbed a bank toward the southbound lanes. No reason to attract too much attention.

"Borrow another car?" Sam, walking backward, raised both palms in the air.

"Unless you want to walk." Tom rubbed his hands together to warm them. Yep, already the reality of the cold weather was coming home again.

They double-timed it to the first crossover where they spotted a car of teen boys. The boys thought it would be fun to throw half-empty bottles at the trio and edged the car toward them until they saw Tom holding his rifle.

DR grabbed the driver's door handle. It was locked, but when he nodded toward Tom, the boy opened the door. "Get out," DR ordered.

Four teens rolled out of the car, hands in the air. "Mister, don't leave us stranded."

Sam jostled around them toward the rear passenger seat. "You should've thought about that before you started throwing things at strangers. Didn't your mother teach you better?" He shook a finger at the boy in his way, then shrugged. "Don't worry. The police will be up the road in a little while. You can tell them we borrowed your car."

Tom climbed into the car. "Can you believe how brazen they were?" Then he sniffed. "And we couldn't have picked a smellier car to borrow?"

"Look what we have here?" DR held up a bag of cocaine, his foot shuffling cans and trash on the floor. "I think I know why they were so brazen."

"I hope they make it to the cops." Sam laughed.

DR turned the car around in the crossover and drove the green Equinox south toward Chicago, passing emergency vehicles racing to the accident scene. "Guess they'll have a story to tell."

At his home on the other side of the pond, Miguel shot Kim a thumbs-up, leaning against a fireplace as she played with Corey on the floor. "Laurie, what great news. I'll pass it on to Debbie and everyone here. Is Tom going to make it home for Christmas?"

"No. We decided he'd stay and help DR. If they don't do something, those children will be lost to trafficking forever, and I, for one, couldn't stand knowing we could've done something about it and didn't."

"What are they going to do?" He walked to the living room window, looking out on all the Christmas decorations and admiring his manger scene and other decorations lighting up the night. "Where are you spending your Christmas? You're welcome to celebrate with us. Debbie is here, and Lorenzo, David, and Cillia will be here. We'd love to have you join us."

"I appreciate the invitation, but the main reason I didn't travel with Tom was to look after my mom and dad. We'll have a quiet Christmas together. As for the guys, first, they have to find where the children are. Then, somehow, take them. DR is afraid they'll try to dispose of them, maybe in Lake Michigan, if they catch wind of his plan. So they have to get them all at the same time."

"Thank you for calling." Surely, DR and Tom could do it—God helping them. Miguel placed his hand on the Bible on the end table near the window, encouraging himself. He drew in a deep breath. "It's been good talking to you. And thanks for the good news. I'll pass it on. I know everyone'll be relieved their prayers were answered. When you talk to Tom again, tell him we're all over here praying for them."

"I will, Miguel. Have a merry Christmas and give everyone our love."

He laid the phone on the same table and summoned Debbie.

After a few minutes, she came down and parked herself on the floor with Kim and Corey. "Is everything all right?"

"I just got off the phone with Laurie. The guys are all right." His chest burned as he gave the good news. "The FBI talked to your friend, the congressman, and he told them everything."

Debbie let out a strangled cry. Then she sobbed, propping up on the sofa behind her, covering her face and eyes with her hands.

Kim slid over and hugged her.

"She said they're still in danger—they're going to find the kidnapped children and get them to safety somehow. We need to keep praying. It seems this Jennings fellow is a powerful man—and a lunatic." Miguel walked over to a globe on a floor stand and spun it. "By the way, Laurie said one of the children—a girl named Amal, one of three sisters—saved DR and Tom from being drowned in Lake Michigan. They took her to Greg and Penny's in Birmingham for safekeeping."

Kim smiled. "Isn't God amazing?"

Debbie took a deep breath. "God? What does God have to do with anything? I don't see God in any of this."

Jennings slammed a fist against his desk, the cool dark room doing nothing to calm the raging heat lighting up his insides. How could Ray and Hughes still be alive? His friends at Circle weren't happy with the situation either, having called a board meeting without him and discussed their options.

"You had one job—*one*. Make POTUS look bad, simple, straightforward, and you failed," the caller said.

"I agree. It was simple. But somehow the man gets free every time, and now I haven't heard from Smithers and company since yesterday morning."

"That's another reason I'm calling. They are dead. Leave the doctor alone. Make POTUS look bad. Who cares about the doctor? We don't."

His heart jolted. "What do you mean dead?" He swallowed the last drink in his glass and reached to pour another. "How do you know?"

"How do you think I know? Because we control most of the media. That's how. The police in Wisconsin tracked two helicopters to them. They leased them in Indiana. One of them was abandoned in a clearing in the forest outside Eagle River. Two bodies were recovered, probably O'Connor and Manning. The second helicopter found a way to wrap itself around a log truck just outside of Eagle River."

Silence.

"It seems your doctor friend and his pals were nowhere to be found at the accident scene, what little was left of everything. But they were in Eagle River—right at the hospital when Smithers killed the congressman."

News of the kill hadn't reached Jennings. He slumped, some rigid tension draining. At least, he had one thing to be happy about. "Don't worry. I'll tie off the loose ends. This won't happen again."

"You've played around with this long enough. The other members aren't too happy about losing Smithers and company. They've always been a capable and invaluable partner. Either kill the doctor now or be finished with this thing!"

The phone went dead.

Jennings slouched back into his leather office chair, swiveling to look out his window. *Who are you, Dr. Ray, and why are you so hard to kill?*

Knowing the answer in his heart, he shuddered, feeling destiny closing in.

FBI Agent Larson drove his bureau-issued SUV to the Nichols's and rang the bell to enter the property.

"How may I help you?" that obnoxious butler answered.

"FBI Agent Larson. I'm here with Agent Riddlehour to see Mr. or Mrs. Nichols. We were here earlier." How he hated dealing with staff. He shrugged at Riddlehour.

"I'm sorry, agent." The man's voice carried a well-practiced and grating drone. "I've been informed to tell you they're going to be out of town through Christmas."

Larson shook his head. A likely story. "We'd like to come in and look around. We have reason to believe a missing child may be on the premises."

"I'm sorry, sir. I'm not at liberty to admit you unless you have a search warrant. In that case, please hold the warrant up to the video camera."

"That won't be necessary. We'll come by later." He backed the Suburban away from the gate, stopping. "I don't believe a word of it. Do you?"

Riddlehour shrugged. "Let's go around the property. Maybe there's a way in out back. I want that bonus. It'll really make my Christmas bright." He pointed at a dirt road going around the outside of the Nichols property. "Let's see where this goes."

Larson followed it down and around the meadow behind the Nichols home. It was around four p.m. and warm, the sun in full array. Spotting a gate behind a horse barn on the rear of the property, he stopped.

Since the fence was chained with a lock, Riddlehour took out a set of bolt cutters from the back tool set and set to work to cut the chain. Moments later, they entered and pulled the gate closed behind them, not wanting to let out the horses.

"Do you hear that?" Riddlehour peeked around the edge of the barn. A young girl splashed in the swimming pool, no one else around. "Let me see that picture."

Larson fished inside his jacket pocket, brought a picture out of a young Arab-looking girl, and handed it to Riddlehour who now had his binoculars trained on the swimming pool.

"Bingo. They lied. She's here—and in the pool alone. Let's grab her." He stepped out, then stopped.

"What's the matter?"

Riddlehour took a deep breath and nodded toward the horses midway in the pasture. "Horses have always freaked me out. I got hurt when I was young because of a colt. Ever since, I get the willies near them."

"Come on. Man up. You're in the FBI, for heaven's sake."

"It's going to take God to get me by them too." Riddlehour, now whiter than Wisconsin snow, stepped out, Larson following.

Larson passed his partner before reaching the horses, helping him by them, and closed in on the pool, now a mere fifty yards away. The horses began to walk, then ran to the other side of the pasture. Stopping, listening closely, he held his hand out to halt Riddlehour.

"What are you stopping for? It's just the girl singing."

But Larson stayed crouched, hand still extended. "Turn around, run." When Larson stood and ran himself, Riddlehour followed.

Soon it became apparent to Riddlehour why they were running, a large ATV with two men on board came roaring by the swimming pool, catching up to them as a warning shot was fired. The agents slowed and stopped, just twenty or so yards from the barn and possibly safety.

"Drop your weapons and put up your hands."

Larson complied, then Riddlehour.

"You're going to be in big trouble." Trying to get a peek at his captors, Larson went to turn. "That girl belongs to a powerful man."

"Stand still." Mr. Nichols pulled the ATV around them after Johnson got off.

Larson cringed. The front of the house had a security gate. "How stupid are we? They had an alarm on the rear gate too." Closing his eyes, he exhaled, disgusted with himself and Riddlehour.

"Of course there's an alarm. Who would have a security gate and leave the back door open? Now march, go into the barn. Johnson, pick up their weapons."

Inside Larson stiffened as Mr. Nichols tied him up, pulled his ropes tighter, then jammed a gag in his mouth.

Mr. Nichols clamped a hand on Johnson's shoulder. "Come on, Johnson. Let's go figure out what to do with these losers."

Johnson laughed. "What a day! This wasn't in the job description."

Man, the green Equinox stank, smelling like cigarettes and filth. With the temperature outside in the mid-teens, DR resisted the urge to roll down the window. It must've been the boys' party vehicle. But it ran, and they were making great time toward home. Needing an escape from the smell and a bathroom break, he pulled into the Illinois welcome center.

"Ah, fresh air." After getting out of the car, Tom stretched his frame.

"Not a moment too soon, either. How can anyone stand to ride in such stench?" DR tossed Sam the keys.

"Druggies can do anything. Carla taught me that." Sam hustled up the sidewalk toward the men's room. The snow and cold hadn't stopped the holiday traffic, so the center was packed, even without any traffic from Eagle River.

A pretty brunette reached out and grabbed Sam by his arm, twisting him around. Their faces came within inches of each other. "Hey, stuck-up. Aren't you going to say hello?"

"Hello, beautiful. Imagine running into you all the way out here. What are you doing in these parts?" Sam's face glowed, and he kissed her right on the lips. "How's that for a hello?"

"Wow. That's what I call a hello. Who are these handsome gentlemen with you?" She tilted her head, not missing much of either one of them.

"Megan, Megan Blackmoor, this is Dr. Steven Ray and our good friend and accomplice, Tom Hughes of London. He flew over for an international marksman competition. You remember DR, don't you? Excuse me. That's just what the good doctor goes by now. Remember Stevie, Stevie Ray?" Sam's eyes slid downward, taking snapshots of the woman. "He went to school with us."

"Oh, I remember Stevie. I think every girl in high school remembers Stevie." She moved over to DR and wrapped her arms around him, closing her eyes and smelling his essence. Then she opened them wide and stepped back. "Let me see you." She spun him around, ogling him.

"This can't be the shy girl from Albion Junior High. Megan, how have you been?" He finished turning. "Pretty as ever, I see."

"It's a long story. I'd love to tell you. You boys want to grab a cup of coffee?" She looked him over again. "I know a place a half mile up the road. My treat."

"Sounds nice." DR pulled at the back of his hair and slanted a glance Sam's way. Yep, his friend seemed to get his feathers all ruffled. "We need to go inside. Meet you there?"

"Sure, Sam knows the place. See you in ten." She strutted down the sidewalk, providing them with something to remember, then glanced back over her shoulder, smiling.

When Sam parked at the coffee shop ten minutes later, Megan had already gotten a booth in the back corner. "Over here, boys." She stood and waved, then got out of the booth, and allowed Sam to sit beside her. But her focus was on the man across from her, DR.

"So, Stevie—I mean, *DR*?—a few days ago, I heard over the radio police were looking for you and Sam. What was that all about?" She placed her left hand on the table, tapping her fingers.

"Just someone setting us up and trying to kill us. Nothing new—lately." DR shrugged. She didn't have a ring. "I'm surprised you're not married, beautiful woman like yourself."

"That's a long story too. Maybe we could talk about it later. How about you? Are you married?"

Sam squirmed, getting left behind and obviously not liking it. "DR, did I tell you Megan and I dated for a while?"

She put her elbow on the table and propped up her forehead, looking at the table for a moment. "Yeah, but it didn't go anywhere. So we stayed friends. Right, Sam?"

The server came over and took their order, hastening away to get their coffee.

"Well..." Sam dragged the word out, then winked, perhaps wanting to shut the door on any other suitors. "Maybe we'll try again. Right, Meg?"

DR's brows rose. "If I remember correctly, you used to hate being called Meg. Just goes to show how we all change with a few years."

"That hasn't changed." Her eyes lasered Sam, and her nose scrunching. "He thinks it's funny. Just one of many reasons coming back to me why we stopped dating."

"Where do you live now, Megan?" As Sam's face reddened, DR changed the subject. "Do you still live in Albion?"

"Nope. I haven't lived there since high school. Like you, besides Sam and Carla, most of us moved away—well, Carla's moved away too, now." She glanced sideways at Sam, the warmth for him no longer in her eyes. "I live in Hastings now, near the Thornapple River. I love it there, especially in the spring. How about you, DR? Do you live close by?" She seemed to be talking with her eyes too.

"I live on Wall Lake." He stretched his arms out on the booth behind him, thinking. "Megan, I have a proposition for you."

Her eyes enlarged as the corners of her lips drew up. "Yes, the answer is yes."

"I haven't asked yet." He shook a finger at her. From Sam's expression, the guy would like her to respond to him in that manner. "We borrowed the car outside and would like to get rid of it. It smells, and the cops are probably looking for it by now."

"Whoa. Hold up." She held a hand before her. "You're in a *stolen* car?"

Tom put his left index finger to his lips. "Shh...We like the term borrowed." He made air quotes around the preferred word. "Besides, the boys in it started throwing trash at us, so we borrowed their car."

"The way I figure it, Megan, you're heading our way. Maybe you can stop in for a minute or two, and we can catch up on old times." DR tilted his head, raising his left brow.

"You're just going to leave the car here?"

"No, of course not." He nodded toward the video cameras. "We'll move it over near the interstate ramp so no one will see us with it."

"Okay, I'll do it." She patted DR's hand. "Let's finish our coffee and get out of here before you're caught with a hot car."

CHAPTER
TWENTY-SIX

The yellow school bus returned to the LMMC Saturday afternoon. Senator Carl Brummengarten, against his wishes, was there to inspect the children and help their caretakers get them back into their perspective living quarters.

"Let's get this done as quickly as possible. Were there any troublemakers?" Benett asked, putting the final lock on the cage in the middle trailer.

"Just the one they call Habiba." Pointing at the last cage, Fast Larry widened his stance as the children tried on their new "uniforms" for New Year's Eve. "She doesn't speak English, so you have to use the language app."

"I know a language she'll understand." Benett headed her way.

Senator Carl put out his arm, stopping him. "Give them a break. They're not animals."

Benett growled but obeyed.

"Did anyone ever find the girl Amal who went missing a week ago?" Carl looked from caregiver to caregiver, the job title Jennings gave them. Each of them shook their head. He sighed. Maybe the FBI would find her. Smithers and company certainly wouldn't. "Keep your eyes open.

Something tells me we're going to have some excitement before New Year's."

"Carl, what about the school bus? You want I should return it?"

"No, we may need it for Fast Larry to transport them to the clubhouse if the temperature drops."

The man looked like a hardened criminal. Carl would have to check his rap sheet before leaving him alone with the girls.

"We got this. Carl, why don't you go home?" Benett made eye contact with Fast Larry.

Home sounded good. "I'm home for Christmas and New Year's, so you'll be seeing a lot of me and my boat. Remember what Jennings said would happen if any of the entertainers are harmed. Jennings has a shorter fuse since Max is dead." Carl suppressed a shudder. "He's questioning everyone's loyalty, including mine after Max left the plantation seeking calmer waters. You've got my number if you need anything."

Carl paused at the window as he walked by outside. Benett stood at Habiba's cage, raking a police baton on the bars. The girl was crying, but she wouldn't bend.

On the drive back, DR spoke on the phone with Greg about the rogue FBI agents. They'd take the agents back to their headquarters and leave them tied up in their vehicle with a note so the agents' families didn't suffer at Christmastime. That would be best for Greg and Penny too.

Megan reached the long driveway to DR's home on Wall Lake, so he wished Greg and Penny well. Megan let out a low whistle and waved at the spread.

Tom, sitting in the back seat with Sam, scooted toward DR's seat. "I've got to hand it to you, DR, like your yacht, this is spectacular." His brow rose, and lips stretched into a quirky grin. "I'll bet you've been skinny-dipping more than a time or two in the lake, huh?"

"Really, Tom?" Sam huffed. "Not in the presence of a lady."

"Why are you Americans all so uptight?" Tom cuffed Sam's arm. "I'm just kidding. But it does sound like fun, doesn't it?"

"Relax, boys." Megan parked her car. "I can take care of myself."

"Well, thankfully, no one burned it down." DR slid from his seat and stretched. The lake shimmered in the evening light as he strolled to the front door, not letting go of any secrets and thankful he didn't have a pet. That could've been bad.

After unlocking the door, he switched the lights on to welcome everyone inside. "Take your coats off and get comfortable. Tom, just your coat." He chuckled. "Just your coat, Tom."

"I see I'm not the only comedian here."

As his guest warmed up, DR righted pictures overturned in the obvious search of his home. Finding nothing visibly missing, he then ensured the others were comfortable. First, he started a fire in the front room fireplace. Then he turned up the furnace to complement the fire and put on a pot of coffee.

"DR, you wouldn't happen to have a bottle or two of the delightful sangria from the cruise, would you?" Tom eased himself onto an ottoman.

"As a matter of fact, we're in luck." DR stood in the kitchen archway, then leaned, and stretched on the frame, feeling Megan's focus on him. "Miguel sent me a case of 'Kim's favorite,' just last week. Megan, Sam— would you two care for a glass?"

"I'm game. Megan, you game to try a glass?" Sam headed behind the kitchen island to give DR a hand.

DR and Gail had entertained infrequently, but he loved the fact that here they could be a part of the conversation while pouring drinks or preparing meals.

"Sure. But just one. I still have to drive home." Megan walked over to the picture window. "It's starting to snow. But isn't that nice? The kids will love having a white Christmas. How about you, Tom? Do you like a white Christmas?"

"Haven't seen many of those. The snow doesn't usually accumulate on the ground, and it only snows maybe once or twice a year, if at all, in London."

"So you never built a snowman or had a snowball fight as a child?"

"Here you are, everyone." DR interrupted their conversation, allowing Sam to slide by him carrying some of the wine. "Four Kim's Favorites, along with a bowl of pepper jack cheese and a pack of herb crackers to bring out the berry in the sangria. Dig in, everyone."

DR took a place on the red chenille sofa. Megan joined him. Sam set the cheese and crackers on the coffee table between them and took a place on the leather love seat, Gail's favorite piece, a deep burgundy complementing the sofa perfectly.

"No snowman or snowball fights? That explains why you were doing all that skinny-dipping." DR couldn't help laughing at his own joke, patting the sofa between himself and Megan in fun.

"So what do you do on all those foggy winter days, when you can't skinny-dip?" She set her sangria on the table and dipped a cracker in the delicious cheese.

"Ohh, I'm sorry. Didn't I tell you? Tom and his wife are best-selling authors in London." DR inhaled the sangria's heady fragrance.

"Really? That explains the overactive imagination. What genre do you write?" Megan's eyes enlarged, and her mouth opened as she dipped her head. "I love to read."

Sam's eyes went beady. He stretched out on the love seat and propped up an elbow to follow the conversation.

"We write suspense thrillers and the occasional romantic thriller. What do you like to read?"

"Basically, everything you said, though I do like a good young adult fantasy now and then." She scooted forward, her skirt catching on the linen cushion. "What's something I might know of yours?"

"*Why Ginny Ran.* It's a romantic comedy. Not really our cup of tea, but it caught fire. One of those influencer whales read it, and the next thing you know, it was a bestseller. Comedy is hard for me to write, but Laurie, my wife, she can put anything into words on a page." After finishing his sangria, he held the glass up and looked inside. Then he stood up. "Time for another. Anyone need anything while I'm up?"

"I'll have another glass." Sam held his glass up to Tom. Poor guy looked ready to pass out from exhaustion. It'd been a long three days.

"Me too." Megan handed over her glass, then cuddled back into the soft chenille. "How about you, DR? Want another glass?" Her eyes sparkled. With her long curly brown hair hanging back over her shoulders, she looked gorgeous.

"I... better not. Not just yet, but thanks. I'm a lightweight." Looking at her, he shuddered, and his granddad's words echoed in his head, telling him: "Stevie, always make sure you're filled with a good spirit and not the kind you drink." Michigan Strong, Mom called it.

An hour later, Sam excused himself after asking DR where he could sleep. DR showed him to one of the four bedrooms, all with some sort of view of the lake. Then he showed Tom where he could sleep as well, whenever he was ready.

Soon, it was just Megan and him, and DR felt the same struggle he imagined Debbie had felt for him. Glad he'd only had two glasses—a third and...who knows?

Senator Carl Brummengarten left the LMMC around eight o'clock Saturday evening, not ready to go straight home, needing to sort this all out in his mind. Maybe a little fresh air would do him good. After checking the fuel gauge on *Providence*, he figured he'd top off the tank before going home. By now, his wife would be a little more than perturbed by his long absence.

"Max, I wished I'd helped you. I didn't think you'd ever run. I'm sorry." He tipped his head up toward the full moon, the breeze pushed against the fifty-foot vessel. His heart pounded. Now, he'd have the chance to walk in the late congressman's shoes. He was supposed to be his friend, but he didn't take the pressure Max expressed seriously enough. And now... here he was.

He pulled into his favorite marina to fuel up. Then he frowned at an acquaintance of Max's. He'd hoped to avoid the fellow, but couldn't since the man saw him coming.

"Evening, Senator. What brings you out so late? I'm used to seeing the congressman here about this time, but not you." The unshaven and raggedy-dressed man caught his dock line to help him tie up.

"I'm lucky. I get to take Max's place at the LMMC."

"Terrible thing that happened to Max, and so young too. Heart just gave up. Just goes to show you never know what's going to happen to you. Fill 'er up?"

"Sure. Yes, you never know what's going to happen." His hands gripped his hips, his feet spread wide, and he rocked off his heels. Then his head tilted again toward the moon and stars. He knew what happened to Max. Was he next? That was the question he wanted answered. He handed the man a fifty. "Keep the change."

"Thank you, Senator." He saluted Carl with the fifty. "Have a merry Christmas."

Carl waved as he boarded his boat. As he set course for home, *Providence*, the name of the boat, wasn't lost on him.

Now that Sam and Tom had retired for the night, DR shifted as Megan became more interested in him, in their past, and in what the night might hold. She'd just finished her third glass of sangria and appeared full of a different kind of spirit. Soon, it could be doing all of her talking. Yet he couldn't deny how he felt. He'd always been attracted to her, even as a young boy.

"Can I ask you something, Steven? You don't mind if I call you that while your friends aren't here, do you?" She crossed her legs and sat facing him on the sofa.

"No, that's fine. I just prefer DR, kind of like how you don't like being called Meg." But his reply seemed to zoom right over her head.

"What happened to you?" She pressed her lips together and leaned closer, eyes narrowing, arms crossed around her chest.

"What do you mean? What happened to me?" He knew.

"I used to have the biggest crush on you when we were eleven. I thought you liked me too. Then one day, you... just stopped coming around. At church, you stayed to yourself. After school, you ran home. It was almost like someone else had snatched your body." She slouched back against the couch, clearly feeling no pain. "I wondered for the longest time if I'd done something wrong."

"No. Megan, you didn't do anything wrong. I liked you too." Realizing how vulnerable she was, he had to look away. "Something happened that I didn't know how to deal with. Still don't, but I'm better. A little forgiveness goes a long ways."

"Remember the day we were baptized? I was so excited. I only did it because you did. What were we? Ten?" She picked up her empty glass and tilted it for the last drop. "I would've gone up later anyway, but sharing that moment with you was incredible—coming up out of the water together. That day I felt like I'd set in motion a life to glorify God."

"I remember how cold the river was. How many of us kids? Four?" He closed his eyes, remembering her, how she looked—happy, innocent, and free of shame. Why couldn't he ever feel that way?

"Why did you go to Spain for college? Were you running from something?"

"I was running *toward* something, only I didn't know it at the time. I met Gail at the Dukes School." He locked his hands together. He'd removed the wedding band when he fell in love with Debbie, but still, it remained there, in his soul.

"I saw her picture when she passed." She pointed toward Gail's portrait leaning against a wall. "She was beautiful. I cried for you."

"Forget it. That was a while ago." No reason to mention he'd just been engaged. He didn't want to go down another dirt road. "How about you? You ever been married?"

"Yes, I married Barry Moore. You remember him, don't you? He was the tight end on the football team in high school." She poured herself another glass. "We were married for three and a half years."

"Vaguely. Um, are you sure you want another? Would you like a bottle of water?" He waved toward the kitchen. Huh, beyond the window, the snow was falling hard.

"I'm just going to nurse it. Anyway, long story short, my best friend, Bethany Mitchell, and I grew up together, tighter than two could ever be, or so I thought. We used to share everything—sweaters, hats, whatever." She gulped more sangria. "Then, one day, I drove over to her house in the middle of the day to retrieve the dish I'd left at church that she'd picked up for me. I found out we were also sharing my husband."

"Oh, wow. That must have been rough." DR stole the glass from her protesting hand and set it on the table.

Shuddering, she blinked big eyes up at him. "I lost my husband and my best friend in the whole world. I was devastated, especially when they moved in together." She reached for the glass. "They're married now."

"Ouch. I'm sorry, Megan." He tried to slow her hand down. "Are you sure you want another drink? You've already had three-plus glasses."

"I'm sure. It will give me courage."

"Courage? What do you need courage for?"

"I want to know what happened to you, why you stopped coming around. Maybe thinking tonight we could rekindle a few of those feelings." She put her hand on his lap, and her eyes seemed to illuminate, staring deep into his soul.

"Megan, it's the alcohol in you talking." He slid her hand off his leg and closed his eyes, every pore in him crying out for more.

"Maybe so, but I wondered about you a lot when we were young. I want to know. That's all." She swayed her shoulders and upper body, enticing him. "Don't you want to know too?"

Then she stood, towering over him. She straddled him and cupped his face with her hands. He didn't fight back.

When their lips met, a rush of hot blood flowed all throughout his body. Oh, how he'd missed this! Then he jerked his mouth free, eased her hands from his face, and pushed back. "Stop, Megan. I want this more than you can ever imagine, but it's not going to happen. I can't."

He nudged her to her feet, and she sat rejected beside him, tears flowing. "What is wrong with me, with you?"

"Megan, it's just the alcohol talking." He huffed a deep breath, but couldn't steady himself. "Look, we haven't seen each other for fifteen years almost. You don't want me. You're just lonely."

"No one is perfect. Maybe I am lonely, but not tonight. What's wrong with having a little fun? Everybody else is. Besides, God will forgive us." She raised her wobbly chin, reviving hope.

"Why don't you go out with Sam? He likes you." Why had he been taught to live Michigan Strong? Seemed most of his struggles involved denying himself the pleasures everyone else exploited.

"Sam?" She propped her head up on her knees, face to the floor. "We went out a couple of times. He was okay. But I ran into Carla—you know she's a druggie now, right? Well, anyway, she told me how Sam changed after they married, how he became a control freak, especially after their third child. How one thing led to another, one day he hit her, and that was the last straw."

"Sam? Sam did that?" DR briefly closed his eyes, tilted his head, and twisted his lips in a grimace.

"Yep, that's what she said." Her eyes admired his physicality. "But you're wrong. I do want you, so if that's not going to happen, I better be going home." She stood, then stumbled, and flopped back onto the sofa.

"Megan, you're not fit to drive in this snow. Come on. Let me help you to the bedroom."

"Now, those are the words I want to hear," she mumbled, fully intoxicated.

CHAPTER
TWENTY-SEVEN

The next morning, DR entered the kitchen, trying to stretch out the sleeplessness.

Tom, pouring himself a cup of coffee, hoisted the pot. "Care for a cup of joe, lover boy?"

"I'd love one." DR parked himself on a padded high-back stool at the island, tracing the pattern with his finger while waiting. Still trying to figure out how to deal with last night.

"How do you take your coffee?" Tom turned, waiting for the answer. Already dressed, he looked like he'd been up for hours.

DR, still in PJs, slumped further against the counter. "There's sweet cream in the fridge. Thanks."

"Got it. Here you are." Tom handed over the coffee and creamer. "So how did things go last night? She seemed into you, and I think Sam's mad."

"Thanks." DR saluted Tom with the cup. "Interested is an understatement." He tested a sip. "I see you used my recipe. Thanks."

"She'll get over it." Tom claimed the chair next to DR and swiveled it to him. "Besides, when was the last time you saw her? I wouldn't lose any sleep over it. But she sure is a looker."

"Yes, she is.... That she is. A good person too. I just hate how things ended."

"How what things ended?" Sam interrupted, tiptoeing across the cold tile floor.

"Nothing. Just talking about last night. It's a shame about Megan's marriage." DR offered Sam the seat on his other side and slid the coffee pot and a cup in front of the seat. "How many times did you two go out?"

"Just a few, several years back. But we decided to be friends, something about how she and Carla used to be friends in school and she didn't want to cross the line." Sam sniffed the coffee, then pushed it away. "Little strong for my taste. Why? What happened last night?"

"We talked for a couple of hours, some of it good, some, uh, not so much. She had too much to drink to drive in the snow, so she spent the night." When Sam's eyes widened and his jaw dropped, DR held up a hand. "In the spare bedroom—alone."

Two hours later, Megan started stirring around in the guest bathroom, probably nursing a pounding sangria headache, but hopefully not like the ones he would get.

"Good morning, sleepyhead." Sam rushed to her rescue with a cup of coffee. "Did you sleep okay?"

"I think so. How much did it snow overnight?" Taking the coffee, she crossed to the window overlooking the lake before she settled on the love seat and pressed her free hand to her head. "Is there any creamer?"

"I'll get that." DR strode to the refrigerator and returned with two types.

"It snowed a couple of inches. Nothing major." Sam slid onto the cushion beside her. "I was surprised to see you this morning." Back on the hunt, he propped up on his right elbow, seeming to admire her.

"DR was gracious enough to put me up in a spare bedroom." Her eyes, appearing none too friendly, fixed on DR.

"Anytime, I was happy to have you." *Whoa. Did I say that?*

Tom chuckled and turned his back to the trio while she glared, her face red and Sam seemed oblivious to everything.

"Yeah... thanks for *having me.*" She huffed, then blew the steam off her coffee.

The phone rang, giving him a reprieve. DR answered his brother's call and listened to his plans for their Christmas get-together, tomorrow being Christmas. During the phone call, Megan finished her coffee and her conversation with Sam and Tom. Now, she was throwing on her coat to leave.

DR held up his left hand and finished his call. "Megan, it was good seeing you again. Hopefully, we'll bump into each other again soon." He went to hug her goodbye, but she turned away. So he just pulled at the back of his hair. "Um, I hope you have a merry Christmas."

"You too. Thanks for everything." Her words were an icy-cold slap. "Bye, Sam. Tom, nice to meet you." She waved at them, shooting DR a woolly eye. Someone rang the doorbell as Megan opened the door, leaving in a huff.

Willie had to make a quickstep aside to keep from getting bowled over. Willie's brow arched, seeming to question the pretty woman, disheveled from spending the night, leaving in a hurry, the snow and the woman's heels making the walk look difficult.

"Willie, hi." Embarrassed, DR tried to cover it up. "What brings you here?"

"I'm sorry. I didn't mean to interrupt anything." She kept her back to him, still watching the woman. "I wanted to drop this off for Debbie...." At last, she faced him. "You haven't heard from her, have you?"

"No. But I talked to the friend she's spending Christmas with." He stepped aside to allow her in. "Won't you come in?"

"I can't. I have other stops. Tell her hi when you see her." She froze, seeming unsure.

"Willie, thanks again for allowing us to stay at your place the other day. I appreciate it, and I will make it up to you, I promise." He hugged her, but she stood stiff, surprised, arms out wide. "Merry Christmas."

"So it would appear. Thanks... Merry Christmas."

Churchgoers and last-minute Christmas shoppers packed Marcie's Place, all making the coffee shop their priority to start Christmas Eve off right. Rachael was running around serving her area when Willie entered.

She rushed over. "I'm sorry. I'm not going to be able to take my break now. We're too busy."

"That's okay. I'm going to find somewhere to sit and get something to eat. We can talk later." Willie scanned the place for a table while Rachael went back to work. All were taken, but one table only had a single patron at it—the lady who'd just left DR's home. Willie headed over to her.

"All the tables are taken, and I was wondering if I might be able to sit with you?" She squinted her left eye and gritted her teeth, pleading her case.

The lady arched a brow. "You're the lady I almost knocked down at Steven's home, aren't you?"

Willie cringed. "Guilty as charged." She extended her hand. "I'm Willie. I work with Steven's, uh, DR's brother at WREAL radio here in town."

"You probably think I'm a nutjob." The woman held out her hand. "I'm Megan. I went to high school with DR, only he was Stevie back then or Steven."

Rachael's coworker brought Megan's breakfast bagel and coffee and took Willie's order.

Megan's eyes lit up as she bit into the bagel. "Um, this is delicious. I've got to come back here."

"You haven't been here before?" Looking the pretty lady over, Willie planted both hands on the table. "Where do you live, if you don't mind?"

"I live in Hastings, not too far to come for something this delicious." Megan waved with the bagel, chewing while talking. "Pardon me, but I'm starving. DR had some pastries, but I had to get out. I made a fool of myself last night."

"I didn't mean to pry." But Megan had obviously been crying. "Are you okay?"

"I hadn't seen him for fifteen years or more, but I felt like the same schoolgirl who had a huge crush on him." Megan dropped her bagel onto its doily and stirred her coffee. "I must be lonelier than I thought."

"I know all about that. Loneliness has become my middle name—and I found myself crushing on him too." Willie patted Megan's hand. "There's nothing to be ashamed of."

"I tried to seduce him." Hanging her head, Megan sheepishly peered up at Willie.

"Well, that explains a couple of things. He didn't respond, did he?"

"I've always wondered what he's like. I even got baptized at the same time as him, just to share the experience with him. I would've eventually anyway—got baptized, that is. I'll never forget that day—the best day ever." A fake laugh tried to conceal her pain. "But months later, something must have happened. He stopped coming around me and the other kids, at school and at church. He was never the same. Still isn't."

"Wait a minute." Willie scooted closer, the tabletop pressing into her middle. "Are you telling me DR—Steven—was baptized?"

"Yes. Why?" Megan popped the last bagel bite into her mouth and swirled the dregs of her coffee while glancing at the glass display case, probably pondering another goodie.

"That means he used to be Christian."

"Sure. Yeah. He always came to church every Sunday. Wednesday nights too, at least back then. His mom and dad are really into it."

"Well, you shouldn't feel bad. You're not the first woman who he's not slept with. His fiancée just broke up with him after he proposed, because he wanted to wait." Willie fiddled with her blouse cuff, not ready to piece together her own feelings. "That's the kind of man a woman should want. At least, that's how I feel." She shuddered DR was saved? *DR was saved! We're not unequally yoked!*

"Believe me, I get that. But I've been married before, so what's the harm? Everybody else is having fun. Why shouldn't I? It's not like I do that sort of thing all the time."

"Debbie said the same thing, about being married." The server delivered Willie's food, carefully sliding everything on the table. Willie rubbed her hands together, ready to tear into it.

"Who's Debbie?"

"His fiancée, ex-fiancée for now. He offered to get married the next day, but something broke inside her, something made her lose her priorities. Now, she's spending Christmas in Italy."

Megan ordered one more cup of coffee, maybe trying to wash away the headache and the memory of her great failure. "I don't know how to feel. I'm glad now nothing happened, but also disappointed nothing did. Does that make sense?"

Willie sank back in her seat, her eyes opening more than ever to her own possibilities. "More than you'll ever know."

By eleven a.m. Sunday, Christmas Eve, DR, Tom, and Sam had made their plan. Tomorrow was Christmas, and the children weren't going to spend it in a cage. Not if they had anything to say about it. They had one clue, the matches from the *Lucky Lucie*. The cover advertised a club in downtown Chicago, The Gauntlet Men's Club.

DR stood by the island. "So the rental company is going to deliver us a Jeep Commander around one. If we hurry, we can drive there in around two and a half hours or so, and the club opens at two. We can find out at least by four o'clock where they are, if we're lucky and play our cards right." Scribbling on a sheet of paper, he paused. What an uncertain plan, especially since they didn't even know where the children were.

"I just hope they're somewhere we can get to them." Tom leaned over to look at DR's drawing of the LMMC trailers. "If they're at the Gauntlet, we'll have to draw up another plan."

Sam slunk back into the love seat, locked his hands behind his head, and scowled at the fresh snow beyond the window. "Watching all those thriller movies, I always thought it would be so cool to do something like this. But I've changed my mind. It's borderline insanity in real life. I guess that's what puts the thrill in it."

They filled up on frozen pizza and sodas waiting for their Jeep. The delivery agent arrived right on time. And after the long drive to Gauntlet Men's Club, they began to follow the plan, for better or worse.

Inside the club door, a tattooed goon took their twenty-dollar cover charges, covering for slow drinkers. About twenty-five tables each had at least four chairs. Girls in various stages of dress cavorted with the two chrome poles on the stage beside the bar, while six men and a woman drank and got rowdy.

As they made their way to a corner table, out of the way and in the back, Sam tripped over a chair, watching the stage over his shoulder.

"Sam, stay focused." Tom chuckled at his new friend.

"What do you think I'm trying to do?" Sam shoved the chair out of his way. "I've got twenty dollars invested."

Sitting so they could watch the entire club and the stage, they waited for their server.

Soon, a pretty redhead in what must've been the club uniform twisted her way over for their drink order. "What would you gentleman like to drink?"

Tom ordered, then Sam, both nonalcoholic.

DR eyed her name tag. "*Bri*"—how appropriately named!—"we're actually on duty. The boss sent us to make sure the children were okay."

She perked up, tilting her head. "Are you here for Mr. Jennings?"

"Yep." DR drummed his hands on the table. "He wanted me to make sure everything was cool."

"They bused them out last night. Didn't think I'd ever say it, but I'm glad they came and got them. What a big pain in the butt. What do you want to drink?"

"I'll have what they're having."

She left, twisting the same way she came. Sam shoved himself upright in his seat, not missing a single step.

"Okay, we'll drink our ten-dollar Cokes and get out of here. Looks like our plan just might have a chance."

They waited on their drinks, taking everything in for clues.

Bri returned, one of the dancers making her way back too.

DR pulled out a fifty-dollar bill, handed it to Bri, and held his hand up to tell her to keep it. Then he followed through on a whim. "Bri, have you seen Shortman lately?"

"Not so much lately. He's only coming in on Wednesday's now. Ever since Cindy got promoted to Jennings's LA club. He's not too bright. He thought Cindy liked him. But she's a professional, and she just did her job well. I guess that's why she's in LA and I'm still here." She shrugged, then twirled a hunk of hair around her finger, one glittery nail flashing. "Anyway, Shortman usually spent half his paycheck on her, never getting more than a kiss. Someone shot him in the leg, and he's playing it for everything it's worth."

"Thanks, Bri. Merry Christmas."

After leaving the club, DR drove toward the LMMC.

Tom jittered in the front passenger seat. "Why did you ask about Shortman?"

"I don't know. It just came up. The club doesn't shut down until eight o'clock. We'd better check first thing to see if the children are in their cages or the club. Then we'll have to wait until closing time."

The only vehicle they could find to transport all the children earlier was a box truck. Though unideal, it would have to suffice. DR dropped Sam off at the rental station, and they met again outside the club fence. Luckily, one of the neighborhood's club members was hosting his friends, and the gate was unattended. When DR punched in the code from earlier, 2580, the gate swung open.

He drove to the far corner of the property and down an incline to hide their movements from the club and cameras. Then he parked beside the school bus, Sam parking the truck beside him.

Tom climbed out of the Jeep and jerked his thumb at the bus. "Wonder if the keys are in it?"

"Let's check it out. It would be better than the truck." Following Sam, Tom worked the bus doors open. "There must be a secret to getting them to open easier."

"It's just because it's an older bus. The newer ones have a key and a pull handle." Sam climbed inside and switched on a flashlight. "We're in luck. The key is in the ignition. We should just take this." He turned the ignition on to check the fuel. "It's got over half a tank of fuel. That ought to get us to DR's house. Want to warm it up?" Sam shone the light in DR's face until DR pushed Sam's arm down.

"Easy with the light." DR slammed his eyelids closed tight, trying to get his pupils to refocus after being hit with the light. "Let's check the trailers out first."

"Sorry."

"Let's do this." Tom pulled his pistol and waved it to get them to draw theirs as well. Then he stormed into the middle trailer, Sam and DR clomping at his heels.

Two girls let out a bloodcurdling scream. Thankfully, they were too far from the club to be heard. Tom held his finger to his lips, quieting the two girls locked in their cages.

Tom and DR recognized the girls from the orphanage. "It's them all right." DR nodded. "I remember these two."

"Good. Let's get them on the bus." Sam shook the cage door, looking for the key.

The girl in the other cage pointed to a table along the opposite wall.

Speaking their native language, Arabic, DR told them what was happening and their plan. Once released, the girls wrapped their arms around DR and Sam. Both began to cry and shake, petrified, but obviously overcome with joyous relief.

DR consoled the girl named Tahira, a fourteen-year-old. "You're not spending Christmas in a cage. I promise."

CHAPTER
TWENTY-EIGHT

The LMMC Christmas Eve party was winding down. Already most guests had left the property. Now DR crouched with Sam and Tom hidden by the trailers as some men in the club—"caregivers" Tahira said they were called—began tying the performers together with nylon cord by their wrists.

"That's so they can't separate from the others," Tahira whispered in Arabic. "But Habiba said she had a plan. She's coordinated it with most of the others. Once they're all outside and walking back to the trailers, they'll each cut themselves free in the dark, then all at once, run for the open gate."

DR squeezed his teeth together, barely having time to translate for the others. If only they'd had better warning, they could help. But already Habiba was giving the signal. Now, twenty-one of the twenty-eight cut their cords, using knives they'd probably taken from the kitchen. Then they all dashed to the open gate. The caregivers, taken by surprise, tried to stop as many as possible, but too many sprinted for the gate. Just as the first children were getting to the gate, it closed.

Jennings had sent a couple G-men over in a car, just in case. He must've a bad feeling about things.

Habiba and her companions were trapped. Once corralled, their caregivers beat her after the trainers, girls given responsibility, pointed out she was the mastermind.

The three rescuers, hidden by the trailers, watched in horror as they punished the small twelve-year-old, afterward having to carry her. It was now after midnight, and Santa should've been on his way, but for these children, it looked like their worst Christmas ever.

"I need a drink. This is BS," a caregiver said. "Jennings needs to do something. It's just too many of them to keep up with. Some of them need to go for a swim or let us take one or two home."

"Aw, shut up. Mention that, and we'll be the ones going for a swim. Let's go."

They turned out the trailer lights, leaving only the faint glow of night-lights to illuminate the interiors so the children could see how to use their chamber pots during the night. At least, in the commotion, the men hadn't noticed the two girls missing from their cages.

Leaving the group, three men went to join up with the G-men now in the club. One of the men nodded to the box truck parked behind the bus, telling the others he'd check it out. They kept going. The cold and snow made everything harder, just as it had hindered the girls earlier.

As the man went around the bus, Tom snuck up behind him and pistol-whipped him over the head before he could holler for help. With Sam's help, Tom dragged the guy over to the Jeep and stuffed him inside.

"Let's give them five minutes to get inside the clubhouse." DR rubbed his hands together, the temperature well below freezing. "Then we'll start transferring the children."

"What about that creep?" Tom nodded toward the Jeep.

"He'll be all right. We'll call someone for him after we get away."

After five minutes passed, DR peered around the trailers, seeing no one coming. "Sam, start the bus. Let's warm it up while we transfer the kids."

Ten minutes later, they were ready to leave, but a caregiver came from the clubhouse. DR crouched to peer from a trailer window. "He's probably checking on his friend. Run and turn off the bus."

The man entered the building and called out. "Okay, pervert. Leave those girls alone." Seeing the cages were empty and his friend nowhere in sight, he radioed the clubhouse. "He's—"

DR cracked him over the head. "We got to go. They know something's not right now." He ran to the bus, signaling to Sam they needed to go.

"Go, Sam, and don't stop for nothing!" DR shouted, scanning the thirty-plus children on the bus.

They had just gotten started when men ran out from the clubhouse, pistols drawn, and fired at the bus heading for the gate. Bullets riddled the bus, breaking glass, striking children.

"Get down, duck!" Tom pulled the nearest into the aisle.

As all the children got down, several with flesh wounds from flying glass and bullets, one child remained sitting up, not moving—Tahira. The boys who had sat on the back bench seat with her were covered in blood.

The children all screamed, and DR covered his mouth and closed his eyes, horrified, remembering his promise to her. Now... she was dead. Heat surged through his veins, and his teeth ground together even as his fists clenched. "Go, Sam, go!"

Two cars started after them.

The caregivers piled into two cars, and the crooked G-men followed in theirs. Sam floored the pedal, but their attackers caught up just as Sam was pulling onto Interstate 90 south.

The passenger in the first caregiver's car fired two shots at the driver's side rear tandem tires. The outside tire blew out. When Tom shot him in the arm, the man yelped and dropped his weapon outside the vehicle. The car fell back and into the fast lane to escape Tom's next two shots. This gave the G-men an opening.

"Sam, get off at the hospital exit. Two of the children need care." DR huddled with the kids, comforting them, avoiding looking at the back seat. This wasn't the result he wanted, but the authorities were tied to Jennings. They couldn't trust anyone.

When the bus approached the exit, the second caregiver's car veered into the emergency lane to push them back onto the interstate. As it banged against the passenger side, Sam had to get back on the interstate to avoid a barrel barrier.

The caregiver's car then raced up the exit. Unable to stop for a red light atop the slight incline, it flew through the air—right into a gasoline rig. The explosion shook the interstate, collapsing part of the overpass, and the bus and two assailant vehicles narrowly escaped the crashing debris.

Tom looked out the busted back window, ducking as men in the G-men's car fired three shots. Two struck the brake lights and the third the inside tire on the passenger's tandem wheels. It exploded. The bus shook. The children screamed, everyone holding on.

DR let off a shot, hitting the car's windshield.

It faded back.

"Find another hospital!" he shouted, holding onto the back of a seat, crouched just high enough to see outside.

The caregiver's last remaining car pulled alongside. Tom squeezed off the remaining six shots in his clip. One struck the driver, a nonlethal shot, but the driver lost control, slammed into the tandem wheels, and knocked the sole remaining tire back underneath the bus. The bus's weight now rested on the car, which became its fourth set of tires. But this slowed the bus dramatically.

Sparks started to spray the car as the vehicle's tires burst while being dragged sideways. The passengers shot at Sam driving the bus, probably hoping to stop it. After reloading, Tom fired and emptied his clip at the vehicle again. A spark hit gasoline somewhere, and the car caught fire.

"Stop the bus, Sam." DR sprang to his feet. "The car is going to explode under us."

The two men inside the car gawked at their looming plight. No sooner had Sam stopped the bus than the flaming car started charring the exterior of the bus. As fast as they could, DR and Tom hustled the children off the bus, unable to get to Tahira's body before the car exploded and the bus jolted into the air. Sam guided the children away onto the interstate's emergency lane.

Tom, still on the bus, banged his hand against the ceiling protecting himself as the two crooked G-men came in behind DR and Sam, holding weapons to their heads, the cold air making their breath show in the air.

The first agent nudged DR's head with the cold barrel. "FBI, drop your weapons."

As Sam's and DR's weapons hit the ground, the other agent pushed his gun to the back of Sam's head. "This was a stupid thing to do. Now we're going to have to kill you."

The children all cowered and hit the ground. DR tried to keep his gaze away from Tom before he gave his friend away, but Tom must be seeing it all, unnoticed. And in his peripheral, DR sighted him sneak got off the bus. Then Tom fired two kill shots, one striking each of the G-men. The children screamed. DR crouched over, and Sam spun around, unsure who had fired until the men hit the ground.

DR's knees wobbled as he let out a hoot. "I'm glad you were the one still on the bus!"

Tom held his shooting pose for a moment as if realizing he'd just killed two FBI agents. "So what's the plan now?"

Willie called Mike, having more questions now after finding out DR was baptized as a young boy. She played with the silver icicles on her tree. "Merry Christmas Eve, Mike. Are you busy?"

"We just put the boys to bed. I've got a ton of toys to put together." He chuckled. "I don't know why Alyssa thinks they have to have every toy in the store—or why she doesn't think 'some assembly required' is a big deal."

"Listen, I'll make this quick. I ran into a woman at Marcie's today who went to school with DR, Megan Blackmoor. Do you know her?" She sat on the edge of an armchair near her smallish but loaded tree.

"Not that I can recall right now, but I was five years younger. Why?" The clank of a tool came over the phone.

"She said she was baptized with Stevie. Can you believe it? DR was baptized. Maybe that's why he had all those dreams, and…"

"Whoa. Don't get ahead of yourself. Mom and Dad never said anything about it, so I don't know."

"Mike, I'm telling you—the woman knew him well as a boy, so well she had a crush on him and wanted to sleep with him."

"I thought you said she was baptized with DR? Doesn't sound like it to me. Of course, that doesn't mean as much to some today."

"Look, I'm not judging, to each their own. I just can't help but think there's something else under all the antireligion thing he has going on. Besides, how many men risk everything for children they don't even know? Something deep inside is pushing him." Maybe this was the biggest mystery on Wall Lake. Maybe, if she solved it, she might get the chance to be the woman in his life.

"You need to give up on all this. He's never going to be more than a friend. You and I both know it. Besides, whatever happened to that Ryan fellow working for DR? Do you still see him?"

"Something's fishy about him. It seems like he can't wait to see me, but then when we're together, something's distracting him." After swinging her legs over the chair arm, she sat down and kicked her feet up on her gray ottoman. "It's like he left something somewhere and needs to go back to find it. You know the feeling?"

"Maybe it's just the Irish in him. They tend to be quirky in their ways, at least when compared to Americans. Willie, I got to go. This bicycle is kicking my butt. I think I lost a spacer."

"Sure, sorry to bother you. Merry Christmas." She hopped to her feet and walked to the kitchen where a bowl of clam chowder awaited in the microwave.

"Merry Christmas. Talk to you tomorrow."

Placing the phone on the kitchen counter, she opened the microwave and set the chowder on the counter. After closing the door, she leaned forward and looked into the glass door, seeing her own reflection. "Who are you, Steven Ray?" She narrowed her eyes. "What makes you tick?"

A trail of death had followed them ever since they were drugged and taken onto the casino boat. Now they'd finish it. No one knew they took the children—yet. Well, unless their pursuers had called Jennings or his cohorts. Either way, their plans now included getting the children to safety. After Sam went back for the box truck, they took the children to the club. It was just too cold to use the box truck to drive them the distance to DR's home, so they went back to the LMMC. The rescue squad arrived at the club, without police escort, thanks to Sam thinking of using the G-men's car radio while he drove back to get the box truck.

"Over here. Habiba has bruises and a cut on her head from falling glass and where someone beat her." DR guided the paramedic to the young girl.

"Abba," she responded, reaching for DR.

"What did she say?" The paramedic was thorough, taking the girl's arm and checking for sprains and breaks in all her limbs.

"She called me father." DR slid from her embrace and approached Sam. "Is the yacht warming up?"

"Yep, she'll be ready to go when we are. We're lucky there's not any ice to speak of on the lake, yet." Sam lifted a girl and helped her put her coat back on, shaking his head. "Good thing they walked them back to the trailers. Could you imagine if they hadn't been wearing their coats?"

"I can't imagine, but then again, I never saw this coming, either. Did you?"

"No."

"We've got everyone taken care of. The two girls with the flesh wounds from gunfire need to be taken to the hospital." Packing up their gear, the two paramedics looked around the room. "You know we're going to have to call this in, right? What did you say your name was?"

"Shortman—Detective Shortman, CPD. Just tell your dispatcher, John will take care of all the paperwork." DR followed the instructions the dispatcher had given Sam over the radio when he called for the paramedics, thinking he was one of the two G-men Jennings had hired.

"Oh, I almost forgot. There's a man in a white Jeep down on the backside of the lot, behind the trailers. He's probably pretty cold by now." DR hugged Habiba. "And one inside the middle trailer. They may need some care."

After the paramedics left, Tom pulled the box truck around back of the clubhouse to make the medics think they took the children on the truck. Then Sam and DR led the children out to the yacht. They balked because they were supposed to "perform" there, but when Habiba explained what her new daddy had told her, the children ran onto the yacht and headed into the casino area.

Sam, who also boated and sailed a lot as a teen, pulled the *Lucky Lucie* out while learning her nuisances, DR came up to help, making their way to Benton Harbor, Michigan. The sixty-six-mile trip would take them about four hours.

By now, everyone was hungry, so Tom led the search for food. DR returned to help as soon as they were underway and found a well-stocked kitchen and pantry. They led the children to the dining room, still not fully heated, making do as it warmed up. The children gobbling down fruit, potato chips, and cakes and drank sodas.

With a sense of relief, sadness, and hope, DR discussed their plans to get the children to Greg and Penny's in Alabama. Already knowing the trouble Jennings had caused them and not wanting to discuss the tragedy. Still, Tahira dying cast a further evil light on the situation.

Arms crossed, DR braced against a server station filled with supplies. Could they finally set the children free now? Or would Jennings continue to their death—and his. The whole Circle thing was hard to understand at first, but the realization that a group of powerful men had come together to shut down a president was looking more and more like reality. A reality DR had no business in, if it weren't for fate.

It was late, eleven p.m., and DR had to make several calls, first to Willie, then to Ryan. The children needed to experience some sort of Christmas to help take some of the sting away. "Willie, it's DR." Grateful she accepted an unknown number and on Christmas Eve, he spoke as soon as she answered. "Sorry to call so late. We did it—we've got the children, and we're on our way to my house."

"Ohh, how wonderful! That is awesome."

"It didn't go as planned, and I'll tell you about it later." He ruffled Derifa's hair. With him speaking in English, she'd have no idea what he was saying. "I need your help. Can you put together something with my family to get some gifts and snacks for the kids? It's already been a terrible Christmas for them, so anything you can scrounge up to put a smile on their little faces would be much appreciated. I'll settle up with you tomorrow."

"I'll call Mike. We work tomorrow, but we'll manage something—I'm working the early part of the shift so he can have Christmas with his family first, then I'll get off at noon. I'm so happy I can cry. You guys are amazing!"

"We just did what anyone with a heart would've done. But thanks. I've got to make another call. See you in the morning?"

"Absolutely."

He called Ryan, speaking with him for fifteen minutes, catching up on the shop, discussing the APB, and enlisting his help.

"Sure, coz. I'll be there. There's nowhere else to go. Besides, it'll be nice to see Tonya. I'll get there early and get things started. What time will you be there?"

"I'm not quite sure, probably between eight or ten in the morning. We still have to arrange for transportation from Benton Harbor to my house. Probably going to borrow a bus."

"Okay, sounds good. I'll get there early and get everything started. Be careful."

Be careful. The words echoed in DR's head. What more could they face?

CHAPTER
TWENTY-NINE

They reached Benton Harbor around four thirty Christmas morning and put their plan to grab a bus into action. DR had searched the internet for the local bus terminal and found one several miles from the lakeshore. Finding a place to dock the *Lucky Lucie* was tricky but doable. DR and Sam left Tom with the children and walked to the terminal.

"Whew, it's cold this morning. We better double-time it, or we'll freeze solid." Sam rubbed his hands together, picking up the pace.

"That's what I miss about Spain. Its winters are much warmer."

"If we get out of this, you'll have to take me there. It sounds fantastic."

"You'd like it, Sam."

They kept their pace, passing boarded-up storefronts and the others that appeared old and unkempt.

"Have you ever noticed that most bus terminals are in the worst part of town? I wonder why that is." Sam took his glove and made a line through the dirt on a window.

"Don't know. Maybe to save costs." DR pointed toward a sign, then smirked. "Looks like we made it, and we haven't frozen to death yet."

The company was closed for Christmas, and the compound locked tight. They could only access one bus out by the dumpster near the building. It was old, probably the reason it wasn't locked up. Sam found a piece of pipe and pried the door open, cracking the glass on one side in the process, but nevertheless, they were in.

"No key—wish I'd paid more attention in automotive class." DR checked for it above the visor and in the storage compartment, to no avail. "Do you know how to hot-wire it?"

"Turn your head. I don't want to give away my secrets." Sam chuckled and ducked underneath the steering column, digging for the ignition wires. "Some of us *did* pay attention."

Moments later, after stripping several wires, he fired the bus up. It was a diesel and sputtered and died out after five precarious seconds of rough idle. It took two more times before the bus stopped dying out.

"Ta-da!" Sam spread his arms out, palms up. "See, I have skills."

"Yes, you do. Good job." DR slid into the driver's seat and wiped the grime from the gauge with a tissue. "The fuel gauge reads three-quarters of a tank, but I don't know whether it's working or not. This thing is so old it must've come over on the *Santa Maria*."

"You might want to stop to get some fuel just in case. It would be bad if we ran out with all the children on the bus." Sam dropped into the first row across the aisle. "*Santa Maria*?"

"You know, the whole Christopher Columbus thing." DR grinned.

"I'm afraid I missed that sailing, my friend." Sam waved in the air as diesel fumes entered through the engine cover. "And at this rate, the *Santa Maria* is going to drown us."

Tom stiffened. A police officer was checking out the *Lucky Lucie*. The officer parked and approached them. Made sense. She wasn't supposed to be docked there. Tom asked the girls to wait inside and took the three American children, one boy and two girls, out with him.

"Merry Christmas, Officer. May I help you?" He put his arm around Melody and Tina, while Riley, a twelve-year-old boy, hung out at his other side.

"Merry Christmas. Sorry to be the bearer of bad news, but I'm afraid you can't dock here." The officer pointed to a nearby sign. "This is for commerce only, even if it is Christmas day."

"We're just waiting for our friends who went to get our bus. Then I'm going to take the vessel up the coast." Tom roughed up Riley's hair. "We're taking these kids, and thirty more orphans to a Christmas celebration this morning."

"Isn't that kind of you? God bless you. Kids are His favorite." The officer took his hat off and waved at the children. "I have four of my own, and I know how much they mean to me. You take as long as you need. It's Christmas. There won't be any ships coming in today."

"Thank you, Officer. We won't be here long. They should be along shortly. I think I see them coming now." Tom waved goodbye to the officer while Sam and DR pulled the bus near the yacht.

The officer strolled away. "Gentlemen, it's a wonderful thing you're doing for those precious children. God bless you." He climbed into his cruiser, and DR and Sam waved goodbye as the car pulled away.

"What did you tell him?" DR planted his feet wide, rubbing his jaw as the car rolled out of sight.

"Half of the truth, plus a little white lie." Tom stuck his chin up and let the three children go, then released his full Brit twang. "Shall we get the others?"

With the bus loaded and only seventy-one miles to travel, Sam closed the door and pulled away. Leaving a black cloud of diesel smoke behind them, the *Santa Maria* sprang to life. "Next stop, Wall Lake."

Willie called DR's parents, Mike, and her own parents, spreading the news that DR and his friends had rescued thirty-one kids. Early Christmas morning, she met her mom and dad, then stopped to pick up whatever they could find at the only store open near Delton, a convenience store. The store carried a small assortment of toys for children, gas tanker toys, jacks, jump ropes, and other small items, along with Christmas cookies and milk—they bought lots of milk.

With the car loaded up and headed out of town, Willie's dad clamped a hand on her arm. "This fellow, DR, and his friends, they sound like my sort of people."

"They are good people, Dad. I'm sure you heard me talk about Gail. DR is her husband—well, was." She steered her car into his long driveway. Finding fresh tire tracks but no vehicle in sight, she craned around as her curiosity rose.

"He sure has a nice home." Mom leaned forward from the back seat.

"I remember now. This is the guy from the cruise. He and his wife found Indian treasure. No wonder he has a nice home." Dad eyed the lake. "I'll bet the fishing is good."

After using the key DR had loaned Mike while he was on the cruise, she stepped inside to the smell of popcorn, bacon, and a mystery odor. Someone was in the kitchen, and now that someone was coming out.

"Ryan?"

"Hi, Tonya. DR told me you'd be over this morning." Ryan hustled around her, apparently seeing her parents loaded down with gifts. "Need any help?"

"There's one more bag in the trunk." Dad laid his load down and reached to shake Ryan's hand. "I'm Tonya's dad, Roy, and this lovely lady is my wife, Christina. It's nice to meet you, Ryan. Merry Christmas."

After shaking hands and exchanging pleasantries with both her parents, Ryan went out for the last bag.

Willie wasn't expecting him. Just how did she feel about spending Christmas Day with him? Well, no matter. It was for the kids, so she'd deal with it. She put the toys and candy in gift bags, trying to spread it out over thirty-one kids, a hard task. "How have you been? I haven't seen you for a while."

"Just working. Occasionally going out for dinner or over to Marcie's. I've seen Rachael a few times."

Puzzled how to continue the conversation since he didn't leave her an out, she quietly packed the bags, watching him, feeling a darkness she hadn't felt before. "Well, that's all the bags. I'm going to put them under the tree."

His gaze lingered on her as she left. This wasn't the man Debbie had described. This man was cold, introverted. Not like the man from the airport, either.

Forty-five minutes later, DR called, "We'll be there in an hour. Have my parents made it yet?"

"No, just Ryan." She hung a glass Santa Claus ornament on the tree. "What's going on with him? He's as cold as ice today."

"You know how the Irish are. They can be moody."

Her dad placed a hand on her shoulder, a finger to her lips, and pointed to the kitchen.

"I never saw Gail like that." Willie dropped her voice to a whisper. "Was she moody too?"

"No, but Gail was raised as a Spaniard, not like how the Irish live in Ireland. I think the weather affects everyone too, and the weather in Malaga is amazing. I've got to get off here. My parents called to say they were just about there. Can you ask Ryan to help them? They brought a lot of food."

"Yep, merry Christmas."

"Thanks. I'll make it up to you all. Merry Christmas, Willie."

She disconnected and repeated, "I'll make it up to you." Eyes narrowing, her lips pursed. "Yes, you will Dr. Ray. Yes, you will." She'd called in a favor late last night, Giggles, the station manager covered her shift, and that came at a cost.

DR edged the *Santa Maria* up his drive, and a black trail of smoke signaled their arrival a half hour after his dad texted to say he and Mom made it and to promise that they, along with the Gotteys and Ryan, set up the food, snacks, and put gifts under the Christmas tree. "Not too shabby if I say so myself for such a hastily thrown-together shindig," Dad had added.

DR parked, and his friends helped the kids out. Soon, Tom opened the front door, and Sam followed him inside, holding one of the girls injured in the melee earlier. "Ho ho ho! Merry Christmas, everybody." Sam set eleven-year-old Baylee down and took her hand.

Following close behind him, thirty other children edged into the house. Tom and DR right with them. Though his home was large, having thirty-one kids and nine adults made it feel small—and crowded.

Mom hustled over, bringing pillows and blankets. "Some of the children can sit on these." She hugged DR tight. "Thank God, you're safe. I've been worried stiff."

"It's not over yet, Mom." He held her at arm's length, then kissed her cheek. "We'll talk about that in a while. For now, we need to get the children settled down."

"Honey, do you have any more blankets or quilts?" She gestured to her hoard. "I got these from the closet near your bedroom."

"There's some smaller ones near the other full bathroom." The enormity of it all hit him, and he dropped onto the edge of an armchair. He'd intercepted a fortune in trafficked kids. This wasn't going to sit well with Jennings.

Only DR understood Arabic, so he had Tom and the others download the app Penny had, helping them speak to the children. Faces began to light up after they could communicate. Willie set to work learning their names and putting name tags on them as they came through the kitchen for food and drinks. After everyone had eaten, they handed out the gift bags, and as each child tore theirs open, laughter and smiles enlivened the Ray home.

DR thanked and hugged Willie, though Ryan looked on suspiciously. "Now this truly is a merry Christmas."

Tina and Melody sandwiched their new friend, Habiba, and her sister, Derifa, the four girls crying happy crocodile tears. Habiba pointed at DR and said something the American girls didn't understand. Willie, seeing them trying to communicate, left DR and took her cellphone to translate. She placed it in front of Habiba and motioned for the child to speak.

The child pointed again, and the phone translated her words. "Abba said he would be our daddy. I knew it, and he rescued me and my sisters again!" She left her new friends, her smile bright, and went to her new daddy.

As she hugged his waist, DR's chest swelled, and feeling her love, he melted.

~

Christmas wasn't merry everywhere. Jennings was unhinged. Not only had the target of his political scheme managed to wreck his plan to embarrass his ex-friend, the POTUS, but also now, he was down a congressman, a club assistant, a mercenary squad, *and* all his entertainers —right before the biggest weekend of the year.

"Incompetent! Is everybody incompetent?" His face heating and temples throbbing, he exhaled and dialed his daughter's phone, shifting between business and family, his only family, an adopted girl he rescued in Russia long before joining Circle and corrupting his empire.

"Hello, darling. Merry Christmas."

"Merry Christmas, Dad. Did you get the package I sent you?"

"Yes, thank you, sweetheart. I'm looking at it now." The picture of his wife Patsy now hung where his picture with his ex-friend and him playing golf had hung for thirty years.

"Are you feeling better?" Her sweet voice lilted. "You've seemed uptight the last times we've talked."

"It's just business. This whole presidential thing has everything upside down." He rubbed his thrumming temples, fighting the urge to ask for her help. He'd never involved her in business, especially with the performers. The less she knew the better.

"Is there any way I can help? Do you need help at the LMMC?"

"Honey, you know I don't like to involve you with business. It's not something you should be involved with." But she'd opened the door. Maybe, just maybe, he should ask.

"You've always been here for me. Let me be there for you."

Like the days leading up to Patsy's death, he felt it coming and couldn't stop it. "I didn't call to talk about this. I just want you to know I love you more than anything and I'm hoping your Christmas will be great. I miss you. I'll talk to you soon."

"Merry Christmas, Dad. Call me."

Laying the phone down, he closed his eyes. How could it have come this far? It was just one yacht, a simple task—blow up the yacht, take down the President. Now everything had changed.

～

After the joyous Christmas celebration, while the children lay down to sleep, all bushed, DR took his friends and family into the kitchen to discuss the next step—getting the children to safety. They had already determined to reunite the other children with Amal at Greg and Penny's home.

DR's parents and Willie's sat on the high-back barstools on the living room side of the island, still covered with pieces of colored paper Willie had cut to make the paper-chain garland. The three heroes leaned against the front, and Willie and Ryan sat on opposite sides on the same high back stools. DR's famous sailors' brew filled the air, along with pure joy.

"We put our heads together to figure out this mess. The only option we can come up with is to send them to Alabama for now. We don't know who is crooked and who isn't. Plus, Habiba and Derifa's sister is there, so we want to get them back together." DR shifted his weight against the kitchen island, speaking softly. "Just so you know, not everything went smooth. One of the girls was killed."

The room went quiet.

"We didn't think to have the kids to get down low on the bus. When Jennings's men started shooting, they fired to hit us at first. That's why two of the girls were hurt." Fighting tears, DR covered his forehead with his hand to hide his struggle. "A little girl named Tahira was killed. She was so scared." Unable to control himself, he left the room, then returned a moment later.

Apparently, he wasn't the only one struggling. There wasn't a dry eye in the room.

Mom hugged him tight. "Steven, you've done everything you could. These children have hope because of you and your friends. It is sad, and I hate that it happened, but Tahira's with God now. You have to finish it now, so the others can have a good life."

As DR relaxed into his mom's love, Sam took over.

"After the three American kids get some sleep, we'll send them back to their homes tomorrow, except the boy." Sam slammed a fist into his open palm. "He'll go to the authorities in his hometown. His stepmother sold him, and he's terrified of her. The girls are from Louisiana. We'll put them on a bus and notify their parents."

"Why such secrecy?" Christina's mouth dropped as she shook her head, leaning forward, arms wide. "No one will ever know who rescued them. Don't you want to share what you went through to save the children? It might help others whose children have been taken have hope."

"No." DR pulled from his mom's hug. "We need our part to end. Tom needs to go back to England, Sam has a hotel to run, and I must talk to my fiancée and get with Ryan here to finish up on the Indian dig."

"You're engaged?" Dad gasped.

"Well, I was, for nine hours. I don't know where that stands now." DR's eye caught Willie's. Why was she eyeing him? Did she still have it for him? He forced a smile her way. "I'm going to call her soon, let her know we've got this situation with the children straightened out."

Willie ducked her head. But her eyebrows rose, and she whispered, "She'd be crazy if this didn't make her want you even more."

Around noon, everyone said their goodbyes, merry Christmases, and left. Only Ryan lingered.

"I'm sorry to hear about you and Debbie." He bent over picking up some paper trash from the Christmas gifts and snacks. "Hopefully, she'll come to her senses."

"It'll all shake out, somehow." DR held a garbage bag open for Ryan to stuff the trash in. "How's everything coming at the shop?"

"Great." Ryan wadded up the last of it. "Everything is caught up, and no sign of Clyde, thankfully. I've learned a lot this last week."

"How are things between you and Willie?" DR tied up the bag. "I couldn't help but notice you two seem a little standoffish."

Ryan shrugged. "I think she has a crush on you. I like her, but I just can't seem to connect."

"Don't give up. She'll come around."

The children started waking up, rested. DR told them of their next adventure, an adventure to freedom and family. First, he called sixteen-year-old Melody's family, letting her tell her folks.

"Mom, it's me—Mel. I am coming home. I've been rescued Mom, set free." She turned, smiling, crying. "I'm taking a bus first thing in the morning."

Then it was Tina's turn. DR remembered the scared fifteen-year-old girl's face when he first talked to her in the club hallway and the fear in her eyes as she talked to Mel, who was far more in control. At the time, DR hadn't known Mel had been in their captivity a week longer than the other children.

After he explained things to the children from Aden, Habiba and Derifa became upset, not wanting him to send them away. "Girls, it's going to be okay," he promised. "I'll join you with Amal in Alabama after I finish this. We don't want any other children suffering, do we?"

They embraced their new dad, shaking their heads. "No."

His chest tightened as he held them. It better be a promise he could keep. He better make it back. He just had to.

CHAPTER
THIRTY

t was nearing eight thirty p.m. in Marsala. DR paced to the window beside the fireplace. Had Debbie thought about him today? Either way, it was Christmas and she and Miguel deserved an update. He felt raw inside, anxious, Tahira dying had taken so much out of him. He knew he ought to be thankful, but his soul felt bare. Maybe this phone call would help. He dialed as joyful voices filled the air.

"Miguel, it's me—DR. Merry Christmas."

"Merry Christmas, my friend. I was beginning to think you'd forgotten us."

"No way. We've just been... busy. We picked up thirty-one hungry and scared kids—had to make them happy." He strolled to his bedroom for some privacy, sat on the edge of the king-size bed, and looked out the window with its full view of the lake below.

"They are there? The Aden children are there? Ha ha ha. Thank God, you found them."

"As far as we can tell, we got them all, but, Miguel, one of them was killed during our escape. I can't get the look of her face out of my mind. I talked to her earlier, and she was so scared. I promised she would be okay...." He rubbed a hand over his face, his gaze dancing from place to place, not seeing. "She didn't deserve to die. I'm going back, and I'm going to end this once and for all."

"DR, you be careful. Don't get in over your head. Meantime—we're all praying for you. But first, someone here wants to speak to you. Merry Christmas, my friend."

"Merry Christmas, Miguel. Give everyone my best. Tell Lo and David I'll call them soon."

"DR?" Debbie's voice laughed through the speakers. Then a gasp shuddered across the miles. "Oh, thank God, you're alive! I've been worried sick ever since I left your house. I'm so sorry. I don't know what's come over me. Can you forgive me... please?"

"Sure." Breathing a sigh of relief, he slumped back to lie on the bed. "But let's talk about the terms of your surrender later. I just wanted to hear your voice and wish you a merry Christmas. We've got a house full, and I need to get back to them. I'll see you in a couple of weeks. Right?"

"Hopefully sooner. What's going on over there? Miguel said someone is trying to kill you and Tom."

He sat up as a deer walked in a stealthy fashion down to the lake's edge for a drink of water, reminding DR of another reason he loved his home. "Remember your friend, the congressman?"

"Max? You're talking about Max Rice. From the surprise party."

"That's the one. He was behind it all, the attack on the yacht, everything. He ran the LMMC for a man named Jennings." Remembering the interrogation, it all clicked. "Debbie, they took the children from the home in Aden again. But I got them. They're all here, with Tom and a friend of mine. Max is dead."

The deer raised its head, right ear twitching, maybe signaling several fawns to come for a drink. A signal its children were safe—Were his, the ones in his care?

Debbie let out a low whistle. "Max was dirty?"

"He didn't have much choice. The man who financed his campaigns turned dirty a few years back, joining something called Circle. So Max got caught in the middle. Jennings hired mercenaries to kill Max, Tom, and me. Anyway, it's a long story. I need to go. I just wanted to hear your voice and wish you a merry Christmas. Can't wait to see you." He pushed off the bed and walked toward the living room, putting one hand on the entryway wall, and leaning against it, thankful for the openness.

"Merry Christmas, sweetheart. I love you."

"I love you too." After ending the call, he put the cellphone in his pocket, and a laugh escaped. All was right between them again. Exhaling, he went and sat between Derifa and Habiba. Maybe their Abba was right. This felt so good.

Early the next day, they put their plan into motion. Sam drove the three American children and Ryan to the bus station in the *Santa Maria*. Ryan would sit with them until the last child had boarded their bus. Then he'd rent a car for DR. Sam continued on with Tom to drop off the *Santa Maria* and get a real bus, at least a more modern version DR reserved online, with a driver.

Two hours later, around eleven a.m., the bus arrived. After saying goodbye to each child, DR waved goodbye. Habiba and Derifa cried boarding the bus, running to their seat to wave goodbye, watching as the bus left the house.

Grabbing a hot shower, DR relaxed under the cascade of the hot liquid and let his anxiety and frustration go. He tried to feel only the pleasant sensation and not think, to give himself a much-needed reprieve. After the relaxing shower, he decided on a quick shave. Then he heard from Ryan.

"Hey, I've got the car. Be there in about a half an hour. I'm going to stop by Marcie's and pick up some éclairs. Would you like a coffee?"

"Uh, no, I'm good, but thanks. See you in a few." DR wiped the steam from the bathroom mirror and leaned in, studying his reflection. Maybe he should let his beard grow. Nah, he'd never been much on growing a beard. His last attempt ended with him itching.

Before he started to shave, a noise came from the great room. Who could that be? Unsure, he tiptoed to the entrance. A strange man was putting his valuable pieces in a sack. Going back, DR pulled on his clothes and shoes, then ran into the room and tackled the man.

After wrestling with the slighter man, DR overpowered him and pinned the man's right hand behind his back. Then he forced the man into a chair and tied him to it with an extension cord, finishing the job with duct tape. All the while, the man kept shouting about explosives.

Wait—What was he saying?

"I just put explosives all around your house. It's going to blow soon. Please let me loose! We've got to get out of here. Now." The man fought against the restraints, but DR had put so much tape on the man, even wiggling was hard.

"Where did you put explosives?" As much as DR didn't want to believe the man, something pushed him to go check.

"All four sides of the house. They gave me enough explosives to send your house to the moon. Mister, you can have the cash they gave me. Just let me go."

DR narrowed his gaze. "If you're blowing up my house, why did you come inside?"

"I didn't think anyone was home. I didn't hear anyone. I figured I could grab some extra bucks out of your stuff. Please, mister, we've got to get out of here."

DR grabbed the guy's shirt. "Who are you working for?"

"Shortman, Detective Shortman," the guy squealed. "Can we please get out of here?"

"I'm going to check your story first." DR headed for the door, going outside.

"There's not time. Please, mister, let me loose." The man's eyes bulged as he fought the restraints, all to no avail.

As soon as DR went around the left corner, his heart sped into overdrive even as his feet rooted him to the snowy ground. It was true. The entire foundation was rigged to explode. He began sprinting, tracing a timer fuse around to the back where a conglomerate of wires and a timer were set to explode at noon. It was eleven fifty-eight. He ran back to the house, standing in the door for a moment.

Less than two minutes.

He didn't have time to set the man free.

As he spun around and dashed down the front steps, he heard the man plead, "Mister, please don't leave me here. Please!"

DR ran as fast as possible, clearing about thirty feet before the explosion ripped the house off its foundation. The blast threw him another forty feet onto a hillside and pummeled him with debris. Part of the exterior front door struck his back and gouged his left shoulder. Another hit his head. Smaller pieces of insulation and splinters from the wooden support beams rained down on him, partially burying him before the shock wave from the blast knocked him unconscious.

"DR, DR, where are you?"

Waking, groggy, pain walloping his body, DR felt a hand pulling on him, then another taking the debris off him. He struggled to imagine, at first, what had happened—the man, the explosives, the explosion!

DR groaned, all of it crashing on his memories. Surely, the intruder died, probably nothing much to find now, but the guy had done it to himself.

Then his teeth started chattering, and DR struggled to get out from under the debris. Who was his rescuer, anyway? Ryan? He hadn't heard Ryan drive up.

"DR, DR, I'm here. Hang on." Ryan hauled him up. "What happened?"

"Ohh, that hurts. Someone tried to kill me." DR sat up, facing the pile of rubble that once was his beautiful home, memories and possessions destroyed.

"Your back is bleeding." Ryan frowned at him. "We've got to get you to the hospital."

"No... I don't want Jennings to know I survived. I caught a man, the one who set the explosives. He's in this mess." DR waved at the debris field extending to the lake. "He's somewhere, and I want them to think it's me. So no hospital, no cops until I'm out of here. I need to get warm, though. I'm freezing." A trembling took hold of him.

Sirens came from across the lake, several fire trucks heading their way.

DR reached up. "We've got to get out of here before they reach the driveway. Help me." He struggled to his feet. Clothes full of debris, he wiped at it while trying to run, half hobbling over to the silver Cadillac. "You couldn't find something less conspicuous?"

"Sorry." Ryan held the door open for DR. "Wow, that was some explosion. I saw it down by the road."

"I can imagine." Dazed, DR patted the dashboard. "Let's go."

The silver Cadillac hit the main road moments before the fire trucks turned the corner and onto the driveway. Soon, news would travel throughout the area about the lakefront home.

~

At WREAL radio, Mike leaned against the studio doorway, sipping his coffee. It might be the day after Christmas, but he was still bleary-eyed after the late Christmas Eve assembly line.

"Hey, Mike." Jogging over, Bobby Joe handed him the notice hot off the news desk's local law enforcement wire. "You may want to see this bulletin just put out by the police and fire departments."

His eyes raced over the report. "Ray home on Wall Lake devastated. DR's home? Is DR dead? It doesn't say anything about children's bodies being found, just part of one man. Maybe they got the children out beforehand. I don't see where it says what caused the blast, do you?" He ran a shaky hand over his face, his insides hollowing. *DR is dead!*

He finished reading the wire, then dropped into his desk chair. "Why couldn't they just leave him alone? He never did anything to them. Yesterday, he said he was going to finish it." No! He didn't want to believe his brother was dead. He blinked, fighting the burning sensation in his eyes. "These people are psychos."

As Bobby Joe sat on the edge of Mike's desk, reading it again for the details she may have missed, he noticed the memorial for the late congressman, Max Rice, of Chicago written on its backside before dropping it on his desk.

"I'm sorry Mike. If you need me to finish your shift, I will."

"Thanks. I need to find out what's going on. Let me think this out. Then I'll let you know." He fished on his desk to find the vibrating cellphone buried by the wire.

"Hi, Willie. I just heard the news." He swiveled in his chair, his back to the door. "I guess you heard too."

"That's why I'm calling. The body wasn't DR. He called me to ease our fears. He doesn't want the police or fire department to know it wasn't him. He's hoping to surprise the man who sent the poor guy."

"What? DR's safe?" Mike pushed the wire in the trash. "What happened?"

He exhaled after she explained what she knew. "So he's all right?"

"More or less. Mike, don't tell your parents he's alive, or else it might get back to the people trying to kill him."

"I can't do my family that way. They'll be torn up." He rubbed a hand over his face. "No, I can't do it."

"You have to. Go to Bobby Joe's desk, get the wire, and show it to them. Don't tell them we talked. That's not lying."

He reached into the trash and took the report back out. "I don't know if I can. Mom and Dad will be devastated, and so will my brothers."

"You have to, Mike. His life might depend on it."

Just after nine a.m. on the West Coast, Jennings smiled. *Goodbye, Dr. Ray. I'll see you in hell.* He called Senator Carl Brummengarten in Chicago, still on a congressional break, while watching birds in a cloudless sky. Yes, it was a beautiful California morning.

"Good morning, Senator. How was your Christmas?"

"Good morning, sir. It was nice, thank you, and yours?"

He sipped from a glass of orange juice, then set it on the glass table beside him. "Uneventful, Michelle is in Atlanta, and I'm here. But I did get some interesting news. One of our entertainers is in Birmingham, Alabama. Two of our boys tried to get her back, but someone intercepted them. We'll have to figure it out." He coughed coarsely, clearing his throat. "But there is good news, and with a little luck, our nemesis will not be troubling us anymore."

"Sir?"

"Our friend, Dr. Ray. It seems he perished in an explosion at his home today at noon. Terrible shame, don't you think?"

"Terrible. That ends it. Now things can get back to normal—right?"

"Yes, if anything comes out of all this, you'll simply testify Max went rogue and started the entertainment at the LMMC all on his own for a side hustle. See how simple that is?" He swatted at a fly. "In the meantime, at the club, I have more girls coming. Eduardo and his men are bringing seventeen entertainers to the club today. I need you there to meet him and his helpers, get the entertainers situated, and ready for work. We have to have them up to speed for the weekend."

"Today?"

"Did I stutter, Senator? Yes, *today*. You've got a lot of work to do. Michelle is coming to help you with the entertainers. I didn't want to use her. But she offered, and I'm in a pinch thanks to your pal, Max."

"What time will they be in town?"

He twisted his watch into view, doing the math in his head. "Six o'clock this evening—your time. And, Carl, make sure the caregivers don't do anything stupid. Especially Fast Larry. I can count on you, right?"

"You know you can."

"Any word on Max's memorial?"

"It's Thursday, sir. Thursday at two p.m."

"Guess I should send some flowers, maybe send Leslie some money too. How are you coming with the impeachment?" The corners of his lips turned up, and a Grinch-like smile came to life as he thought of his old friend the POTUS scrambling for his political life, now a sworn enemy.

"It's not. There's no crime, but I'll do what I can to make it look like one."

"Good. Use the media. Six o'clock, Senator, don't forget." He then hung the phone up, mumbling to himself, "Don't let me down, Senator. Don't let me down."

Mike didn't want to break the news to his parents, but sooner or later, someone would say something. Better from him than just anybody. Right after work, he went over to their house, taking the wire report with him, struggling with Willie's instructions.

Mom must've seen him pulling up to the house. She came out to meet him, appearing to be babbling all the way. "Hi, honey. Did you forget something yesterday?"

He hugged her, building up the nerve to break her heart. "No, I didn't forget anything. I don't know how to tell you, so I'm just going to let you read this." He handed her the report.

"Okay, this must be bad." Her brows arched upon seeing the news, but she didn't react the way he had expected. "Congressman Rice, isn't he the man Steven saved in Wisconsin? Yes, it says here his heart failed. I wonder if Steven knows. That was the morning your brother was cleared. We better let him know."

"No, Mom. Read this." He turned the report over.

Her knees went weak. If not for his quick reflexes, she would've fallen on the gravel driveway. She started to scream, but Mike couldn't finish it this way. He had to tell her. He gripped her shoulders. "He's not dead, Mom. He's not dead."

Dad came running. "Is everything all right? Why does your mother look like that?"

Mom had lost all her color. The fear of losing her firstborn must have ripped her heart open.

"What's the meaning of this, Mike?"

"Someone tried to kill DR, but he escaped. He asked Willie to let me know. He needs you to believe this for a day or two, until the DNA report on the dead man comes back, so it doesn't seem suspicious." He gritted his teeth, hunching his shoulders. "Willie said he wanted the killers to think he was dead. But I couldn't do it. I knew how bad it would hurt you, but you've got to play the part—otherwise, he may get killed."

"We'll do whatever we need to do." Dad slid Mom from Mike's grip. "If someone calls or comes by, we'll do our best."

Good thing Dad held her so tight. She still looked feeble.

"Does Steven know about this fellow dying?" Mom pointed out the notice on the other side. "Yesterday, they acted right proud about how they helped save his life. I don't think he knows. You might want to ask Willie to let him know. It could be important."

Dad let Mom stand on her own, but he took her hand.

"Mom, Dad, I've got to get home. Sorry for the scare, Mom. Remember, you don't know anything, okay?" He climbed into his car.

"Mum's the word."

Driving out of the driveway, he called Willie and stopped before pulling onto the main road. "I couldn't do it. Mom got hysterical, and I buckled under pressure."

"Oh man. You really can't keep a secret."

"I couldn't hurt Mom and Dad like that. Besides, the killer's probably never going to hear anything about it. Mom told me to tell you about the other story on the printout." He unfolded the sheet. "It was about the congressman DR helped save. He's dead—died the same day DR was cleared, Mom said."

"Thanks. I'll let him know."

"Willie, why is he calling you? Why doesn't he just call me? Do you two have something going on I don't know about?" He tossed the paper aside and toggled the car heater.

"You know better. He can't call his family. They might be monitoring all your calls, besides, he's using Ryan's phone, maybe he doesn't remember your numbers?"

"Okay, that makes sense. I've got to get off here. Dinner's waiting."

He twisted his grip on the steering wheel. What happened when the killer found out DR was alive? How many more times could his brother escape?

CHAPTER
THIRTY-ONE

After stopping by DR's shop, making sure it was secure, and grabbing a wad of emergency cash from the safe as well as a few firearms and other fun toys, DR and Ryan drove to Chicago. They got a room on the upper north side of the city in Edison Park, as close to the LMMC as possible. The swanky hotel was almost completely booked. Only Debbie's connections got them in.

Just after four p.m., Ryan received a call from Willie. He winked at DR as he answered it. "Hi, Tonya. What's up?"

"If you see DR, let him know the congressman is dead. It may be important."

He huffed, his shoulders hunching in. "I hoped you were calling to talk to me." He moved to the hotel window. "He's here with me. I'll put you on speakerphone."

"Thanks. DR, I just found out the congressman you guys saved still died that same morning. Did you know that?"

"No, I didn't. Maybe that's why there was a lot of commotion at the hospital. Four people were killed, apparently for no reason, maybe it was a cover-up." He checked one of the 9mms he'd picked up, perfect.

"The wire said the memorial is Thursday. I better let you go, keeping the call under a minute. Sorry for the bad news."

The line went dead.

DR paced. Maybe Leslie might have information on Jennings's whereabouts.

"Ryan, you better step up to the plate soon. She's a keeper." DR handed him a walkie-talkie, then pulled on a heavy coat. The temperature had dipped near zero as a cold front came through. "I'm going outside to check their range. Keep it on."

"You want me to go?"

"I've got it. You stay here. I can use the fresh air to think this thing through. Especially after hearing about Max's death." He flipped his walkie-talkie's switch on, then closed their room's door behind him.

Running thoughts of that night's struggles through his mind while going outside, he replayed getting Max to the hospital and the gun battle with the helicopter on the road back to Chicago the next morning. None of it made sense. Why did they want Max dead so badly, especially after dumping Dingleman in the lake? "This wasn't about me, Dingleman, or Max. It's an obsession. The man is obsessed."

"What did you say?"

"Sorry, Ryan. I didn't mean to hold the talk button. I'll explain when I get to the room." At least the radio worked.

Senator Carl Brummengarten arrived at the LMMC around an hour early, wanting to get it over with. He hated having anything to do with Eduardo, a coyote who'd kill his own mother for a few dollars. All their meetings had been uneasy at best, and now, here he was, doing business with the outlaw.

And since he knew the extent of Jennings eavesdropping on him, even in DC, things had changed. He kept playing over and over in his head what Jennings told him earlier: "Just remember what you told Max. Just shut up and do your job. It's not rocket science and not nearly as hard or bad." The man's laugh sealed it.

The caretakers turned the heat on in the trailers after receiving word of the girls' arrival, but the stench from the chamber pots wafted from the cages. Poor girls. What was he doing? He was supposed to be protecting people, not aiding their destruction. *Just shut up and do your job. It's not rocket science.*

His phone rang, and Eduardo's contact flashed before Carl gritted his teeth and swiped to answer. "Hey, amigo. It's been a long time."

Carl pulled the middle trailer door shut and went to check the first. "It has been a long time, but not long enough."

"Come on, Senator. Why the hostility? We're business partners, no?"

"No, Eduardo. Jennings is your business partner. I'm just someone in the wrong place at the wrong time." Someone who'd stepped too quickly into Max's reluctant shoes.

"So you don't want the girls, amigo?"

"You know what I mean. No, bring the girls. Jennings wants them." Carl stopped at the pang of guilt, the dehumanization of it all, the thing that probably consumed his former colleague.

"You sure, amigo? I don't want to hurt your feelings."

Eduardo laughed, and more laughter in the background raised the hair on Carl's neck.

"We'll be ready at the trailers. Hurry up and get this over with." Carl motioned to Fast Larry to empty a chamber pot.

"Dude, that ain't my job."

"Do it!"

"What did you say?" Eduardo asked.

"I wasn't talking to you. Hurry up, Eduardo." Carl disconnected, imagining how the coyotes were laughing it up.

He talked aloud to himself, recalling Scripture. "'A little leaven leavens the whole lump.'" Only he didn't know who the leavening was—himself, Jennings, or Eduardo. Was this just buyer's remorse? Each had played their part. "I've got to go back to church."

The next morning, Wednesday, DR and Ryan had their plan. As DR drove them to see Leslie Rice, Max's wife, Ryan opened up about himself and Willie, apparently taking a chance on DR's forgiveness, hoping it wouldn't be the end of him in DR's life.

"I've done some things—things I'm not proud of. I owe some people a lot of money in Dublin, and here—now. That's why I have a hard time with Tonya. She's so… so, good. She deserves a man who is too."

DR checked the side-view mirror. "Ryan nobody is perfect, not even Willie."

"What I'm trying to say is I can't reconcile being with her and how I feel about myself. Besides, the people I owe will do anything to get their money, anything, even if it means hurting someone I care about."

"You can't owe that much. How much do you owe?" DR frowned at Ryan's sullen expression.

"Nearly six hundred thousand American dollars now, thanks to a bad-luck streak."

"Ah, you like to gamble. Where did you get the money for my cruise, if you don't mind my asking?" Maybe this story had a bright side. "I wondered how a Catholic church administrator had that kind of cash lying around."

"You don't want to know."

"Why did you come? Don't get me wrong—I'm glad you did, but it seems expensive for a guy in your shoes." DR sipped out of a hot cup of coffee, peeking over the top as he drove.

"It was stupid." Ryan squirmed. "I got scared after the casino sent some boys by the church to rough me up. I saw your advertisement in that trade tweet, and my aunt bought me a ticket to fly with her to Malaga. Next thing I knew, there I was."

"An impulse? Okay. Let's just keep this our secret. We'll talk about it later. Here's Leslie's home coming up." Parking in the driveway, DR took a deep breath. Would their meeting with her be as informative as the drive over?

Ringing the bell, DR could see into the living room. A few boxes lined the floor.

"Hi, DR. Won't you come in?" She held the door open, turning sideways to allow the visitors to pass.

"Hi, Leslie. This is my friend Ryan. We're so sorry to hear about Max." DR reached out for her hand to console her. "You must be devastated. How are your children?"

"We're taking it day by day. We learned so much about what was going on. I hoped we could start fresh, but Max's heart just stopped. The doctors still haven't told me anything." She held his hand for a moment, then showed them to a seat. "After you called, I dug these boxes out of the garage. They have all his notes and correspondence, nothing classified, just his quick notes and things."

"How much did Max tell you about the men's club and the children?"

"It wasn't just that. He said this Jennings fellow was pushing him and some of his colleagues to take down the POTUS, that it consumed him. The kids from Yemen were the last straw. Max said he couldn't continue down that path. After they tried to kill you, he knew they would come for him." She wiped her eyes with a tissue. "He knew too much and wanted out."

"I'm sorry to bring all this back, but that man blew up my home yesterday morning. I was lucky to escape." He rose up and looked over the boxes, probably a plethora of dead ends. "I've got to finish this."

"Here's his secretary's name and number." She handed him a card with the congressional seal on it. "Maybe Mary can help you find what you're looking for, but as far as I know, he never visited Jennings's home in California. He only met the man once. Mary will be in town tomorrow for Max's memorial service. Maybe she could meet with you then."

"Thanks, Leslie." He held the card up and tipped it at her in gratitude. "I was wondering—How can we get in early to pay our respects?"

"I'll leave word with the ushers to let you in. If you don't mind, I have an appointment I can't miss. Trying to tie up some loose financial ends." She rose and reached for DR, hugging him. "Thank you for all you did in Wisconsin."

He let go of the hug. "You're welcome. We just wish the outcome had been different."

On the way out to the car, Ryan took the card. "Why didn't you tell her about the cafeteria and heliport attendants being killed?" He gave the card back.

"At this point, it wouldn't help her grief. No use opening that today." DR dialed the number on the front of the card for Mary Hipple, assistant to Congressman Max Rice. "Hello, Mrs. Hipple?"

"This is she. How may I help you?"

"Ma'am, I'm sorry to bother you, but I need your help. It concerns the late congressman...."

Ten minutes later, after lots of back and forth, she agreed to meet him briefly at the memorial service—before the public entered the service—keeping their meeting secret.

In Birmingham, Greg and his wife awaited the charter bus. At last, it grumbled up the drive, reportedly carrying twenty-eight children, Tom, and Sam. The paid driver rang the bell to announce themselves, and Johnson opened the gate. Now, as it drove up, Greg and Penny stood on their oversized front porch with its fluted columns. Amal snugly tucked under Penny's right arm. Unable to hide her joy, the child was bouncing up and down.

As soon as the bus door opened, Amal shot away, then tried to get onto the bus. "Whoa, whoa, whoa, little lady." The driver held up a hand. "Let's let everyone get off the bus."

Not understanding his words, but seeing his hand stuck out, she stepped to the side, right outside the door, waiting and bouncing. Penny and Greg approached, and she put her arm around Amal, as much as a restraint as an emotional hug. After half the bus had unloaded, a bruised and bandaged Habiba followed their other sister, Derifa, down the bus steps and out onto the driveway. Penny let Amal go, and Greg breathed in deeply, happy to see the sisters reunited, safe from harm.

Still, he couldn't help being overwhelmed by the number of kids coming off the bus. This would take the special effort they'd planned, at Penny's urging, to accommodate everyone. By the time Tom had exited, the kids covered the porch and driveway, Sam leading them away from the bus.

"Greg, Penny, it's so good to be back." Breathing in the warm Alabama air, Tom turned around in a circle to take it all in.

Greg robustly shook Tom's, then Sam's hand. Penny was kneeling and fussing with the kids and trying to listen too. She reached for his hand and nearly fell over. "Thank you, thank you, all. I can't tell you how much this means to me, seeing these kids free. God must've been with you."

The three men looked at each other before Sam spoke up. "I believe you're right. At every turn, we should've been dead, yet here we are."

While awaiting the bus, Greg had helped his wife gather up as many sleeping bags, quilts, and blankets as they could, along with pillows. Johnson stocked the kitchen with an abundance of snacks and fruit, and along with Penny's sister and brother-in-law, was cooking a hearty Alabama stew for lunch. The smell of baking bread already filled the home, making everyone wait less patiently. Amal was chattering to her sisters and the other children, probably telling them what she'd been through and, hopefully, how good they'd been to her.

Tom called Willie. As planned, she'd agreed to be their contact point.

"Hello. Is that you, Willie?" He smiled at Habiba. A bruised eye, cuts, and scrapes did not slow her down from loving on and playing with her baby sister.

"Tom, you made it?" Willie's voice came through loud. Tom must've put it on speakerphone since the kids were so noisy. "That was fast."

"Yes, got in about half an hour ago. How are things up there?" Tom leaned against the wall, staying out of everyone's way while looking on.

"They blew up DR's house. He barely escaped. There's nothing left but a pile of rubbish."

"What?" Tom held up his hand to get everyone to quiet down.

His chest muscles tightening, Greg edged closer as Willie related the story. He let out a low whistle. "That man must have nine lives, and thank God, for every one of them."

"Absolutely," Willie responded to Greg. "The other man was killed, and DR is going to let authorities believe it's him, maybe buy some time to strike back. How are the children?"

"They're good." Tom goggled at Greg, seeming just as in shock as Greg was. "Especially after joining up with Amal again. We're getting ready to eat. Would you let DR know we made it okay?"

"Sure. Talk to you soon."

"See ya." Tom tilted his head toward the floor on his right side, rubbing at his other temple, obviously collecting his thoughts. Then he placed his hand on Greg's shoulder and motioned Sam over, keeping his voice low probably to keep from scaring Penny and the kids since a few of the girls understood a little English. "I'm afraid it's not over yet."

～

The temperature continued to drop as the day wore on. Meanwhile, a steady stream of souls confronted the harsh conditions to see the girls at Club Gauntlet in Chicago. DR and Ryan waited in the car until the club had been open for an hour, around four p.m., before going in to find the detective, vowing to get to the bottom of this.

"Thanks for the clothes. I didn't have anything that would fit in," Ryan said. "How do you plan to get him out without anyone knowing the better?"

DR waved his pistol. "Just a little friendly persuasion. Something tells me this guy will do anything to stay alive. Eat his own arm off if necessary." He stepped out of the warm car, and the cold reality hit him. "Brrr. Hard to believe someone would leave a warm home to come here today."

Ryan double-timed it toward the club. "Priorities, I would guess."

"Tells you a lot about society." DR caught up with Ryan. "Oh well. To each their own."

Inside the club, the tattooed man wasn't working. Today, a petite black-haired girl with a pretty smile greeted them. After paying the cover and letting their eyes adjust, they spotted their target, Detective Shortman, sitting at a dark and out-of-the-way table on the club's far side. A crutch leaned against the wall nearby.

Walking around the club, not allowing the detective to see them first, DR moved in behind the man while surveying the room out of the corner of his eyes. "Hello, Detective. It's been a while." He pushed his gun in the man's back through his overcoat pocket. "Care if we join you?"

When the detective turned to see, his jaw dropped, and his eyes widened. Then he mumbled, stuttering, "Sure, b–but you're not supposed to have a gun in here."

"Ha ha. Sorry. Don't mean to break any rules. It's nothing personal." DR retold the man's words back to him.

"What do you want?" Shortman craned, nervously looking for help, but not finding any with the male bouncer not on duty today.

"Stay calm, and everything will work out. We don't want to get crazy because this gun fires really easy. All we want is some information. After we have a drink with you, the three of us will leave together." He stopped.

A performer was making her way back, following a server. After taking their order, the server left, leaving the performer there.

"Hello, gentleman, and you too, Detective." She was twisting to the music in her own seductive way. "You fellows look like you could use a table dance."

"Maybe later, sweetheart." DR watched her smile turn to a frown. "We haven't seen our friend here for a while and have some catching up to do."

"Are you sure?" She gave a special twist. "I think you'll like my dancing."

Ryan's eyes bulged out.

DR smirked. "I know we will. Come back later."

"You must have ice water in your veins." Ryan huffed, his gaze following her seductive saunter to the stage. "How can you keep from watching her?"

"Don't think a part of me doesn't want to. I just know it's harder to stop a rolling wheel than it is to hold the brake before it starts." As the server came back with their drinks, DR passed Ryan a fifty to give the young lady, then jabbed the gun against the detective's ribs.

Ryan ogled her as she delivered the drinks, admiring her uniform, and lack of it. "Here, sweetheart. Keep the change."

She checked the bill, beaming. "Thank you, gentlemen. I'll come back to check on you soon."

"You do that, honey."

DR shook his head, learning more about his cousin-by-marriage than he cared to know. So much for his feelings for Willie. "Come on, Shortman. You're going to lead us out of here. Remember, I'm not afraid to use this."

"Where are we going?" Shortman reached for his crutch.

"Somewhere we can talk privately." DR pushed to his feet. "And don't try any funny stuff."

Back at the hotel, they entered through the garage not to garner any attention and arrived unfettered at their room. After securing the detective to a chair, DR pumped him for information about Jennings, Max, and the LMMC.

Shortman kept tight-lipped, not saying anything—at first.

CHAPTER
THIRTY-TWO

Thursday afternoon, the line for Congressman Max Rice's memorial service stretched for a block, hundreds braving the brutal late-December weather. During his time as a construction contractor and congressman, Max had made friends with many of Chicago and Illinois's top public figures. Some spoke of backing him to leave the House of Representatives and run for the Senate in the next election, joining Chicago's favorite son Carl Brummengarten in leading America out of the icy hands of the conservative maniacs.

Arriving early, DR and Ryan followed Leslie's instructions and were allowed to enter. They visited with the family and viewed Max, before taking a seat in the middle of the sanctuary. Mary Hipple arrived shortly after, coming in just before the public was granted entry. After spending time with Leslie, Danny, and Dawn, she made her way back to them as the public started coming in.

"Dr. Ray, it's nice to meet you. Leslie shared with me your situation and how you helped get Max to the hospital." She nodded to Ryan.

"It's nice to meet you too, Mary. This is my friend and associate, Ryan McNeilly. Thanks for taking the time to help us." DR surveyed the room, not seeing anything suspicious.

Then she handed him a manila envelope, stuffed almost to the point of not closing. "I was able to retrieve this from Max's personal safe. You should find something in there to help you."

"If I can find out anything about this Jennings fellow, it'll be a help. We don't have a clue where he is—or even who he is."

"He used to call Max a lot, and Max called him often—so much so I was on a first name basis with Kat, Jennings's personal assistant. He had something over Max and a lot of others, the best I could tell. Max feared his calls."

She fidgeted her feet as people streamed in, then stiffened. "I see Max's friend and colleague, the senator." She pointed to the head of the review line. "I better go say hi. Good luck."

"Thanks, Mary. Be safe." DR rubbed his jaw as she snaked her way to the front. "What a strange expression on the senator's face, don't you think?" DR locked eyes with the man.

"His friend died. You never know what kind of feelings that will bring up."

"Guess you're right." But feeling something in his bones, DR tried to keep the envelope under his overcoat secret and away from prying eyes.

After conversing with Max's family and Mary, the senator took a seat five rows in front of them, pulled out his phone, and took a selfie.

"Strange. Why would anyone take a selfie at a funeral service?"

"Maybe for reimbursement, to prove they came. Who knows? People do crazy stuff."

When Senator Carl's text arrived, Jennings opened the photo while keeping their call connected. "Are you sure, Carl? You saw Mary hand Dr. Ray an envelope?" He studied the selfie the senator just sent him, then slammed his glass on the desk, orange juice flying everywhere.

"Yes, sir. Ray stuck it under his overcoat as fast as she handed it to him. Mary may have given him confidential information."

Jennings swiveled in his chair, ignoring the day's pressing business on his desk. "How does this guy keep surviving? I just don't get it, Senator. I just don't get it. It feels like I'll have to take him down myself." He picked the glass up, taking a hard swallow of orange juice and glaring at a picture of himself and Carl on the senator's boat.

"I don't know either, sir. When our guys had them all trapped on the bus, they did everything to that bus *but* kill him. So what do you want to do—about Mary? She's going to be a smoking gun, a loose end."

"Agreed." Folding his hands in front of his face, he covered his mouth as he exhaled. "What time is her flight back to DC?"

"Five forty-five this evening. I'll get back to you with the flight number."

"No need. There won't be another flight leaving east at the same time." A bird flew off the ledge of the building. "Bang."

"Sir?"

"Nothing."

"What are you thinking, sir?"

"Eduardo can take care of our little pigeon. He likes to try out our new toys. I'll give him one of those you just sent me. That should take care of our rat problem." The tightness in his chest increased. The doctor warned him about stress.

"We can get Mary another way. Then we'll get the doctor."

"Maybe, maybe not, but it's a shame he's not working for us. I could use a doctor like that."

DR headed back to the room after picking up Chinese takeout down the street. Riding up the open escalator, he caught the smell of a wonderful fragrance, soon spotting the source checking in at the front desk. The woman was beautiful, but more than that, her perfume was a fragrance that captured his senses, one not easily forgotten.

"Hope everyone likes lo mein. They were all out of fried rice." He called out as he entered the room. Back at the table, he opened the bag to expose three Styrofoam containers. He set one before the detective and one on each side of him. "Don't try anything stupid, Detective, and you'll live to see tomorrow."

Then DR's jaw dropped, and his eyes widened. "I know why the senator took the selfie! He works for Jennings. He wasn't taking a picture of himself. He was taking *our* picture. Mary—Mary's in trouble." He reached for his phone. "I've got to call her now."

"Wait a minute." Ryan gripped DR's arm. "Are you sure? How would he do it?"

"Ha ha, probably shoot down the plane—if I know him," the detective mumbled, stuffing lo mein in his mouth.

The color left Ryan's face as he connected the punishment to the crime. "There's around five hundred people on those planes. He's not that big of a maniac, is he?"

"He didn't become a member of Circle playing with Pixy Stixs." Shortman hunched his shoulders and gave them a friendly roll, raising his right brow. "Besides, the girls have arrived at the club, and the senator has to get them ready."

"Girls?" DR spoke over the cellphone before getting an answer. "Hello, Mary? Are you okay? We think the senator told Jennings about our meeting. I think you're in danger."

"I'm fine. I've got to go. My plane's almost finished boarding."

"No, Mary—no!"

But the phone went dead.

"That didn't sound promising."

"She hung up. Said her plane was boarding."

Shortman kept calmly shoveling food into his mouth.

DR paced to the window. "I hope you're wrong, Detective."

"About what—the plane or the girls?"

"Both. What girls are you talking about? We already took the children somewhere safe." His blood rising, DR took a deep breath.

"Eduardo, Jennings's main supplier, brings them across the border using NGOs. Plus, he does all sorts of favors, for a price. He brought them, yesterday."

"Chicago PD knows about this?" Ryan finally opened his dinner, apparently having been too enthralled by the whodunit.

"Not officially. I do, and all this is off the record. Police work doesn't pay zilch, especially in this era of defund the police." The greasy guy wiped his mouth. "So most of us have to get a side hustle, helps with the bills, and you never know, they just might defund us."

"More kids." DR hardly dared voice it. "They're getting them for this weekend, aren't they?" He held his breath, afraid of the answer.

Shortman nodded. "They're already at the club. They start entertaining tomorrow night. Not all of them are kids."

"You're disgusting." DR balled his fist at his side, fighting the anger, his rage building. "How can you let this happen to them right under your nose?"

"I feel you, Ray, but what can I do? He doesn't have a problem getting rid of troublemakers, so we all take the money and keep our mouths shut. It worked well until you came along, and the congressman grew a conscience."

"Jennings killed him too, didn't he?"

Another nod. "So what are you going to do with me?"

"We're not killers. After we go, we'll leave word at the front desk tomorrow night to set you free."

"For what it's worth, I'm sorry I took you out on the boat, but it was you or me. Better watch your back. That Eduardo is a tricky one."

Willie was meeting Mike at Marcie's Place for an early dinner. His wife and kids having gone to her mother's home for the day while the kids were on Christmas break, Mike wanted the latest update. How odd that Willie, who once had a raging crush on DR, was his only outlet to communicate now.

"Hi, Rachael. How was your Christmas?" Mike grinned, nodding at her daughter playing up front by the shop's Christmas display.

"It was nice. I'm sorry about your brother. We're all terribly sorry."

Right. No grins. No one knew it wasn't his brother in the explosion at his house. "I'm holding out hope. They haven't named the man they found yet. Mom and Dad are in pieces."

"We'll just have to keep praying, then. Are you ready to order?"

"If you don't mind, I'll wait on Willie. She should be here any minute... *and* it appears she's coming in the door."

"Okay. I'll come right back." She went over to Willie, hugged her, said something, then joined her daughter.

Mike rose and squeezed Willie's shoulders. "How's it going?"

"Do you mean with me or DR?"

"Both, I guess. You first."

"I'm okay, just a little weary, trying to maintain my own peace. As for the other, it's like I told you earlier. The bus arrived in Alabama yesterday, and they're going to take the kids somewhere else. I talked to Tom again today. They think the FBI agents they caught told Jennings about Amal. So they're not chancing it." She flipped through the menu. "What are you having?"

"I'm going with the bacon cheeseburger. I don't get the chance to indulge myself when Alyssa is around." He patted Willie's hand. "This is my treat by the way."

"You don't have to do that."

"I know, but you've been such a good friend to me and my family. It's something I want to do. Any more news?"

"Ryan and DR are in Chicago." She filled him in on the goings-on there before Rachael came for their orders.

"That's a lot." Mike handed over his menu.

"Things are moving fast. They have to, or Jennings will catch up to them."

Mike studied her. Was the crush the real thing, or it was a two-way street now? "Don't you find it odd that you're the one he trusts to relay the news to everyone?"

She shrugged. "I'm probably the only one who can. The FBI must still have tracers on everyone else."

"We interrupt this WXON-EZ Chicago television programming with a special report. We're coming to you live over Lincoln Park from Air Bird 1, where it appears a 747 bound for Washington International was shot down this evening by a surface-to-air missile at six p.m.

"Reports are hazy, but several eyewitnesses say a rocket streaked toward the airliner and made a direct hit that divided the plane in two. Both parts fell into Lake Michigan less than a thousand yards from the shoreline. Our reporter, Manny Hernandez, is on the scene at the lake's edge."

"Turn that up." DR shushed the detective as Ryan used the remote to raise the volume.

Ryan sat down, stunned. "I thought you were kidding!"

"Don't underestimate Jennings." Calmly scooping another bite, Shortman shifted toward the TV. "Look what he did to sink you all in the Indian Ocean, not just anyone could make that happen. Jennings is obsessed with bringing you down. He thinks you made him look bad to his counterparts in Circle. The longer this goes on, the more he's going to do to get you. Everyone I know is surprised you're still alive."

The reporter continued speaking. "Tonight's flight from Chicago ORD airport to Washington International carried four hundred and sixty-three passengers and fourteen crew members including two pilots. Although no information is available, it appears unlikely there were survivors. Police, as you can see behind me, are watching the coastline for any debris or bodies that may come in with the tide. Six of the twenty-one sectors of the coast guard are either en route, being dispatched, or have reached the wreckage area.

"Police and coast guard are setting up a communication center, and as soon as more news is available, we'll bring it to you live on site. This is Manny Hernandez, reporting for WXON-EZ Television, Chicago."

"Mary." DR paused, closing his eyes, taking a deep breath. "He killed almost five hundred people—just to get to Mary?"

"I told you."

"We'll have to keep hitting him where it hurts until he comes out of his slimy hole. Then maybe we can show him some fun games."

"Good luck. The man is untouchable. All of Circle is. They own the DOJ and the media, not to mention half of Congress. That's why he doesn't care who he hurts."

"Everybody has something they'll fight for, someone they'll protect. He must too."

～

Friday morning in Birmingham, Alabama, FBI Agents Larson and Riddlehour returned to the Nichols home, this time with six other agents and a search warrant for Amal Saeed, age unknown, origin Aden, Yemen.

When Larson rang the bell at the gate, that butler answered. "I'm sorry, but no one is home."

"We have a warrant to search the premises," Larson replied, feeling the back of his head where he took a vicious blow last visit.

"Hold it up to the video camera."

After he showed the warrant in the video camera, the gate swung open. Moments later, his and the other three cars pulled to the front porch, and all agents climbed out. Johnson met them on the front steps.

"You could've made this easier if you'd turned the girl over when we were here the first time." Pushing by Johnson, Larson pointed for the agents to spread out, two this way, another two that way, and two more to the barn out back. Then he and his partner went upstairs to check the bedrooms and extra baths.

Fifteen minutes later, the agents met on the front porch, all of them finding nothing. "Where did they take the girl? She's a minor. Mr. and Mrs. Nichols are violating the law."

"Why didn't you just ask me earlier? Before you trespassed and tried to kidnap the girl, maybe I would have told you."

"You know we'll find her. It's just a matter of time. Make it easy on yourself."

"Like I said, I don't know where she is, nor the Nichols. I'm just a hired hand. They don't tell me where they're going."

Larson looked back into the house, scanning the property. "Tell the Nichols this isn't the last of this. They're dealing with powerful people, people who won't stop until they get their way. Their friend, Dr. Ray, found out the hard way. How many more of you will have to die?"

Friday, the cold front eased up, and the temperature hovered around freezing all day. The news of the LMMC bringing in new performers disturbed DR. He hadn't stopped anything. Rather, he'd caused a different set of victims to be brought forward. This and the shooting down of Mary's flight was more than he'd prepared for. Now he had to figure out what would get to Jennings more than anything.

"Ow. You gotta let me off this chair. It's killing me." Shortman tugged against the cords, to no avail.

"Would you rather be tied to the bed?" DR jerked a thumb toward the frameless bed. Just how would he tie him up there?

"Anything is better than this."

"All right. We'll give it a shot. First, I'm going down to get us something to eat. After breakfast, we'll move you to the bed." On the way out, DR stopped by the bathroom where Ryan was shaving. "I'll be right back."

Going down the escalator, he smelled the alluring fragrance, the same as the evening before. Ahead, the woman and two large men entered the lobby elevator. Tall and slender, she'd dressed to impress in a glittering gold dress split at her thigh.

He shook his head. *Why is she so captivating? This isn't like me.*

Still, he leaned forward to get one last look. Minutes later, when he carried their breakfast back to the room, what sounded like a helicopter whirred overhead. Then its shadow fell on the hotel hallway floor.

"What's that look on your face?" Ryan, having finished dressing, was combing his hair.

"I don't know what you mean." DR set the food tray on the table and passed the goodies around. He pushed a handful of creamer and sugar into the middle of the table. "Hope you like your coffee strong."

Ryan untied Shortman's right hand so he could eat. "There. No funny business."

"Did you hear a helicopter take off from the roof? I think a celebrity's staying here. I saw a lady get in the elevator. She might've been who took the helicopter." DR huffed out a breath. *Got to stop this. You're engaged.* "Being near a celebrity has never awed me before, but there's something about this one."

Ryan sipped his coffee, eyeing it as if to decide how much cream and sugar to add. "So did you come up with anything of Jennings's to bring him out of his hole?"

"I was thinking about the casino yacht. Nothing bothers the wealthy more than going after their wealth or their children." DR bit into his blueberry bagel, the cream cheese coating his tongue. "And we don't know where his children are, or if he even has any."

"So the *Lucky Lucie*, it is." Ryan drummed his hands on the table. "Shortman, does Jennings have any children you know of?"

"One."

"So, that was helpful." Ryan shook his head theatrically.

"What do you want from me? I've only seen her once. He doesn't involve her with his business."

"Is that all you know?" Sitting back into his seat, DR waited as he finished chewing.

"Just rumors. That's all I know. Word is she's a rescue from his days before Circle, back when he was a good man. Now can I finish eating before we continue fifty questions?"

Holding the bagel in his right hand, he stared at his bite mark. *If I bite Jennings where it hurts, can I really stop the man from finishing what he started? Or will the man finally get lucky?*

CHAPTER
THIRTY-THREE

Senator Carl Brummengarten opened the helicopter door, and a pair of beautifully sculpted legs stretched out to meet the helipad. The lady in the sparkling gold dress exited, smiling. After clearing the chopper's blades, she met him with a hug. Then they went from the roof pad downstairs into the club. The helicopter took off, leaving no traces of its delivery.

"Michelle, welcome. It's so good to see you. What's it been—three years?" He held her at arm's length, taking a good look. "I like your hair this color."

"Thanks—it's been four. Sorry to say I wish it was more, but Dad has gotten worse since he joined Circle. Playing politics, gambling, and trafficking is all he does anymore." She flattened her lips into a tight frown.

"I know. Did you hear about Max?" Carl took her coat and hung it in his office in the hallway to the kitchen, once Max's, then returned.

"I did. What happened to him?" She turned in a circle, checking out the club's dance floor and bar, pushing back her light-brown hair, now in a curly do.

"His heart just stopped. The coroner doesn't know what caused it. It just lost its electrical pulse."

"What a shame." She touched his arm. "So you're running the club now?"

"Unfortunately. My wife's not crazy about the idea. Good thing she doesn't know what's going on here." He nodded toward the trailers. "He just brought seventeen in from Mexico. Most are from Honduras. Eduardo used an NGO to get them in the country."

"Eduardo? Didn't you two get into a scuffle a few years back? Eduardo probably fits right into the left's business model." She nodded to a blank space on the wall.

"The picture's gone. Your dad didn't want any reminders to the members about his past association with the President. It's all about business." He jerked a thumb toward where a picture of Circle's members now hung.

"Well, I better get to it. I've got an event to plan."

"Dressed like that?" He arched an eyebrow.

"It'll give the girls something to aspire to."

"Don't get your hopes up. These girls were a last-minute addition. Someone stole our other performers—all thirty-three of them."

"How could someone steal them?"

"They're crazy. They busted in and took out the caregivers, then killed two FBI agents and three of our guards during a high-speed chase through downtown Chicago, escaping with all the performers. Your dad was pissed."

"This sounds complicated. I'll get with you later, and you can tell me everything."

Michelle Jennings walked to the trailers.

Carl tsked his tongue. "Poor kid. I didn't think the old man would ever involve her."

Forty-nine miles from Birmingham in Tuscaloosa, Greg spoke with Johnson on speakerphone. Greg's brother and sister-in-law were in the next room playing You Say, I Say—a game Penny made up using her app to translate Amal's language, Arabic, so she could understand. The children would say a word, and then the Nichols would repeat it after the phone translated it. Now he shifted, catching Penny's gaze, Sam and Tom also listening quietly.

"You were right," Johnson said. "Those rogue agents came by today with six more agents and what appeared to be a valid search warrant. But I didn't tell them anything."

"I knew it." Greg held the phone out so everyone could hear. "They didn't find out about the others, did they?"

"No, but they seem pretty determined. I doubt this is the end of it."

"I'm sure, now that we have all thirty-one. Once DR gets back, we've got some real figuring to do. Thanks for holding down the fort, Johnson. I'll call you again tomorrow to check on things." He hung up and slid his phone in his back pocket.

Penny slipped her arm around him. "Good thing we paid attention to our premonitions."

Greg could sense where this was going, but maybe Penny was right. Something—or Someone—had helped them escape harm every time. Maybe it was time to look into it. "Let's go see what those kids are into now."

"Good call, Greg, good call bringing them here." Sam patted his shoulder.

In the family room, despite the tragic circumstances, the kids were laughing. A serious game had turned into a game of craziness thanks to the children's desires to have fun. The kids kept coming up with funny words to play and learn with.

Tom laughed. "Looks like we may have a few authors here."

"Why ruin the fun?" Penny poked at Greg, grabbing him by the waist and laughing as the children cut it up.

Like his lovely wife had said just months earlier—good friends like these were worth several crappy trips.

On the television muted on the back wall, a special news report flashed. Police reported two American children, kidnapped early this year, were returned to their homes in Louisiana by a secret group of rescuers from Michigan. Video of the happy reunions shared their joy.

～

Friday afternoon in Chicago, DR and Ryan checked their firearms, their walkie-talkies, and their plan. Though simple, the plan required a lot of things to go right. After spending two days with Detective Shortman, they had a better grasp on how the LMMC operated, along with the casino in the *Lucky Lucie* and the "entertainment."

"Let's go over this one more time." DR walked to the window overlooking the street. "To get in, we pretend to be the security for the people in the vehicle in front of us. If that doesn't work, we go to plan B."

Ryan raked his red mop of hair back from his forehead. "What's plan B?"

DR winked. "We'll figure that out if plan A doesn't work. Once inside, we park as far away from the main building as possible. Then, right before the *Lucky Lucie* sets sail, we board her." He left the window, retrieved his pistol, and stuck it in his concealed holster. "From there, we play everything by ear."

Shortman shook his head. "Do you really think the two of you can pull this off? There will be at least twenty of the club's best men on the yacht—that's three to sail the yacht, ten to run the casino, three to keep up with the entertainers, and four for security, and some are off-duty cops. And that's the minimum."

The high-stakes stress clenched DR's now-healing abdomen as apprehension tried to push in. "I didn't say it would be easy, but if our distraction works, we might succeed. Nobody's going to expect us to try to get these girls with all the security, so we'll have to rely on the surprise element."

"Don't forget about me. Tell the desk to set me free." As the door closed shut, Shortman held a cup of Coke with a long straw in the air with his secured right arm.

In the cloudy night sky, the moon and stars kept shuttling in and out of view, at times providing the cover of darkness, and at others the light to get it done. Several vehicles in the line to enter the LMMC had already passed through the security check. DR listened intently as the driver before them, a black Rolls Royce, barked out the passengers' names.

Now, the gatekeeper asked their identity.

"Mays and Smith, security for the Antonins."

"I'm sorry. You're not on the list. I can't let you in."

DR checked the man's name tag. "Chris, if you can't let me in, you better go get the Antonins. They don't travel to any parties without us, their security."

When Chris's coworker shrugged, Chris stepped aside. "All right. Go ahead."

"Thanks." DR drove through the gate. "Whew, plan A is working so far."

Ryan exhaled. "That was quick thinking."

DR followed the Antonins toward the club until the men at the gate resumed checking the others entering. Then he pulled their car over to the far side. The tuxedos he'd rented helped them blend in. As he parked, he nodded toward the lake. Two, not one, vessels docked behind the clubhouse. The *Lucky Lucie* and *Providence*.

"What's the senator's boat doing here?" Ryan asked.

"That boat is everywhere. It was in the Indian Ocean. That's the boat the kids were being trafficked in." His jaw dropped. One and one finally equaled three perpetrators. "He's behind it all. I'll bet he knew about Mary, maybe even ordered it. That was why he took the selfie, to finger us out. New plan. I'll sneak on the *Lucky Lucie*, and you take *Providence* out after we set sail. Give us about fifty yards before you follow."

"Are you sure? How will you get all the children together by yourself?"

"I'll figure it out. But this way, we'll have a place to take them and a way to get them to safety once I get them away from those parasites. When the moon goes behind the clouds, go down and check her out. See if the keys are still in her. Once the *Lucky Lucie* starts to pull out, start her up and let her run until we get out fifty yards, then follow at a safe distance." DR patted Ryan's shoulder, then shook his hand for good luck. "Oh, make sure to turn on your radio after you get aboard."

Ryan ran to the *Providence* in a crouched position, alert for security but finding none. Soon he was on the boat and headed to the helm. Radio on, he checked in. "All clear. Key in the ignition."

Crouched under a set of steps behind the LMMC, DR awaited his turn to run, startled as the men, the children, and an unexpected guest walked to the dock, a familiar aroma wafting his way.

"No way. *She's* part of this?" Then he sighted something else going on further to the right of the *Lucky Lucie*, glad he'd brought his miniature binoculars. A small inflatable dinghy with six men drifted ashore. Three hopped out and went into a storage building, soon carrying out something akin to a handheld rocket launcher.

"Ryan, can you hear me?"

"Roger that."

"We've got company. Somebody just loaded what might be a rocket launcher on a motorized dinghy. Probably Eduardo. Remember what Shortman said, how Eduardo probably did Jennings's dirty work? Well, looks like he's got plans for tonight too."

Three men, dressed in black and appearing heavily armed, marched to the *LL* and boarded her.

"Ryan, Ryan, come back."

"I'm here."

"Three men went on board the yacht—all carrying assault rifles. Make sure you watch for the other boat before following. We can't clue them in on our plans. Okay, here I go. The moon's getting ready to go behind a cloud. Talk to you on the other side."

On board the *Lucky Lucie*, Michelle worked out how to make her own plan. Ready to risk it all. The girls only understood Spanish, so she could talk to them without the caregivers or security knowing what they're talking about—hopefully, glad for her own language skills now.

"Once the caregivers assign you your cabin number"—she spoke in rapid Spanish—"each of you go toward that cabin, but instead of going in the door, go to the downward steps at the back of the boat. Go down two sets of steps. I'll meet you there, and we'll lock ourselves inside the dry-goods hold for the rest of the cruise. They're not hurting you, not on my watch."

As they were breaking up, a girl in the back spoke. "Can I pray for us before we leave?"

Michelle made her way to her and took hold of the girl's small right hand. "Please, Maria, pray for us."

"Everyone, hold hands and close your eyes. Dear Lord, I don't know what Your plan is or who this lady is, but thank You for sending Your angels to bring her to us. We ask for Your protection and blessing, and, Lord, help us escape tonight. In Jesus's name, we come to You, amen."

"Amen." Michelle squeezed the child's hand. "Okay, girls. Remember, go toward the room you're assigned but don't go in. Instead, go to the back staircase and make your way down until you see me. It's going to be a few minutes until they bring your assignment, but don't worry. It's going to be all right. Take this time to snack on something so you won't be getting hungry."

She left them in the makeup room. Closing the door, she leaned against the corridor wall and shut her eyes as well. "Dear God, I couldn't let these girls get abused. But what have I gotten us into?"

The back of her eyes burned, tears making their way down her cheeks. She took a deep breath, righted herself, and wiped the tattletales away before heading downstairs.

In a few minutes, her life would change forever. What would her dad do?

DR hid himself behind the same canvas covering Amal had hidden behind over two weeks earlier, leaving a small crack to watch for Eduardo and his men. Their dinghy must be following at around thirty yards. He could barely hear its motor.

"Ryan, can you hear me?"

"I'm here."

"See Eduardo and his men? Make sure they don't see you."

"I'm on it."

"See you soon. Just watch yourself."

Then he made his way down to the yacht's second-floor berths and found himself in a long hallway of cabins. He put his ear to each door, listening for voices. Nothing. Maybe with the party going upstairs, the girls hadn't come down to the rooms.

He headed to check the next floor down where the ship's storage and extra refrigeration was. He balanced his weight on each the step, feeling the yacht slowing, then dropping anchor.

At the hallway's backend, a voice called out behind him. "Who are you?"

"DR. Who are you?" He put his hands up, not realizing the woman didn't have a gun. The perfume that had drawn him so enticingly before now surrounded him.

"Put your hands down. I don't have a gun. I'm here to get the girls off the yacht."

"That makes two of us. What's your plan?" Taking notice of her beauty, he turned his head to steady himself.

"I was planning on locking the girls—"

Gunfire erupted two levels up.

She spun toward the sound. "What is that?"

"Eduardo's men are out to rob the cash cage—or so I suspect. We've got to move. Where are the girls?"

"They should still be in the makeup area. I don't think they've received their assignments yet."

"Let's go." He used his hand to urge her to lead the way.

"DR...DR." His walkie-talkie crackled. "It looks like the men on the boat are getting ready to fire the missile or rocket or whatever it is. You better hurry."

He fumbled to speak into his radio. "Ryan, loop behind the boat and pull to the side they can't see, the starboard side. I'll bring the girls up there. Be careful."

The beauty paused while running up the stairs. "Who was that?"

"Our transportation."

The dinghy behind the yacht sped to within a good firing range of the *Lucky Lucie,* hoping for a better shot. Forgetting to watch for the sentries posted on the yacht, they took on gunfire.

"Eduardo, watch what you're doing. Don't get too close."

"Shut up. Who's in charge here?"

Inside the yacht, Eduardo's other men followed their instructions and shut down the helm to ensure the casino cash wasn't locked down. "The cash cage won't open until the yacht stops. Make sure you take the helm first. Over."

"Okay, Eduardo. The helm's secure, dropping the anchor."

"Go get our money." Eduardo backed the dinghy away, responding to the warning shots. The sentries let their guard down.

Three armed robbers confronted the young lady in the cash cage with their firearms pulled, speaking in broken English. "Open door. We rob you."

She held her hands in the air in a show of cooperation while stepping on the panic button. A bulletproof steel partition dropped partly from above and another half came from the floor, halting the robbery. Security was immediately alerted.

Moments later, the three men from Mexico lay dead, along with two security personnel.

"Jose, Jose? Come in, Jose." Eduardo, no longer feeling the euphoria from earlier, called out his brother's name, but no answer came. "Get that rocket ready to fire."

Security from the *Lucky Lucie* fired at their boat and called the helm to get underway, but no one was on the helm to hear them. If not for the waves, their shots may have found their targets.

Frigid weather now worked against the men from the south, making operating the keypad and hardware nearly impossible as the dinghy rocked hard side to side. By now, six shooters were dead on the deck of the *Lucky Lucie*, and an occasional bullet was fired from the boat.

Eduardo grew impatient, going to the front to help launch the missile. "Jose, you've got one minute before we blow the yacht. If Jennings finds out we tried to rob him..." He yanked the launcher from his man. "Give me that launcher. He'll feed us to the fish."

With the yacht's security detail focused on Eduardo and his men, DR and Michelle led seventeen scared girls up to the front starboard side, handed them up on the rail, and told them to jump. Ryan had dropped anchor and was catching each girl as they dropped from the yacht's higher level.

With Michelle and DR helping the girls, they were on board *Providence* in under two minutes.

"Help me let down the lifeboats."

DR looked at her. "There's not time for that. We've got to go."

"Not until I tell the others inside."

They lashed two boats to the side, then went in to tell those who were oblivious to the attack. Maybe they'd thought they'd been hearing party poppers. After only managing to convince a few, DR caught her hand and pulled her toward the lifeboats. "We've got to go. They are firing a missile at us."

He switched on his radio. "Ryan, can you hear me?"

"Loud and clear."

"Pull up the anchor. You've got to go as soon as this last one boards." DR sent Michelle to the lifeboats, then stopped by the cash cage, retrieved the scared girl, and instructed her to go jump on the *Providence*. While she ran outside, he reached into the cage, grabbed three bags, and held them up in a toast. "For my house and yacht."

Out on the deck again, he slung the bags across the water into the back of *Providence* that was just beginning to make way. Then he spoke into his walkie-talkie. "See you back at the hotel room, Ryan. Take the girls in the back way so no one sees them. We'll take them somewhere in the morning."

A light flashed.

"Oh, shoo—"

Shock from the missile blast threw him into the air, off the yacht toward the lifeboats. Then everything went black.

CHAPTER
THIRTY-FOUR

As he piloted his craft back toward their van, Eduardo cursed all the way, mourning his brother and friends, while trying to nurse his fingers that smashed against the dinghy's trim when the rocket fired from the FIM-92 launcher. His companions lay in the boat, fingers and hands almost frostbitten because of their struggle working with the launcher. One of the security guards had shot Garcia in the shoulder. He now lay writhing on the boat's bottom, holding a cloth to stop the bleeding.

"Get in the van!" Eduardo shouted to Hernandez, his cousin. "Let's get out of here before the cops come. We can't let Jennings know we sank his casino."

He hauled the dinghy behind bushes in a cove. Then the two men limped to the van, helping Garcia.

"What are you going to tell the boss?" Hernandez asked. "He's going to want to know what happened to our guys."

"Shut up! I'm thinking." Eduardo propped his elbows on the steering wheel, hands clamped against his face. "If the yacht sinks, we'll blame it on that gringo Jennings has been trying to kill. I aimed the missile for the back of the yacht. It was supposed to hit the back. I aimed for the back."

"I told you—it was for shooting down planes!" Garcia shouted from the back seat, still clutching at his wound.

"It worked, didn't it?" Eduardo grunted. "We'll blame it on the gringo. Yeah, we just have to hope the yacht sinks before anyone gets to it." He squealed the tires onto the highway, leaving behind the burning yacht, his dead brother and friends, and the promise of easy money.

"You think Jennings will raise her up and find our boys?"

"That all depends on who's going to raise her and how much money he had on her. He won't want someone digging around on board and finding the girls. We'll just lay low, and if the boss allows, we'll get our payback. Jennings isn't invincible, and neither is the gringo."

Ryan hadn't been a part of DR's earlier exploits, close encounters, and illegal doings, but sometimes, in doing good, you have to break a few eggs. Much like DR and millions of others before him, Ryan guided *Providence* across the lake, grateful when he stumbled upon the coast near Benton Harbor.

Having seventeen Hispanic girls on board and knowing very little Spanish himself, he knew communicating would be difficult at best. He resorted to drawing crude pictures to explain what he was doing. Fortunately, his cellphone hadn't died, and he went onto the rear deck and was able to call Tonya.

"Hello. Ryan?"

"Sorry to call so late, Tonya. But there's been an accident, and I need your help." He found the three bags with the *Lucky Lucie* crest on them and hauled them inside the helm while on the phone, hoping not to lose the signal.

"What sort of accident? Are you all right? Is DR all right?"

"I'm fine. I have seventeen Mexican girls with me on the senator's boat. I don't know where DR is. I don't know whether he's alive or dead."

"What? What happened?" Her sob came over the phone.

"We were rescuing these girls, but someone else, probably a cartel gang, tried to rob the yacht's casino—Can you believe that timing?" He dropped into the captain's seat. "Well, things got chaotic. Once I had the girls, DR motioned for me to get underway, and I'd just started to veer off when they fired a—get this—a *missile*."

Silence. Then low-volume crying.

"Look, Tonya, I didn't want to tell you this tonight. But I don't know what to do. I have seventeen Spanish-speaking teen girls here, with no transportation, no hotel. I need to figure something out before we leave the senator's boat and its warmth behind." He hefted one of the casino money bags. They were almost full. He tried to open a special clasp, to no avail.

"I know a Spanish-speaking cleaning service. Maybe they'll help. I'll call them in the morning. Can you find a bus? DR, Sam, and Tom had brought the other girls to his house on a bus. Where are you?"

"A warehouse wall on the dock says welcome to Benton Harbor." He searched the helm for something to put the casino bags in.

"Hold on. Let me find you on the map and find out where the bus station is."

"Tonya, I know you care for DR—I do too. So don't jump to conclusions and don't give up hope. And please—don't tell anyone else until we know more."

"I won't say anything. Found it. The ad says the station opens at nine a.m. I guess you'll have to spend the night on the boat. Do you want me to make reservations for you?"

"Would you, and hotel reservations too? That would be awfully kind and sweet." *Maybe it's not too late for us. Take a bag or two of the casino's money, settle my debts, and see what the future holds.*

"Okay. Give me a minute. I was in bed getting ready to go to sleep. I'll text you the information."

"Thank you, Tonya. You're wonderful. I can't wait to see you again. Good night."

"Bye. Wait—How do you want to pay?"

"I have cash. I'll pay when I check in." After hanging up, he found a screwdriver and a hammer. *Now to get this thing open.*

～

Three hours later on the West Coast, the news finally reached Mr. Jennings, interrupting a romantic night. The hotel in Chicago had also just found and released Detective Shortman when the senator called from the LMMC.

"This better be good. I'm in the middle of something here."

"Mr. Jennings, I have bad news. You might want to sit down."

"I was lying down—but not anymore. What's so important to call me at this hour?" Jennings swung his legs over the edge of the bed and slid his feet into a pair of slippers, leaving his companion to go into another room for privacy.

"It's the *Lucky Lucie*—someone *sunk* her. Looking at the video, I'd say it was probably Eduardo and his men. There were no survivors, according to the coast guard."

"Michelle?" He gasped, feeling like the final piece of decency in him was about to be shredded and die. "Is Michelle all right?"

"There's been no sight of her either, sir."

Silence.

"The video shows Eduardo and five of his men, dressed in black. They came to the dock in a small dinghy. While a trio boarded the *LL*, Eduardo and the other two took out a stinger—yes, a *stinger*, sir. That's gotta be what sunk the yacht."

"Hell knows no wrath like the fury of a fool."

"There's more."

He scratched at his thinning hair. "Go on. What can be worse?"

"Ray was on the yacht as well. He came with another man, and the other man stole my boat."

"Ray? What's he doing on my yacht?" Coughing, sounding like he was going to gag, Jennings closed his eyes and gritted his teeth, unsure what he felt most—anger, sadness, or devastation? Maybe all of them, his emotions running the gamut. Hatred for an old friend had started it all. *Who are you, Dr. Ray, and why do you keep haunting me?* "So it was Ray in the selfie. Who did they find in the lake?"

"I don't know. It hasn't been reported anywhere yet. I guess it's too early."

"Let me know if anything else comes up." Hanging up, his eyes burning, Jennings sat in a leather armchair and stared at his deceased wife's portrait.

His young companion slipped out of his bedroom door, moving quietly down the hallway to another room, dressing. He heard her but let her leave, his romantic encounter would have to wait.

Why? Why do You have to take everything from me—everything I love. Haven't You taken enough? Why Michelle? His chest hurt. His soul felt drained.

~

A flickering light and warmth from a nearby fireplace caught DR's attention, and a pounding headache reminded him of the night before. After he took several minutes to regain his senses, his eyes sought to unravel the mystery he found himself in. Wait—he was naked under the covers.

"You took a nasty blow to your head."

The voice, the perfume—the lady! He struggled to rise. "How did I get here?"

"I put you here. You've been out for nearly ten hours." She sat beside him and felt his forehead. "You had a temperature too, but that probably came from being hit in the head by the flying boat paddle. I didn't think I was going to be able to pull you into the boat."

"Ow, my head feels like it's cracking open." He reached up to probe his injury, then regretted it. "How did I get naked?"

"I had to get you out of your wet clothes before you caught pneumonia. Don't worry"—she snickered—"I didn't take any liberties with you."

He laid back, closing his eyes, exhaustion almost forcing him to sleep.

"No, no, no. No, you don't. Don't you go to sleep. You likely have a concussion. We need to prop you up and get some light in here." She got to her knees and hauled him up, fluffing the pillows up behind him. "It's okay to close your eyes, but not in the dark." After getting to her feet, she opened all the cabin's curtains. Exposing a broken glass pane on the entrance door.

"Did you break in here? Where am I? Where are we?"

"Yes, it was life or death, and I preferred life. I'm not sure where we are. Somewhere south of Chicago... maybe? We drifted a lot while I was paddling. I'd never rowed a boat before." She leaned back against the wall, bracing herself beside the window. Outside, snow was still falling fresh over the lakeshore, a mere hundred feet away. "It was all I could do to get us here. On top of that, a powerful storm blew in just as we went out on the water yesterday. There's a good foot and a half of snow out there now."

The fire started to die. She used the poker to stir it up. "I need to go outside. There's wood stacked under a lean-to about twenty-five yards away. I'll be back in a few minutes." She wrapped herself in her coat and tied hand towels around what used to be her high-heel shoes, the heels already broken off. She shoved against the door to knock the blowing snow out of the way. Then the brave lady left the cabin's warmth.

While she was outside, he struggled to his feet. Woozy, he wobbled to the fireplace to retrieve his clothes where the lady had hung them to dry. He pulled his underwear, pants, socks, and shirt on, but his shoes, coat, and bow tie were laid on the other side of the room.

Lying back down, his head banging even harder after the slightest exertion, he closed his eyes.

Ryan received Tonya's text—and after following her instructions—arrived at a hotel reminiscent of an old Super 8. Their rooms wouldn't be ready for hours, but the limousine service's van had to go straight to its next call after unloading.

He stepped off the van first, smiling at the lady waiting for him. "Tonya." He scooped her into a hug. "Thank you for helping out. I would've never thought about something like this." Holding his hand out, he helped each fearful girl out.

"You're welcome. Come... come with me." She led the girls down the snow-covered sidewalk, the wind whipping the powdery precipitation around.

After everyone was snuggled into the hospitality room, he settled up with the driver and carried the three bags of cash inside a pillowcase stuck inside another.

His teeth chattered with his shivering. "I'm not a fan of these Michigan winters. I thought we were going to get stuck coming across the lake. It's starting to get icy."

"Ryan, don't you think you should call the authorities?" After helping the girls get settled, Tonya jammed her hands on her hips and turned in a full circle as if counting the girls. "And where did these young girls come from? They all look underage."

"First off, no. I'm not going to call the authorities. I don't know whether DR is alive or dead. So the last thing I want to do is show up with seventeen underage, illegal migrant girls I know nothing about. That is DR's thing, not mine. Is anything on the news?" Using sign language, he gestured to his mouth to ask the girls if they were hungry.

They all nodded.

"Sigueme, follow me." Tonya motioned and took them into the room in the back where breakfast was just about over, but there was still food to be had—muffins, cereal, and fruit. Just enough to knock the edge off. The desk clerk, Molly, looked on, none too happy, appearing to whisper something to herself.

"I reserved seven rooms. We can put four girls in each room, and in the fifth room, one of the girls can share with a caregiver."

The girls all shirked at the word *caregiver*.

"Don't use that *C* word. That's what the club called the men who kept them locked up." Ryan craned down a corridor, then grabbed an apple. "I'm glad the room entrances are inside. When will the, uh, attendants be here?"

"In a couple of hours. What are you going to do? These girls need more than this to eat."

"You act like I've done this before." Sitting at a high-top table, he put his elbows on the table, propped up himself, and tousled his hair.

"I'm sorry. I forgot—you've been up almost all night." She twisted her watch into view. "I can run by Marcie's and pick something up, if you like, before I go home."

"That would be great. Pick something up for the hotel clerk too. I think she's going to blow a gasket." He handed her two hundred dollars. "Is this enough?"

"Yes... But where did you get all this cash?" She extended it, and her right brow arched.

"It's not mine. It's DR's. Well—technically." He gripped her shoulder. "Remember, don't say anything to DR's family until we know for sure what is going on. Thanks, Tonya. You're a lifesaver. I'll make it up to you. I promise."

She snorted. "Yeah. Seems I've heard that a lot lately." Then she tipped her head toward the girls. "As long as they're all right, we're even."

Ryan stifled a shiver. They'd gotten the girls out, but could he promise Tonya no one would be coming after them?

After sleeping several hours, DR awoke to a sulfuric odor. The cabin was much brighter as the sun rose and the clouds pushed out. Or did the young woman moving around in front of the fireplace brightened the place so?

"What's that smell?" He cringed, unable to place the odor.

"Quite possibly dinner, breakfast, and lunch." Stirring the concoction, she grinned at him. "There's not a lot of food here. I guess the hunters took it all with them to keep wild animals from sniffing around. The cabbage was outside in a root cellar, frozen, but edible."

"I still don't know your name. I'm—"

"I know your name. You said it on the boat." She opened a cabinet and retrieved plates and forks. "We're lucky this was here, DR. Otherwise, we'd be in a tight spot. My name is Michelle, Michelle Jennings."

"What?" He jolted upright, his heartbeat thudding. "Did you say Jennings?"

Dare he believe his luck? Had he just found what would get Jennings out of his hole? "*You're* the daughter of the man trying to kill me?" His temperature and temper rose. "Do you know anything about that?"

"No... I mean, what? No, I didn't know anything. Why would he be trying to kill you?" Her gaze locked on to his. "Besides, if I was in on it, why would I have saved you?"

"I don't know!" He started to rise, then thought the better of it. "But in the last three months, he's used terrorists to blow up my yacht, had henchmen attempt to drown me and a friend, and kidnapped thirty-plus children, and the ones we saved last night. He's blown up my house, hired mercenaries to kill me, *and* he killed Max Rice. Other than that, I don't know what else. Oh... and shot down a plane with almost five hundred people aboard."

She ladled the boiled cabbage on two metal camping plates, then handed him one.

He pushed her hand and the plate away. "I don't need my killer's daughter to feed me."

"Better eat this." She didn't relent. "Or else no one's going to have to kill you—you'll have killed yourself."

He huffed, finally taking the plate of boiled leaves. "How can you eat this... this stuff."

"I've eaten far worse. Look, I don't know what my dad is doing now. That's why I was on the yacht." She scooped a bite and seemed to enjoy it.

Holding a bite up on his fork, he eyed it long and hard, then stuck it in his mouth. "Mmm, this isn't bad. Where did you learn to cook like this?"

"You mean boiling down cabbage? It's nothing. On the street you learn all sorts of ways to feed yourself."

"On the streets?" His gaze drifted over her. His senses recognized the perfume once again. Even while enraged she was his enemy's daughter—adopted daughter—he couldn't help this untimely attraction.

"When my dad found me, I had survived on the streets of St. Petersburg for seven months. And that was all it was—survival." She set her plate down. "Want some coffee? It's probably stale, but it's hot and loaded with caffeine. There's not any creamer, though."

He held up his right hand. "I'm good. Maybe later. Go on. Tell me more."

"There's not much more to tell, at least that I want to remember. My parents were taken into custody, but before the KGB came for them, they hid me. They charged my parents with a religious insurrection and hung them three months later. The US didn't do anything to help them, and I didn't come out of hiding for fear. Who knows, the US may have not known about it." While eating her meal, she walked to a window and sipped her coffee.

"How did you survive? Where'd you go?" He couldn't direct his anger toward her, even though her dad had done what he'd done, even though she was right here. She'd saved his life.

"I was fortunate. It was the end of spring, so street life, while hard, wasn't deadly... at first. But looking back, I don't know how I did it. The only thing I can say is God must've had His hand covering me." She came back over and sat across from him in a plastic lawn chair.

"God. Give me a break. You're not going to play that card."

"What? You don't believe in God? How do you explain last night? You helped rescue those girls."

"Yes, I helped, but that wasn't the real reason I was there. Jennings has been after me for no reason. I don't even know what the man looks like. I thought if I could get something of value to him, it might bring him out of his hole. So we were going to take the casino money." As he reached for the coffee, his head began to throb. "But I have something even better now."

"What's that?"

He peered over the coffee cup. "You."

CHAPTER
THIRTY-FIVE

D R lowered his cup as Michelle hopped up from her plastic seat, appearing horrified by the news. But for some reason, he didn't sense she was upset he'd harm her. Maybe she was having troubling believing what her dad had done?

"DR, have you ever believed in God?" Finished with the cabbage, she sealed it in a plastic bag she'd found under a cabinet.

"When I was young, before I realized it was just some people's way of covering their misery or writing off their mistakes." He scraped the last of his bowl—Had he really eaten all that? He shifted, stretching out his legs and crossing them at the ankles. "Why did you help let the girls go?"

"I didn't want to see anyone harm them, especially after what I lived through." She dropped back into her chair. "Just because Dad is backslid doesn't mean I will. I learned a valuable lesson on the streets." She shoved back her hair, a long scar revealed under her hair, until she tilted her head back, fanning it out.

"Yeah?" He scooted forward, letting the whole Jennings thing go, for now. Instead, he *needed* to know this beautiful woman's story.

"Dad, Jim, has turned, and he's running from God. Ever since his wife —my mom, Patsy—died, he's been angry with God. She was diagnosed with cancer ten years ago, several years before he found me. She had the best doctors and thousands of people praying night and day. Their faith was the cornerstone of our home." She sipped her coffee. "I fit right in because, instead of running from God, I ran to Him when I was on the streets. My faith grew, and He—*God*—was all I had."

He shook his head. "Isn't that always the story? We pray, pray, pray, and people still die."

"I'm not going to dispute that, and it's heartbreaking. But no one knows why or how long or if He's already given us more time or less. Have you ever read the Bible, DR?"

"No. In children's church, we had a simple picture version, but that's all. Why?" He started to get up but sat back down just as quickly. "I'm a little woozy, but I would like more coffee. It was so good. Would you mind?"

"Stay there. I'll get it. You shouldn't exert yourself until the headache goes away." She scooted over to the fireplace and, using a towel, picked up the pot and poured a scalding cup of coffee. "If you'd read the Bible and understood God and your role, you might not judge others so quickly— or harshly."

"I've got my reasons. How do you know so much about concussions?" He reached for the cup, peeking at her hairline again.

"I've had plenty of them, especially on the street." Her hand rose, an involuntary response, hiding her scalp while she bent close to hand him the cup.

"Is that how that happened?"

"How what happened?" She fluffed her hair up.

"The scar on your hairline. Did someone hit you?" The only imperfection he could find, and she was trying to hide it.

"I don't remember what happened. A street gang trapped me in an alley, wanting me. This is one of the souvenirs." She slid her index finger over the protruding evidence. "I woke up three days later in critical care. That's where Dad found me."

"How many concussions have you had?" He pointed at her scalp. "Was that the last one?"

"This is one doctors called chronic, partly by the force, the number of times I'd had them before, and my age. It took me nearly a year to get back to normal, somewhat. I've gotten them different ways, but usually by the same boys or men." She pursed her lips and forced a smile, but unable to squash every tear, she rose and went back to the window. "This is getting personal. Do you mind if we change the subject? I'll give my testimony when it gives God glory."

"I'm sorry. So that fueled your need to help the girls the other night." He drummed his hands on the small table beside the bed. "I understand, believe me. My friend should have them safely tucked away by now. So what happens now?"

She pivoted and braced a shoulder against the wall. "We have to get you better. Hopefully in the morning, your headache will be gone, and we can discuss walking out of here. There's a road at the end of the driveway, about a hundred yards. I don't know where it goes, so we have to be fed, warm, and healthy. We might get to the road and go the wrong way, so you must be stronger." She glanced from one corner of the cabin to the other, several times. "Does that sound about right?"

Just for a moment, he saw the same fire that was in his Gail. It was the first time he'd seen it since she passed. "I think so." *What am I doing? I can't be thinking this way.*

"That's it, no comments, no suggestions? Ha ha."

"Why are you laughing?" He raised his right eyebrow, tilting his head sideways.

"I don't know why God brought us together, but He's up to something."

DR held up his hands. "Truce on God?"

"That's between Him and you. I've made my decisions."

Noon, New Year's Eve in Delton. In the thirty-six hours since Ryan had seen or heard from DR, he'd begun to have trouble keeping the girls under wraps as the helpers they enlisted became suspicious. But at least the girls were having fun, finally trusting he was their rescuer—no ugly intents.

Unable to sit still—unable to sit on the situation any longer—he called Tonya at work. "I'm thinking of taking or sending the girls to Greg and Penny. What do you think?" He nudged the drape aside. Out in the parking lot, a security guard made the rounds.

"They're not home. A few bad FBI agents tried to claim Amal, so they took all the girls on a trip. I don't know where they are, and obviously, they can't say over the phone."

"I've got to do something. The girls need new clothes, and fast. They only had what they were wearing on their backs. Can you please help me?" After letting the curtain fall back, he sat on the edge of his bed. "I need to go home, take care of things. Any way we could get more people to help?"

"My break is over. I'll get them the clothes and call the agency when I get off. Get all their sizes and meet me at Marcie's. We'll discuss your costs for next year over a meal." She chuckled. "See you around six thirty."

The phone went dead.

Hooting, he slammed a fist pump into the air. "Yes!"

He downloaded the same phone app Penny used to communicate with Amal. Down the hallway from his room, he spoke to two of the ladies he'd hired to help, let them know he had to leave and would be back soon. Then he went to each of the girls' rooms, got their sizes, and assured them everything was okay.

Leaving the hotel, he had an errand to run first. This time, he'd start the New Year off fresh. He opened a cash bag and removed two hundred and fifty thousand dollars, kissing one of the stacks of hundred-dollar bills. Lady Luck may have just landed on his lap, especially if DR never came back.

"I just have to play it cool. Here's to dead heroes. Ha ha."

DR had rested for almost two days. His headache was gone when he awoke Sunday. The storm had also passed through, and the moon was rising over the trees out front. Michelle sat in front of the fireplace. He almost held his breath, trying to figure her out before speaking.

"A penny for your thoughts."

"I was praying, asking what God has in mind for me now. I'm not sure how Dad will react when he finds out I didn't go to help him, but to rescue the girls."

"Oh, that again."

She slid sideways in the seat to face him. "Do you believe in Providence?"

"At least the boat. I've been on it three times now." He smoothed his hair out and stretched his arms behind his head.

"I'm serious. What does all this mean to you?"

"I'm serious too. Everywhere I go, I see that boat, *Providence*. It's almost like having a puppy following you. It just doesn't stop. I've even dreamed about it, during the cruise—and last night." *Is that a sign? Oh man, I never thought of that.*

"Have you ever heard people say God uses your experiences, good and bad, to help people around you? At church, people give their testimony to glorify God, and rightfully so, and most of them have found their life's work, service if you will, in their tragedies." Her eyes lost their glimmer.

"I would think being the daughter of a rich and powerful warlord you'd already have your path set." Oops. He grimaced at a bad dig.

She sprang to her feet, looming over him. "Is that how you see me? A spoiled rich kid who traffics kids? I'd have thought the last couple of days together would've changed your perspective. I guess not." Shaking her head, her hair slipping past her scar, she started toward the coffeepot. "I need some coffee. Would you like some?"

"I'm sorry. I didn't mean that. It was ugly and I apologize. And, yeah, thanks. I'd love a cup." Feeling guilty, he stood, testing himself. "I think I'm okay to go on that hike now."

"It's too late today. We'll have to start the new year off here in the cabin." Pouring their coffee, she frowned. "I had hoped the new year for the girls would be better than this one."

"And it still may. Something tells me they've had a terrible year."

"Where do you think they are now?" She handed him the coffee.

"Hopefully in Delton. I don't know where else Ryan would've gone. But if he talks to Willie, she'll help him figure it out. Money won't be the problem."

"How was standing? Did it cause you any problems?" She leaned over to view the back of his head where the paddle struck him. "Is your bump feeling any better?"

"Yes, if I leave it alone. Hopefully, none of my brain fell out."

"I can't speak to that. I don't know what you were like before the paddle hit you. But if I were a gambler, I'd say this little detour has enlightened you." Her face brightened, and the corners of her mouth rose, revealing a beautiful smile. "I'd like to help children. It seems I keep getting caught up in these trafficking scenarios anyway." While she ran her finger along the rim of her cup, her gaze met his.

He didn't respond right away, drinking his coffee dregs.

"What about you, DR? Would you like to turn the bad things in your life into something good for others and maybe discover a destiny? Maybe start an agency for human trafficking or a home to help the kids."

"When I was on my cruise, before your dad interrupted it, I dreamt about the kids we rescued. Then after the attack, I was laid unconscious beside the oldest of three sisters. She was unconscious too. We both had the same dream, and a voice spoke to us, telling her, Habiba, that I would be her new dad. Now, being here with you, I feel like it is my destiny, and I don't know how to feel about that. After we rescued her again from your dad, she kept calling me her daddy, and I kind of liked it."

Michelle's jaw dropped. Then the biggest smile took over. "That is incredible. You do have a heart." She poked at him with her hand. "There's nothing like the feeling of love. Maybe we could work something out—together—to help all those kids."

"Your dad is obsessed. He'd kill me first. I don't know—"

She touched his arm, halting him. "We'll figure out a way to get around that, somehow."

He looked down at her hand, the urge to take her in his arms almost overwhelming him. He shuddered, and she jerked her hand away. She must've seen it in his face. "Okay... Let's think about all this and discuss it in the morning."

Was that disappointment in her eyes? He didn't know, but it must be in his.

"Sure. We better get some sleep." She stood.

Someone was shooting off fireworks down the shoreline.

"Look, there. Fireworks. It must be close to midnight." She crossed to pick up the watch on her coat by the door. "Three minutes till."

After struggling to his feet, he sidled up alongside her by the window, the temptation returning. His hand on her shoulder, he stood at her side. He could hear her breathing. She was only a couple inches shorter, and when her eyes met his, he hovered over her, unable to control the urge. The moment was incredible, electric.

Then she put her hand on his chest, pushing herself away. "I want to kiss you so bad, but not like this. Not tonight." She exhaled a shaky breath. "Let's get some sleep."

Embarrassed he had desires for her and had let his desires get the most of him, he stepped aside, and the disappointment hit, his whole body deflating. They didn't kiss, but all those emotions often swept away reason. "Good idea. Happy New Year, Michelle."

They hugged like old acquaintances saying goodbye. Then she left the embrace and went to lie down, leaving him standing by the window.

After watching the fireworks, he lay down, but sleep didn't come for a while, his earlier excitement wouldn't die. *Am I in love with Debbie? Will she come back?*

The questions didn't feel quite as pressing several days earlier, but now?

He rolled over to look at Michelle. Her eyes were open, and she was already watching him.

⁓

Willie arrived at the hotel around six thirty New Year's Eve, bringing with her clothes, shoes, and coats for seventeen girls. She'd also called in a special order at six o'clock for pizza and soda from the local pizzeria, having it delivered at their earlier closing time due to the holiday. Now, its tempting aroma wafted from the hotel's food area where the girls all camped out, looking out the window as fireworks sounded all around.

With Delton such a small town, there weren't any fireworks visible from the hotel, but several residents on nearby Wall Lake had joined together and were now launching fireworks over the lake. Occasionally, one flew high enough and caused a big enough bang to get the girls excited.

The hotel clerk, Molly, no longer treated them with malice. Willie had included her in all their girl things for two days, and now she helped Willie, even going out to her car and carrying in some of the packages.

"Willie, thanks for the pizza. Fred didn't do anything for us this year.

He said it's been a slow time." The girl loaded up, carrying a double stack of shoes, two wide by four high. "I hope he doesn't have to sell the place."

"Things will pick up. You just have to keep your hopes up. By the way, do you go to church?" Willie balanced the other nine shoeboxes in her hands as Ryan came running out to help without a jacket. He scrunched up, feeling the bite of the cold air.

"Better wear your jacket next time. I don't want you to get sick before I get my dinner out of you." She winked, trying to support the boxes without dropping the top one. As he man-hugged the remaining bags of clothes, she followed Molly, then turned to see if he had the rest. "Got it?" He'd surely drop half of it. She quickened her pace, her load shifting.

"Yep. Let's go get some of that pizza. It smells amazing." He ran crouched over, maybe realizing he should've made two trips.

"Wow, the temperature sure has dropped since the storm passed through. Brrr." She laid a double load of packages on the high-top table, caught the falling packages that didn't fit, and placed them on another table while he unloaded as well. Then he reached for her.

She returned his hug, having seen how he treated the girls with kindness and love. Maybe there was a chance for the two of them. She'd just take it slow. "Thanks. That was a load. The kid at the store gave me a woolly eye for making him bring it to my car. Ha ha, but he liked your tip." She leaned on the oldest of the girls who came over to check out the packages.

"My tip? Oh yeah. Thank you, Tonya, for everything." He spread out his arms to indicate the hotel's dining area.

"Everyone's here." Willie clapped. "Let's destroy this pizza before it gets too cold." The girls gathered in and grabbed a slice, and she picked up one from a pepperoni pizza, waved it in the air, and shouted "Happy New Year!" in Spanish.

After returning her blessing, the girls bowed their heads and gave thanks while Ryan looked on.

The joy of the new year was gone, distinguished in a flash by Michelle's disappearance, his daughter of fifteen years. Jennings was taking a hard look at himself in the mirror of life. Having all the power he could ever dream of had brought him nothing but to the depths of frustration and sorrow. While money had become no object, he had no one to love, no one to share his fortune with.

Something from his past teased the edges of his consciousness. Yes, that's it. "Little children, keep yourselves from idols."

Confused, angry, and alone, he didn't want to confront his past. God had abandoned him. Or so he thought, but now he was going to have to settle it, one way or another.

"You left me. You said You would always be with me, but You let Patsy die. *Why?*" He went out onto the master bedroom balcony, overlooking the valley and river below, every bit of him numb, rathering he was the one to die, not Michelle.

"Why did You give her to me after allowing her to be treated so badly, only to take her away? Was it to twist the knife deeper in my soul?" Leaning on the ornate concrete wall enclosing the patio, he propped his elbows on its top, cradled his head in his hands, and cried.

"It's all Ray's fault. You sent him to torture me, didn't You?" He thrust his head back, crying out at the sky, and peered above him, trying to find God in the clouds. He couldn't.

"Well, Job was right. 'Man who is born of woman is few of days and full of trouble.'" He rocked his head side to side, reflecting on his past. "Leave Michelle, take me—if You've got to take anyone, take me!"

He heard laughter in his spirit, on one hand—a cold evil laugh. And he also felt naked, stripped of all pretenses on the other, standing on a precipice. "Why God, why?" he asked for the thousandth time since his Patsy had died and now his Georgia peach had disappeared. He could almost imagine all the goodness inside him had been smashed with a sledgehammer.

Stone-faced, he went back into the house, alone, the inevitable upon him. He readied himself for the new year, and a spirit howled inside him. "I don't know where you are, Dr. Ray, but I will get you."

CHAPTER
THIRTY-SIX

New Year's Day, the wind had finally laid down, and the snow was no longer blowing. By seven a.m., DR awoke to smell the same coffee he'd braved brewing once again in the old-fashioned percolator Michelle had found in a cabinet. Grateful, he watched her as she stood by the window while waiting on the coffee.

As if sensing his gaze, she turned. "Hello, sleepyhead. How did you sleep?"

"It took me a while. But I slept well." He raised a brow. "How about you?"

"After a while. Look, I'm sorry about last night. I still struggle with—"

"No, don't be," he interrupted. "I shouldn't have gotten so close. I am —or was—in a relationship, and I shouldn't have allowed myself to tempt us. I have struggles too, so let's forget about it. At least for now. Okay? Deal?" He reached out his hand.

She took his hand and shook. "Deal." A smile softened her tense features, the relief shining in her hazel eyes. "We need to figure all this out before we leave this morning. There's going to be a lot of pushback from my dad, and we have to decide how and what to do with the girls, if your friend hasn't already notified authorities." She went to the fireplace and poured two cups of coffee.

"I've been thinking about Habiba." He reached for his hot cup. "Maybe I should adopt them, once your dad stops trying to kill me."

"Yeah. I'll have to work on that. It may take a while, though. It sounds like he's obsessing about you." She shook her head rapidly. "The coffee is getting harder and harder to drink without my French vanilla creamer."

"Obsessing?"

"It sounds like some sort of spirit has gotten to him. You do believe in spiritual warfare, right?" She surveyed the cabin. "Or is that something you never heard of?"

"What are you looking for?"

"Just wishing there was some creamer or something to eat with the coffee. We have to leave this morning, the cabbage is gone, and with your head feeling better, we better go before the lack of food catches up to us."

"You've done an amazing job keeping us filled. Thank you, Michelle. I hope you'll give me the chance to make it up to you."

"Let's plan on meeting on the thirty-first of this month. It will give me time to work on Dad and figure out how to use all this for good. Prayer— lots of prayer—is what it's going to take, whether you believe or not." She shuddered, then forced herself to take another sip of coffee.

"You do what you do, and I'll do what I do. The thirty-first sounds great. We'll both have time to figure things out. Do me a favor?" He tilted his head, gritting his teeth, and closed one eye in a pleading manner.

"Maybe. What is it?"

"Don't wear that perfume."

"Why not?"

"You are already pretty enough, but with it on, you're intoxicating, irresistible."

She chuckled. "Isn't that the whole idea?"

Two hours later, after waiting for an hour that might find someone on the road, they pulled on their coats and took the linen from the cabin's bed and pillows. She wrapped her modified high heels in the pillowcases and plastic shopping bags stored under the sink. He wrapped his feet in the bags too. They divided the bed sheets between them to wrap around their upper bodies. Then they left the cabin.

"Brrr, it's freezing." He scrunched himself even tighter in the sheet.

"See what I've been braving just to keep us warm and fed?"

Walking up the snow-covered driveway, he snuggled beside her and put his arm under her sheet to share their body heat. It felt wonderful.

"That's better." She leaned into him.

Not knowing if it felt better to be warm or cuddled together—he pushed on and on. At the end of the driveway, one set of tire tracks, freshly made, stamped the snow.

"I hope whoever made the tracks is still close by." Watching their breath intermingle, he took a deep one.

"How do you feel? Are you okay to go on?" Looking over at him, her eyes began to water.

"I'm fine. We've got to do this."

The going was slow, and every step required effort to push through the snow, even in the tire tracks. Half an hour later, they saw a small house on a hill, up a long unplowed driveway.

"Thank You, Jesus," Michelle whispered, her fitness being put to the test.

"Laying around these days has drained me. I hope I can make it up the hill."

"You'll make it, even if I have to carry you." She squeezed her arm around his middle. "We've got to take care of those children."

The phone rang on Willie's bed stand. When she reached over to answer, Tom's contact flashed on the screen. Relieved to hear from him finally, she took the call. "Happy New Year, Tom. How are things?"

"Hi, Willie. You too. Things are a little chaotic, but we're surviving. I'm looking forward to getting home to my wife—that much I know. How are things there? Did DR and Ryan succeed in their mission?"

She swung her feet and legs over the edge of the bed to sit up. "Ryan made it back with seventeen more girls, all speaking Spanish." She exhaled loudly. "We don't know if DR is even alive. He disappeared after the casino yacht was blown up by a missile."

There was a long silence.

Then Tom huffed. "He's alive. I know it. He's part cat. He has nine lives and hasn't used them all yet."

Was he being brave, or did he have a premonition? She didn't know. "You're right. We've been praying and keeping our hopes up. I'm glad you called, though. We need to do something about the seventeen girls Ryan saved. Right now, they're in the hotel here in Delton. Do you have any ideas?" She shuffled into the kitchen, unearthed a piece of paper and a pen in her clutter drawer, and took down the number he dialed from.

"I'll get with everyone here, and we'll put on our thinking caps. We took our children to a hotel too. So we'll have to come up with a plan soon. Maybe get the authorities involved."

"We'll see. Hopefully, DR will come back and have a good plan. I've been praying."

"Oh, yeah... Well, Penny's been praying here in something she calls tongues. Greg is beside himself, said she's becoming like his grandmother."

"Good for her." Willie jabbed the air in triumph. "I can't wait to meet her."

"I've got to get off here. Don't want to be traced. I'll pass on the news. Thanks for everything, Willie. Can't wait to see you again."

She hung up the phone, whispering, "What are You up to, God?"

After struggling halfway up the long hilly driveway, Michelle collapsed in his arms, having fed him better than herself. It was his turn to rescue her. Inching up the hill, calling on his will to live, he finally reached the porch, but the effort caused him to start to perspire, not a good thing in ten-degree weather. Shivering against her, he pushed on the doorbell while holding her up. After waiting for a minute, he decided to knock, and finally, someone scuffled around in the house.

"Who—What are you doing out there in the cold? Come in. Please, hurry." The stranger held the door wide for them, then gripped Michelle's right arm to help DR guide her in.

Obviously seeing them nearly frozen, he shut the door and showed them to the gas fireplace. "Martha, come here. There's a couple here nearly frozen to death."

"Fred, grab some blankets out of the hallway closet. I'll go get them dry clothes."

An hour later, having thawed out, they shared their story, what of it they could, while nursing a hot bowl of leftover beef stew Martha had made for their dinner the night before.

"If your house had been any further, we wouldn't have made it. Thank you for everything." Shoveling the last spoonful into his mouth, DR realized how close he'd come again.

"God was looking after you." Martha rubbed his shoulder. "We were supposed to go to the church and clean up, but because of the snow blowing last night, I didn't think we should go out."

Michelle, still drained, sank back into her easy chair. "God has a way of showing up at just the last moment. That's for sure."

The grumbling whir of a snowplow clearing the road broke a brief silence.

"See? Just in time." Michelle winked a weary eye toward him.

At three o'clock, an Uber driver showed up, and they thanked their gracious hosts and hugged them. They climbed into the Jeep, ready to start their plan, meeting on the thirty-first, in Atlanta. He was grateful for her kindness, care, and love—and she for his.

The Uber dropped them off at their hotel. Even though their rooms had been emptied, there were still loose ends to tie up. Hugging, resisting the urge for more, they exchanged numbers they said goodbye. Then went to call their loved ones.

Over the next weeks...

After settling back into his life, DR made a lot of tough decisions. On the kids' part, he, along with Greg, Penny, and Michelle, worked out a plan with federal authorities to keep the children from Aden, Yemen, in America. They'd be the first children to dwell in the new Tahira's Home for Children, named after the teen from Aden killed in their escape.

Of the seventeen Spanish-speaking children, six were returned to their families in Mexico, but the others would stay in Tahira's Home, having been illegally transported from other countries into the United States through NGOs.

Michelle couldn't find a way to tell her dad she'd saved DR's life without giving him critical information about their plans. Rather, she told him DR had saved hers, which he did at the end.

But the unrelenting spirit in Jennings still insisted someone had to pay for making him look bad, so Ray wasn't off the hook yet.

Debbie came back to Delton after New Year's for several days to pick up where they left off. They could not. She went back to Chicago after discovering she needed more time to sort out her "new" Christian beliefs and how they could fit with his Michigan Strong.

Greg and Penny rediscovered their Christian roots, and Greg began praying in the Spirit, just like his grandmother had predicted, in their backyard.

Tom returned home to Laurie. They started writing a new international thriller, *Live to Die Another Day*, part of their Nine Lives series.

Sam reconnected with his children after DR's encouragement. Now, he began weekly visitation and ensured they were getting proper care, rather than just sending half his paycheck.

Willie gained a new respect for Ryan, so there might be something in their future, and Ryan returned half the money in the bags to DR—after secretly settling his gambling debts, in America and Ireland. Now, he's hoping Willie never finds out.

Simon Crouch, the casino manager, noticed the trademark bands around the cash Ryan McNeilly used to pay his debt, so Simon alerted the LMMC, a business courtesy.

As for DR? He's watching in the mirror for Jennings and waiting for Debbie to work out her issues. Meanwhile, he's sharing his newly leased home on Wall Lake with three lovely girls, soon to be his daughters, and working closely with Michelle to build the home in Atlanta. Willie comes over often to look in on the girls, or so she says that's why she's coming over. His mother's dream came true, in Alabama.

"Dreams really can come true, can't they, Daddy?" Habiba's dark-brown eyes glowed as Derifa and Amal played with their new puppy, Bubbles.

DR's heart had never felt fuller. "Yes," he whispered. "Yes, Habiba, they do."

The End

To be continued in Obsessed Intentions - Book Three

Find Lee's other books at:
https://www.amazon.com/author/leewimmer

Visit www.leewimmer.net for a free bonus chapter, discussion questions and special PDF bookmark downloads.

GROUP DISCUSSION QUESTIONS

1. One of the first topics in this book is forgiveness. How does DR view forgiveness, and where did that view come from?
2. How does forgiveness affect his story after the point of his forgiveness?
3. Who did his forgiveness free the most?
4. The main driver of the first novel was DR's parents not going to the police, afraid people would talk. Was Stevie's reaction too harsh? Should he have confronted his parents?
5. When Debbie stormed out on their relationship, DR didn't become irate. Instead, he still wanted to continue with their relationship. Is that a form of forgiveness or something else?
6. DR is willing to forgive Debbie and continue their relationship. What do you think?
7. Was Debbie challenging DR's conviction to live his Michigan Strong? Or was she overreacting to her pressure to choose right from wrong according to society or God?
8. Is Ryan ever going to be a good match for Willie?
9. Is Willie over her crush on DR, or is it still under the surface, ready to pounce at the right moment?
10. Why can't Mike keep a secret? Is he a gossip, or does he think he's helping the situation? How do people like Mike make you feel in real life?

11. Mr. Jennings is still trying to kill DR even after the spotlight of the presidency is taken away. What could drive that sort of obsession?

12. In light of what's happening around us now, is this type of obsession unrealistic?

13. Do you see Jennings obsession as demonic, fueled by a desire for power, or both?

14. Jennings became a member of Circle before going off the deep end, so to speak. What do you think Circle is, and do you see a relevance in today's society?

15. The portrayal of Congressman Max Rice and Senator Carl Brummengarten as felonious co-conspirators with Mr. Jennings is central to the story. Do you see examples where members of today's Congress may be behaving similarly?

16. In this novel and often in movies such as *The Fugitive*, the portrayal of a cop shooter gives the authorities a shoot-first, ask-questions-later theme. From what you have witnessed, is that a fair assessment of today's law-and-order establishments?

17. Child trafficking is central to this story. Can you see this happening in our society today?

18. One of the storyline Scriptures is Romans 8:28. Here, God has taken the tragic instances in DR and Michelle's lives and turned them around for good, to help other children in harsh circumstances. Do you see it this way as DR and Michelle discuss opening Tahira's Home for Children?

These are just a few of the questions to answer. If you would like to share your questions or suggestions, leave Lee a comment at www.leewimmer.net. Be sure to join for the free short stories and other special offers just for email subscribers in connection with this novel.

VISIT LEE

Visit Lee:
https://www.leewimmer.net

You'll find the free bonus chapter, Disgraced,
and inspiring printable bookmark PDF files free to download, plus free
short stories, novel news, and Lee's blog.

Find Lee's published books at:
https://www.amazon.com/author/leewimmer